Praise for Car

'Genuinely unputdownable books are rare in my experience. This is one . . . A brilliant, original comedy'
Daily Mail

'I have a feeling Caroline Hulse might be a genius, this book is so brilliant. Funny, clever and original'
Lucy Vine, author of *Hot Mess*

'Razor-sharp comedy'
Sunday Mirror

'Witty, whip-smart and wincingly observant, pure entertainment from start to finish. A Caroline Hulse book is a reading highlight of my year'
Cathy Bramley

'I loved *The Adults*! Funny, dry and beautifully observed. Highly recommended'
Gill Simms, author of *Why Mummy Swears*

'A deliciously dark comedy of manners'
Daily Express

'*Like A House On Fire* is everything I love in a book. A sharply observed study of relationships packed with subtle wit . . . What a triumph!'
Josie Silver, author of *One Day in December*

'Brilliantly funny'
Good Housekeeping

'A very funny writer and a wonderfully compassionate
observer of human frailty'
Kate Eberlen, author of *Miss You*

'Packed with sharp wit, engaging characters and off-beat
humour, this is a fresh and feisty thrill-ride of a novel'
Heat

'Painfully astute and brilliantly funny,
Like A House On Fire is a triumph of a novel'
Beth O'Leary, author of *The Flatshare*

'I loved it – funny and sad and relatable and deeply human'
Harriet Tyce, author of *Blood Orange*

'Acutely observed and brilliantly funny. Very Nina Stibbe'
Clare Mackintosh

'Sheer delight from start to finish'
Lesley Kara, author of *The Rumour*

'Such a breath of fresh air! Witty, intensely human and
(dare I say it) relatable'
Katie Khan, author of *Hold Back The Stars*

Caroline Hulse lives in Manchester with her husband and a small controlling dog. Her books have been published in fourteen languages and optioned for television.

Reasonable People is her fourth novel.

By Caroline Hulse

The Adults
Like A House On Fire
All the Fun of the Fair

REASONABLE PEOPLE

Caroline Hulse

ORION

An Orion Paperback

First published in Great Britain in 2023 by Orion Fiction.
This paperback edition published in 2024 by Orion Fiction.
an imprint of The Orion Publishing Group Ltd.,
Carmelite House, 50 Victoria Embankment
London EC4Y 0DZ

An Hachette UK Company

1 3 5 7 9 10 8 6 4 2

A CIP catalogue record for this book is
available from the British Library.

ISBN (Mass Market Paperback) 978 1 4091 9730 0 ISBN (Export
Trade Paperback) 978 1 4091 9729 4
ISBN (eBook) 978 1 4091 9731 7

Typeset by Input Data Services Ltd, Bridgwater, Somerset

Printed in Great Britain by Clays Ltd, Elcograf S.p.A.

MIX
Paper from
responsible sources
FSC® C104740

www.orionbooks.co.uk

REASONABLE PEOPLE

PART ONE

PART ONE

I

It was the sound of running water that woke Roy up that night.

He ran his arm under the duvet on the other side of the bed. Still warm. Lynn sometimes went for a fresh glass of water in the night, preferring not to drink from the one Roy always placed on her bedside table. She'd spent too many nights listening to a lapping cat.

The cat had died last year but – old habits.

Roy waited for the sound of running water to stop.

After five decades together there were many old habits. How Lynn always switched the television on and Roy always switched the television off. Lynn turned the central heating up, and Roy turned it down. Lynn always used the same handbag, a boxy purple one their daughter Claudia had sent from Singapore – and Roy always used the same ancient Sainsbury's carrier bag, one once illustrated with bright fruit which had paled to pastel, the Red Delicious apples fading over the years to Pink Lady.

Lynn always let Roy deadlock the front door when they went to bed, for convenience (hers) and peace of mind (his). If Roy was ever served cake in error, he slipped his piece to Lynn in a wordless sleight of hand. On Sundays, Lynn cooked the dinner and Roy did the drinks and the carving, the two moving around each other in a practised kitchen dance.

Roy pulled himself up onto his haunches. The water was still running.

Lynn wouldn't be washing up or having a bath. If Roy couldn't sleep, he might have done either, but Lynn had no such need to optimise all waking hours. She'd once come upon him ironing during the night and asked, 'What, exactly, are you atoning for?' But efficiency was Roy's lighthouse. When retirement from the biscuit factory loomed, Roy applied to become a magistrate. Now also retired from the bench, he was a fit seventy-eight and, as a result, the house's guttering had never been cleaner. The radiators shone with fresh paint; the waste-paper baskets got regularly emptied.

Roy listened to the running water. A burst pipe, maybe? If so, he'd have to phone Phil. It felt intrusive to phone a plumber in the middle of the night, but when that plumber was your son, he'd get crosser if you didn't.

Or perhaps they had been burgled by a particularly heartless crook – one who left the water running for a twisted kick? Roy had always taken extravagantly anti-social acts into account when sentencing. Such people deserved to have the book thrown at them, and Roy Frost had happily thrown it.

The water was still running.

Fear pulled cold at Roy's stomach. It was the ordinariness of the sound, rendered extraordinary by the circumstances. Like the ring of the phone at night: a noise he wouldn't give a second's thought to in the daytime, but which took on a disquieting implication at this hour.

Roy looked across the room, to the outlines of furniture discernible in the darkness. He'd gone to bed with clothes draped over the back of his dressing chair. Where there had once been a belt there now hung a snake, the leather pooling on the seat into a cobra's hood. Moonlight reflected from the snake's buckle in a monstrous eye, glinting back at him.

He sat up and switched on the bedside lamp.

Instantly the snake became just a belt, the burglar's water just a running tap.

Roy looked at the dress hanging on the front of Lynn's wardrobe: a burst of sun-orange sheathed in protective plastic. 'I do have other dresses – yes,' she'd told him twelve hours before. 'But how often do we get to go to a wedding these days? And look!' She waggled a cellophane package holding an incomprehensible mix of metal and feathers. 'It has a fascinator!'

Roy shoved his feet into his slippers. 'Lynn?'

He pulled at the toggle at his waist, adjusting his pyjama bottoms higher on his hips. He pushed his feet into his slippers and padded down the stairs towards the kitchen, irritated by his own ridiculousness.

A belt was just a belt, and water was just water. Nothing was wrong. Nothing was—

Roy took it all in at once.

The cold tap, gushing into the unplugged sink.

The glass tumbler, broken in half on the kitchen floor.

And Lynn, the woman he'd loved for half a century. Lying on the cold tiles, her dressing-gown cord undone, one arm twisted crookedly overhead. Her decolletage visible above the pink roses of her nightdress as she stared past Roy with empty eyes.

2

Janine's day started as it always did – looking at her phone in the work canteen, inching forwards with Sal in the coffee queue.

'Listen to this one!' Janine read out from her phone. *'Am I the villain for calling the police after no one picked up the kid I was babysitting?'* She batted Sal's arm with glee. 'Can you imagine?'

'I still don't understand who writes these things.' Sal pulled her card out of her pocket. 'Who honestly thinks *Yes, today I'd like to be judged by a bunch of batshit strangers?'*

Janine's phone vibrated in her hand.

She tilted her screen so Sal could see the name. *Marky.*

Sal wrinkled her nose. 'Don't answer.'

'But what if he's dying or something?'

Sal took a second. 'But what if he's *not* dying?'

Janine answered the call. 'Early for you, Marky.' Through the floor-to-ceiling windows she watched slow-moving traffic circle the roundabout. 'Don't tell me you got a morning gig?'

'I've got the solicitor today, so I need that answer. Are you buying me out or not?'

Ahead in the queue, two men in suits took their coffees. Janine shuffled forwards. 'Marky—'

'I'm going to assume you're not.'

'Can you give me a bit longer to find the cash? You don't need the money.'

The barista put Sal and Janine's cups on the counter. Janine smiled thank you and pressed a lid onto her cup awkwardly with one hand.

'That's not the point.'

'I know that's not the point.' Janine fiddled in her pocket for some cash. 'But maybe, in a tiny way, it is?' She dropped a pound in the tip jar. 'When you're talking about selling your daughter's home out from under her?'

Sal made eye contact with the barista. 'It's her ex.'

'J?' Marky's voice was crisper than usual. 'I need an answer.'

Janine took a large swig through the hole in the cup's lid. Her attempt at casualness had made her reckless: a concentration of too-hot coffee burned her lip.

'Janine?'

'I thought, maybe,' Janine pressed the back of her hand to her lip in an attempt to soothe the pain, 'since we both know I paid the whole mortgage when we were together, you'd cut me some slack now you've found a cash cow to fall back on.'

'Don't call Molly a cow.'

'A *cash* cow. A benefactor.' Janine walked with Sal towards the lift. 'Don't twist it. Molly seems genuinely nice. Way too good for—'

At Sal's warning hand on her arm, Janine stopped.

The situation was infuriating. For the five years of their relationship, Marky had pursued a less-promising-by-the-year 'musical career' – his guitar had played too big a part in Janine's life for her liking. They split up, and Marky had found a new girlfriend within weeks. And still got to be a 'professional musician', and never did have to get that job in a call centre. The day Marky had met Molly, a woman who'd inherited great skin, a generous manner and, crucially, her parents' import/export business, was the worst day of Janine's life.

It was the day Janine had finally learned life's fundamental lesson. Life really – really, *really* – isn't fair.

'If you're not going to buy me out, I'll have to put the house on the market, Janine. Today.'

'Do what you've got to do.'

Janine switched the phone off and stared at Sal.

Sal shook her head sadly. 'Told you he wouldn't be dying. You'll find the money,' Sal said.

'People say that, but how does that work? You can only *find* money if you have it already.' Janine's heart was going like she'd been running. 'And now Marky gets to do fuck-all, and live in a house with remote-controlled lights, and *still* gets to go around telling people he's a musician for a living. You know what he said to me the other day? *Life is for living your dreams, Janine. If you just believe, things work out. I always told you that.*'

Sal sniffed. 'Prick.'

A notification flashed up on Janine's phone.

Urgent. Meeting at 9 a.m.

'Huh.' Janine stopped walking. 'Weird email.'
She opened it.

Hello Janine,
Please would you make yourself available to attend a meeting in Room 7 at 9 a.m.

If you wish, you may have a colleague or union rep present. Please confirm your attendance by reply.
Thanks,
Scott Gregory
Head of Retail Sales

'Scott's invited me to a meeting in ten minutes time. I can have a union rep present.' Janine stopped in front of the lift and looked up. 'Do I want a union rep present?'

Sal pressed the lift button. 'I reckon you're pretty good at representing yourself.'

The lift dinged.

'A union rep, though. In a meeting room on the *ground floor.*' Janine stared at the email. 'Why the ground floor?'

'Maybe they're making you redundant?'

'I bloody hope so. Can you imagine?' Janine gave a dreamy sigh. 'Sitting around, getting all the naps in, getting paid! If they ever offer me that brown envelope, I'll snap their hands off.'

They reached Sal's floor.

'First thing would be a holiday.' Janine followed Sal down the corridor. 'And then – well. Everything would be different. I'd cook proper food. I'd become one of those people who soak chickpeas.' She smiled at a passing member of the facilities team. 'I'd get fit, like Jane Fonda.'

Sal opened her office door. 'Isn't she about ninety?'

'I'd go on protests.' Janine followed Sal into Sal's office. 'I'd write letters to my MP about refugees and zero hours contracts. I'd get jobs done. Paint the radiators. I'd even fix the fridge door. Wow.' She scratched her cheek. 'I never thought I'd ever fix that fridge door.' She tried to imagine opening the fridge without having to do the usual jerk-and-lift. It felt like magic.

Of course, if Marky sold the house, someone else would get the benefit of the fridge door, but there was no space for reality in Janine's fantasy.

Sal sat at her desk. 'None of this sounds massively like you.'

'No, I would, though, Sal.' Janine moved a water bottle and perched on the edge of Sal's desk. 'I'd be a better person if they made me redundant. I'd *have time* to be a better person.'

'I hope they're not making you redundant. Our coffee runs have been the only good thing about my workdays for fifteen years.'

'You don't need to worry.' Janine patted Sal's arm. 'They can't sack me – who'd be Scott's Bad News Bear if I left? What, he'd have the difficult staff conversations himself? Besides.' She gave a sad smile and pushed herself up. 'I'm just not that lucky.'

'To summarise' – Scott spoke into the piece of paper, staring at it with a fierce intensity – 'because of these consolidations, your role is now at risk of redundancy.'

Janine stared at him, across the desk.

Scott deliberately didn't look up from reading. 'The three-month consultation period starts today.' His wedding ring flashed faintly, catching sunlight from the window. 'We understand it's a lot to take in.'

Janine pushed her tongue into her cheek until it hurt.

She pulled her tongue back. 'What?'

Scott stared at his paper.

'Redundancy?'

Scott's wedding ring flashed again. The paper in his hand trembled faintly.

'You mean – *redundancy* redundancy?'

Scott put his paper down and wrote something. 'There is information about next steps in the briefing pack I'm giving you.'

Janine took a deep breath. 'Scott!'

Finally, Scott looked up.

'I bought you fancy knives as a wedding present! I wrote you a reference for this promotion! For fuck's sake, Scott, I'm your Bad News Bear!'

Scott started writing again.

'What are you writing? Show me.'

Janine leaned over the table. She pulled the piece of paper towards her.

Between the typed words, Scott had handwritten:

What? Redundancy? You mean – redundancy redundancy?
I bought you fancy knives as a wedding present. I wrote you a reference for this promotion. For fuck's sake, Scott, I'm your Bad News Bear.

'You're only meant to write down the gist.' Janine pushed the paper away. 'And you don't want HR to know I'm your Bad News Bear. Not if you want them to have any respect for you at all.'

Scott pulled the paper towards him and wrote those words too. He cleared his throat. 'As a result of this consolidation, new roles have been created and you have been placed in a selection pool.'

Janine sat forwards. 'Pool? What pool?'

'This pack of information contains details about your selection pool and—'

'I'm the only sales manager in the north-west. There can't be a pool.'

Scott put his finger up in a *one-minute* sign. He wrote again.

Janine shuffled in her seat. She didn't do cliff-hangers. She pulled the information pack towards her and found the details.

Pool G: North-West Sales Lead x 1
2 roles to 1
Current incumbents: 1 x North-West area manager and 1 x North-West area support

'Lee works for me. We're different bands.' Janine looked up. 'He can't be in my pool.'

Scott said nothing.

'Get him out of my pool, right now, Scott. Write that down on your little pad. *Get him out of my pool!*'

Scott stared at his paper. 'There's been a job resizing exercise and—'

'Get him back in the changing rooms, get him back in his *little outfit*' – Janine could hear herself over-annunciating – 'and *get him out of my pool!*'

Janine took a breath. She watched Scott write. Was she making things worse?

Of course she was making things worse. This was what Janine did when she was in the right. Built the fire, lit the match, fanned the flames. Got incinerated in the fall out, leaving nothing but charred, righteous remains.

Classic, *classic* Janine.

'Please.' She jerked forwards, her weight on her elbows. 'I need this job. Phil's self-employed and we're losing our home. Katie needs to eat and stuff. Write that down. No, don't.' She felt a sharp immediacy in her nose – tears threatening. 'Actually, do.'

There was a time for dignity, and this wasn't it.

In her bag next to her foot, Janine felt her phone buzz.

Scott picked up his paper again. 'We understand this is upsetting, so we suggest you go home for the rest of the day. There will be opportunities for further questions as part of the consultation process.'

Janine stood up. 'That's it?'

Scott nodded into his paper.

'You make a shit Bad News Bear, Scott. You didn't even think to bring my coat down. Write that on your little piece of paper.'

She wrenched the door open and banged it on the way out, just because. She took a deep breath, smiled at the receptionist, and hurried out of the building with her things before the first tear came.

She walked towards the bus stop and jerked her phone from her bag.

Three missed calls from Phil.

Had he felt a vibration across the ether?

She rang him. 'Phil! This is the worst day ever. Marky's said he's turfing us out of the house, and work are making me redundant!'

Phil didn't speak.

'I feel such a fool. *Please would you confirm your attendance by reply*, when has Scott ever said that?' Cold whipped through Janine's thin blouse, icing her shoulder blades. 'And we never have meetings on the ground floor – only visitors get the good tea and fancy hand towels. And I *still* didn't get it.'

The other end of the line was silent.

'He didn't even bring down my coat. If I get hypothermia on the way home, make sure Scott comes to my funeral.' Janine took a breath. 'The only good thing, of course, is this is definitely what I want.' The acid feeling in her nose sharpened. She sniffed.

Was that a sniff from the other end of the phone? Was he sniffing in sympathy?

'Phil?' Janine tried to pull it together. 'We'll be OK. I promise. We'll be OK.'

'No, it's . . .' Phil's voice sounded emptier than she'd ever heard it.

'Phil?'

'My mum collapsed in the night. She's dead.'

3

Janine's bad news was firmly eclipsed by Phil's. They didn't talk about the redundancy or the house move. When an estate agent hammered in the For Sale sign outside the house, Janine just watched through the window with folded arms and narrowed eyes, storing up her fury to hiss at Sal later, when Phil wasn't there.

Janine did all the washing, and all the washing-up. She helped Katie make a printed photobook – *The Book of Nana Lynn*. She left gaps in conversation for Phil to talk and, when he didn't, told stories about his mum instead. How Lynn liked to sing show tunes in the car, with special sub-Mariah trills when she thought no one was listening. How *she'd once seen* a soap star on the train and *had* got him to sign Phil's birthday card. How she'd once asked a waiter for a Molotov cocktail when *she'd* meant a mojito.

And Janine didn't say anything when, in the night, she felt Phil getting up next to her, knowing he was going downstairs to drink wine until dawn.

Three weeks later, the cremation was short and perfunctory. Roy's street was busy with cars, his house full of people. Janine stood among the throng in Roy's front room, smoothing down her shirt dress with one hand.

15

'Brie parcel?' She held her tray out to a woman walking past. 'They're from M and S – they're fancy.'

The woman looked at the tray. 'Do you have coleslaw?'

'What?' Janine frowned. 'No. Why would you . . .'

The grandmother clock chimed four, and Janine turned automatically to look. The clock was too big for this seventies semi but it was inherited, which meant it had to stay for ever. Katie was holding court on the sofa, inexplicably wearing a frog head shower cap, showing some cousins her *Book of Nana Lynn*.

The coleslaw woman walked away. Janine watched her mother stride towards her and tried to look pleased.

'It's a shame Katie's wearing that shower cap,' Mum said.

'I think it's fine.'

'She'd look prettier without it.'

Janine didn't say anything. Today wasn't the day.

'She's been such a tonic. Made the whole day so lovely and cheery.'

Janine shook her head in mild reproach. There'd been no need for Mum to come, as Janine had told her, but her mum had an inexplicable love of funerals. *It's about respect,* she'd once said, while reapplying her lipstick in a bereaved friend's hallway.

Janine held her tray up, but Mum raised the palm of her hand with the firmness of a lollipop lady. Rita Pierce hadn't eaten pastry since 1984.

'That grandmother clock.' Mum nodded towards it. 'Make sure you get it properly valued when the time comes.'

'Mum!'

'I'm just being practical!' Mum laughed in apparent surprise. 'You've always been so squeamish about death.'

'What a ridiculous thing to say.' Janine offered her tray to

an elderly woman, who appeared to have brought a Jack Russell on a trailing lead. Should Janine say something? Weren't
wakes usually for humans only? But then, she couldn't care
less about tradition, and Roy wouldn't see the dog anyway.
He hadn't left the kitchen. Today, he was a drinks-serving,
snack-fetching Terminator of hospitality.

'You are. You're *extremely* squeamish about death.'

Janine shook her head. It was irritating her mum had noticed that, especially because Janine went to great lengths
to hide it. She pretended she understood that life was more
precious for being finite, and that death gave life meaning,
that the Circle of Life wasn't just a *Lion King* song. Still,
she felt embarrassed that, at the age of forty-two, she
hadn't quite got her head round it. She made the right
noises, but her fear came out in subtle ways, such as never
being able to bring herself to carry a donor card – just in
case she still needed her organs for some future she didn't
believe in. She understood Lynn was gone, but couldn't
quite fathom that *Lynn was gone.* Her own irrationality was
infuriating.

'I'm pleased I've got you alone.' Mum's voice was low. 'Phil
tells me Marky's selling the house out from under you. But
you'll be fine. You've got something alternative planned, of
course.' She asked the question with no question mark. 'And
your job is nice and secure.'

Janine scratched at something caught between her teeth
and didn't answer. She didn't need to. Mum had a way of
asking questions that came with the answer rolled in, pre-
emptively removing any possibility of dissent or bad news. If
Janine were to correct her in this situation – *no, definitely not
fine; no, we have no House Plan B; no, my job's not secure, I'm
about to be made redundant* – Mum would just give a pained

frown as though Janine had spoiled everything, and move on to telling Janine about another part of her life that Mum had decided was also wonderful.

'If you get stuck, you can always use my old caravan. That's why I've kept it. For family emergencies.'

'That's kind, Mum. But we'll be fine.' Janine nodded towards her daughter. 'Katie's trying to get your attention.'

Mum beamed. 'She is?'

Janine watched Mum walk away, a bounce in her step. Those kitten heels were new, and what Mum called *dancing height*. Concerning on a day like today – but then, Janine wasn't her mother's keeper. Thank Christ.

Janine put her tray down and headed for the kitchen.

Roy was at the sink rinsing a glass, his shirt sleeves pushed up, a tea towel over his shoulder.

'Can we do that later, Roy? I'm sure everyone's got a drink by now.'

'Gavin needs a fresh glass.' Roy's voice was gruff. 'He's put his down somewhere.'

'I'm sure people can wash their own glasses.'

'No.' Roy whipped the tea towel off his shoulder. 'And I've got everything under control, so don't fuss.' He buffed the glass to a squeak.

Well. She'd tried.

She found Phil alone in the garden, sitting on his mum's padded garden chair, staring at his feet, inching the footrest in and out. Lynn and Roy each had their own chairs in a matching rhododendron pattern, but only Lynn's chair reclined. Roy didn't believe in reclining – he considered the action morally suspect.

Janine made her voice light. 'You hiding?'

'Maybe.' Phil kept looking at his feet. 'Times like this, I

wish I still smoked.' He ran his finger over the plastic chair arm. 'This was Mum's chair.'

Janine left a respectful gap. 'Katie's wearing a frog shower cap. I'm not sure where she got it. Is that a problem?'

Phil inched the footrest out. 'Mum would probably like it.'

'I thought that. Also, there's a Jack Russell in the lounge.'

Phil took a second. He shrugged.

Janine sat on the bench opposite. 'You told Mum about Marky and the house.'

'She offered us the caravan.' Phil sniffed. 'I said, Rita, I know people make strange decisions when they're grieving, but we're not living on your driveway.' He looked up. 'Is Dad all right?'

'He's washing up. Intensely. So I think so.'

Phil shook his head. 'I told him not to have the wake here.'

'He makes such odd choices.' For a man obsessed with efficiency, Roy always took the path of most work.

Phil's sister Claudia approached from the back doorway, her face half shaded by the sun. 'Can I join you?'

'Of course.' Janine shuffled over on the bench to make room.

Nobody spoke.

Janine tried to think of something to say – something meaningful and intimate, something beyond bland politeness. Problem was, she didn't know Claudia. Claudia lived with her family in Singapore, and this was the only time she'd flown home in the four years Janine had been with Phil.

Still, Janine knew all about Claudia. Roy and Lynn were full of information about her musical children, her impressive job in corporate finance, her powerful new air conditioning. Roy even did a daily background sweep of Claudia-adjacent detail and, when anyone mentioned the weather in the UK, was ready to counter with *It's eighty-nine degrees today in Singapore, sixty-four per cent humidity.*

'This is so hard.' Claudia sat down. 'I should have come back sooner.'

Janine left a pause for Phil to reassure his sister.

When he didn't, Janine leaned forwards. 'You didn't know this would happen, Claud.' Nope, too overfamiliar. She'd go back to Claudia next time.

'And I feel so upset to be leaving Dad so soon. I've got to get a taxi to the airport at four.'

Phil brushed something from his trousers.

Claudia stood up. 'I'll go and check on Dad.'

Phil watched her walk back inside. 'I thought at least she'd stay a few days.'

'She'll bring her family to visit your dad when it's not so raw.' Janine hoped it was true.

They both sat in silence. Janine listened to the rustle of the trees. She studied Roy's perfectly trimmed hedges, and his lawn. It was immaculate, the freshly mown stripes evident even in grief.

She glanced at Phil. 'You look handsome in a suit, you know.'

He gave a faint smile. 'Can't wait to get it off. The collar chafes.'

Janine glanced at the redness under his jawbone. 'You can't tell.'

There was a too-loud peal of laughter from the kitchen. Her mother's laugh.

Janine screwed up her eyes. 'Sorry.'

'What?'

'Doesn't matter.' If Phil hadn't noticed her mother's gaiety, she wasn't going to point it out.

She listened to the rustling trees some more. She watched a blackbird hop across the top of the fence.

Eventually, Janine put her hand in Phil's. 'Shall we go back in?'

Phil didn't say anything.

'Come on.' Janine squeezed his hand. 'Let's go back in.'

4

Roy waited for the house to empty. He accepted hugs from his guests while pressed back against the hallway table, trying not to disturb the photograph frames with his rear. He made all the right noises, again and again.

'Thank you – yes, you too.'

'Thanks for coming.'

'Safe journey.'

Eventually, there was just family left. Roy had managed to dispatch Claudia back to the airport in a taxi, but Phil and Janine were more stubborn.

Roy flapped a determined tea towel in their direction. 'Go!' He flapped his towel again. He was a ringmaster – and one with particularly stubborn lions. 'You've helped me get the glasses into the kitchen, now be gone. I'm fine!'

Phil glanced at Janine and back. 'But . . .'

Roy squared up to him. 'Don't I look fine to you?' He directed the words at the bridge of Phil's nose. He couldn't risk looking him in the eye. He couldn't risk his gaze hooking on anything like sadness there, for fear his own eyes would reflect it. Reflect it, and escalate it, creating infinite mirrors of grief.

No. No infinite mirrors of grief for Roy this afternoon. That was *not* how this was going to go.

'If you feel up to looking after Katie this weekend, we'd appreciate it.' Janine kissed Roy's cheek. 'But let me know.'

'Of course I'm happy to have Katie.' Roy knew Janine didn't need a babysitter. She was trying to give him a focus.

Katie blinked up at Roy from under her frog cap. She held up *The Book of Nana Lynn* – the book she'd been brandishing all afternoon, a book he couldn't even glance at. Not if he had any chance of getting through the day.

He made his voice soft. 'Thanks, Katie. It's wonderful.' He took the book and placed it on the hallway table.

He stopped smiling. He flapped his ringmaster's tea towel at Phil for a third time, with a hostility bordering on aggression. 'Go!' He reached for Phil's shoulders and physically turned him towards the door. 'I've got things to do! Be gone!'

Phil glanced at Janine.

'Right.' Janine pushed her heavy fringe to the side. 'We'll see you at the weekend, Roy.'

Finally, they left.

Roy shut the door behind them. The house buzzed softly with quiet.

He replated the remaining sandwiches and cake slices, winding them in what Lynn would have said was too much cling film. He washed the guest glasses and placed them back in the display cabinet. He placed the best china back in its original boxes and slid the boxes into the cupboard under the stairs where they had sat for fifty years.

Roy wiped the surfaces and put the tea towels over the maiden. He poured some water into a (non-guest) glass, and sat down in his armchair. He rested his head back against one of many squares of fabrics Lynn had placed on headrests, giving his furniture the feel of airline seats.

He could get rid of those silly squares of fabric now, of

course. Roy had won that argument. He was the last man standing.

But he knew now, with certainty, that he never would.

Roy looked down, to the crisp creases of his trousers. The creases Lynn always teased him for ironing in.

He swallowed.

He gripped and closed his hands.

He strode through to the hallway and swiped his keys from the bowl.

Roy walked and walked. Up the estate, towards the T-junction, past the cemetery. Past the bus shelter with the smashed glass and the bubble-letter graffiti.

Looking for anything to distract him, he stopped to read the advertising cards in the newsagent's window.

Volunteers needed at the library. Flexible hours.

And somehow, that registered.

Five minutes later, Roy stood at the library desk in front of Tessa, the reliably unfriendly manager who'd been ground down by years of overdue returns.

'We'll be closing soon,' Tessa said, by way of greeting.

'I understand you're looking for volunteers, and I'd like to apply for the position.' Roy rocked back on his heels. 'I was shift leader at the biscuit factory and then a magistrate. I recently gained a distinction in an Open University degree in Philosophy.' He indicated Tessa's computer. 'If you look at my records, you'll see I've never once returned a book late.'

Tessa nodded. 'I'll get you a form.'

'I'm available immediately. I can start tomorrow.'

Tessa paused. She took in his clothes.

Roy looked down at his smart black funeral suit. He said nothing.

'Bring this in tomorrow.' Tessa handed him a form. 'And we can talk.'

Roy walked back from the library and let himself into the house.

He took his suit jacket off and placed it back on the hanger. He placed the jacket back in the cupboard, rustling Lynn's sun-orange dress in its plastic cover.

Roy looked at the dress for a moment. He adjusted the still-cellophaned metal-and-feather-hat-thing attached to the hanger, making sure the feathers weren't squashed. He closed the cupboard with a soft click.

He went back down to the front room. He switched the radio on to the sounds of Rachmaninoff's Piano Concerto No 2. And, now he knew he had at least one appointment in the future, Roy rolled up his shirt sleeves and set up the ironing board.

PART TWO

Six months later

5

Phil strode through the house in his work overalls, searching for his wallet, phone and van keys. He found Janine sitting opposite Katie at the kitchen table.

Katie was eating breakfast.

Janine definitely wasn't.

'And how many racoons are there?' Janine had her elbows on the table, leaning forwards and holding out a letter. She looked at Katie with the air of a TV cop interviewing a suspect.

Katie, unruffled, picked up another square of toast. 'All the Year One girls are dancing racoons.'

Phil looked at the space next to the breadbin and found his wallet.

'And what about the boys?' Janine asked. 'What other animals are in the play?'

'There's crocodiles.' Katie ripped the crust from the toast. 'Penguins. One frog and some tigers.' She laid the crust on her plate. 'And there's a shark in the bath scene.'

Phil picked up some post from the side and looked beneath. No phone; no keys. He wondered idly what kind of play this was, where Antarctic animals met tigers, and sharks took baths, and the world was overrun with dancing racoons.

'Phil!' Janine whacked the back of her hand against the

letter. 'The school say I've got to send Katie in base layers for a racoon outfit for that play this afternoon. I've only just found the letter. What colour do *you* think a racoon is, Phil?'

From the double use of his name, Phil suspected he knew the answer. 'Black and white?'

'Oh, no. Oh no, no, *no*, Phil! Racoons are *pink*!' Janine waved a stiff arm. 'They only want me to send her in in a pink T-shirt and trackie bottoms! To play a bloody racoon!'

Phil tried not to notice how much calmer breakfast had been when Janine used to leave early for work. 'The school probably think they're making it easy for us.' Phil surveyed the surfaces. 'They'll think we have pink trackies hanging around.'

'Well, that's even worse, isn't it?'

Phil took one last glance around the kitchen. No phone or keys.

'Phil. Look.'

Janine held up a phone. He was about to say *thanks*, when he saw it was *her* phone. On the screen a racoon looked startled, holding up its paws in a furtive scurry.

Phil took in the image. 'Brown and white, then.'

'Not pink, though. Definitely not pink.'

Phil glanced around the kitchen for a final time.

'I'm not buying anything new.' Janine put her phone back on the table. 'We're not the kind of family who can buy new clothes for a one-off play, and it's not right for the school to expect it.'

'Katie's friends might have spare pink clothes.'

'I'm sure they do.' Janine sniffed. 'She can go in that free T-shirt from when they were handing out cereal at the station. It's pink enough.'

Katie looked up at Phil, her eyes wide. *Save me!*

Phil gave her a friendly pat on the shoulder. *I know, mate. I know.* He walked into the lounge to continue his hunt.

On the TV in the corner of the room, a breakfast reporter read the news.

'Pink's a broad spectrum.' Janine followed him, her too-long pyjama bottoms catching under her feet. 'And colour's in the eye of the beholder. The cereal T-shirt will be fine. And I can put her in her old leggings.'

Phil picked up a sofa cushion and – success! – found his phone.

'Phil?'

He turned.

'The fruit bowl.' Janine dangled his keys. 'You maniac.'

'Thanks.'

'Wait there.'

Janine hurried back into the kitchen. She came back holding a lunchbox and thermos.

Phil paused. 'You didn't have to.'

'I know, but . . .' Janine blew her sharp fringe out of her face. 'I've got time.'

Phil took the lunchbox and thermos. 'Thanks.' He tried to look grateful. Janine's new Superwife thing was quite unnerving – this new routine where she handed him a bag of food at the door in the morning, and Phil thanked her for something he didn't want. Yes, he was getting a lunch and a thermos made. But it was a shit lunch, and he was getting a thermos made by *a stranger.*

'Do I need to get your dad a ticket for Katie's play?' Janine said suddenly.

'He bought it directly. He said it would be easier for us.'

Janine raised her gaze. 'We could have bought him a ticket for a fiver.'

'I know but – you know Dad.'

'I do.' Janine left a meaningful pause. 'I do.'

Phil decided not to find the pause meaningful. He didn't have time for *meaningful* at seven thirty.

But Janine did. 'Of course, I love your dad. He's so good to us, helping with the pick-ups. And those amazing Sunday lunches he does!'

'He said he didn't want to stagnate.' After Mum died, Dad had applied himself to learning 'Lynn's jobs'. He now excelled at all household tasks, and tackled each with the sincerity of a bomb-disposal operative.

'And his gravy never tastes like it's from a packet,' Janine added.

Phil inched his phone out of his pocket. 'It won't be from a packet.' Janine's company had once put her on a Crucial Conversations workshop. Hearing Dad's good qualities listed was a sign Janine was moving through bread layers and about to hit the filling of the shit sandwich. Phil always knew his day was about to get worse when Janine approached, kindness in her voice, and said *You know how much I love you and how much I really appreciate everything you do around the house . . . ?*

'I just wish he didn't tell Katie she looks pretty quite so much.'

And there it was.

Phil glanced at the time on his phone. Seven thirty-seven. He needed to go. 'Is this definitely about Dad? Are you sure it isn't about the pink racoons?'

'Right now, we're on your dad.'

'He's trying to show an interest.'

'And that's fine,' Janine said. 'It's brilliant. But can't he talk about her maths or something?'

'He could . . .' Phil tried to find the right corner of that logic to unpick. 'But it would be a bit of a leap. When she never mentions maths.'

'He could try harder to compliment her on something that isn't her appearance.'

'You want me to ask him to . . .'

'No, I just want him to stop on his own.'

'I'm not sure he will. Old dogs, and all that.'

Janine shook her head.

Phil took a small step towards the door. 'I just don't understand what you want me to do, J, if you don't want me to speak to him?'

'I just want you to notice. And agree with me.'

Phil said nothing.

On the TV, the news reporter said, *'The energy price cap increase will mean bills going up by seventy-four per cent.'*

Janine and Phil both turned to stare.

Janine shook her head. 'Evil.'

'We'll be fine,' Phil said, in the firm tone he used to convince himself.

'Yes, we will,' Janine replied in the same tone. 'Because I'm going to get that job.'

'Yes,' Phil said.

'And I'll take whatever salary they offer. I have no pride.'

'And, as so few consumers are on fixed rates, the increase will affect the vast majority of Britain's twenty-eight million households.'

Janine reached for the remote control. 'I picture those energy guys as Mr Monopoly.' She switched the TV off. 'The guy from the game with the big hat.' She gestured above her head.

Phil nodded.

'There's stuff we can do. I've been looking into getting a heated gilet.'

Phil was finding it hard not to look at his phone again. Breakfast time used to be about coffee and toast. Not financial planning.

'I'm going to get one to wear around the house in the daytime. I can maybe get one of those big heated slipper boots you put both feet in. I can hop from room to room, it'll be fine. Good for my core. I can't have the heating on when it's just me in the house now.' She threw the remote onto the sofa. 'Now I'm not a proper person anymore.'

Phil gave a weak smile. He'd never got used to these conversations. *You have a pudding, that's fine, I can't justify pudding now. You have a pint, I'll just have a half now I'm unemployed.* Seeing his previously strident partner calling herself *not a proper person* was as jarring as her handing him a packed lunch at the door.

From the other room, Janine's phone rang.

Katie shouted. 'It's Daddy!'

Phil and Janine made eye contact.

'It'll be fine.' Janine rubbed her arms, self-soothing. 'It'll have fallen through.'

Phil nodded. 'Of course.'

'That's what he'll be phoning to say – that it's fallen through. House sales always fall through, don't they? *Always.*'

'Hi, Dad!' Katie's voice was singsong. She was the only person in Janine's life who still felt any pleasure about hearing from Marky. That Katie felt like that was a good thing, obviously.

'Tell him I'll call him back after I've done your school run!'

Phil squeezed her arm. 'It'll be fine.'
'I know.'
'It always is. We always are.'
Janine nodded hard. 'I know.'

6

Janine walked Katie in the direction of school. She'd given back the work car two months before. They'd let her keep the car for the whole of her garden leave, which was pretty decent of them – if you overlooked the fact they'd stitched Janine up over the redundancy, which Janine definitely *could not*. Janine still woke up in the night, teeth clenched about the unfairness of it all.

Janine's phone beeped. A message from Marky.

Talk in person? Meet you in the café round the corner from the school at 9?

'Mum, did you just make a face?'

'Of course I didn't.'

Janine tapped a reply.

OK

'Who was it?'

Janine slid her phone back into her jeans' pocket. 'Wrong number.'

At least he'd picked a convenient location. Did Marky know she'd had to give up the car? Probably. Katie was super leaky. A lovely girl, of course – but a proper little grass.

'Mum?'

Janine looked down at Katie and smiled. 'Yes?'

'You and Daddy aren't going to argue, are you?'

'Of course not.' Janine adjusted Katie's Power Rangers rucksack, moving the weight on both shoulders equally. 'We never argue. We respect and admire each other hugely. Just because we don't love each other anymore, doesn't mean we don't like each other.' Was this gaslighting? 'Please don't worry.' If it was gaslighting, was it a good kind? 'See you at home time.'

Janine watched Katie pick up pace and hurried towards her group of friends. She turned, hoping to do a quick getaway. It was essential not to make eye contact.

'Hi Janine!'

Janine didn't stop. She just smiled, gave a vague wave to whichever mum had spoken, and hurried towards the café.

It was something Janine had started to worry about lately – gaslighting Katie. She couldn't help noticing how regularly she did it. Santa, the Easter Bunny, the Tooth Fairy. And the other kind of gaslighting: about how the world worked. The *if you work hard, you get rewarded* kind. The *grown-ups know best* kind. The *everything's going to be fine* kind.

Were they really doing kids any favours?

Janine pushed her hands into her coat pockets. She never used to think about this stuff. It had been so much more straightforward when she'd always been in a rush, and had a million excuses for being shit. Since the redundancy, she'd *had time* to think, like she *had time* to prepare vegan food and *had time* to source products in recycled packaging. It wasn't a good thing. Six months at home, and she *still* hadn't fixed the fridge door. Every time she went to get milk and did the special jerk-and-lift, she despised herself that bit more.

Janine entered the café. The bell above the door rung.

She looked at the handwritten chalk board above the counter, and tried not to look at the prices. Coffee shops added an extra quid per drink if there was a chalk board. She was about to walk towards the counter, but thought *fuck it – Marky's idea, he can pay.*

She settled into a table in the corner, moving an old newspaper. She glanced idly at the headline.

At Least 60% of Households Projected To Be In Fuel Poverty By Autumn.

She turned the newspaper face down.

Marky was late, of course. *Artist's time*, she used to call it. When such things were a cute personality quirk (for the first few months), rather than evidence of a core selfishness (forevermore).

She picked up her phone and flicked onto the *Am I The Villain Here?* forum.

Am I the villain for putting salt in my own milk because my housemate kept stealing it?

'You're not usually here at this time, Janine!'

Janine looked up. It was Lexi's mum – the one with a grey streak at the front of her hair, who always wore a yellow rain-coat. She looked wholesome. Smiley. A woman completely without edge.

'Hi . . .'

Janine didn't know Lexi's mum's name. She'd been told it, of course – but that wasn't the same as *knowing it.*

'Beth.'

'Beth, of course, Lexi's mum.' This was why you needed a bit of edge, so people would remember you. Schools, workplaces, takeaway places – everyone knew Janine's name.

Beth indicated behind her, at the group of mums gathered round a large table, nice-arguing about whose turn it was to get the coffees. '*Absolutely not, you got them on Tuesday and Thursday last week.*' '*Megan, don't make me fight you.*'

'Do you want to join us?' Beth asked.

'I'm waiting for someone.' Janine's smile didn't waver. 'But thank you.'

'How's the job search going?'

'Oh.' Janine jiggled her head. 'You know. I'm waiting to hear.'

'You're always welcome to join us,' Beth said. 'We come here most days. Tomorrow we're doing plans for the school quiz, if you'd like to join?'

'Ah, thanks so much for asking me!' Janine gave her warmest smile. 'I *so* appreciate you asking.'

Beth smiled back.

'But I don't want to lie and keep making excuses that demean us all. I'm just not that kind of mum. No shade – I'm just not. I'll be back at work soon but, in the meantime, I'm not working. It's pretty humiliating really.'

Beth's smiled faded.

'That's not the humiliating bit,' Janine said hastily. 'It's that I'm a *working mum* who's not working. You can see it – it's obvious! I'm the *bring Aldi cakes for the bake sale, send my kid in with the wrong kind of flour, my kid's waiting on the step of after-school club* kind of mum. So it just wouldn't work.' Janine gave her warmest smile. 'But I really appreciate you asking me.' She put her hand on her heart. 'It means loads.'

Beth nodded. 'I didn't want you to feel left out.'

'I hope I haven't offended you.'

'No problem. See you at the play. Our girls are going to make very pretty racoons!'

Janine smiled as Beth walked over to the other table. Her smile faded.

The bell jangled as Marky entered the café.

In sunglasses. At nine in the morning.

Janine's stomach pulsed.

She knew she really shouldn't feel this irritated by a pair of sunglasses, but there was something about this man that gave her a physical reaction. It had got so much worse since he'd got lucky with Molly. If he said anything about *living your dreams* or *manifestation*, Janine was walking out.

Marky made a coffee gesture and Janine nodded.

She looked down at her phone again.

Am I the villain for putting salt in my own milk because my housemate kept stealing it?

I'm very organised and don't like to run out of anything. All my housemates swear they don't take my milk, but I often find an empty carton in the fridge. So I started marking it with my name. And still the milk went. I'm sick of it.

Last week, I marked my milk as normal, poured salt into the carton, went to work, and waited.

When I came back from work, one of my housemates accused me of trying to poison him. But salt isn't deadly. And it's his fault for stealing in the first place.

Am I the villain for putting a harmless substance in my own bottle of milk?

You're the villain here
Not the villain here

With satisfaction, Janine clicked *Not the villain here*.

Marky placed a coffee down in front of her.

She put the phone away. 'Thanks.' Janine blew on her coffee, making a hole in the foam. *Make this quick.*

Marky took his sunglasses off and folded the arms in. 'So we're all good to go.'

Janine stopped blowing.

Marky put his sunglasses on the table. 'I had confirmation late last night – we've exchanged contracts.'

'It hasn't fallen through?' Janine stared at the foam hole. 'I thought it was going to fall through?'

'Why did you think that?'

'Because everything falls through.' Janine raised her gaze. 'What about the survey? What about the state of our damp course? What about it needing a new roof, were the buyers not looking properly?'

Marky smiled. 'They didn't mind. I didn't even need to knock money off! People are desperate! Have you seen the state of the market?'

'Yes,' Janine said pointedly.

'It's a seller's market, Janine!'

Janine stared at Marky's sunglasses. She wanted to sweep her arm across the table, send them skittering across the busy coffee-shop floor.

'The market is so buoyant right now, I was even wondering whether I should pull out and keep the house as an investment!'

Janine glanced up. 'With us living in it?' The idea of Marky as their landlord was hideous. The other option was worse.

He frowned. 'To rent out properly. For profit.'

Janine stared at her cup's handle.

'I thought you didn't believe in making money from property?' She kept staring at the handle. 'I thought you were a Marxist. Or was that just when you were poor?'

Marky chuckled. Of course, he was able to be good natured. That's what money gave you – the ability to take a joke. The ability to wear topics lightly, rather than having them weigh you down like a waterlogged cloak. 'You never did understand me, did you, Janine?'

Janine saw Beth and the others looking over. She smiled back reassuringly.

'The exchange date is Friday. They want to move in on Saturday.'

'*This* Saturday?' Janine banged her cup down. 'That's too soon!'

'They're getting pressure down the chain. You knew it would be soon.'

Janine said nothing.

'I'll see if they can wait until Sunday. Have you found somewhere yet?'

'What do you care?' She couldn't stop herself.

'Of course I care where Katie lives! But that's why I wanted to talk. I'm much more settled than I used to be. If you're finding it hard to get somewhere you can afford that's appropriate . . .'

Janine clamped her jaw till her cheek throbbed.

' . . . then we can work something out. Do you want Katie to move in with us while you find somewhere?'

'No.'

'Just temporarily.'

'Still no.'

'Molly and I would be delighted to have her.'

'Thanks, Marky, I appreciate the offer. I've found somewhere.'

'That's great!' Marky's eyebrows softened. 'So where—'

'And I need to take this call.' Janine held up her unringing phone. 'It's about a job. Thanks for the coffee.'

Janine grabbed her handbag. She placed the phone to her ear and walked out of the café. She waved at Marky through the window, pretending to speak into the phone, with the last of her self-respect draining away – only stopping fake-talking when she was a good distance down the road.

7

That afternoon, Roy strode into the bustling school hall for Katie's play, with a faint feeling the world had done too many turns.

This was the school Roy had attended. The same school hall. Perhaps even the same dusty floor he had sat cross-legged on seventy years previously, buttocks cold and numb, pulling absentmindedly on his regulation black shoelaces while a wizened reverend ranted about hellfire.

Roy suspected assemblies here didn't go in for hellfire these days.

'This is my first school play for decades.' He handed his ticket to the young man on the door, one he tried not to notice had a glittery beard. 'Is there a seating etiquette, like at weddings?'

The man smiled. His beard twinkled. 'Are you family?'

'Not biologically. Step-grandfather.' Roy wondered whether the man wasn't well. 'And that's not strictly accurate, my son and his partner aren't married, but it's there or thereabouts.'

'The seats are for family only. We're massively oversubscribed.'

Roy nodded. Rules were rules.

He gestured to the back of the room. 'Then I stand there, I presume?'

'Jesse!' A woman came striding over. 'What are you saying to this gentleman?' She turned to Roy. 'Of course, we can find a seat for *you*.'

Roy gave a smile of appreciation. He was about to thank her – and realised.

He switched his smile off. 'Don't find me a seat.'

'Someone will give one up for you, I'm sure.'

'No need.'

'We can always make exceptions for our elder—'

'Rules are there for a reason.' Roy straightened up. 'And I will stand at the back, like everyone else.'

With dignity, he walked to the back of the room. He stared straight ahead, refusing to acknowledge the woman waving in his eyeline.

He couldn't see Phil and Janine anywhere.

It was only a good time later, as the lights went down and a teacher walked onto stage, that Roy recognised Janine's angular mousy bob and fluffy-hooded jacket as she and Phil jogged past, hunched over, each with a hand lifted in apology.

Among the sea of lifted phones, Roy watched the play.

Boys dressed as frogs and monkeys jumped onto crash-mats and tumbled across the stage. There didn't seem to be any arc to the narrative – no evidence of Aristotle's three-act structure – but, still, Roy was happy to go with the flow. He hadn't been expecting Ibsen.

The latest set of roaring animals left the stage, and the woman at the side spoke into her microphone. 'And here come our talented dancing racoons!'

Around Roy, there were whispers of anticipation. Phones moved higher.

A line of five-year-old girls skipped sideways onto the stage, holding hands in an inexpert Riverdance, to an audible ripple of *aahs* from the audience. The racoons' fluffy ringed tails trailed behind them.

One Riverdancing racoon caught Roy's eye. Pride swelled in his chest. Katie!

Except . . .

Except.

Roy's chest contracted.

Katie's face was painted like the other racoons, and she had the same tail. But, while the other racoons were all in pink T-shirts and trousers, Katie's T-shirt was – orange. And what was that illustration? The logo of a cereal company?

If that wasn't bad enough, Katie's leggings were too small, beige, and riding high up her calves. Dancing next to the other perfectly dressed kids, Katie looked like some kind of . . . street urchin.

Roy put his hand to his mouth.

He knew Janine and Phil were struggling. But *this*!

He had been worried for a while. Now, it was getting serious. Here was the evidence, dancing in front of him in too-short leggings and an orange Corn Flakes T-shirt.

Roy was *really* starting to worry.

The play finished. Rows of animals came out to take their bows, to a level of feet-stamping that suggested David Bowie was about to play an encore.

People milled past as Roy strode up to Phil and Janine. 'What happened? Why were you late?'

'My fault.' Janine blew her fringe out of her eyes. 'I had some stuff to sort out.'

'Why were you standing at the back, Dad?' Phil frowned. 'I know *you* won't have been late.'

'Seats were for biological family. Common-law step-grandparent didn't count.'

Janine glanced up. 'They said that?'

'In spirit, if not in word.'

'But you *are* family, Roy.' Janine crossed her arms. 'I wish you'd told us. I would have given them a piece of my mind, especially with you being—'

'Here she comes!' Roy said overloudly.

Katie barrelled up to them, her fluffy tail sweeping the floor.

'Amazing work, Katie!' Janine said.

'What moves!' Phil shook his head in apparent wonder. 'I was like – *is that our Katie dancing, or is it Rhianna?*'

'Wonderful! A sense of rhythm like that, you could do Shaftesbury Avenue!' Roy tugged a lock of Katie's hair. 'And *what* a pretty racoon!'

Did Janine stiffen? Did Phil look away?

Katie beamed back at Roy.

A woman came over, holding a bowl of crisps. 'Now, Katie, be a good little helper and offer these to our audience.' She placed the bowl in Katie's hands. 'I'm asking all the racoons to help.'

Janine stared at the teacher.

And there it was again – an unexpected crackle of tension.

'And the crocodiles and monkeys?' Janine spoke more slowly than usual. 'Are they helping too?'

'They can help if they want.' The teacher looked over at the stage. 'But better we let them let off steam, isn't it?' Roy followed the teacher's gaze, to where boys dressed as crocodiles and monkeys dived onto crashmats. The teacher shook her head fondly. 'If we ask the boys, they'll only drop the bowls.'

Roy smiled.

Janine moved her bottom jaw an inch to one side. She leaned down to Katie. 'Would you like to play on the crashmats instead of helping?'

Katie shook her head. With both hands, she held her bowl of crisps up to Roy.

Janine looked back to the teacher. She looked like she wanted to say more, but the teacher walked away. Janine stared after her.

It felt like there was a charge in the air today.

But Roy could make things normal. He beamed at Katie, who was still holding up the bowl. 'Thank you very much.' He took a crisp, though he didn't eat them – crisps being a food-like invention of Big Hydrogenated Fat and Big Salt, and only to be eaten in emergencies. 'What a wonderful waitress. And *such* a pretty racoon.'

And there was that tension in the air again. Not a crackle, this time – a freeze.

Roy wasn't imagining it. And it had happened a few times lately. It must be the redundancy, that must be why Janine was looking so . . . stiff.

Katie turned to the group next to them, offering crisps and accepting compliments.

Roy smiled at Janine to show there was nothing to be tense about.

Janine stared at Phil, as though she was waiting for something.

Phil coughed. 'So, Katie's maths.' He turned to Roy. 'She's great at maths, you know.'

'That's wonderful.' Roy put the crisp in his mouth and confirmed what he already knew. Not food.

'She's not *great* at maths, to be fair.' Janine glanced round to check Katie wasn't listening. 'But she does *do* maths. And other stuff too. She doesn't just go around looking pretty all the time.'

'Well, that's lovely, Janine.' Roy looked around for a napkin to wipe the grease from his fingers.

'Roy. You know I really appreciate everything you do for us?'

Slowly, Roy looked up.

He glanced at Phil.

Phil stared at a wall of posters with unnecessary intensity.

'Would you mind . . .' Janine leaned forwards . . . 'Not calling Katie pretty *quite* so much?'

Roy blinked at her.

'As a favour,' Janine added. 'To me.'

Roy pulled his handkerchief out of his jumper sleeve. He wiped his fingers, one by one, waiting for the conversation to make sense.

It didn't.

'I know it seems like a tiny thing,' Janine continued, 'but the world has moved on.'

Roy folded his handkerchief. He edged it precisely back into his sleeve, evenly distributing the cotton under the wool. He smoothed the bumps till the area around his cuff was smooth.

Roy cleared his throat. 'If you say so, Janine.'

'Thank you. Much appreciated.' She smiled. 'I'm going to talk to that teacher.' She strode off.

Roy turned to Phil. 'What was that about?'

Phil gave a tiny shrug.

'And why's poor Katie in orange?'

Phil glanced over Roy's shoulder and Roy followed his gaze. Janine seemed to be remonstrating with the teacher by some metal catering urns.

Phil turned back. 'The letter got bunched up in her school bag. We didn't realise till late. We had to improvise.'

'But Janine has so much time on her hands now!' Roy always knew when Phil was lying. 'This is about money again, isn't it?'

Phil paused. 'Pink's a broad spectrum. And colour's in the eye of the beholder.'

'Please can I help you with money, Phil.'

'Dad. I'm forty-four.'

'Yes, but with Janine out of work—'

'Dad, please. Not today. It's not a good one. Marky's exchanged contracts on the house. We need to be out by next weekend.'

Roy stared at him.

'Dad. It's fine.'

'That's not enough time to buy!'

'We can't buy anyway. We can't get a mortgage without Janine having a job.'

'But renting is just throwing money away!'

Phil shoved his hands in his pockets. 'We don't have a choice, Dad. And it's fine.'

'You do have a choice.' Surely *now* they'd let him help? 'Maybe I can get a mortgage for you?'

'They only give mortgages to people of working age.'

'Really?' That was a jolt to Roy's heart. 'Not that, then, but you know I have two spare rooms! This is madness!'

'We'll sort something.' Phil appeared fascinated by

something over Roy's shoulder. 'We're going to look at a place straight after this.'

'You don't want to eat into your house deposit by renting or you'll never be able to buy!'

'Dad. *Please.*'

Phil deliberately turned to speak to the man on his left.

Roy shook his hands in frustration.

The crowd of proud relatives started to disperse. Roy, Phil, Janine and Katie collected their coats.

They edged out of the hall together, past racoons jangling charity buckets with *Donations Please!* on the front.

'Only the racoons, *again,*' Janine muttered, to no one.

Phil started to reach into his back pocket.

Roy put a restraining hand on his arm. 'I'll put in for all of us. I have to, I've only got a twenty.' Roy got out his wallet and surreptitiously fingered past small notes.

'That's very generous, Roy.' Janine smiled at him. 'Thank you.'

Roy smiled back. It must be because Janine was stressed about money – that must be why she'd been so odd today.

Which was one of the many reasons Roy couldn't let this situation go on any longer. He couldn't stand idly by and let his family suffer.

It was decided. Whether Phil wanted him to or not.

Roy was going to *do something.*

Roy drove home from Katie's play, tapping his hand against the steering wheel.

Here he was, fortunate enough to be born in history's golden era, with a final salary pension and a naturally austere mindset. He'd retired from his shift leader's job at sixty, in good health, with many good volunteer years ahead of him to do his civic duty as a magistrate. He knew he'd been lucky.

If only he was allowed to share this good fortune with his family!

It was a fact of life that your children were meant to be better off financially than you had been. That it wasn't the case here was so galling. Roy had failed at the most fundamental part of parenthood.

Phil was being selfish. And Katie was the one who suffered, going to school plays in cereal T-shirts and too-small leggings. A little girl, being driven around in *a van*, now they didn't even have a car. They were nearly homeless – and Phil still wouldn't let Roy help!

Ahead, the big traffic lights turned amber.

Roy brought the car to a stop.

A scruffy man in a bobble hat leapt in front of the car. Roy shrank back.

He registered the squeegee. The bucket. The man's soapy sponge, dangerously close to his windscreen. 'DON'T!'

It was essential the man heard. If no sponge touched windscreen, there was no psychological contract.

Roy opened his window. 'Not today, thank you.'

The man stared at him, water dripping from his sponge onto Roy's pristine bonnet.

'You know,' Roy said kindly, 'you might like to ask before you put your sponge on a stranger's windscreen. You'll get into fewer awkward conversations.'

The man continued to stare at Roy.

Roy gave him his friendliest smile. He glanced at the traffic light. Still red.

'I'll get into less awkward conversations?' The man's voice

had an edge of menace. You're telling me how to do my job?'

'*Fewer* awkward conversations.' Roy beamed at the man. 'But we're both correct, of course, because such conversations will also be *less* awkward.'

The man put his sponge in his bucket and placed both on the tarmac. He leaned on the bonnet and stared at Roy with an intensity that made the back of Roy's neck prickle.

Ahead of Roy, the lights turned amber.

Roy put light pressure on the accelerator. The car gave the politest hint of a roar.

He doffed an imaginary hat. 'Have a nice evening.'

'I knew it!' The man slammed his hands on Roy's bonnet. 'It's *you*!'

There was a long beep from the car behind.

The windscreen man slammed his hands down again. 'You're the judge twat who fucked up my life! I was wrongly accused! I lost access to my kids because of you!'

There was movement in Roy's peripheral vision. The driver behind manoeuvred into the next lane.

'Say sorry!' The man shouted. 'Admit you made a mistake. You fucked up my life!'

Roy looked in his rear-view mirror.

He shoved the gearstick into position and reversed hard.

The windscreen man jogged forwards. 'Hey!'

Roy span the car round. He felt a crunch under the wheels.

He scrunched his eyes shut. *Not his foot, not his foot, not his foot . . .*

'You've run over my bucket, you arsehole!'

Roy sped back in the direction he'd come from. He didn't dare look back for at least a minute.

Finally, he risked looking into the rear-view mirror. The

man wasn't chasing him. He just needed to breathe. He just needed to—

A horn blared.

Roy snapped his gaze to the front – and into the rapidly flashing lights of the oncoming car.

He jerked the wheel to the left. He slammed his foot on the brake.

He just had time to take in the warning red of the post box before it came up to meet him.

8

Phil parked round the corner from the house they were due to view.

Janine jumped from the passenger side, continuing her phone conversation. Katie picked up her tail and followed Janine down.

'No, Mum.' There was strain in Janine's voice. 'We really appreciate the offer, but we still don't want your caravan. We've got it all under control.'

Phil tried not to react. Rita's caravan was a rusty, fussy curtained thing from the nineties. Worse, it was parked permanently on Rita's drive – the very opposite of a great *location, location, location.*

'I need to go. We're viewing a house right now.' Janine switched the phone off and looked at Katie. 'Don't you want to take your outfit off?'

Katie shook her head. She picked up her tail and swung it in a circle.

Phil saw the house and slowed. He took in its narrowness. The missing glass pane in the front door, replaced by board. The peeling window frames and broken gutter.

'It can't be that one.' Janine looked at the instructions on her phone. 'Oh.'

Katie trailed behind. 'Will the new house be bigger than our old house?'

Janine glanced at Phil. 'It'll be *better* than our old house.'

'Will it have a swimming pool?'

'We wouldn't want our own swimming pool, Katie. We'd have to clean it out constantly.' Phil shook his head. 'We'd have to keep putting in chemicals, sampling the water. Imagine the hassle.'

'You could do that though,' Katie said. 'I want a house with a swimming pool.'

Janine glanced at her. 'Do you know *anyone* who has a swimming pool?'

'August at school. And she has a stable of ponies, an underground ice rink, and a magic cup that fills itself.'

'No, she doesn't.' Janine smiled at the man waiting with a clipboard. 'Hi!'

'Hi.' The man's suit bunched at his ankles. 'Janine and . . .'

'Phil. And Katie.' Janine paused. 'Katie's a racoon.'

The man indicated with his clipboard. 'I didn't know racoons ate Corn Flakes.'

'They do, all the time,' Janine followed him towards the door. 'Famous for it.'

Katie stopped. '*This* house?'

Janine patted her shoulder. 'It's the inside that matters.'

Katie turned to Janine in the kitchen. 'The inside is *worse*!'

Janine's voice was singsong. 'It's fine.'

'It smells like a hamster cage!'

Janine smiled at the clipboard man. 'Don't be ridiculous!'

Katie picked up her tail, like she didn't want it trailing on *this* floor. 'I thought we were moving somewhere like Daddy's.'

Janine didn't answer.

Katie gasped. She shrank back, behind Janine's legs, and pointed.

Phil looked. Under the single, battered counter, there was space for something electrical. Where that something had once been, there was now a nest of stringy, dirty cobwebs, and a single withered Monster Munch.

Katie reached for Janine's hand.

'We'll remove the cobwebs,' Janine said. 'And the hole will be covered up.'

Katie's lips trembled. 'But we'll *know*.'

The clipboard man looked from one to the other. 'It's for a washing machine. I assume you have a washing machine?'

Janine and Phil exchanged glances.

'Do we?' Phil asked.

'I don't know.' Janine put her hands on her hips and studied the kitchen. She crouched opposite Katie. 'There's been a mistake.' She flashed Katie a smile. 'We're not living here.' She stood up, turned to the clipboard man and switched the smile off. 'We're not living here.'

'But, in your budget, the only options are—'

'Later.' Janine smiled at Katie again. 'I'll phone you later.'

Katie held her tail up high and followed Janine out of the house. 'I don't want to move now. Let's just stay where we are.'

Phil shoved his hands in his pockets. He'd let Janine take this one.

Janine put her sunglasses on. 'We can't stay where we are, lovey.'

'Why?'

'Your father and I have decided to sell the house. It's the right decision.'

'Could we live at Daddy's?'

Janine's response was instant. 'No.'

'He's got loads of rooms he doesn't use.'

'I'm sure he needs them all.'

'He has one room that's just for his guitar. And one room just for exercising. My bedroom there is bigger than our whole—'

'We can't, Katie. I'm sorry. It doesn't work like that.' A tear rolled out from beneath Janine's sunglasses, carving a glistening path down her cheek.

Katie stared at the tear. She frowned.

'It's just the sun.' Janine wiped her cheek with the back of her hand. 'In my eyes.'

Phil reached for her hand.

'And I've got one of my migraines coming on. But I'm fine.' Janine beamed at Katie. A fresh tear flowed down her cheek. 'And you're going to love the next house I show you.'

They drove home in silence. They were nearly there when Janine's phone went.

'Janine speaking.' She paused. 'No, he's here though. He doesn't always answer his phone.'

Phil glanced down at his phone in the cupholder. Several missed calls: fairly standard. If he answered all his calls, he'd never get any work done.

Janine's voice changed. '*What?*'

Phil jerked his head round.

Janine wiggled a hand for Phil to pull over. 'But is he going to be OK?'

Phil pulled the van up at the side of the road.

'Please tell him we'll be right there.'

Phil stared at her. Katie stared at her.

Janine took a second. 'So.' She glanced from Phil to Katie. 'The important thing to remember is that Roy's going to be absolutely fine.'

Half an hour later Phil sat opposite Dad's bed in the hospital.

There was something about seeing Dad on a bed. He *never* saw his dad in bed. When had he got so small?

'I didn't have a fall,' Dad said quickly. 'It was a car accident.' He touched the swelling on his cheeks. 'It's just bruising, from the airbag.'

'What about the other car?' Phil asked. 'Are they OK?'

Dad paused. 'It's a long story.'

Dad was released from hospital that evening.

Phil was helping Dad out of the van when Sal came out of the house next door. 'Roy! Your face!'

'I'm fine.' Dad's voice was gruff. He strode up his path and went inside.

'Car accident.' Phil spoke in a low voice so Dad couldn't hear. 'He's shaken up, but he's all right.'

'Anyone else involved?'

'No, thank God.' Phil paused. 'It seems he drove into a post box.'

Sal raised her eyebrows a fraction.

'He's got a bit of bruising from the airbag but otherwise he's fine.'

Sal made her voice lower still. 'And will he be giving up the car?'

'Apparently the answer is definitely, definitely not.'

Sal and Phil had a conversation with their eyes.

Phil shrugged. 'He won't be able to drive for a few weeks,

anyway. But he won't let me stay over tonight so can you keep an eye on him?'

'Course, mate.'

'Thanks.' Having Janine's best mate living next door to his dad was a godsend sometimes. Not least because it was how Phil and Janine first met, at one of Lynn's *Come one, come all!* sangria barbecues.

'Has Janine heard about that job yet?'

Phil shook his head. 'I've got a good feeling about it though. I think.' He scratched his cheek. 'Or a desperate feeling. Which is the same thing, isn't it? Kind of?'

Sal raised an eyebrow.

'She's . . . getting worse.' It felt like disloyalty. Was it disloyalty when it was *her* friend he was talking to? 'She asked Dad not to call Katie pretty at the play. She asked just now if the Tooth Fairy was gaslighting.'

Sal lifted her chin. 'She does have a bit of a thing about gaslighting.'

'She says she's going to get a heated gilet. Says she can't have the heating on at home alone now she's not a proper person anymore. Can't justify it.'

Sal winced.

'She says she's going to get one of those heated old people boots, and hop from room to room.'

There was a long pause.

'She'll get that job.' Sal's voice was firm.

Phil nodded. 'Yeah.'

'And I'll check on Roy later.'

Phil touched her arm. 'Thanks.'

9

The next morning Roy shaved carefully around his bruises, trying not to notice the black eyes staring back at him in the mirror. He'd been prepared for swelling, and greeny-purply bruising. But he'd woken to see the skin round his eyes as funereal black as Katie's racoon make-up, giving him the masked air of a scholarly, Third Age Batman.

A Batman who drove into post boxes.

He picked up his carrier bag of books and left the house half an hour earlier than usual. He had to walk the long way into town, if he was going to avoid the windscreen man's crossroads. Which he definitely was. For ever.

'You been fighting again, Roy?'

Roy looked across the street. The young man from over the road, Darsh, had his eyebrows raised.

Roy gave a faint smile. 'You know me.'

'I should see the other guy, right?'

Roy kept his smile fixed.

'Did you have a fall?'

Roy snapped his smile off. 'Car accident.' He sped off towards the library before having to explain that, in this case, the other guy was a post box.

Walking was fine. Roy could do everything adequately on foot and public transport. Still, he hoped he'd get his car back soon. He'd seen too many friends stop driving after a *something*. Something medical, a bump, a loss of confidence – whatever it was, the evidence was overwhelming. If you stopped driving a car for too long at seventy-eight, you didn't start again, and Roy refused to be a burden. Being a burden, and being Roy Frost, were two very different states of being.

Roy shook his head as he walked. The whole thing was unsettling.

Not just Roy's lapse in concentration, though that was bad enough. Also that the bobble-hatted man had called Roy *that judge twat* – which, while it wasn't the ideal synonym for *magistrate*, did suggest this wasn't a case of mistaken identity.

Surely Roy couldn't possibly have ruined this man's life with an incorrect decision?

If someone said you'd ruined their life – whether it was true or not, you'd at least expect to remember them.

And then there was the other problem. His soon-to-be-homeless family.

Eventually, Roy reached the library's entrance. The familiar noise of his footfall on the wide entrance steps, echoing against the stone wall, had a soothing effect.

Everything felt manageable at the library.

It was something about the lovely calming hush of a community of people improving themselves. Which was one of the reasons he never understood why the manager, Tessa, could look so unhappy.

Roy strode up to where Tessa stood at the counter with another volunteer – her mother, Yvonne. 'Ladies.'

'*Roy!*' Yvonne sucked in her breath. 'Your face!'

Roy made a made a *pff* noise. 'Airbag.' He got it in before anyone could say *fall*. 'Looks much worse than it is.'

Tessa peered at him. 'Surely you'd rather be at home today, Roy?'

'I'm absolutely fine.'

'We could easily have coped without you.'

Roy balked. 'A Frost meets his commitments, Tessa.' He walked to the staffroom and tucked his bag into the cupboard next to the sink. He headed back to the counter. 'So what do we have planned for today?'

'There's new stock to input.' Tessa's tone was flat, for what was such excellent news.

'That's wonderful.' Roy could be enthusiastic enough for two. 'And what does the new stock comprise?' Most people said *comprise of* these days, but Roy liked to keep the accurate use in circulation.

'The new stock is fiction.' Tessa's voice had an edge. 'Romance, crime, historical. The stuff our customers want.'

Yvonne looked between Tessa and Roy, beaming. She was an elderly woman who smelled of cigarettes and synthetic roses, with a seemingly endless parade of fluffy pastel jumpers. She had a compliment for everyone, and never stopped smiling. That she was Tessa's mother was something Roy found as unfathomable as Tessa's lack of enthusiasm for new books. There had been a clear failure of both nature *and* nurture.

'Tessa.' Roy stood straighter. 'Have you had a chance to ponder our chat last week, about whether to get in more non-fiction books – in particular, philosophy?'

'We've discussed this.' Tessa glanced at Yvonne and back. 'And I told you the buyers make the choices centrally.'

'I listened to what you said – that it would be here

somewhere. But I've systematically reviewed the catalogue and I can't find anything about Thomas Aquinas. Which feels like a big gap to me.' Roy left a pause. 'As I'm sure it does to you.'

Tessa glanced at Yvonne again.

Yvonne kept smiling.

'Roy.' Tessa's voice was firm. 'If I suggest we need anything to the central buyers, it will be more large print erotica. But thanks for the input.'

Roy nodded with apparent capitulation. He had anticipated this.

A young man in a hooded sweatshirt approached.

Roy rocked back on his heels. 'Yes, sir. How can I advise?' This was his favourite bit of the job – the opportunity to make recommendations. *Well, if you like Milton, it's just a short hop to Spenser.*

'The printer's stuck.'

Roy felt his smile wobble. Still, he followed the man to the computer area.

Five minutes later, the man in the hooded sweatshirt was quite irate, and Roy stepped back to let Tessa take over. Tessa removed the piece of paper that was inexplicably jammed – well, how was Roy meant to find *that* door?

Roy called out as she marched back to the desk, 'Wonderful job, Tessa.'

Yvonne appeared at his side. 'The printers do get easier.'

Roy watched Tessa wrench her ergonomic keyboard towards her and type what must be a venomous message. 'Do you think Tessa enjoys her job? I feel like we both enjoy being here so much more than she does.'

'I suppose we don't have the responsibility she does.'

'That must be it. Yvonne, did you know the world's oldest

known library was founded sometime in the seventh century BC?'

Yvonne smiled. 'I didn't know that, no.'

'It was built for the royal contemplation of the Assyrian ruler Ashurbanipal.'

'How wonderful!'

'Mum!' Tessa sounded strained. 'Can you help this lady with the encyclopaedias?'

Yvonne touched Roy's shoulder and walked away.

Later, Yvonne collared Roy in the Young Adult section. 'Roy, I've been meaning to ask. What was in that plastic bag you furtively brought in earlier?'

'I wasn't furtive. I was deliberately not being furtive. Wait here.'

Roy hurried to the staffroom and came back with his bag of books. 'I suspected Tessa wouldn't order any philosophy books, so I took it upon myself to buy some. I'm making a donation.'

Yvonne pulled the books out of the bag, smiling. *How to Think. Great Minds. Beyond Good and Evil. Philosophy Through the Ages. The Little Book of Thinking. Big Ideas and Open Minds. Thought Experiments: Philosophical Puzzles for Young and Old.*

Yvonne looked up. 'You bought these yourself?'

'For the greater good. Tessa can't mind, can she?'

'How could anyone mind a donation from a volunteer?'

Roy didn't say *Tessa could*. If Yvonne wasn't aware of the psychology of her own daughter, Roy didn't want to disappoint her.

Tessa came over. 'I thought we'd processed all the new stock already.'

Roy smiled. 'Not quite all.'

'But it took you ages, Roy.'

'I had a little something up my sleeve.'

'And it's such a simple task.'

'We have more new stock.' Roy took a deep breath. 'Because I have made a philanthropic donation.'

Tessa followed his gaze to *Thought Experiments: Philosophical Puzzles for Young and Old*. She walked away.

Roy looked at the *New in Stock!* stand. There wasn't any room on the top shelves, and he didn't want to push his luck. He placed *How to Think* and *The Little Book of Thinking* on the bottom.

He wondered how long it would take for some eager punter to snap them up. And whether it was appropriate he hover by the stand, so he could congratulate them on their good taste when doing so.

Roy was in charge of the trolley of returns, placing the books back on their original shelves. He looked at the last one – *Cooking on a Budget* – and turned it over.

Would it be intrusive to get this out for Janine? After all, she had a habit of looking gift horses in the mouth. *Glaring* gift horses in the mouth.

Yvonne stopped next to him. 'Cookery's top shelf, near the DVDs.'

Roy looked down at the book. 'I was wondering whether to take it out.'

'I didn't know you cooked, Roy! How wonderful!'

'I was actually wondering whether to take this out for my daughter-in-law. But . . .'

'But?'

Roy stared at the sparkly brooch on Yvonne's baby blue cardigan. 'It's delicate.'

When he looked up, Yvonne was smiling. 'Coffee?'

In the library's back office, Roy and Yvonne sat across from each other on low spongy chairs.

He hadn't meant to tell her anything.

He'd told her everything.

'I see your conundrum.' Yvonne made her cigarette-rasped voice thoughtful. 'People get ashamed when times are hard. That time I was hiding from the rent collector, I always put on my best dress and my biggest smile.'

'But they won't let me help! And with Janine out of work, they can't even get a mortgage!' Roy felt his neck stiffening. 'It's little Katie who loses out when they don't ask for financial help!'

'I didn't realise that little Corn Flake racoon was your Katie. My heart went out to the poor love in orange.' Yvonne leaned forwards; a miasma of synthetic florals caught in Roy's throat. 'What about Katie's father? Can he help?'

'He's a waste of space.' Roy moved back in his chair. The concentration of perfume was still strong. 'He's a man in his forties who plays guitar at a bar two evenings a week and calls himself a professional musician. His maintenance payments were always late until he met a wealthy lady.' Roy shook his head. 'His name's Mark but he calls himself *Marky*. He doesn't even *try* to get a proper job, though he has a child to support, and he's forty-five. *Forty-five*. And Mark-*y*.' Roy said the last syllable with emphasis. 'Isn't that all you need to know about the man?'

Yvonne shook her head. Her long earrings jangled like a collection of gaudy paperclips. There was something about Yvonne that put Roy in mind of a fortune teller.

'Phil and Janine have to be out of their house by the

weekend. And I have two spare rooms! But they're too proud to move in!'

Yvonne lifted a finger in a *wait* gesture. She seemed to be studying Roy carefully.

Roy shifted self-consciously.

Eventually, she spoke. 'Your car's in the shop for a while?'

Roy nodded.

'Well, there you go.' Yvonne nodded. 'Say you need them to move in. To help you with shopping and stuff.'

Roy pulled his eyebrows together. 'Oh.'

'Say you're feeling vulnerable after the crash. Milk those black eyes.'

'I can't say that.' Roy sat up straighter. 'Because I'm not vulnerable at all.'

Yvonne raised her eyebrows. 'And you say *they're* too proud?'

He looked at his shoelaces.

'Roy, *of course* you're not vulnerable. This is a teeny white lie for the greater good.'

Roy thought about this. 'You don't think it's too … cunning?'

'I'd say *shrewd*. Shrewd, like a fox.'

Roy sat back. He turned the idea over in his mind.

'Shrewd like a fox.' Roy jerked forwards and gripped both Yvonne's hands. 'Thank you!'

'Not just a pretty face, see?' She beamed at him. 'Even if I don't know anything about Syrian libraries.'

'*Assyrian*. I'm going to phone Phil right now.' He half sprang out of the spongy chair and threw open the staff-room door. 'Very clever, Yvonne!'

*

That evening, Roy sat opposite Phil and Janine at Roy's kitchen table.

'It feels like a *huge* deal,' Janine said.

'It's not,' Roy said. 'It's killing two birds with one stone.'

'Surely you don't *really* want us here?'

Roy paused. 'I'm not quite feeling myself.' He stared at the wall calendar, so he didn't have to meet their eyes. 'After the bump.'

Janine frowned.

'I might get dizzy standing up. What if I can't even iron a shirt?'

Janine looked at Phil and back. 'Neither of us know how to iron, Roy. I don't believe in it.'

Roy frowned. He looked at Phil for corroboration.

Phil shook his head too. 'We don't even have an ironing board.'

'It's not the ironing.' Roy reeled from this revelation. 'It's the cooking. Though I'll still do most of that. And the cleaning. Though I'll still do most of that too. And having access to a car – though, of course, in the Altrincham conurbation we are adequately served by public transport. No, it's having you there, really. If I'm feeling' – he licked his lips – 'vulnerable.'

Janine looked at Phil.

'And you'll be able to keep your money for a deposit for when Janine gets a job, rather than having to throw it away on rent.' That was *much* more comfortable ground.

Phil stared at the kitchen table. 'We'd have to give you *something*, Dad.'

'I wouldn't hear of it.' Roy leaned onto his elbows. 'You can do some shopping and some jobs for me around the house, how about that?'

They all sat in silence.

Phil glanced at Janine. 'I really don't like it when he goes up on the roof.'

'If you're worried about privacy' – Roy tried not to look victorious – 'the previous owners had lodgers, so the bedroom doors have locks. I will distribute all the keys.'

'I'm sure that wouldn't be necessary,' Janine said.

'You don't have to decide tonight.' Roy pushed himself up from the table. 'But why don't I show you your rooms?'

Janine and Phil were given a full tour of the rooms in Roy's house – including an introduction to where all the door and window keys were kept, a demonstration of the central heating timer, and a detailed explanation about how to use a shower with an immersion heater. Eventually, they were allowed to leave.

Janine's head was full as she walked down the path. Could she do this?

No.

No?

No.

She glanced at the house next door. 'Will you pick up Katie from Marky's without me?' She touched Phil's arm. 'I need Sal.'

On Sal's sofa, Janine cradled the cup of coffee, not drinking. 'Phil thinks we should do it, I can tell.'

Sal ripped open a packet of chocolate digestives and placed it on the table.

'Would you move into your father-in-law's house? It's worse than him moving in with us. Isn't it? Because it'd be *his* house. And he winds me up.' Janine went to take a sip, and stopped. Sal made her coffee so strong you could taste the anxiety. Not what she needed right now. 'Though everything's winding me up at the moment. What colour do you think a racoon is, Sal?'

She looked up. Sal didn't answer, just kept crunching her biscuit.

'Pink, Sal. At the school play, they made all the girls wear pink.' Janine sighed. 'But then Roy was there, making it worse, so I snapped at him. I don't want to snap at Roy – I *like* Roy. And best way to keep liking him is to live in a different house.'

Sal held up a finger. 'Listen.'

Janine listened, out of respect to the finger. Mournful guitar music came from upstairs.

'Alfie's listening to Joy Division now. Can you believe it?' Sal reached for another biscuit. 'I bet it was on a TV show. That's usually how it happens. Fifteen years old and he's playing Joy Division. I feel quite proud.'

Janine nodded. 'And Roy stood at the back through the whole play, when anyone would have given him a chair if he'd just said. And he called Katie *pretty* for the millionth time.'

'You know Roy gets everyone's bins in if we forget? The whole street. We call him Bin Captain.'

'Yeah, I know, he's great.'

'That time he went to Anglesey, you should have seen it out there. Bins everywhere. Brown ones, blue ones, green ones, black ones – every shit colour of the rainbow, all blocking the kerb.' Sal indicated the biscuits. 'You having any?'

Janine shook her head. 'Roy's great, obviously, and he's lonely and he's been shaken by the car accident and I feel sorry for him.' Janine used one fingernail to pick dirt out from another. 'But I don't think we're on the same wavelength. He does such strange things! It's not just calling Katie *pretty* all the time or standing at the back of the play like a martyr.' She leaned forwards. 'You know Lynn died in the early hours, but he didn't tell Phil till nine a.m.? Roy just called the police, then sat there, alone, with no support. All night.'

Sal raised her eyebrows minutely.

'He said he would have phoned Phil if it had been a plumbing emergency, but as Lynn was already dead it could wait till office hours.'

Sal sniffed.

'He drives me insane. But he's a good man, so I *feel bad* that it drives me insane, which means I feel bad twice over. Bad *squared*.' Janine took a breath. 'And I'm the only one who'd be there with him in the daytime. I already feel bad about not having a job, so I'd feel bad *cubed*. I don't want to feel bad cubed, Sal. I'm not in the right place to feel bad cubed.' She bit some loose skin from her lip. 'Let's talk about something else. How's work?'

Sal shrugged.

'Have you seen Scott the redundancy snake lately?'

Sal shook her head and indicated the biscuits. 'If you're not having any, I'll put them in the kitchen.' She took the biscuits away and came back.

'Who's Scott got as a Bad News Bear now? Don't tell me he's dealing with his own messes.'

'Sales and operations don't really interact; you know that.'

'But surely you see him in the canteen sometimes.' Sal wasn't off the hook like that. 'Do you glare at him? Do you send him subliminal messages of hate?'

'No.'

'No?'

'Not my circus. Not my monkeys.'

Janine gave a deep intake of breath. 'Sal! This is your circus! I *am* your monkey!'

'Nope.'

'I am your monkey,' Janine mumbled.

'Stop dwelling. Didn't you have an interview last week? How did it go?'

Janine sighed.

'You sigh a lot at the moment.'

'I do?'

Sal nodded. 'It's like you've got a new thing.'

Janine sighed again. 'It went OK. I wore a skirt suit and tights, like a professional lady of business. I banged on about stakeholder management and upskilling.' Janine stared at Sal. 'Anyway. Roy's house.' Janine leaned forwards. 'What would you do?'

Sal paused. 'I'd go home and talk to my partner.'

'Yeah, I suppose.' Janine stood up. 'Yeah.'

Janine let herself into the house to find Phil and Katie watching TV. On screen, a man in a tweed suit priced up a clock. Phil had an amazing capacity to watch anything that was on.

Janine threw her bag next to Katie on the sofa. 'Have fun at school?'

Slowly, Katie turned to Janine. She looked – empty. 'Everyone was playing with special pens they got given at Ava's party at the weekend.' Her voice was drained of joy. 'Everyone in the playground was pen twins. Except me.'

There was a stab in Janine's chest. 'Oh, no, love.'

'It was a special pen. With a fluffy tail.'

'Not everyone gets to go to every party, I'm afraid.'

'The ink was silver.'

'We can buy you a silver pen.'

'When you shook it, little hearts in water went up and down.'

'We'll search for it online and get it.'

Katie shook her head to show such a thing would be futile. She pushed herself up from the sofa. 'I'm going to look at my stickers.'

Janine watched her daughter leave the room with slow, dignified steps. 'Did I miss an invitation in the school bag? Or did they just leave Katie out?'

'She'll have forgotten by tomorrow.' Phil patted Janine's leg. 'Half the kids will have lost those pens by now.'

'I wonder if the party was a drop-off. I'd be gutted if I missed a drop-off.' Even with free time on her hands, a drop-off was still the parenting dream. 'Do you think they left her out because I don't make enough of an effort with the mums?'

'No.'

Janine snuggled further back into the sofa cushions. 'It was fine before, when I worked. But now it looks like a slight that I don't join in with their coffees and PTA stuff. Like I'm looking down on them or something. When they're actually living what is, of course, an absolutely appropriate and equally valid kind of life.'

Phil stared at her. 'Are you still talking to me?'

Janine frowned. 'What?'

'You sound like you think you're on the radio.'

'I need to make more effort.' Janine straightened a cushion behind her. 'I've told the parents to save the date for Katie's birthday party, but you know what? I will give those parents the precious gift of a drop-off. That's got to be worth some points.'

Phil patted her knee. He stared at the screen.

'But parties are so expensive these days.' The cushion was still uncomfortable; Janine placed it to the side. 'It's so different than in our day – a pass-the-parcel and a block of Neopolitan with jelly won't cut it anymore. Six-year-olds have bucket-list parties now. Anyway.' It was time. 'What do we do about your dad?'

'It's your call.' Phil looked casual, staring at the screen, but he was scratching the fingernails of one hand against his thumb.

'Why?'

'My dad. Your call.'

'I don't want to move in there.'

'I know.'

'Would you move in with my mum?'

Phil's eyes widened briefly. He scratched harder.

'You wouldn't. I know you wouldn't.'

'There wouldn't be space. Not with all her jewellery and kettlebells.'

Janine smiled. 'I love your dad but he's . . . you know.'

Phil glanced at her. He looked back at the screen.

'I think it'll be a disaster.'

'Then we won't do it.'

'I think you want to.' She jiggled on the sofa in agitation. 'But you won't say it because you're making it my decision. You always make the hard things my decision. It's always all on me!'

Phil turned to face her.

She knew he wanted to say she was being dramatic, but he didn't say it, so they couldn't have a row. Janine couldn't pick up Phil on what he wanted to say – *thought crimes* weren't the same *actual crimes*. Janine had learned that in Crucial Conversations.

Though she was pretty sure Crucial Conversations hadn't called them *thought crimes*.

Still, feigned neutrality wasn't fair. This was definitely Phil's circus, and these were *born* his monkeys. 'You saw me and your dad at the play. Look what happens when we spend too much time together.'

Phil said nothing.

She scratched the back of her neck. 'And I know I made it worse when I brought up the *pretty* thing. It was ... suboptimal.' Janine might not be in the workplace anymore, but she could still use its vocabulary. 'I'm worried if we move in, it'll ruin things for ever.'

Phil appeared to be concentrating on an antique clock.

'You think we should move in.'

'All I think ...' Phil turned to face her '... is that we're homeless from Sunday. Not an exaggeration. We literally have no home.'

Janine looked at her lap.

'And it's just while we sort ourselves out and Dad recovers. If we had anywhere else to go, we could. But we haven't.' He held her gaze. 'So it's a win-win.'

'Or a lose-lose.'

The dishwasher beeped. Phil got up in a Pavlovian response.

'Leave it.' Janine got up. 'It's my job, now I don't work.'

'J. I can empty the fucking dishwasher.' Phil walked through to the kitchen. He opened the dishwasher door and pulled out some plates. 'Think about it. Look how scared Katie was of the house we could afford.'

'Kids adapt.'

Phil leaned against the counter. 'It wouldn't be for ever.'

Janine started unloading cutlery, so she didn't have to look him in the eye. 'You think we should do it.'

Phil pushed the dishwasher door shut. 'Yes.' He put his hands round Janine's waist. 'I think we should. But it's your call.'

Janine straightened up. She took in the warmth of Phil's hands through her T-shirt.

She gave a long sigh – and, remembering Sal's comment, stopped. She didn't want to be a sigher, on top of everything else. She wasn't one of life's defeatists. Janine was dynamic. A trooper. Decisive, even. It wasn't that long ago a company used to *pay* her to make decisions.

'I'll go to see your dad on my own. Tomorrow.' Janine looked in his eyes. 'And I'll decide.'

The next morning, Janine dropped Katie off at the school gates. She looked at the mums milling around. Which woman belonged to the kid who'd had the party, Ava?

Was she the mum with the pram, and the grumpy shih tzu stashed underneath where a nappy bag should go?

Was she the one all in lycra with a high ponytail, and those special sculpting leggings and a white – *white* – gym hoodie?

Or was she the one walking away, the one with the reality TV eyelashes and cheek fillers who made a laugh noise in words to show she found something funny – '*huh huh*' – and had never, to Janine's knowledge, actually laughed?

Janine focused on Lexi's mum, with her streak of grey hair and yellow raincoat. The woman with no discernible edge. *Beth*.

'Hi, Beth!' She strolled over. 'I just wanted to ask you – there was a party at the weekend. Ava's party. Do you know anything about it? Katie didn't get an invitation.'

Beth's eyebrows scrunched together. Janine took in the

firmness of her forehead. She was at least a decade younger than Janine, despite the streak of grey. 'She didn't get an invitation?'

'Maybe. You know kids lose things.'

Beth turned to the woman with the pram and the grumpy shih tzu. 'Do you know anything, Megan?'

Janine tried to sear the name onto her memory. *Megan. Shih tzu Megan shih tzu Megan.* She assumed there was a baby in the pram and it wasn't just a shih tzu carrier, but she'd save that question for when she was running out of conversation another time.

Megan smiled at Janine. 'Zara definitely put it on the WhatsApp group.'

Janine closed her eyes briefly. 'That'll be it. Thanks, Megan.' So it was Janine's fault.

'It was all over WhatsApp, wasn't it, Cass?' Megan said to the woman in the white hoodie.

The white hoodie woman – *Cass* – nodded. 'There were loads of messages back and forth.'

'I muted that group.'

Beth lifted her chin. 'It can be useful, you know.'

'Yes but …' What could Janine say? She couldn't bear to let all that non-stop tedium sluice into her life. All the conversations about lost cardigans. The PTA. Presents for teachers. *So many* lost cardigans.

'Thanks.' Janine nodded to Beth. 'I'm sure it is.'

'Do you want to join us at the café today?'

'I can't. Thanks.' Janine wondered how this woman had the energy to be so nice to someone who didn't deserve it. 'I'd really like to, this time, but I said I'd go to see my father-in-law. He's been in a car accident.'

'Is he OK?'

'He wants us to move in with him.' Janine blurted it without thinking.

Beth raised her eyebrows in an *eek* face.

Cass and Megan did the same.

'Yeah.' Janine smiled at the women. 'Awful, isn't it?'

They got it. That was something.

WhatsApp aside, maybe it was possible she could become friends with these women after all?

Half an hour later, Janine stood with Roy, surveying his spare bedroom. There wasn't much to survey.

They'd be able to get one wardrobe in here. Maybe a chest of drawers. The rest of their furniture would have to go into storage, but then – you only really needed a bed. And a wardrobe. And when you went camping, you didn't even have those, did you? It was fine. She and Phil were troopers.

'Remind me how long before you have to move out?' Roy said gently.

'A few days,' Janine said.

Roy left a pause. 'There's a lot to organise in finding a new house.'

'Tell me about it. *And* I keep forgetting to sort Katie's birthday.' Janine pressed her lips together. 'I sent a message telling everyone to save the date, but that's all. I need to give Katie a really good party to get in with the mums. It's going to have to be a drop-off.'

Roy looked up. 'If you move in here, I can arrange Katie's party too.'

'No, Roy. Anyway, I've been given a recommendation of a party guy. Party Vince.'

'I like organising things. And I want to be a bigger part of

Katie's life and do nice things for her. Even though I'm not biological family.'

Janine turned to look at him. 'If this is about you having to stand at the play, Roy, those people at the school were bang out of order. You're proper family to me and Katie – inner circle. When the apocalypse comes, we'll spend our last minutes crying and sheltering together.'

'I'd really like to get to know Katie better. Ideally, not in an apocalypse scenario. And I could spend more time with her, if you lived here.'

A wave of tiredness washed over Janine. She looked around the room – at the late-nineties terracotta walls. At the jaunty curtains with their matching, lacy-edged tie-backs.

Why was she still fighting? Giving in would be so much easier. And while this felt like a decision, so many of Janine's more positive decisions were clearly awful. *Marky*. So what did she know?

The wave of tiredness ebbed. She felt smaller in its wake.

She nodded. 'OK. Thank you, Roy. It's a very generous offer. We'd love to move in.'

11

In an ideal world, homelessness would have been enough of an incentive. Roy wouldn't have had to deceitfully overegg some notion of vulnerability. Still, in extreme cases, the ends justified the means – didn't they? Occasionally?

Roy tried to ignore his views on political philosophy. He'd always thought Machiavellianism the cad's branch.

Roy watched Phil and Janine carry a chest of drawers through the front doorway, his eyes widening with alarm at the proximity of the wood to his freshly painted banister. He hurried towards them. 'I'll take that end.'

'Dad . . .' Phil's voice was strained. 'Back off, please. We're moving in to help *you*!'

Roy moved out of the way, and tried not to listen to the chest's journey upstairs. Later, he tried not to notice the new scuff marks on the wallpaper, or the newly chipped paint on the landing skirting board.

Moving day was taking its toll on Roy's house – and on Roy.

Katie's smile dropped when she saw the boxroom. 'This is my room?'

'It'll look better when it's got your bed in it. And your teddies, and such.' Roy had spent the morning in there, washing blinds and wiping down skirting boards.

'It's not for ever.' Janine turned to Katie. 'Think of it like camping!'

'My clean boxroom is nothing like a tent!' Roy tried to keep the heat out of his voice. He turned to Katie. 'Your auntie Claudia grew up perfectly happily in this room.'

'Why are there holes in the carpet?'

'Those marks are from where my furniture was. They'll go soon.'

He turned to walk downstairs.

Katie followed. 'Why do all your plants sit on frilly bits?'

'They're plant coasters. Lynn crocheted them. You have to protect the wood.'

A minute later. 'Why do all your chairs have cloths on the back like in trains?'

'Lynn liked them.' Roy still couldn't ditch them. This was the home Lynn had made. This was how it would stay.

'Why's your TV so small and old?'

Roy didn't answer that. Katie was young. She didn't know what she was saying.

Katie drew in a sharp breath. Her face screwed up with fear. 'The witch!'

Roy closed his eyes. He'd forgotten the witch – the markings Katie saw in the branch of the old oak tree. He looked out of the kitchen window at the offending branch. 'I'll sort it.'

Katie edged back behind the kitchen door, not taking her gaze from the tree.

'I'll do it tomorrow.' Roy made his voice soft. 'I promise, Katie. Tomorrow, the witch will be gone.'

There was silence. Katie stayed in position, behind the kitchen door.

'Now, then,' Roy put his hand on Katie's shoulder, 'To help you settle into your room, why don't we go and read a story?'

'You can't.' Janine shoved the box under the alcove with her leg. 'Her books are all in storage.'

Roy frowned. *All of them?*

She shrugged. 'Mummy said I had to make choices about what was important.'

Roy shook his head in wonder. 'Then it's a very good thing I never throw anything away, isn't it?'

Roy found the box easily in the garage, congratulating himself on his labelling and storage system, uncorrupted by the decades. He carried the box up to Katie's room and sat next to her on the bed.

She didn't look as happy as he'd like.

He clicked his fingers and smiled at Katie. 'I told your mummy I'd arrange you a special birthday party! With all the trimmings. Did she tell you?'

Katie's face opened up. 'I'm having a proper birthday party?'

Roy nodded. He'd offered to arrange it so that he could pay for it, in another Machiavellian move. Janine had been too distracted to notice.

'Can I have costumes that aren't homemade?'

'You absolutely can. In fact, I insist on it.' There'd be no repeat of the shameful Corn Flakes T-shirt incident. Not on his watch.

Katie gripped his arm. 'Mummy said I couldn't have a proper costume.'

'Well,' Roy said carefully, 'I'm in charge now.' The whole thing was so confusing. Yes, money was a factor for this family. But Roy kept reading in the papers about the pressures on mothers, and how they were all always competing to be the best. Yet sometimes it felt like Janine was competing to be the *worst*. She'd once told Roy she was making Katie crisp sandwiches for tea – and said it with something like pride.

'Look, isn't moving fun?' Roy opened one flap of the box. 'It's an adventure! And you have a whole set of new books now!'

Katie side-eyed the box's contents. 'They don't look new.'

'New *to you*.' Roy tapped his handwritten label on the box. 'Can you read that?'

Katie concentrated. 'Phil and Cla ...' She stopped. 'Cla ...'

'*Clau*dia. It says *Phil and Claudia's books*.'

Roy sat on the bed next to Katie and opened the other box flap. The smell of mothballs wafted up.

Katie wrinkled her nose. 'What's that?'

'Mothballs. It's a nice smell.'

Roy ignored Katie's still-wrinkled nose. He pulled the top book out. 'Ah, yes.' He hurtled through decades in his mind, back to that beach in Norfolk, sheltering behind the windbreak with Phil. 'This one is—'

Roy looked more closely at the *Little Sambo* cover. He stopped.

The illustration showed a black boy, carrying an umbrella and wearing very little. The boy had bulging eyes, and massive red lips.

He frowned. It couldn't have always been illustrated like *this*? Surely there was some mistake?

Katie looked at the cover. She looked at Roy.

Roy turned the book face down. 'It was a different time.' He picked up another, showing a floating boy in impish green. 'Aha! That's more like it – *Peter Pan*!' He held it out with pride. 'Have you ever read *Peter Pan*, Katie?'

Katie shook her head.

'It's got a fairy in it. And pirates. And a man with no hand. And a crocodile that swallowed a clock.'

Katie lifted her chin with interest.

Roy leaned back against the headboard. 'Snuggle in, then.' He patted the bed beside him. 'And we can get in a few chapters before I cook tea.'

Roy left Katie in her room, sorting her animal stickers, dealing them into sets with the solemnity of a croupier.

He started making spaghetti bolognaise, cooking to the unfamiliar sounds of a busy house. A toilet flushed without Roy's palm on the handle. Doors opened and closed on a floor where Roy wasn't. Whole conversations took place that Roy only registered as the mumble of voices through the ceiling.

Roy looked at Lynn's handwritten recipe book. *Cook in shallow roin brown dish with crimped edges.* He traced Lynn's handwriting with his finger. She had written these instructions for herself, of course. But, now she wasn't here anymore, it was like she'd written messages just for him.

Roy placed the steaming dish of bolognaise on the mat on the kitchen table.

Janine walked in. 'Smells delicious!'

'Sit anywhere!' Roy paused. 'Except the chair opposite the window.'

Phil and Katie took their seats. Roy started serving.

Janine didn't sit down straight away. 'Wine, I think.'

Roy couldn't help it. 'On a Sunday?'

'It's a special Sunday, moving-in Sunday. It's an occasion.'

She went to the cupboard where she'd placed wine bottles in front of Roy's condiments, and pulled one out.

She opened another cupboard. She closed it, and tried again.

'Wine glasses are in the top cupboard to the left of the kettle,' Roy said.

'Thanks.' Janine got three glasses out. She tried to place one in front of Roy.

Roy shook his head. 'Not on Sunday evening.'

'Fair enough.' Janine poured glasses for Phil and herself.

Roy put a plate in front of Katie. 'It's dark, with that blind drawn. Can you put the big light on, Phil?'

Phil stood up. 'Why's the blind down?'

Katie whimpered.

Janine mouthed to Phil. *The witch.*

Phil flicked the main light switch on.

'Wow.' Janine blinked. 'We'll definitely be able to see what we're eating, won't we?' She blinked again. 'But it looks delicious.' She raised her wine glass. 'To the chef.'

'Cheers.' Roy raised his glass of water. 'And welcome to your new home.'

12

Janine raised her glass to Roy and took a sip of wine. Immediately, she took another, larger one. She took a large bite of Roy's (excellent) spaghetti.

Did Roy usually eat in a room lit up like an operating theatre?

It was one of the first things she'd noticed when she'd moved in – the lighting. There was so much of it – and it was so harsh. Strip lights in the kitchen. Floor-standing task lights next to armchairs and sofas, glowing orbs burning bright like mini suns.

With the harsh glare above, Janine could see the old juice stain on Katie's jumper. It was almost better, Janine decided, to have your house in soft focus.

Janine was feeling homesick. For a home that didn't exist.

Phil took a bite of spaghetti. A shadow crossed his face and he put his knife and fork down.

Janine frowned. 'Phil?'

'Just having a moment.' Phil stared at his plate. 'It tastes just like Mum's.'

Roy looked up. 'It's her recipe.'

Janine reached under the table and squeezed Phil's hand. 'It's delicious.' She looked across at Katie. 'Have you been settling in?'

'We've been having fun, haven't we, Katie?'

Katie nodded. 'Roy's been reading with me.'

'We can watch a film later.' Roy beamed. 'I borrowed *The Little Mermaid* DVD from the library. It's one of the modern Disneys.'

Janine took another bite. Was there a fleck of tomato sauce on her chin? She felt Roy staring at her.

She swallowed. 'Sounds great. Maybe a different film though?'

Roy tapped his chin. 'You've got something . . .'

Janine nodded *thanks*. She wiped her chin with the back of her hand.

'There are napkins,' Roy said. 'On the sideboard.'

Janine nodded *thanks* again. She took another forkful of food and swallowed. 'That film has dangerous messages. A girl chooses give up her voice to win a prince?' She sniffed. 'When Katie got invited to a *Little Mermaid* party, I made her go as the crab.'

Katie was concentrating on twirling spaghetti round her fork.

Roy looked up. 'Dangerous messages?'

'Crabs have more fun.' Janine made pincer gestures. 'Their feet aren't welded together, for a start.'

'But surely they've sanitised the original Hans Christian Andersen story?' Roy's eyes were wide with alarm. 'The mermaid won't be walking in agony, *surely*? She can't die and dissolve into foam at the end?'

'I'm pretty sure Disney will have changed it,' Phil said.

'I wish the mermaid *had* dissolved into foam.' Janine rubbed her chin again, feeling an echo presence of the already-wiped sauce. 'That would have been a better lesson.

So.' Janine smiled at Katie. 'So what were you two reading this afternoon?'

'*Peter Pan*.' Katie looked up from her fork-twirling. 'It's Roy's book.'

'I guessed that.'

'I like pirates now.'

'Good for you.'

'I want to have a pirate party for my birthday.'

Janine nodded. 'Good. You can have whatever you want. And a pirate party is a much better choice than a *Little Mermaid* party. We could even recycle your crab outfit.' She made finger pincers again. 'You could add an eye patch, be a pirate crab.'

Katie stopped smiling. 'I want proper costumes for my party. Not homemade.'

'Oh.' Janine put her fork down. 'Katie, but you know, this year—'

'Janine, we discussed this.' Roy gave her a firm smile. 'You've got too much on as it is, so I said I'll organise Katie's party. No discussion required.'

'Oh, no.' Janine looked at Phil. 'He's doing too much.'

'*He* wants to. And it's already in train. I spoke to the man you suggested, Party Vince, and he's got the date provisionally held. I'm meeting him tomorrow.'

Janine kept looking at Phil.

Phil shrugged.

'I want Roy to do it,' Katie said.

Janine wished her daughter had a shorter memory. The Corn Flake T-shirt had a lot to answer for. She turned back to Roy. 'You know kids' parties can be a bloodbath.'

'You always did have a knack for exaggeration, Janine. I've held many a children's party in my back garden.'

Janine took another mouthful of spaghetti, and didn't point out it must have been over three decades since he'd organised one. 'Let me tell you what's changed. Kids don't like plastic these days.'

'Good for them,' Roy said. 'Right-minded little citizens of the planet.'

'That means no plastic party bags. Or straws. It's not like the old days when you could throw any old' – she glanced at Katie and stopped herself saying *shite* – '*stuff* in party bags. Kids these days can be judgy.'

Roy got up. 'Hold that thought.' He got a telephone pad and pen from the side table. Janine watched him flip the pad open, click the pen on, and write *No plastic*.

He gave a queenly wave. *Continue.*

'Some kids get judgy about glitter too. Though other kids love it, so good luck with that.' Janine forked a pile of spaghetti. 'And no books in party bags. Kids don't like books as gifts.'

Roy didn't write that down. He looked up, making eye contact with Janine. 'Really?'

Janine nodded.

'If you say so.' Roy picked up his pen. Slowly, he wrote *No books as gifts*.

Janine swallowed. 'Kids never notice the details, so take a broad-brush approach and don't faff with the small stuff. Don't bend over backwards when the RSVPs start coming in about dietary requirements – that way, madness lies. You can't please all of the people all of the time.'

Roy nodded. 'I'll defer to the wisdom of J. S. Mill.' He gave Janine a pointed look. 'The greatest happiness for the greatest number.'

Janine nodded. It was fine. A bit of condescension came with the territory.

She poured herself another glass of wine. 'Put some dietary options out if you can but, worst comes to the worst, a kid doesn't eat for an afternoon, no one's going to die. Nuts are the only dealbreaker – nothing with nuts.' She jabbed more spaghetti. 'If any kids are sugar-free, don't be swayed into getting sugar-free cake. It's *not* the same and Katie is only six once. Sugar-free cake does not equal *party*.'

Katie's eyes widened in panic.

Roy wrote *sugar-free cake ≠ party*.

Janine smiled at Katie. 'He's writing it down. Look.' A hot shame pulsed in her chest. 'Roy . . .'

He looked up from his pad.

'I'm sorry if I can sometimes be a bit sharp.'

'I've never noticed,' Roy said gallantly.

The shame in Janine's chest melted to warmth. 'Party Vince will help with the details. He's got a good rep, and I'm sure he does pirate parties.'

Roy wrote down *pirate party*. He added a question mark.

Janine leaned forwards. 'Rumour is he's receptive to offers, so haggle.'

'I'll haggle like I'm in an Egyptian Souk. Thank you, Janine.' Roy closed his notebook. 'And leave it all to me.'

Ten minutes later, Janine's wine glass was empty, and the warmth in her chest had dissipated. 'You *have* to let us wash up!'

'Out of the question.' Roy leaned over the table to pick up her plate. 'Not on your first night as my guests!'

'We're not guests, we're living here! And you cooked!' Janine watched him take her plate to the sink. 'I thought you couldn't cope in the house on your own? I thought that was why we were here?'

Roy stopped moving. He put the plate back down.

'You're right, Janine.' Roy wiped his hands on a tea towel. 'Some help would be nice. I will watch television.'

He walked out.

Janine switched the big light off. Without the operating theatre ambience, the place felt calmer.

She poured another glass of wine and gave Katie a bright smile. 'See?' Janine reached for the washing-up gloves. 'Isn't this nice? All of us together.' She squeaked the gloves on with difficulty. It appeared Roy had the tiniest hands.

'Isn't this nice?' Janine said again. She nodded to herself – hard. 'I really think this is going to work.'

13

At five thirty a.m., Roy got up, grabbed a plastic tub and went out into the dewy garden to pluck the slugs off his marigolds. He took the tub to the park and released his prisoners, making sure he stood equidistant from all the surrounding houses.

Roy returned home and washed his tub. He watered the plants and filled the birdfeeder.

He made scrambled eggs.

He sat in his armchair and read the newspaper.

Eventually, he heard a door open. The flush of the toilet.

'Katie!' Janine's voice. 'It's time!'

Roy listened to the muffled bumps and conversations of a family getting up, it had been thirty years since he'd last heard these noises in his house. It was strange. Comforting, but strange.

Roy finished reading his newspaper. He got his glass spray and microfibre cloth from the cupboard under the sink. He pushed himself up onto the counter and started cleaning the inside of the kitchen window.

There were footsteps down the stairs.

Janine's hair was at an angle, her glasses skew-whiff. 'What are you doing up there?'

Roy indicted his cloth and spray.

Janine pulled her long T-shirt down self-consciously. 'I didn't realise you'd be up.'

'I've been up for hours. You have to be early if you want to outwit the slugs.'

Janine flicked the kettle on. 'Coffee?'

'I've had my two cups already. Can I make you scrambled eggs?'

'Of course not, Roy! Have you got any cereal? I haven't unpacked ours yet.'

'I do.' Roy crouched at a bottom cupboard and pulled out a box of All-Bran.

Janine looked at the box with a raised eyebrow. 'I mean, I'll try it on Katie, but ...'

Ten minutes later, Katie took her first bite of All-Bran. She put her spoon down and looked at Janine with outrage.

'I can't find our cereal.' Janine rubbed Katie's back through her white school shirt. 'I'll dig it out before tomorrow.'

Janine asked Roy how to use the washing machine and, after politely listening to an extended introduction to its idiosyncrasies, she put the washing in and took Katie to school.

By the time she got back, Roy had finished cleaning the windows and mirrors, and was polishing the glass-fronted cabinets in the front room.

Janine threw her handbag onto the sofa and looked at the remaining boxes, stacked in the corner of the room. 'OK if I start putting some more stuff in the kitchen?'

Roy looked at the boxes and frowned. 'Can I help?'

Janine shook her head. 'You've done so much already.'

Roy stood in the lounge polishing the wood, listening to

cupboard doors opening and shutting, and the spin cycle of the washing machine. He tried not to notice that Janine didn't ask which cupboards he kept things in. Or notice the clinking sounds of his own products being pushed to the back.

He finished polishing, and moved on to darning socks.

Janine called from the kitchen, 'Do you have a basket for the washing?'

'Under the sink.'

Janine came into the front room, holding his laundry bucket. She started draping underwear and T-shirts on the radiator.

Janine saw him looking. 'It's just quicker this way.'

Roy put his sewing to one side. 'It's no problem to get you the maiden for outside.'

'This is a shortcut. They'll be done in a couple of hours, and you'll never have to see our clothes again.'

Roy gave a tight smile. He didn't say anything about the moisture that would be generating, or the risk of damp. He just gave a brisk nod, opened the window, and picked up his sewing again.

That afternoon, Roy sat in a café opposite Party Vince, a man whose orange sweatshirt and bright blue jeans gave him the air of a children's TV presenter.

The waitress put down their pots of tea on the table between them.

'I usually do this over the phone,' Vince said.

Roy balanced the strainer over his cup and poured. 'I prefer to conduct my business affairs in person.'

Vince poured his own tea, not bothering with the strainer. 'Let's get to it.' He grabbed an A4 clip file out of his bag. His hand had a mottled effect from a long-ago burn. 'How old's your granddaughter?'

Roy took a breath. *Not specifically my granddaughter, my step-granddaughter, except they're not married, but there isn't a word for—*

'She'll be six.'

Vincent opened his file. 'The six-year-old girls – that's a slam-dunk. They love the princess party.'

Vince flicked through pictures of toadstool seats around a lake made of a slippery, silky fabric, with girls doing ring-a-ring-o'-roses in long dresses and crowns. The dresses were ruffled, pastel, and looked alarmingly combustible.

There was also a pink structure like a large Wendy house, with turrets and floaty gauze and fairy lights. The sign said *Princesses Enchanted Castle.*

Roy took a sip of his tea. An apostrophe was missing – but from where? 'How many princesses own the castle, Vince? One or several?'

Vince blinked at him.

Roy waved a hand generously. 'No matter.' He could put a real-life punctuation learning opportunity into the party programme. 'You know, it's funny. I've been reading Katie *Peter Pan*, and Janine – that's the mother – encouraged her to ask for a pirate party. Can you imagine?'

Vince frowned. 'A pirate party?'

'Exactly.' Roy put his cup down. 'I think that says more about Janine than Katie.'

Party Vince paused. 'Some of the mums are . . . you know.' He leaned over his cup and lowered his voice. 'I don't want to say *uptight* but . . .'

Roy nodded. 'You know, Janine asked me not to call Katie *pretty*?'

Vince widened his eyes. He sipped his tea.

'She said *the world has moved on*. And, apparently, when Katie went to a *Little Mermaid* party, Janine made her go as a crab.'

'These mums.' Vince gave a small shake of the head. 'Some of them look for the harm in everything.'

'Exactly!' Still, it was important to be loyal. 'Janine is a wonderful mother in other ways.' He tried not to remember the Corn Flakes T-shirt or crisp sandwiches.

'If you really want to look at it, the pirate party is our cheapest party. Extremely competitively priced.'

Roy readied himself. *Egyptian souk*.

Except – why would he bother haggling on this price of this party? A pirate party was completely unsuitable for a group of six-year-old girls – and Roy knew it. Vince knew it.

Everyone knew it – except Janine.

But Roy could go through the motions. 'Let's look at the pirate one quickly, then. Get it out of the way.'

Party Vince flicked to another page. Roy looked at pictures of boys in eye patches and bandanas, holding plastic – *plastic!* – swords.

Vince tapped the page. 'The costumes and props are much simpler. It's mainly walking the plank. That's why it's so cheap. People don't want to spend so much on costumes for boys.'

'I see. No cat o' nine tails?'

Vince paused. 'Not in the twenty-twenties, Roy.'

Roy peered more closely. Was that piece of wood raised off the ground on two bricks meant to be *the plank*?

Vince saw him looking. 'Elf and safety,' he said, in an exaggerated Cockney twang.

'I'm not giving Katie a pirate party – and especially not one with a plank on the ground.' Roy turned the page. 'The princess party is *much* more suitable.'

Vince picked up a supermarket carrier bag and placed it on the table. 'I have sourced realistic jewels for the crown-making exercise.' Vince brought a stiff cardboard crown out of his bag. 'And special stencil cutters so all the girls can have different crowns. Girls like individuality, see. More than anything, they want to feel special.'

Roy tapped the crown. Impressive. 'No glitter.'

'*And* it's recyclable.'

Roy nodded his approval.

'The kids never want to throw away the crowns anyway. I know a princess who's still wearing hers five years on!'

Roy nodded. 'Claudia loved making crowns. That's my daughter. She lives in Singapore.'

He turned the crown over in his hand. He pictured Katie's delighted face as he placed the crown ceremonially on her head. *Arise, Princess Katie of Appleton School.*

'I'd need a deposit immediately.' Vince met Roy's gaze. 'In this gig, I've been burned too many times.' He moved closer, conspiratorially. 'I get a lot of calls.'

Roy smiled. 'I'll give you the deposit now.' He wasn't going to haggle. After the Corn Flakes T-shirt, Katie deserved something nice. And that meant something full price.

'Great.' Party Vince sat back in his chair. 'Imagine the birthday girl's surprise when she turns up expecting the boring plank and eye patches her mother told her she wanted – and finds she's got a full princess adventure, with crowns and enchanted castles!'

Roy watched Vince get his card machine out of his bag.

'That's a good point.' Roy got out his chequebook, and Vince's smile faltered. 'I'll tell Phil and Janine, but I won't tell Katie I'm getting her a princess party. It'll make it a lovely surprise.'

14

They were twenty hours into all living at Dad's and Phil was still pretty sure this was a good idea.

The bed wasn't great – Phil and Janine had kept rolling together on what Phil suspected was a forty-year-old mattress. And they'd need to get better curtains. Since dawn, Phil had had to keep the duvet flapped over his eyes, his breath bouncing wetly back at him like heat in a steam room.

But they were all getting on all right, weren't they? Moving in and out of each other's paths, being respectful of each other. Just a couple of mini hiccups.

That morning, Phil had passed Janine on the stairs and come into the kitchen to find Katie in front of a full bowl of All-Bran, her spoon on the table, her eyes wide with outrage.

'You look very pretty in your school uniform, Katie,' Dad said.

Phil screwed his face up. He wished Janine had never pointed out his dad's *pretty* stuff. Once you'd seen it, it was impossible to unsee it.

Dad beamed at Phil. 'And what can I get you for breakfast?'

'I'll grab something at work. I don't eat breakfast.'

'You used to. You did when you lived here.'

Phil didn't point out it had been a quarter of a century

since he'd lived there and, back then, he'd also had a Sony discman, a shoegazer's fringe and a twenty-a-day habit. 'I'd love some coffee though.'

Katie watched Dad get a cup from the cupboard. 'Shall I show you my whistle?' She pursed her lips and gave an airy blow. 'This is "Little Donkey".'

It wasn't a whistle. Still, Phil watched politely.

Dad stirred Phil's coffee and handed it to him. He turned to Katie, smiling, saying:

> *A whistling woman and a crowing hen,*
> *Are neither good for God nor men.'*

Katie paused, mid-blow. She nodded.

Phil blinked at his dad, wondering where to even *start*, relieved Janine was still gathering washing upstairs.

Dad headed out of the room to pick up his post.

Janine came back into the kitchen with an armful of washing.

Katie started whistling 'Little Donkey' again. She stopped. 'Oh.'

Phil felt the fingers of tension patter up his back.

Katie turned to Janine. 'Roy says God doesn't like me whistling!'

Phil put his cup down. He bent over the sink, simulating checking the water pressure.

'We don't do God in this family, Katie.' Janine dumped the washing on the floor and looked at Phil. 'I didn't think Roy did either?'

Phil shrugged and stared at the running water, grateful Katie wasn't any more specific about whose whistling, in particular, God didn't like.

And Janine didn't even know – but she still didn't give it up. 'Don't listen to Roy. Keep whistling, Katie.'

'I've finished now.'

'No, keep whistling. And I'll protect you from God.'

Dad came back with the post.

Janine looked up from the washing machine. 'Where do you keep your fabric conditioner?'

Dad shook his head. 'We don't believe in it.' He went into a long explanation about the machine's different spin and rinse settings while Janine clearly zoned out.

Phil watched them interact, sipped his coffee, and thought – *yes*.

Yes, he was pretty sure this was still a good idea.

Phil's job that day finished early, and he didn't start another. There were some benefits to being self-employed.

When he got home at three-ish, there was no one downstairs. 'Dad?'

There was a shout from the garden. 'Hello!'

Phil walked outside.

Dad was up a stepladder he'd placed against the old oak tree. He wore safety goggles, and was holding a chainsaw.

'Dad?' Phil strode over. 'What the hell?'

Dad lifted his goggles. 'I wanted the witch branch gone before Katie got back from school.'

Phil shook his head. 'You've got to be careful after your accident, Dad!'

Dad made a *pfft* noise.

'Let me do it.'

Dad hesitated. He climbed down the stepladder anyway.

'Which branch?'

Dad tapped the lowest branch. Phil stared at it. If you

squinted at markings on the bark long enough, you could see a pointy hat and long jaw maybe. Maybe those knotholes could be eyes. But Katie was definitely reaching.

He stepped up the ladder. Dad handed him the saw, and Phil got into position.

'Phil?'

Dad pulled the safety goggles from his head, pulling a section of hair up. The wisp floated down, settling slightly above his crown like tumbleweed.

He handed the goggles to Phil. 'We might have to rearrange the kitchen cupboards later.' Dad stepped back onto the patio to watch. 'It's all got quite crowded.'

Phil put the goggles on awkwardly with one hand. 'OK.'

'And I'm not sure there's much of a system. We might have to prioritise. For the greater good.'

'No problem.' Phil wondered how long he was going to be up this ladder holding this chainsaw.

'I've just met with the party man. Vincent. So you'll be pleased to know that's all sorted.'

'Well done, Dad.' Making a point, Phil switched on the saw. It roared into life, vibrating in his hand.

Dad raised his voice, still talking. Phil caught the words, *'because that's infinitely more suitable.'*

Phil turned to the tree. He lined up the blade against the branch.

'. . . so I'm not going to tell Katie in advance.'

Phil concentrated on cutting.

'I'll make it a wonderful surprise!'

The branch shifted beneath Phil's saw. It fell to the grass with a light bounce, the leaves shivering with reverberation. It settled.

Phil switched the chainsaw off.

Dad dusted off his hands. 'Ding dong, the witch is dead.'

Phil jumped off the steps. 'I'll take it to the tip.'

'No, Phil.'

At the disappointment in Dad's voice, Phil looked up.

'Firewood. Of course.' Phil started the chainsaw again.

Phil found Janine in their new bedroom, half lying on the bed, propped up against the headboard. 'All right?'

Janine looked up from her phone. 'Was that the chainsaw?'

'Dad was removing the branch that scares Katie. I took over.'

'That's nice of him.'

Phil sat on the bed. 'What are you up to?'

Janine raised the phone in her hand. 'I was just looking up *Peter Pan*. I wanted to see if it's OK – what people think about it now. Today people, I mean.'

'And?'

'It's not too bad actually. No blacking up or golliwogs.' Janine threw her phone onto the bed. 'The main girl, Wendy, gets to go on the adventures. And the nurse is actually a dog, so that's ... something?' She shrugged. 'I followed a few links about old kids' books and went into an internet hole. It turns out *The Tiger That Came to Tea* was about the Nazis.'

'Right,' Phil said.

'But I'm not sure I believe it.'

Phil nodded.

'Does your dad have *The Tiger That Came to Tea?*'

Phil stared at her.

Janine stared back. 'OK.' She pushed herself up from the bed. 'I'll go and make a start on tonight's food.'

Phil decided not to point out it was three in the afternoon.

She turned. 'You know, your dad bangs on about waste, but he puts the heating on and then throws all the windows open anyway. What's that about?' She picked up a hoodie from the bed and pulled it on. 'And I can't believe he doesn't have fabric conditioner, that's why his bedding feels like sandpaper. We'll have to get our duvet covers out of storage.' She stared at the duvet. 'It smells wrong too. It's hard to sleep in something that smells wrong.'

Phil nodded. He picked up her phone to check the time, to see the screen was open to Janine's most recent searches.

Is Peter Pan problematic
Do ears get bigger as you age
How old is Jane Fonda
Am I depressed
What does arthritis feel like
Normal sized portion of pasta
Does death hurt
Cost to charge a heated gilet

In his hand, an email notification pinged. A message slid across the screen.

Your recent application.

'You've got an email about that job!'

Janine took the phone from Phil. She screwed up her face, not looking.

'It'll be fine,' Phil said.

Janine sank onto the bed. Her eyes widened. 'No!'

Phil tensed.

'I wore tights for that interview, Phil!' Janine jumped up from the bed. *'Tights!'* She looked up, her big eyes imploring. 'And a skirt suit! I cosplayed a professional lady of business!' She threw her phone down. 'And I still didn't get the job!'

'I'm so sorry.' Phil gave her a firm hug.

'I changed for them! I wore my *don't scare the horses* outfit. And I still scared them!'

'I'm sure you didn't *scare* them. They will have loved you. There will have just been someone . . . more suitable.'

'I hate the word *suitable*. There's nothing worse than suitable.'

Phil didn't reply.

'Tights!' Janine mumbled into Phil's shoulder.

Phil traced circles on her upper back, wondering if he was being soothing or annoying. 'Shall I make you a sandwich?'

Janine shook her head into his shoulder.

Sal had given him the sandwich tip. Said it worked on her son, Alfie. *No one can stay angry when someone's made them a nice sandwich.* But Janine never seemed to want a sandwich. And if someone said *no* to a sandwich and you made them one anyway, that made them even more annoyed, Phil found.

Janine stared up at him with sad eyes. As always, she looked wonky-lovely, her fringe thicker on her left side, her left eyebrow more curved than her right. Phil had read somewhere that classic attractiveness was about symmetry. Janine did not do *classic*.

He felt a throb of warmth. 'I'm so sorry, J. You deserve to be snapped up. You're *ace*.'

'Even superheroes don't wear tights anymore. I changed myself for that job and they *still* didn't want me. *And* I laughed at a shit joke. My future not-boss's shit joke.'

'Laughing at a future-new-boss's joke is fine.'

Janine shook her head. 'I demeaned myself.'

'You didn't. Look, I'll go and get a shower and give you space, OK? I'm sorry about the job. I'm sorry about the tights.'

He walked into the bathroom, unbuttoning his overalls. It crossed his mind that there was something he meant to ask his dad about – but then he got into the shower and his thoughts turned to Janine's job rejection, and what it meant for how long they were going to have to live here, and all thoughts of the conversation outside slipped away.

15

Janine hadn't got the job. Her fallback job. The one she didn't even want.

She chopped an aubergine for the moussaka, glancing towards the crowded top cupboard she'd designated an overflow.

Was it too early for wine?

Roy beamed as she placed the moussaka on the table. 'Smells delicious. Fresh vegetables. And I heard all the chopping – cooking from first principles!' He smiled at Janine. 'Wonderful.'

Of course, Janine liked to be complimented. But there was something about Roy's approval, sometimes, that made her want to scratch the back of her neck, hard.

Roy watched her refill her glass. 'Are we celebrating *again*?'

'We're commiserating. I didn't get that job.'

She held out a glass to Roy.

'The fools.' He shook his head. 'I'm very sorry to hear that, Janine. Their loss.'

'So now I've got no irons in the fire. Nothing at all.'

'It's just a bad time.' She felt Phil reach for her hand under the table. 'Someone will snap you up soon.'

'Yes.' Roy cleared his throat. 'Yes, I'm sure they will. Janine, don't let the' – Katie walked in. He mouthed *bastards* – 'grind you down.'

Roy using a swearword was so rare, Janine smiled. 'Thanks, Roy.'

As the week went on, there were many nice moments with Roy, Janine thought.

If only they weren't punctuated by . . . the other kind of moments.

Because there was one worse thing than living with a retired person when you were unemployed, and that was living with a *busy* retired person.

However early Janine got up, Roy got up earlier. While she was still in her night T-shirt, he was always fully clothed. And active. Ironing. Cleaning out the oven. Defrosting the freezer. Advising.

'Are you sure you don't want the main light on if you're reading?'

'Oh, you choose to buy beans in salted water?'

'Are you sure you don't want me to fetch the maiden?'

How could everything need cleaning so often? How could so many things need fixing? Janine thought about the fridge door of her old home, how she hadn't repaired it for five years, and self-hate bloomed in her stomach like a thistle.

On Thursday morning, Janine sat in the front room on her laptop, looking at the *Am I The Villain Here?* forum.

My aunt doesn't believe in veganism and has been known to sneak meat into my food. Am I the villain for refusing to go there for Christmas?

Janine clicked *Not the villain here*. The screen changed.

Thank you for your response!
Current status:
You're the villain here: 36%
Not the villain here: 64%

'Excuse me.'

Roy reached over Janine's head and pulled a rumpled blanket from behind.

Janine moved obediently forwards. Still, the blanket caught her hair. 'I'm not an invalid, you know. You don't have to adjust my pillows.'

'It just all looks so much neater with the blanket folded.'

'Then I can do it!' Janine watched him fold the blanket. 'You have to tell me what you need, Roy.'

Roy shook his head. 'You are applying for jobs. I don't want to interrupt you.'

Janine smiled weakly. She tilted her screen away.

'And it's just a blanket,' Roy said.

'Of course it's just a blanket. *I know* it's just a blanket.'

Janine wasn't even allowed to help with soft furnishings – or Katie's party. Roy had waved away all her efforts to let her help with that weekend's pirate party because *it's a delicate balance, and all under control* and *too many cooks spoil the broth.*

Of course, it wasn't all Roy's fault. But Janine's pointlessness bounced back at her from every corner of the room.

Janine rested back against the blanket. Her phone beeped. Marky.

What's your new address? Where should I pick Katie up from tomorrow night?

Janine wrinkled her nose. Of course, she had to tell Marky eventually.

12 Consul Street. See you then.

It was nothing but the truth. Not the whole truth. But nothing but the truth.

On Friday after school, Katie was getting ready to leave for two nights at Marky's. Janine was in her own bedroom, hiding from Roy's busyness, psyching herself up to start making a lentil cottage pie. She'd lost enthusiasm for it, since Roy had told her how thoroughly he approved. She knew he'd make congratulatory noises while she was cooking, so she didn't want to make it anymore – and how old was she, *seven*?

She heard a squeal from Katie's room. 'He's outside!'

Janine wasn't sure why that merited a squeal, until Katie added, 'Daddy's got a new car!'

Janine closed her eyes.

'Look, Mum! Come and look out of the window!'

Janine took a moment. She walked slowly across the landing and looked out.

Marky was wearing sunglasses, of course, though it wasn't even bright. He shut the driver's door of a low, fancy sports car that Janine didn't know the variety of, and hoped she never learned.

The car had two doors. *Two doors.*

Katie hurried downstairs and opened the door.

'All right, munchkin. What do you think?' From a floor away, Marky sounded as excited as Katie. 'Bring some sunglasses and I'll take you for a spin with the top down.'

Janine walked to the top of the stairs. 'She doesn't need sunglasses. It's dusk.'

Marky didn't look up. 'Shall we call your friends, tell them to look outside, do some drive-bys?'

'It's a fancy car.' Janine reached the bottom of the stairs. 'Two doors, I notice.'

'We've still got Molly's Audi too, don't sweat it, Janine. And, before you ask, I've put the booster seat in.' He gave Katie an eyeroll. *Your mother, hey?*

'What have you done with your old car?' Katie asked.

'Nothing yet. We'll sell it soon. Luckily, we have room for three cars on the driveway.'

Janine stared at him. Could he *hear himself*?

'We haven't got a car here.' Katie's voice was monotone. 'We have to use Phil's van.'

Janine put a restraining hand on Katie's shoulder as another thistle bloomed.

Marky looked at Janine. 'Where's your car?'

'It was a work car. I had to give it back after the redundancy but the van's fine. So . . .' Janine smiled brightly. 'Katie, are you ready to—'

'Can we have your old car if you're not using it, Daddy?'

'Go and get your schoolbag, Katie!' Janine realised how harsh she sounded – she softened her voice. 'And take a few minutes to tidy your room because I need to speak to your father.'

Katie ran upstairs without any protest. Janine's demeanour must have told a story.

Marky waited until she was out of earshot. 'You don't *even have a car* anymore, Janine?'

'No one really needs a car. Anyway, we've got a van.'

Marky shook his head. 'I'd have to speak to Molly about the old one.'

'We don't want your car. Katie said that, not me. She said it because she is a child. I want to make it clear no adult has asked for your car.'

Marky looked around the front room. 'This place isn't too bad, you know?' He shoved his hands in his pockets. 'Not really your style, though. I'm surprised you took it furnished.'

Janine smiled weakly. 'It wasn't exactly like that.'

'It's a bit dated, of course, but it's good you've got somewhere.' He peered at the sideboard. 'Your landlord left all their photos and ornaments? You don't mind?'

Janine took a breath. 'No, it's . . .'

There was a shuffle from the kitchen. Roy was listening.

'I'm getting a retro vibe. Wow, can that television get more than three channels?'

'It still works perfectly.' Roy strode in from the kitchen, dusting his hands. 'This house may not be to modern tastes, but everything here is in good working order.' He held out his hand, his tone pleasant. 'Mark, I presume?'

Marky shook his hand. 'Marky.'

Roy gave a faint smile. 'I'm Roy. Phil's father.'

'Oh, are you visiting?'

'No.' Roy looked at Janine. 'While you're busy here, I'll get things started for the shepherd's pie.'

'I said I was making it, Roy!' Janine called after him. 'So please don't!'

Still, she heard the cutlery drawer open and shut. The rustling of packaging.

Marky frowned at her. 'Janine?'

Janine's palms felt sweaty. 'Did I not mention it?' She wiped her hands on her jeans. 'This is Roy's house and we're staying here. Briefly.'

Marky stared.

'Just while we work out something more long term.' Janine pushed her fringe out of her eyes. 'It's fine. I've got so many job irons in the fire. Too many, it feels like sometimes. Managing all those irons – well, it's practically a full-time job in itself!'

There was an audible sound of scraping from the kitchen. Roy might move with small, precise movements, but he did some tasks at a surprising volume.

Marky held Janine's gaze.

'I said it's fine. So that's that. KATIE!' Janine turned to the staircase. 'YOUR DADDY'S READY TO GO!'

Roy came into the room, holding a half-peeled potato and an ancient peeler, its handle wound with string. 'How many ounces of potato in this recipe, Janine?'

'I don't really work in ounces.'

'I can do grams.'

'I mean, I don't really do measurements. I do it by sight. But please leave it, Roy. I'll do it when Katie and Marky have gone. Please.'

Katie came down the stairs with her rucksack. She held her head high as she descended, like a debutante at an eighteenth-century ball.

'Just think,' Roy smiled at her, 'when you come back here next, it'll be to your own birthday party! See you on Sunday, birthday girl!'

Katie beamed. 'Bye, Roy!'

Janine gave Katie a kiss. 'Love you.'

She stood on the front step and waved Katie off, trying to keep eye contact without absorbing any information about the new car.

Marky would be asking Katie about Roy, already. About the arrangements in the house. But what would Katie say?

Janine walked back into the kitchen.

Roy looked up from peeling potatoes. 'Why don't I put the kettle on?'

'I'll do it.'

'Of course, we're none of us going to have cars soon,' Roy said, with the air of someone continuing a conversation that was already in mid-flow. 'Nobody really needs a car. And not in this kind of conurbation.'

Janine put the mugs down. 'No.'

'Especially not a sports car. Has the man really bought a car with only two doors?'

Janine nodded.

'He'll be sorry. When he needs to take a neighbour's family on an airport run.' Roy scraped his potato. 'It's obscene how he never got a proper job and yet he's fallen on his feet.'

Janine smiled faintly. She put the kettle on.

Roy stopped peeling. 'I know we should be happy for Katie, that her father's life is stable and that she gets to go on nice holidays.' He looked up. 'But there's something about seeing someone so undeserving get such an abundance of good fortune. It feels . . . . just wrong.'

Janine smiled at Roy – a proper smile now.

'And he really doesn't need sunglasses at this time in April.'

Janine gave a sniff of laughter.

Roy held out the potato peeler. 'Yours, I think.' He gave a bow. 'I hope I haven't trodden on toes.'

'Thanks.' She reached for a potato and started to peel. 'You know, your house is lovely. And there's nothing wrong with your television.'

Roy gave a firm nod. 'Thank you.'

She watched Roy leave the room, and concentrated on trying to peel with the ancient, strange-angled peeler. She ignored how hard it was to use, as a mark of respect.

Yes.

Yes, they could do this.

After tea, Janine took the rest of that night's bottle of wine upstairs.

The meal had passed pleasantly enough but, without Katie there, the house felt even more claustrophobic.

She sat on the scratchy, wrong-smelling duvet cover – she couldn't face going to the storage unit. Seeing all their life's accumulation of stuff in one place felt humiliating.

She poured another glass and scrolled through kitchen tools online.

Phil came upstairs.

'I'm ordering a new potato peeler.' She pressed *buy* and looked up. 'I'm not going through all the boxes.'

He sat on the bed opposite. 'I reckon we can afford a potato peeler.'

'I can't face being sociable tonight. No offence to your dad.'

'We're not guests. We don't have to socialise.'

Janine shuffled over to make room.

Phil sat next to her. 'We need a telly in here really.'

Janine looked at the careful piles of clothes on the chest of drawers. 'There's nowhere to put one.'

'We can use the laptop.' Phil got the laptop and placed it on the bed between them.

He didn't open it. The air was charged.

Katie was away. It was Friday night.

The knowledge pulsed between them.

'I'd offer you wine, but we're all out.' She nodded towards the bottle in the bin. 'Shall we have—'

At the footsteps on the stairs, she stopped.

Roy walked past the door, studiously not looking inside.

Janine waited a minute. She turned to Phil. 'Shall we—'

Roy walked past again, having changed his jumper and chinos into a white T-shirt and tennis shorts. He kept his gaze firmly ahead.

Janine was silent until she could hear Roy was firmly back downstairs. 'I like how respectful he's trying to be of our privacy.'

Phil got up. 'Speaking of privacy . . .' he gently pushed the door closed – 'it's Friday.'

'I know.'

Phil sat next to her. 'But we don't have to.'

Janine looked at her socked feet. She stretched her toes to a bumpy point.

They always had sex on Friday nights when Katie was at Marky's. *Spontaneity's great, and all,* Janine always said, *but a plan means it actually happens. We're like Pavlov's dogs. Sex is like a muscle – use it or lose it.*

But Roy was right beneath them.

She stared at Phil's leg. 'Do you want to?'

Phil looked at his feet. 'Do *you* want to?'

There was a soft knock at the door. How was a man who peeled potatoes so loudly so stealthy on the stairs?

Phil raised his voice. 'Come in!'

There was the sound of wood against carpet as the door pushed slowly open. After an overly respectful period of time, Roy's head appeared. 'Just to say I'm—' He looked at the wine glass on the bedside table. 'I'll get you coasters.'

'It's fine, Roy. We're not really coaster people,' Janine said.

'You'll get rings on your good furniture. I didn't realise you'd need coasters.'

'We didn't and, anyway, the bottle's empty.'

Roy looked at the empty bottle sticking out of the bin. He took a step towards it.

'Roy.' Janine kept her voice even. 'It's fine. We can clear up after ourselves.'

But Roy had already picked up the bin and left the room.

Janine glanced at Phil. 'He wanted to say something about drinking in the bedroom.'

'He restrained himself though. He's trying really hard.' Phil paused. 'We all are.'

Roy walked back into the room, empty bin in hand.

'Thanks, Dad.'

Roy placed the bin down. He clicked his fingers. 'Coasters!'

He turned abruptly and left.

Janine and Phil didn't speak.

When Roy came back, Phil got up to greet him. 'Thanks.' He took the coasters from Roy, and shut the door slowly, but firmly.

Janine waited a moment. She turned to Phil. 'So. Friday night.'

Phil said nothing.

'OK, I'll say it. I don't want to, not with your dad down-stairs. It's too weird.'

Did Phil look relieved? 'Right.'

'I'd love to, of course. If your dad wasn't down there.'

Phil massaged her thigh. 'That's how I feel too.'

There was a soft knock at the door.

Phil closed his eyes momentarily. 'Come in!'

Roy pushed it open, agonisingly slowly. 'I didn't actually say what I came in to say. I'm off out.' Roy stepped into the room. 'I do Tai Chi on Fridays.' He gave a demonstrative knees-out squat and swiped the air with one arm. 'I'll be a couple of hours, at least. You have the house to yourselves!'

Phil smiled faintly. 'Have a good time, Dad.'

There was the sound of light footsteps. The scrape-up of keys from a bowl. The front door opening, and clicking shut.

Janine and Phil said nothing for a long time.

Janine looked up at Phil. 'I can't. Not now. Not here. It feels too weird.'

'I know.' He patted her outstretched leg and opened the laptop. 'I know.'

16

Sunday was party day, and Roy had picked up party cakes and bought balloons and decorations. He'd bought a new set of garden chairs. He'd shaped his ornamental hedges to perfect fat globes, and mown the lawn in parallel lines, giving the effect of a freshly vacuumed carpet.

His family had been here for nearly a week now, and everyone was settling in perfectly. Though there had been one hairy moment on the Thursday evening, when Roy had been on the sofa with Katie.

Katie turned to him. 'Can I borrow your phone?'

Roy smiled. 'No.' He got up to pick up a log from the grate.

Katie's eyes widened. She screamed.

'Katie?' Janine called from the kitchen.

'*The witch!*' Katie gripped the sofa cushions. '*Roy's holding her head!*'

Roy looked down at the log he was holding, its 'face', pointing in Katie's direction. 'No! No, it's—'

In panic, Roy pulled back the fireguard and threw the log on the fire.

It landed at an unfortunate angle. Face up.

Katie screamed even more.

Janine hurried in, holding a basket of washing. 'What is it?'

Katie pointed. 'She's burning!'

'She'll be gone soon.' Maybe Roy could distract Katie by making this situation educational? 'In the seventeenth century, witch-burning was actually—'

At Janine's hand on his arm, he stopped.

Katie buried her head in Janine's jumper.

'I'll tell you when it's safe.' Roy watched the flames lick the 'face'. 'Nearly. Almost gone. Nearly.' The flames took over the log. 'And – gone!' Roy said brightly. 'For good! Witches can't come back from a burning, that's why the Restoration fellows did it!'

Katie pulled away from Janine's jumper. She ran upstairs.

'Imaginations run wild at that age.' Janine took the washing basket to the radiator. 'She'll get over it.'

Roy watched Janine drape socks and T-shirts over the radiator, his lips pressed into a line. 'Are you sure you don't want me to get—'

'I'm fine without the maiden, Roy. Honestly.'

Roy wrung his hands. He strode across the room and pointedly opened the window, letting out the moisture – and all his precious, expensive heat.

But that morning, Roy was optimistic. He cleaned the kitchen and front room. He hosed the patio.

He was blowing up balloons with the helium canister when Janine and Phil came downstairs.

'Are you sure we can't help, Roy?' Janine said, for the hundredth time. 'There are so many balloons!'

'Yes, but I'm not blowing them up myself.' Roy tapped his canister. 'I borrowed this from the party shop, so it's not exerting. Imagine I'm driving with power-assisted steering.'

Janine looked at Phil. 'I can't just be here and not help.'

'Let's go out,' Phil said.

'Where?'

'Somewhere. Then we can pick up Katie and bring her back for the party.'

They left. Roy finished blowing up the balloons and arranged them in the back garden. He put pink netting in the trees and strung fairy lights over the plant pots.

He stood on the clean patio and studied the results of his work.

Roy wasn't artistic – Lynn had been the artistic one, she'd always done the presents and parties. She was famous in their dinner-party circles for her napkin origami.

Still, he was happy. The garden looked fit for a princess.

Roy moved his focus back inside the house. He laid out the party plates and bowls, the cakes and the cutlery. He put together the party bags, placing in each a princess mirror, a jewelled bracelet, and a packet of sugar-free sweets. He stacked the party bags in a grabbable line on the hall table. He tied silver balloons to the front gate and arranged gold cardboard stars on the front door with Blu-tack.

With an hour to spare, he had a bath. He towelled himself down, moving awkwardly round the obstacles in his bedroom. So much of the usual floor space was taken up by the computer table he'd moved out of Katie's room. Still, he managed to get dressed without incident, in the smart grey suit he had bought for weddings. He sprayed himself with the aftershave Lynn had bought him, the one she said made him smell *like a handsome sailor on shore leave.* He combed his hair carefully and tied his tie in a pristine Windsor knot.

Roy looked at himself in the mirror. He nodded.

It was time.

*

Vince pulled up in a red van with *Party Vince* in huge bubble letters on the side. He stepped out, wearing the suit Roy had requested.

'You look very smart.' Vince's suit was shiny from wear, not quite well fitting around the shoulders, and a non-celebratory black. Roy suspected it was his funeral suit.

'I feel trussed up like a chicken.'

'But a *very smart* chicken.' Roy peered at Vince's neck. 'Now why don't I help you straighten your tie?'

Together, Roy and Vince connected the joints and poles of the enchanted castle. It reminded Roy of his summers in St David's, putting up a tent while Lynn sunned herself on a deckchair with a paperback.

Roy and Vince laid out the slippery lake. Roy switched on the fairy lights.

Vince stood back. 'Grand.'

And it was.

Roy stared at his transformed garden, watching the twinkling fairy lights ebb and flow, shimmering through their routine.

He lifted his camera from round his neck. 'The calm before the storm.' He took a photo for Yvonne. 'These princesses are going to have a wonderful day.'

17

'Why does he even put the fire *on*, if he's going open the windows?' Janine said to Phil, from the van's driver's seat. They'd picked up Katie from Marky's and were on the way back to Roy's. 'It's such a waste.'

It was Janine's first time driving the van, and she felt a throb of power from being so high up.

A voice piped up between Janine and Phil. 'The fire shouldn't be on at all. And we shouldn't use radiators. Everyone should just wear more clothes, because of the planet.'

Janine glanced down at Katie. 'I'm not sure you mean that.'

'I do.'

Janine looked back at the road. 'We wear loads of clothes already, Katie.'

'You don't. You don't even wear a vest.'

'I wear a bra. That's like an adult vest.' Janine glanced at Phil. She needed to stop gaslighting her daughter, but it came so easily. 'And I've ordered a heated gilet for when I'm alone in the house!' That, at least, was true. 'Heat the human, not the house!'

Katie gripped Janine's leg. 'Do you think there'll be cutlasses today?'

'No doubt,' Phil said.

'And treasure?'

'A whole chest's worth, at least!' Janine parked outside Roy's house. She took in the balloons and gold stars on the door of his Seventies semi. 'Party time!'

Katie whooped.

Roy threw open the door and hurried out, followed by a man with a badge saying *Party Vince*.

Janine jumped down from the van. She took in their suits. 'Very dapper.'

'It's a big occasion, turning six!' Vince looked at Katie, wearing her *Six Today!* badge. 'Do I see the birthday girl?'

Katie stood up straighter. 'Yes!'

'Our guest of honour.' Party Vince did a deep bow. 'Follow me, my lady.'

Janine raised an eyebrow at Roy. 'Suits?'

'My idea.'

Janine smiled at Katie. 'You're so excited, I can actually feel you shaking. Fizzing, even.'

Roy looked up. 'You know, I think I might be fizzing a little too.'

Janine smiled. She watched Katie toddle into the house.

Sal came out of the house next door. 'I've come to take a look at this pirate party. I've been listening to the extensive preparations all morning.'

'Roy's been taking it very seriously.'

Janine and Sal followed the others inside.

'I might just walk the plank before any kids turns up,' Sal said. 'For old times' sake.'

Roy's voice was audible from the kitchen. 'We have fifteen minutes before the other guests get here. Fifteen minutes to have your party to yourself, birthday girl! So let's just get you into your dress.'

In the kitchen doorway, Katie went slack. She stared out of the kitchen window. She'd stopped fizzing.

Katie turned slowly back to face Roy. 'My dress?'

The word *dress* registered. Janine stopped moving forwards.

'Yes!' Roy picked up a Barbie-pink dress with ruffled sleeves. 'We're having a surprise princess party, and this is your special surprise dress! It's much grander than the other princesses' dresses. It has a longer train and . . .'

Roy trailed off.

'No.' Katie looked at Janine and back. 'I'm going to be a pirate.'

'No, no! You don't understand!' Roy leaned forwards and stroked Katie's arms roughly. 'It's a princess party! It's a surprise! *Much* better than a pirate party!'

Katie's eyes got shiny.

Janine stared at her. She didn't quite understand. Because surely Roy hadn't . . . ?

Sal got it. She patted Janine's shoulder and, without speaking, turned and walked out. The front door clicked shut.

Upstairs, the toilet flushed.

Phil hurried down the stairs. 'Shiver me timbers!' He jumped the last two stairs and landed at the bottom with a thump. 'Let's grab some cutlasses, me hearties, and—'

Phil stared out of the window.

Janine looked where he was looking.

Roy's back garden was *pink*.

Pink netting in the trees. A pink castle thing on the lawn. Next to it, a silky lake that was clearly blue – yet also managed to have a sheen of pink.

'This isn't a pirate party!' Katie's eyes filmed with tears. 'I said I wanted a pirate party!'

Roy stood statue still.

Katie started to whimper.

Phil crouched beside Katie. 'Hey. Hey, Katie! It's OK!'

Katie stopped whimpering. She stared at Phil with a new, utter blankness. The blankness of a soldier who'd seen war.

The doorbell went.

Roy stumbled back, against the kitchen counter. He put his hands behind to steady himself.

Phil's voice was a whisper. 'Dad, what have you done?'

Janine still hadn't moved.

The doorbell went again.

'ANSWER IT!' Janine pushed her fringe out of her eyes and made herself lower her voice. 'We can't send the kids home. To retract the offer of a drop off party would be in-humane.' She looked at Phil. 'Take the kids through the side gate. And don't let anyone else in here, kids or parents. Get the parents to drop off and piss off!'

Phil pulled Roy's arm and ushered him out of the room.

Katie burbled through tears. 'MUM!'

Janine crouched down. She put her arms round the sob-bing Katie. 'I know.'

Katie vibrated against her. 'I said I wanted a *pirate* party!'

'I know.' Janine rubbed Katie's back. Phil came back into the room. Janine stared at him over Katie's shoulder. 'I know.'

Phil wrung his hands. 'Dad's taking the girls out to the garden through the side gate. Some of the mums are asking after you.'

Janine shook her head.

'I think there's been some kind of mistake,' Phil said carefully.

'Yes.' This was one of those occasions where Janine had to step up and be an adult. She couldn't just scream what she thought. 'A mistake.' She pulled away from Katie and made eye contact. 'It's a real shame the pirate party wasn't available. But this still looks lovely, doesn't it? So much fun.'

Katie shook *no* with her whole body.

'We'll just take a minute to ourselves. Your friends are all arriving, and I can see them through the window. They look really excited to see you! And they're carrying such big presents!'

Katie didn't even look up at *that*.

'So how about we take a moment and then get your dress on –' Janine glanced at the pink polyester ruffles of her nightmares – 'and join the other girls in the' – she could barely make herself say it – 'enchanted castle?'

Katie puddled to the floor.

Janine looked at the trays of cupcakes decorated with pink and gold sparkles. They all had words on them. *Thoughtful. Kind. Loving. Helpful. Pretty.*

Roy's hopeful face appeared in the window of the back door.

Janine picked up a *Pretty* cupcake. She looked from it to Roy. She held his gaze.

She dropped the cupcake onto the tray, icing down.

Roy blanched and reversed out of view.

Katie looked up from her puddle. 'I want to go home.'

'No, you don't, Katie. Not really.' Janine shaped a smile. 'I know it's not exactly what you wanted but it's still your birthday and it's time to have fun! It's a paaa-rty!' She jiggled her hips. She shook invisible maracas. 'All your lovely friends are here!'

Katie shook her head.

Party Vince edged across the garden in their direction. He put a minimal slice of face through the doorway. 'Maybe if we make the crowns first? Everyone likes making crowns. Maybe the birthday girl would—'

Katie gave the loudest sob yet.

Phil gave Vince an agitated waft away.

Party Vince pulled the door closed behind him. He turned to stand in front of the group of princesses and brought a squirrel puppet out from inside his suit jacket.

'This is Tails. She lives in the enchanted wood. What's that, Tails?' Vince put the squirrel to his ear. 'You want to make a magic wand? But you've lost your special fairy dust and you need some princesses' help? You need . . .'

Roy opened the back door and let himself back into the house. He looked from Katie to Janine.

'Katie,' Phil looked serious, 'why don't you come upstairs. I want to show you something.'

Katie let Phil tug her to standing, limp and doll-like. She followed him up the stairs.

Janine whirled round to face Roy. 'What have you done?' She sounded barky, but that was fine. She *felt* barky.

Roy looked down at his hands. 'I thought it was more suitable.'

'She said she wanted PIRATES!'

'I know she said pirates, I just thought this was . . .'

Janine folded her arms. 'I can't believe you'd do this! I can't believe you'd overrule what she wants, just so you can make her have the kind of party *you* think she should have!'

'Claudia loved making crowns.'

'Claudia's forty-six and lives in Singapore, Roy! Claudia has sciatica and varicose veins!'

Janine looked through the window. The party guests in their princess dresses had made a long chain and were following Vince, skipping in the direction the squirrel puppet indicated with his paw.

That the other girls were clearly enjoying this made Janine only boil hotter. This shit was *insidious*.

'You just won't stop with your *pretty* this and your *pretty* that and your *pretty bloody racoons!*' Janine strode over to the tray of cakes. 'Loving? Helpful?' She picked up a *helpful* cupcake. 'When does Katie get to have the adventures? You think she's a supporting character?'

'No.' Roy frowned. 'No, I just made a mistake.'

'What was your mistake? Getting Katie the wrong party? Or treating her like a passive support human?'

In her anger, Janine started to eat the cupcake. She realised what she was doing and dropped it onto the counter.

'If . . . no, I'm not sure what . . . but this isn't a time for semantics.'

Roy had never said *this isn't a time for semantics* before. He was a man who'd corrected the vicar's syntax after his wife's eulogy.

Phil and Katie came downstairs, Katie crying harder. 'There was nothing upstairs to see up there!'

Phil raised his palms in despair. 'I thought a change of scene might help.'

Janine crouched in front of Katie. 'Let's see if we can make the best of a bad situation.'

Katie shook her head.

'Let's stay half an hour and see how you feel about the party then. See if you feel like playing with your friends.'

Katie whimpered.

Party Vince came to the patio door, holding the squirrel puppet, its head held questioningly to one side. 'Let's all just take a deep breath and calm down.' Vince inhaled and exhaled performatively. He indicated with the puppet for the rest of them to do the same. 'Let's all just calm down and—'

'Calm down? *Calm down?*' Janine squared up to Vince. 'I swear to God, if you come near me with that squirrel . . .'

Vince widened his eyes and stumbled back to the garden.

Janine looked outside at the sea of pink and pastel. 'Katie, do you want me to ask the other girls to take off the princess dresses?'

Katie nodded.

Phil coughed. 'But, Janine, the other kids . . .'

Janine stared him down.

Phil tried again. 'Party Vince said he'd saved the best Princess dress for Katie. The pink one has a long train. And a cone thing –' He pointed to his head '– and a veil.'

Janine swallowed. 'I didn't realise it had *a train!*' She took a second to compose herself. 'Katie, doesn't a train sound lovely?'

Katie shook her head with her whole body. She wouldn't enjoy herself now, Janine knew it. Not if a boatload of *actual pirates* turned up with a chest of treasure.

Janine looked at the clock. It was two thirty. 'Right. Let's have some party food. And if you still don't want to play in half an hour, we'll go somewhere else.'

By three o'clock, Katie's cries had given way to hiccups.

Janine looked through the window. Party Vince led Katie's friends in a dance around the lake, the girls doing some kind of ring-a-ring-o'-roses, holding hands and dipping up and down in a circle like passive fairground horses.

Party Vince caught Janine's gaze. He looked back to the ring of girls. 'Now, princesses, who wants to visit an enchanted castle?'

The princesses cheered.

Janine muttered to Phil. 'Look at them. Brainwashed. Stepford girls.'

Phil held out a plate to Janine. 'I've made you a sandwich. Well, I haven't made it, it's from the tray, but—'

Janine pushed the plate away and turned to Katie. 'Do you still want to leave?'

Katie nodded.

'Even though your friends are all here? Even if we took all the pink away?'

Katie nodded again.

Janine kissed her on the head. 'Come on, then.' She grabbed the van keys from the side and turned to Phil. 'I'm taking the van. Do what you want, I don't care. I'm not staying here another second. Me and Katie are going to the cinema.'

18

Phil watched Dad stand at the front door, his back to the hallway table, smiling at his guests as the house emptied, handing out party bags.

Phil reached for a party bag. 'Do you want me to—'

Dad swatted him away. 'No!'

Phil shoved his hands in his pockets. This was Dad's Titanic, and he was going down as a one-man orchestra.

The last girl and parent reached the door. This girl's crown was too big, sitting lopsidedly, a heavy 'ruby' pulling it down so it covered one of the girl's eyes. 'That was the best party ever!'

'Thank you.' Dad looked up at the mother. 'I'm so pleased she enjoyed it.'

'I'm sorry I didn't get to thank Janine.'

'These bugs come on so suddenly.'

'Please tell her Beth said thank you.'

'Thanks for coming. Safe journey!'

Phil and Dad helped Party Vince pack up his equipment and put it in his party van.

Vince slammed the door. 'Well, I never.' He shook his head. 'A little girl who doesn't want to be a princess!'

They watched Vince drive away. Slowly, Dad closed the door. And there was just him and Phil.

'I don't need your help to tidy up.' Dad's voice was aggressive.

'I don't want to leave you like—'

'Ridiculous!'

Dad stormed into the kitchen and out to the garden. Phil followed.

Without speaking, they popped balloons with scissors. They pulled the remaining pink netting from the trees. They removed every scrap of confetti from the garden and rear-ranged the furniture.

Phil helped Dad replate the remaining food.

They washed up in silence.

'Now,' Dad threw his tea towel down aggressively, 'I will make this up to Katie. But what do I do about Janine?' He put his palms flat on the kitchen counter. 'I've tried to call but she's not answering.'

Phil unplugged the sink. He watched the water circle down, the suds collecting at the plughole. 'It's good you want to apologise.' He ignored the fact Dad hadn't actually said that. 'But maybe leave it till she's calmer.'

Phil refilled the sink with fresh water.

'It just sounded like a much more suitable party.' Dad picked up the cloth and wiped the surfaces. 'It *was* a more suitable party. I hadn't realised how much Katie liked pirates. And I told you it was going to be a princess party, Philip.'

'What? Of course you didn't!'

Dad stood up straight. 'I *did* tell you. Quite clearly. And you had ample opportunity to warn me if you thought it was a terrible idea.'

'*When?* When did you tell me?' Phil stared into the washing-up water. That was the wrong question. He should have stuck with blind denial.

'Right after I met Vince. While we were taking the branch off the tree.'

Phil's balloon of certainty popped. 'When I was using the chainsaw?' He raised his voice in panic. 'But it doesn't count if I was using the chainsaw!' He took a breath. 'Why did you do it, Dad?'

'I thought it was more suitable! *And* I told you about it. I thought Katie would prefer it.'

'This is the problem! You think Katie must prefer to be a princess, because that's what you think she should want, and you ignored what she asked for. You need to stop with all the sexist stuff. And all the *flirtys and prettys* – Janine says it drives her wild.' This was Dad's mess, pure and simple. No way Dad was going to palm his guilt off on Phil.

'I made a mistake today. But that's nothing to do with calling Katie *pretty*. Phil, Janine can't just take things that aren't related and mix them together!'

'Janine doesn't do that.' Phil made his voice firm with loyalty. That was absolutely what Janine did.

'Katie likes it when I say she looks pretty!'

Phil shook his head.

'Janine's being completely oversensitive. Yes, I got the party wrong. But that's all! It was one mistake! You know Janine makes every tiny issue bigger than it needs to be.'

Phil shook his head again. 'No, she doesn't.' He spoke as firmly as he could for someone who agreed completely.

'Well.' Dad stared at Phil. 'I *was* prepared to apologise, but now I've changed my mind. I'm not going to apologise for a whole lot of things I haven't done. I just didn't know how keen Katie was on pirates.' Dad threw his *Llandudno hardd, hafan, hedd!* tea towel onto the maiden. He picked up a fresh towel covered with tumbling oranges. 'That's the extent of any apology I'm going to give, but that won't be enough for Janine, so why bother?'

Phil watched his dad dry a bowl roughly. His shoulder blades were visible through the back of his shirt. He was getting thinner, as well as smaller. 'Are you OK?'

Dad's cheek flickered with irritation. 'Of course I am. Now leave me alone.'

Dad started flicking his tea towel in Phil's direction. Phil knew how it went from here. He walked up the stairs to his old bedroom with heavy feet.

Phil sat on the bed, half watching a series on his laptop. He could hear Dad watching the news downstairs.

Half an hour later, the front door went.

Phil tensed.

'Come on, quick.' Janine's voice was low. 'If we go straight upstairs, we can open your presents before bed.'

Phil heard two sets of feet hurry up to the landing, go into Katie's room, and shut the door.

Half an hour later, Janine came into their bedroom. She threw her handbag and a bottle of red wine onto the bed, and pushed the door shut. She held a glass from the bathroom – the glass Dad kept his toothbrush in.

Phil paused the episode. 'Hi.' He shuffled up the bed. 'So that was a balls-up. How is she?'

'I put her to bed. We had popcorn and ice cream at the cinema. Then a Nando's. An expensive solution, but fuck it. She stopped crying eventually.' Janine picked up the wine bottle and stared at it. 'A fucking cork.' She dropped the bottle back on the bed. 'The absolute pricks.'

'Do you want me to get a corkscrew?'

Janine shook her head. A moment later, she nodded.

Phil walked past Dad in his chair without speaking. He got a wine glass and corkscrew from the kitchen and headed back up.

Janine was still standing where he'd left her.

He pushed the door closed. 'J—'

Janine walked to the window. 'I don't want to talk about it.' Roughly, she pulled the curtains closed.

Phil sat on the bed. He unscrewed the cork.

'That fucking man!' A piece of her fringe caught on her eyelashes; she pulled the hair away. 'Did you tell him? Did you tell him how out of order he was?'

Phil poured Janine a glass. He handed it to her.

'He hasn't even apologised.' She took a large swig. 'He hasn't even come up.'

'I told him to leave you alone tonight.'

Janine gestured with the glass. 'He had plenty of time to apologise today!' Red wine sloshed up the glass's sides.

'I think he said sorry to Katie.' Had he? Phil wasn't sure.

'Wait.' Her eyes narrowed. 'You told him to leave me alone tonight?'

'I just thought it wouldn't help.'

'In case tonight I'm *irrational*?'

'How's this my fault?' *You were using the chainsaw.* 'I

thought it'd be better if you had some time—'

'To calm down?'

'Definitely not calm down,' Phil said quickly. 'To take the heat out of things. To make sure you were in the right mind-set to say what you wanted to say.'

'Fuck off, Phil.'

'Hey!'

Janine put her glass down on the bedside table, next to the coaster. 'Did you try and make him feel better about his fuck-up?'

'He was upset, J!'

Janine sniffed.

'And he's doing us a favour! Two favours! With the party and moving in.'

'Those are favours we didn't even bloody want! It's not a favour if it's forced on you.'

Phil winced.

'Why are you wincing?'

'Your voice is quite loud. With . . .' *Dad downstairs* '. . . Katie trying to sleep.'

Janine shook her head. She tossed back the rest of the glass of wine.

'We had nowhere to live, Janine.'

'We would have found somewhere.'

'So what do we do now?'

'He's crossed a line. He can't be allowed to think this is acceptable.'

'Am I meant to shun Dad now? Just because you're cross with him?' He saw Janine's face. 'Not *just*. I didn't mean *just*. The man's bereaved! He's not himself.'

'No, Phil.' Janine indicated for him to pass the bottle. 'Lynn died six months ago, and I know that doesn't mean he's fine, but the problem is he's *very much himself*.' She poured more wine. 'He thought princesses were *more suitable*, and didn't tell us. What kind of man would do that?'

Phil had to say it. 'He said he'd told me.'

Janine narrowed her gaze. '*Did* he tell you?'

'Of course not. You think I would have agreed to that?'

Janine eyed him some more.

'I'm not the bad guy here! There are no bad guys, in fact. Dad just made a mistake. A really stupid, infuriating mistake. He's really upset and sorry.'

'He just doesn't do *sorry*s out loud.'

'He wouldn't look me in the eye. He knows he made a mistake.' Janine's wonky-lovely face didn't look so lovely with her eyes this hard. 'But there are always two sides. Nothing is ever completely clear cut.'

'You're taking his side?'

'No. There aren't any sides.'

'Aha! You just said there are always two sides, Phil!'

Phil felt his face flame. He wasn't as good at arguing as Janine. 'He's been a dick. But he's my dad, J.'

'Just because he's doing us a favour, doesn't mean he can do stuff like this.'

'He's my dad,' Phil repeated.

Janine sat on the bed. 'If you won't support me, other people will.'

Phil stared at her. 'What does that even mean?'

Janine shook her head.

Phil shook his head back. If that's what it had come to, he could do *it's not worth it* pass-agg head-shaking all day.

'Let's talk tomorrow.' Phil turned on his side, his back

facing Janine. He reached for his headphones from the bedside table.

He put his headphones in, brought his laptop closer towards him, and pressed play.

19

Janine lay on her side next to Phil, the faint buzz of TV gun-fire audible through his headphones.

She was meant to be grateful? No way Janine was going to be grateful.

Favours weren't favours when they were dumped on people. It was like receiving an unwanted present. Nice and all, but if that present turned out to be a piece of rotting roadkill, it was fair to say the situation wasn't net positive.

Janine felt herself rolling back into Phil on this decades-old mattress. She braced herself, keeping a tension in her body, clinging on to the uphill section. Touching felt too conciliatory for tonight.

This whole thing would be so much easier if Roy was *always* an arse. Everyone complained about people being so binary on social media, but at least you knew how to sort people. It would save so much effort if everyone could be either a genius philanthropist, or responsible for a genocide. Dolly Parton – fine. Hitler – also fine. (In this limited context.) Life should be like a panto, with clear indicators of when to cheer, when to boo.

But Roy was more complicated, which meant Janine couldn't just cut him out of their lives. Not that Phil would let her anyway. He was going to try to play piggy in the middle.

Phil didn't get to be the pig. *No way* Janine was going to let him be the pig.

She tried to look at her phone without lifting her head, holding it at an awkward angle so the screen didn't flip to horizontal.

She stared at the *Am I the Villain Here?* forum.

Am I the villain for playing Barry White loudly when my house-mate is having sex?

It was always housemates, on forums like this. And that was because living with other people was a Really Bad Idea.

Janine let her phone droop against the duvet. She wished she could go next door to Sal's, but she couldn't, not without seeing Roy.

Janine wanted Sal to tell her she was in the right to be incensed.

Though she didn't need Sal's opinion – not really. When you were in the right, you didn't need anyone else to agree. It was enough to have that unshakeable inner glow.

It would be nice though. To be reassured of her own righteousness.

Janine looked at her screen. It had flipped to the wrong angle again.

She flipped it back. She scrolled down the *Am I The Villain Here?* screen.

She glanced back at Phil.

She shuffled up against the pillows and her screen flipped the right way round.

Janine clicked *New Post*. And, with the determined fingers of someone knowing she was doing the right thing, she started to type.

PART THREE

Am I the Villain Here? Post 35915

CantBeArsed8: Am I the villain here for being furious my partner's father changed my daughter's pirate party into a princess party?

My partner's father is always telling my daughter how pretty she looks, and buying her pink things, and expecting her to be passive. I have made several hints that I don't want her getting these influences and asked him clearly to stop calling her pretty after he said my daughter made a pretty raccoon. He hasn't stopped. And I don't think he forgets — he just chooses to ignore me.

I want us to have a good relationship. He's a widower, and I want to support a lonely man. He means well, and he's been really kind to us in lots of ways. We are currently living with him because of a brief blip in our housing situation. It's harder to pull someone up on their behaviour when they're doing you a favour.

Recently, he offered to arrange my daughter's birthday party. She'd asked for a pirate party, but when she got there, he'd changed the party theme from pirates to princesses because he thought it was 'more suitable'. My daughter was devastated.

Am I the villain for pulling him up on his sexist outlook, when he's the one in the wrong? Is it fair to be furious, when he's doing me all these 'favours'?

Am I the Villain Here? Post 35915

CantBeArsed8: Am I the villain here for being furious my partner's father changed my daughter's pirate party into a princess party?

741 votes, 6 days left
You're the villain here: 5%
Not the villain here: 95%

Latest reply:

@oatcakes79: You are absolutely in the right! He needs to be told. That is one twisted favour.

20

The next morning at five Roy crept to the bathroom, and did his ablutions as quietly as he could. He waved his razor slowly in the water to rinse it of shaving cream, rather than giving it the usual aggressive waggle. He sat down to urinate – an act he frowned on in the able-bodied male as vaguely dishonourable.

He put his coat and shoes on before making his toast, ready to abandon his meal at any sound of stirring.

It all stayed quiet upstairs.

Roy washed up his breakfast things. He took his newspaper and headed into town, walking the long way round to avoid the windscreen man. He sat in a noisy café, reading, until he could take no more cups of tea.

When Tessa finally arrived at the library, she found Roy on a bench outside, his coat buttoned up against the morning chill.

Usually, all Roy's problems felt that bit further away when he was at the library.

Not today.

Not only could he not stop thinking, he had to be on constant alert to avoid Yvonne. He darted away every time he saw a high nest of hair bobbing among the stacks.

She cornered him eventually, at the bottom of the DVD shelves. 'Roy!' Her face loomed above an armful of books, her feathered earrings dancing forwards. 'I can't keep up!'

Roy gave a weak smile.

'So? I'm all ears!' Yvonne put her books down. 'Did Katie love her special party?'

He stood up slowly. 'Yes, she did.'

'*Of course* she did. Have you got photos? I want to see that enchanted castle!'

Roy dusted his hands on his trousers. 'I haven't plugged the camera in to download them yet. Excuse me.' He looked over Yvonne's shoulder. 'That lady looks like she needs some help with the printer.'

Roy pretended to help a bemused customer with the (clearly functioning) printer. He stayed in the printer area and avoided Yvonne for the rest of his shift. He left early, for the first time in library history.

There was only one person he could talk to.

'So there it is, Joseph – my predicament.'

Roy sat further back on the nursing home's sofa and looked into his friend's eyes. 'You'd never think children's parties could cause such a fuss, would you? But you know Janine.' Roy shook his head at the idea of Janine's unfortunate disposition. 'I *could* apologise, of course. But *should* I?'

Joseph gripped his pudding bowl. He scraped intensely at the remnants of something gelatinous.

Roy waited. He knew by now not to come between Joseph and his puddings. 'There's an opportunity for an apology, of course. But does that mean it's the right thing to do?'

Roy waited again. A structural engineer of award-winning

mathematic excellence, Joseph, free range, had been as sharp as a scythe.

But he was no longer free range. Roy took Joseph's bowl and placed it on a side table. 'After all I've done for Janine, is an apology really sending the right message?'

Joseph hunched his torso over his lap. He appeared fascinated by one cuff of his sweater.

In the over-heated lounge, Roy pulled his handkerchief from his sleeve. Everything here was unsatisfactory. The sofa springs too soft; the radiator temperature too high. Even the painted furniture was too bright and institutional – more suited to a primary school than a dignified home for award-winning structural engineers with brains like scythes.

'Yes, I made a mistake, but that's surely outweighed by the fact she moved into my house.' He wiped his forehead. 'And she never even said *thank you* for the party. It cost me four hundred pounds!'

Joseph's attention was still caught by the cuff of his sweater.

He had deteriorated since coming here. Roy had told Joseph's daughter at the time it was a mistake. *'We have to help him fight, girl!'* But Sue lived two hundred miles away in Bristol with her own family, and she'd moved Joseph out of his house after an extremely minor fire. Which was really the company's fault for putting so much packaging on their ready meals and, as Roy said at the time, *'unless they use large font to expressly state to take the cardboard off before putting in the oven, I don't know what they expect!'*

The fire had been contained to the oven, but Sue had called it *the final straw,* and used it as a reason to incarcerate Joseph in a place so fundamentally unsuited to someone with Joseph's independent spirit, it had made Roy cough away tears.

'I see what you're doing, Joseph.' Roy folded his handkerchief carefully and inched it back up his sleeve. 'And your silence speaks volumes. You're right. I can't apologise.'

A young nurse came over to collect Joseph's pudding bowl. 'All gone again!' Her blond hair was collected messily onto the top of her head, forming a lopsided ball. 'You do enjoy your blancmange, don't you, Joe?'

Joseph looked up from his sweater cuff.

'He goes by Jo-*seph*,' Roy said.

The nurse turned to Roy, ball of hair bobbing. 'Most of our guests lose weight when they get here but Joseph loves his puddings!' Her badge said *Elena*. '*Such* a good eater!'

Something about this woman's tone made Roy reply, 'He was a structural engineer. Award-winning. He designed that bridge over the M60 near the old viaduct.' He gave Elena a nod of dismissal.

'How lovely!' She remained standing with the pudding bowl, unaware she'd been dismissed. 'It's great you visit so often.' The nurse indicated the table to Roy's left. 'He likes those books, you know.'

'We're in the middle of an important philosophical conversation.' Roy glanced at the books. They were picture books, and mainly about flowers and animals – not Joseph's areas of interest at all. 'But I'll bring a suitable book next time.'

Elena walked away with the bowl.

Roy didn't remember Joseph having a sweet tooth. 'Are they good puddings here?'

Joseph gave him a peaceful smile.

Behind Roy, the buzzer went. There was a deep metallic ratcheting of locks.

Roy watched Elena greet the visitor. The ratcheting sound made him want to flee for the door, but Joseph didn't notice.

Roy had to accept it – his best friend was an indoor bird now. He didn't get offended by his confinement, or even the primary-coloured chairs all around him. He'd lapsed into Stockholm syndrome, seduced by the crafty deployment of puddings.

'Returning to our earlier conversation . . .' Roy left a pause. 'We are, as always, sympatico. An apology without sincerity has no value. The path ahead is clear, and your wise counsel is appreciated, my friend.' He patted Joseph's arm. 'There will be no apology.'

Joseph became re-entranced by his cuff.

'I'll be back in a day or two.' Roy stood up and dusted his trousers down. 'And I'll bring a much more suitable book. In the meantime, keep your spirits up.' Roy lowered his voice. 'Don't let the bastards grind you down.'

Roy stood up, feeling better for having made his decision. He signed out of the visitors' book, gave a faint shudder at the sound of the ratcheting locks, and strode out of the nursing home.

21

That morning, when Phil and Katie went downstairs, Janine found many reasons she needed to remain in the bedroom. It was essential she cut her toenails – and do it right that second.

Phil came back upstairs in his overalls. 'He's gone out already.'

Janine put the scissors down, one foot still to go. 'I'll make coffee.'

Janine walked Katie to school, slowing when she saw the mums at the school gate.

She needed to befriend these people. This was her life now.

But she couldn't face them. Not after yesterday.

'Just run that last bit on your own, Katie. I'll watch you. Run.' Janine pushed Katie towards school and turned.

'Hi!' The mum who always wore gym leggings and a high ponytail – Cass – fell into step beside her. 'Thank you so much for yesterday. Betty had such a lovely time!'

'That's great, Cass!' Janine smiled and didn't slow her pace. 'I'm so pleased.'

'I had a little afternoon nap, thank you for that gift! Between you and me, Betty hadn't been looking forward to the party. She'd got it into her head that it was going to be a pirate party. But she said it was wonderful.'

Janine slowed. Was this woman not going to mention Katie at all?

'It sounded magical! A princess castle *and* an enchanted wood!'

Janine gave a tight nod.

'And a squirrel with fairy dust to sprinkle onto wands!' They stopped at a pedestrian crossing. 'What a lovely touch!'

Janine jabbed the button, hard. Cars whooshed by with no sign of slowing.

'Katie must have been over the moon.'

Janine froze. She looked up at Cass.

'I know it hasn't always been smooth sailing with the other girls,' Cass said, 'but this will really help, her being the one who threw such an amazing party.'

Janine shook her head in wonder. Turned out her daughter – this *Betty* girl – was a selfish snake. She didn't even care enough to mention the birthday girl didn't go to her own party! Betty was an actual psychopath!

'Katie wasn't there.' Janine ignored the woman striding fast to join them at the crossing. 'We told the girls she had a tummy bug, but she didn't. Katie asked for a pirate party. She was devastated when it turned out to be a princess party.'

'What?' Cass crumpled her eyebrows. 'Oh no!'

The other woman looked up from her bag. 'A *pirate* party? Instead of a princess party?' The woman had a thoughtful expression.

Janine had a bad feeling. 'No, not a pirate party.' She gave Cass her warmest beam and walked faster. 'If you'll excuse me, I'm in a hurry.'

*

Sal didn't look delighted to find Janine on her doorstep.

Janine smiled. 'Got a minute?'

'You know it's Monday? Not the weekend?'

'You always used to have time for me in the workday.'

'We used to work together though. It was different. We had real stuff to talk about.'

'Nope.' Janine made deep eye contact. 'Our conversations were ninety-five per cent ranting about idiots.'

Sal took a second. 'Fair. I'll have to keep an eye on my emails though.' She took a step back to let Janine in. 'And I'm expecting a call.'

Sal sat on the sofa with her laptop, looking at her work emails with disgust. Janine felt a throb of envy. *She* wanted to be the one looking at work emails with disgust.

She heard the shuffle of footsteps down the stairs. 'Alfie's not in school?'

'He's got a cold.'

'Hi, Alfie!' Janine shouted.

'Hi.' The reply sounded an effort.

'Teenagers.' Sal looked to Janine. 'So, you want to tell me about yesterday?'

'I do, because you won't fucking believe it, Sal. Katie asked for a pirate party but Roy got her a princess one. He thought it was *more suitable*.'

Sal glanced down at her emails and back. 'I guessed that. From all the pink.'

'And now I have to live there! At the scene of the crime!'

'Sal indicated her screen. 'I have to look at this. There's a shitstorm.'

Janine gave a fond sigh. 'I used to love a good shitstorm.'

From the kitchen, there was the mechanical sound of a toaster lever depressing.

Sal's head shot up. 'Don't eat all the bread, Alfie!' She looked at Janine. 'He's had about six slices already. I know they say *feed a cold*, but Alfie takes it too far.'

Janine shook her head. It was fair enough, Sal being distracted by shitstorm emails. But it was a bit of a cheek when even Alfie's toast got more attention.

She waited until Sal finished scrolling. 'And I'm meant to be grateful? All these favours Roy does us that we haven't actually asked for? And Phil won't discuss it, he thinks I should just get over it. And I'm not sure that's fair. Which is why I've put it on *Am I The Villain Here?*'

Slowly, Sal looked up.

Janine scratched her neck defensively. 'What? It'll help.'

'Have you told Phil?'

'It's fine. I'll tell him later.' Janine gave her neck another defensive scratch. 'When I can show him people think I'm right to be furious.'

Sal studied Janine.

'It's fine. It's all fine.' Janine stopped scratching. 'Tell me about work.'

'Scott asked about you the other day. Then panicked and asked me not to tell you he'd asked.'

Janine narrowed her eyes. 'Has he got a new Bad News Bear yet?'

Sal's phone started flashing. 'I need to take this.'

'The shitstorm?'

Sal nodded and pressed to answer. 'Keri.' She listened for a moment. 'I know. He's made a right balls-up and now we have to dig him out. Same old.'

Sal kept talking, and Janine tried not to sigh. She pulled out her phone and checked the forum.

Seven hundred and forty-one votes already – 95 per cent of which agreed with her.

Janine gave a sniff of success. Sal clearly thought Janine was one sock short of a full wash, but Janine was fighting the good fight, wasn't she? Fighting for a fairer future for Katie. She might not be able to get another sales job, but she could make the world a better place. Which was much more important, when you thought about it.

A notification shot across the top of Janine's screen – a message from a newsletter she'd subscribed to when feeling desperate.

Networking Event on Wednesday!

Janine gave a different kind of sniff and put her phone in her pocket. She wasn't *that* desperate.

With Sal still on the phone, Janine wandered upstairs to see Alfie.

She knocked at his door. 'Alfie.'

She knocked again. She pushed the door open.

Alfie sat on the bed, headphones on, typing into his phone, a laptop open on his knees. On the laptop screen, a naked woman on her hands and knees was having her hair pulled back painfully.

'Alfie!'

Alfie's eyes widened at Janine. He scrabbled to shut the laptop.

There was silence.

Alife sat completely still, like that might make Janine go away.

Janine shook her head. This kid was her *godson* – or would have been, if she or Sal did God. She'd bought that kid baby clothes and wooden toys! She'd taken him to monster truck rallies!

She indicated to Alfie to pull his headphones off.

He did. 'Someone sent it.' Alfie stared at the bookcase. 'I wasn't even watching. I was on my phone.'

'That video's not OK, Alfie.' Janine sat on the bed. 'Not all porn is created equal. I know you'll watch porn – lots of porn probably, I imagine you're watching it all the time—'

Alfie looked towards the door, as though help might be coming.

'Porn is fine if it's respectful and made responsibly. But that woman wasn't happy.' Janine tried to make eye contact with Alfie, but it wasn't happening. 'She wasn't enjoying it, Alfie. This society doesn't care, but you should.' Janine shook her head sadly. 'Give me the laptop.'

Alfie took a second. He gave his head a tiny shake.

'Give me the laptop and I'll find you better porn, so you can see the difference. It'll be just as sexy, I promise.'

Alfie shook his head more vehemently.

Janine reached for the laptop.

Alfie clung on.

'Please,' Alfie whispered. 'Please, leave me alone.'

'I'm your godmother, kind of. I'm helping you grow. So I'm not going to tell your mother that you watch porn.' Janine let go of the laptop. 'You're fifteen. She knows. But I am going to set you some homework.' She watched Alfie stare into his bookcase. 'By the weekend, I want you to show you've found some responsible porn. Where both parties are equal and fulfilled.'

She waited. She got nothing back.

'I'm not enjoying this either, Alfie.' Janine patted his leg. 'But you'll thank me. There's nothing more sexy than respect.' She stood up. 'And we can also talk about realistic images. Normal labia and pubic hair, that kind of thing.'

Janine nodded goodbye and headed downstairs, enjoying the inner glow that came from being a good role model. She waved to Sal, and let herself out of the house.

It was a shame, in one way, that Janine thought *fuck no way* about having more kids. It was the boys who needed educating even more than the girls, and Janine's boys would have learned about this stuff from birth. Her boys would have always checked for consent; they'd sit with legs close together on the bus. They'd never have talked over their female colleagues, they'd have campaigned against domestic violence, *and* they'd put their own plates in the dishwasher.

Janine walked up the path to Roy's. She listened at the front door.

There was no sound.

She peered through the letterbox. Roy's house slippers were neatly tucked next to the door mat.

Tentatively, she let herself in.

When all she could hear was the ticking grandmother clock, she relaxed. She flopped onto the sofa to read the 95 per cent favourable replies.

Yesterday, Janine had been frustrated. Today, she was channelling that frustration for the common good.

In one way, Janine thought, you could view her as an un-employed, homeless woman – annoying her busy friends, giving unsolicited advice, and hiding from an elderly man.

But, in another, more meaningful, way, Janine Pierce was changing the world.

22

The day after the party, Phil heard his dad leaving the house long before the rest of the family got going.

It was a relief.

Phil found Janine in the kitchen. 'What have you got planned today?'

Janine walked towards the stairs. 'I've got loads on.'

Phil rounded up his keys, phone and wallet. He opened the fridge, just in case.

No lunchbox.

He looked to the counter.

No thermos, either.

Apparently, Phil wasn't getting a shit lunch, or a thermos made by a stranger anymore.

Phil's shit lunchbox days were over.

Phil went to work on the new estate, working with a bunch of lads he knew well. He even managed to forget about the party.

But too soon he was back home, standing outside his dad's front door. He took a breath, briefly contemplated the sky, and let himself in.

Janine stood at the kitchen counter, slicing tomatoes. Katie was doing something on Janine's phone at the table. There was no sign of Dad.

Katie held up a picture of a car to show Phil. 'That's Daddy's new car.'

Phil threw his keys onto the worktop. 'Nice.'

'It parks itself.' Katie held the screen up higher. 'He pushes a button and it goes backwards. The steering wheel turns like there's an invisible man turning it.'

Phil glanced up at Janine. 'Sounds scary.'

'If you press another button, the seats get too hot and it feels like you've weed yourself.'

'I can see why it was so expensive.' Phil placed a hand on Janine's shoulder. She kept slicing.

'When I grow up,' Katie placed the phone back down on the table, 'I want to be a musician.'

Phil looked at her. 'Because of the car?'

'Yep.'

'I think what you're saying is that you want to be Molly.'

Janine sniffed appreciatively. 'I've made a warm salad. Ten minutes.'

Phil took his wallet out of his pocket and placed it on the sideboard. 'I'll tell Dad tea's ten minutes, shall I?'

Janine said nothing, so Phil took that as a *yes*. Anything else would be ridiculous, surely?

Phil went upstairs and had a shower.

Afterwards, he knocked on Dad's door. 'Dad?'

'Come in!'

Phil pushed the door open. He looked around in surprise.

Dad was sitting against the headboard, one leg crossed over the other, a book in his hand. His room was tightly packed. There was even less floor space than in Phil's and Janine's room. A computer desk was jammed between the bed and the wall, and the contents of the spare-room book-shelves were piled up on Mum's dressing table.

He felt a flare of guilt within. 'Can you live like this?'

'It's perfectly fine.'

'Janine's made tea.'

Dad didn't reply.

'It's a warm salad. Right up your street.' Phil looked at the shirt on the hanger on the front of the wardrobe. Dad used to be a large, but this was a medium, at most. 'We'd love you to join us.'

'We?'

'We.'

Dad folded in the arms of his reading glasses. He gave a small nod.

Phil led Dad downstairs, like a chaperone.

Janine didn't look up when they entered the room. 'Roy.'

Dad pulled his chair in. He carefully shook a napkin over his lap. 'Janine.'

Janine placed a plate in front of Dad.

'Thank you.' Dad spoke in a tone of absolute neutrality.

'You're welcome.' Janine spoke in a matching tone.

Phil smiled at Katie. 'Well, this is nice.' He sat in the chair that had been Mum's. Janine put a plate in front of him. 'Looks great!'

He noticed Katie poking her food suspiciously. He looked at his own plate. Lettuce leaves were turning damp, sweating under hot rocks of butternut squash.

Time to rally the troops.

He took a bite. 'This is delicious.'

'No, it isn't,' Janine said. 'It's fine, but it's not delicious.'

'It is, it's – wholesome. I can feel all the goodness soaking in.'

Katie stared at her plate. 'It's salad.'

'It's *hot* salad though,' Janine said. 'It doesn't count as salad.'

Phil looked at Dad, waiting for him to say, 'besides, salad can make an excellent, nutritious meal.'

Dad didn't.

Phil turned to look at Katie. 'Did you have fun at your dad's at the weekend?'

'It was great!' Katie eyes widened with excitement. 'We drove everywhere!'

Phil glanced at Dad. 'They've got a new car. A sports car.'

Dad loaded up his fork with vegetables. 'I know.'

'It's electric!' Katie said. 'All electric, so the planet is happy.'

'It looked very fancy,' Dad said.

Katie turned to Phil. 'Is your van electric?'

Phil shook his head.

Katie shook her head.

Phil said, mildly, 'You can't fit many tools in a sports car.'

'Marky didn't pay for the car, obviously. It was Molly's money.' Janine glanced at Katie. 'Which is fine, of course.'

'The car's got room for Daddy's guitar.'

Phil didn't have to look up to know Janine would be rolling her eyes.

'Have you heard my daddy play guitar?' Katie asked Dad.

Dad smiled politely. 'I haven't had the pleasure. But how wonderful, to have a father who's so *creative*.'

Janine made a twist of her mouth.

'Daddy's really funny too,' Katie said.

Dad glanced at Janine and back. 'I'm sure your father is a *wonderful* man. Who's had quite a lot to put up with over the years.'

Janine lifted her gaze. Finally, she looked at Dad.

Phil stared too. He remembered Dad's rants, pre-Molly,

every time he'd heard Marky's maintenance payments were late again. *The man has responsibilities! What kind of man wouldn't get a reliable job with a child to support?'*

Katie picked up her knife and fork. She made them dance, like they were high-kicking legs.

Phil smiled at her. 'They're doing the can-can!'

Janine smiled too. 'That's brilliant!'

Katie shrugged and kept kicking the 'legs' out.

Phil put his knife and fork down. 'So I'm looking forward to this school fundraiser on Friday!' He saw Katie's face – *school, at night?* – and added, 'not for you, don't worry.' He turned to Dad. 'Are you looking forward to it?'

Janine looked up. 'Are you still coming to the fundraiser, Roy?'

'You invited me, Janine.'

Roy, Janine, Roy, Janine. It was like they couldn't stop using each other's name.

'It will be great to have you there, Dad.' Phil spoke hurriedly.

'I'm sad.' Katie poked her food with a limp fork. 'I've been through my presents from my birthday, and I didn't get any animal stickers. I'd told everyone that's what I wanted.'

Phil glanced at Janine. He'd really hoped they could have got through this teatime without talking about Katie's birthday. 'Sorry to hear that.'

'Will you buy me more stickers?'

Before Phil could say *yes*, Janine cut in. 'You got lots of other great presents and we can't afford to buy you more, love.' She gave Katie a flat smile. 'I'm not working now. We have to think carefully about each purchase and whether it's important.'

'Stickers are important.'

Janine shook her head sadly. 'Heating's important. Food is important.'

Katie turned to Phil. 'Phil, will you buy me more stickers?'

'Your mother's made a decision.'

Janine put her knife and fork down in a clatter. She stared at him.

'What I mean,' Phil turned back to Katie, 'is it's your mother's decision and she's made it, and it's a good decision, and she says *no*, so I say *no* too.'

'I'll ask Daddy.'

Janine picked up her knife and fork. 'Don't do that, please.'

'It means I won't get the stickers till the weekend though.'

'No, Katie.'

'Which is a long time to wait.'

Janine gripped her knife and fork tightly. 'Katie, *I said no!*'

The table went silent.

Katie looked at Phil.

Phil looked at Janine.

Janine stared down at her plate of sweating salad. 'Sorry.'

They finished their meals without any more conversation. Phil started stacking the plates. 'Dad, why don't you read Katie a story?'

'But check first it's not racist, please.' Janine pushed back her chair; there was a screech across the lino. 'I saw something horrific in that box.'

'And Janine, you can sit down,' Phil kept talking, as if she hadn't said anything, 'and I'll do the washing-up.'

But Janine wasn't in the mood for sitting down. She wouldn't let Phil wash up on his own, and now she was scrubbing those pans *hard*.

'Why didn't you support me with Katie just then?' *Hard scrub.* 'About the sticker business?'

'I did support you.'

'When you're being back-up, you should just nod. You improvised.'

Phil glanced at Janine. A piece of her fringe had caught on her eyelashes. 'I can't always nod. I have to mix it up.'

Janine tried to blink the piece of hair out of her eyes. Phil pushed her fringe gently to the side.

'Then be careful. *It's your mother's decision and she says no so I say no too?* Do you think that's helpful?'

Phil held his tea towel in a flag of surrender. 'I could have put it better.' Janine's ability to remember exact phrasing was one of Phil's least favourite things about her. 'But I definitely didn't say it in that wishy-washy voice.'

Janine kept scrubbing the pan. 'You should support me more.'

Phil paused. 'Is this still about the stickers?'

Janine slammed the pan into the rack without rinsing, something she always told Phil was lazy. 'Your dad needs to learn that his behaviour is not OK. Everyone agrees. *Everyone.*'

'Everyone?' Phil turned to look at her. '*Everyone?*'

Janine's mouth was a thin line.

'Oh for fuck's sake, don't tell everyone about this, Janine! This is our family business!'

Janine threw a soapy spoon on the drainer. 'He still hasn't apologised! And you know I'm in the right.'

'Of course you think you're in the right! But there are two sides to everything. And we live here now. You've got to get over this.'

Janine looked up slowly.

'I mean it!' Phil dried the spoon and placed it in the cutlery drawer. He slammed the drawer, harder than intended.

'You're not on my side, then.'

'If you're going to be like this, then I'm going to be Switzerland.' Dad and Janine could argue like humans if they wanted, but Phil could be a whole, magnanimous *country*.

Janine narrowed her eyes. 'You don't get to be Switzerland.'

'I am. I'm Switzerland.'

'Even Switzerland doesn't stay neutral anymore! Besides, you're my partner! You're meant to be on my side. You're meant to support me.'

'You're asking *a fuck* of a lot, Janine.'

Janine turned to face him, the washing-up forgotten. She folded her arms. 'Do you really want to be *that guy*?'

Phil shrugged. He wasn't going to ask who *that guy* was. Just in case he was *that guy*.

'Don't you want to stand up for what you believe in?'

Phil shook his head, incredulous. 'Am I meant to think the same as you on absolutely everything?'

They stared at each other.

'Dad fucked up. No one died.' Phil threw the tea towel down. 'This is ridiculous – I'm off to get some air.' He scooped his keys off the counter and paused. 'And from now on I'm Switzerland.'

Tuesday

Am I the Villain Here? Post 35915

CantBeArsed8: Am I the villain here for being furious my part-ner's father changed my daughter's pirate party into a princess party?

2,289 votes, 5 days left

You're the villain here: 9%
Not the villain here: 91%

Latest reply:

@itspronouncedrafe: I bet he voted for Brexit.

23

Roy sat on his bed. He listened to the running water, brushing of teeth and muffled conversations indicating his family were getting ready for the day.

He'd intended to be out before they got up. The problem was, the shops would be shut at this time. The library was closed. And he didn't really want to sit on a bench again. It turned out there was a nip in the air before the workday started in April.

At least he was able to call Claudia. The good thing about having a daughter living in Singapore was being able to call before the socially acceptable UK phoning window opened. The only good thing.

'How did Katie's birthday go?' Claudia asked.

Roy looked down at his wedding ring.

'Dad?'

'It was fine. All in hand.' There was no need for Claudia to get embroiled in Janine's ridiculousness. The idea of both his children having an opinion on this was abhorrent.

His children. Roy still thought of Phil and Claudia as *his children*. His neurons flared with dissonance at evidence of paunches and professional qualifications and sciatica. Especially with Claudia, because the gaps were so long between them seeing each other. He had a moment of alarm when he'd met her at the airport – at this woman walking towards him who looked like his little girl but also, inexplicably, like his own mother. Whose knees crunched like a packet of crisps when she crouched and who, when choosing from a menu in a restaurant, now asked Roy if she could borrow his reading glasses.

'Anyway, Claud, I'm phoning about your mother's ashes.' He heard the front door slam. That was Janine and Katie gone. Good. 'We said we'd take them to the beach close to her birthday, didn't we?'

There was a pause.

'Claudia? Are you still there?' He didn't trust internet-based phone services.

'It's just hard to organise, with work and school.' She was still there. 'I can't just hop on a plane for a weekend from here.'

'Of course. Let me know when you've picked the dates.'

There was another silence.

'I don't mean to put you on the spot today.' Roy registered the faint brush and click of his letterbox. 'Just let me know. Ideally in the next week or so.'

They said goodbye and Roy hung up. He went to the front door to collect the freshly delivered post – but there wasn't any. There was just a single piece of paper on his doormat, folded in two.

Roy crouched. He unfolded the paper.

It was a slim note, written in black biro in plain block capitals.

HAVE YOU SEEN JANINE'S POLL? HAVE YOU SEEN WHAT SHE'S SAYING ABOUT YOU ON THE AM I THE VILLAIN HERE? FORUM?

Roy pushed himself to standing. He turned the key in the door and wrenched it open.

The street was nearly empty.

There was just one lone figure, walking away in the direction of the high street. Darsh, the young man from over the road. The two men had barely interacted, beyond the courteous. And it hadn't always been *that* courteous – Roy knew Darsh referred to him behind his back as *Bin Captain*.

This was a time for action, not reflection. 'Darsh! Wait, please!' Roy hurried up the road in a half-jog.

'It wasn't me at the weekend.' Darsh removed some tiny earpieces. 'With the party and the music.'

'No, no, I . . .' Roy waved a hand. 'Sorry to trouble you, Darsh. Did you just put something through my door?'

Darsh took a moment. 'No?'

'Something about Janine?'

Darsh shook his head. 'Still no.'

'Did you see anyone else put a note through? Was there anyone here when you came out?' Roy tried to keep the frustration out of his voice.

From the look on Darsh's face, it hadn't worked. Darsh shook his head.

They stood in silence.

Darsh's expression was deadpan. 'Was it a good note or a bad note?'

'It was an anonymous note.'

Darsh raised his eyebrows a millimetre.

Roy was so confused, so uncharacteristically in need of a second opinion, that he held the piece of paper out.

Darsh took it. 'Whoa.'

'So.' Darsh pressed the note back into Roy's hands. 'I need to . . .' He jerked one thumb like a hitchhiker.

'But what does it mean, Darsh?'

Darsh sighed. 'OK.' He let his rucksack slip off his back, placing it down on the pavement. 'Do you know a Janine?'

'My daughter-in-law. She's staying with me at the moment. We've had a –' Roy pressed his lips together briefly – 'minor disagreement.'

Darsh jiggled his earpieces in his hand. 'And what was it about?'

'Some confusion over a six-year-old's party. Whether the theme of the party should be pirates or princesses.'

Darsh's eyebrows moved up another millimetre. He got his phone out of his pocket and started typing.

Roy jerked his hand out, placing it over Darsh's screen. '*No!*'

Darsh looked up. 'No?'

'I don't want to know.' Roy kept his hand over the screen. 'What people say about you is none of your business.'

Darsh studied him. 'The high road.' He gave a slow nod. 'Nice.'

Roy stood a little straighter.

'Good on you, Roy. You're the bigger man.' Darsh picked up his rucksack. 'I'd better go.'

Roy nodded. 'Have a wonderful day at . . . work.' He didn't know what Darsh did for a living.

Darsh hitched his rucksack onto his shoulder and put his earpieces back in. He turned and headed for the bus stop.

Roy watched Darsh walk away with an unbalanced gait, his right shoulder slumping under his rucksack in a way that suggested he had visits to a chiropractor in his future.

Roy watched Darsh round the corner, out of sight.

The rest of the street was empty.

Roy placed the note in his pocket and strode back to his house.

Thinking.

24

'Why are we going in so early?' Katie asked Janine as they walked. 'It's only school.'

'The early bird catches the worm.'

Katie stared at Janine – *at* her, and into her soul. 'Is it because you don't want to be at—'

Janine gave Katie her best gaslighter's smile. 'No.'

They walked in silence. Katie scraped the soles of her shoes in a vague gesture of defiance.

But Janine was happy to ignore vague gestures. 'We're here!' She waved Katie towards the building. 'Have fun!'

Katie hurried across the empty playground.

'Hello!' Janine made deliberate eye contact with parents. She was going to become popular with these mums if it killed her. She leaned down and talked to a passing kid. 'That's a very nice duffel coat.'

The kid looked at her. In confusion, he looked at his mum. He hurried into school.

Janine straightened up. Lexi's mum, Beth, was joining a group at the gates. Janine spotted the woman in the gymwear, and the woman with the shih tzu in the pram. Cass and Megan.

Janine walked up to them. 'Hi, gang!' Ugh. *Gang*. Janine

knew she had to try to get in with these people, for Katie's sake, but did she have to act like a twat?

Cass smiled and pointed behind. 'There's Danny!' She waved.

Janine looked.

Danny Carswell was ambling past, a bottle dangling from each hand. Danny was a stay-at-home dad, and determinedly so, always armed with emergency layers, better pens, and unprocessed snacks. His kids were aggressively hydrated.

The rest of the women waved at Danny too. Nobody cooed, but a coo was implied.

Danny waved back. 'Hi, everyone!'

Janine felt her eyes narrow. This guy positioned himself as a stay-at-home mum, but better. She'd felt obliged to follow him back on social media, and in December learned he moved his Elf on the Shelf to a resourcefully creative place each day. By Christmas Eve, Janine wanted to punch that elf between its flirty eyelashes.

Megan rocked the shih tzu pram, smiling at Danny. 'Are you joining us in the café today? We're making plans for the school quiz.'

'Can't, I'm afraid.' Danny kept walking. 'Busy day!'

'That's fair. You do *so* much.' Megan turned to the others. 'He does so much.'

Janine couldn't help it. 'So much, *how*? More than you?' She hated everything about the situation. The women, Danny – the world and everything in it. *Burn it down. Burn it all down.*

But – no. She had to think of Katie. Parents made sacrifices for their children.

'I was thinking.' Janine turned to Beth. 'Are you all going to the café today?'

*

Janine sat with the other mums, sipping her expensive flat white.

It was a bad decision – she should have got a latte. You got double the drink for the same price. These were the kinds of decisions Janine should be making by instinct now. She was still thinking like someone who had a job.

'It's great you came.' Beth clinked her coffee cup with Janine's. 'I've been wanting to talk to you. We were horrified when Cass told us Katie didn't go to her own party.'

Megan nodded in sympathy, rocking the pram with one hand.

'You didn't know?' Janine stirred her coffee so she didn't have to make eye contact. 'I can't believe none of your kids had told you.'

'Ah, you know what they're like at that age. They forget the most important stuff, they were just excited about the party. Anyway.' Beth looked at the others. 'We all think you did a really decent thing.'

Janine raised her gaze.

'Going ahead with the party anyway.'

'I wouldn't dream of cancelling a drop-off. That would be barbaric.'

'We're very grateful. And we're thinking of putting a couple of mum teams together for the quiz,' Beth looked at Janine. 'If you're interested?'

'That sounds great!' Janine gave her coffee an unnecessary stir. 'We separate into mum teams and dad teams, do we?' It wasn't ideal, on lots of levels. She could picture the blankness on Phil's face if she asked him to join a dad team. *You want me to . . .*

'Oh, the dads aren't really interested. It's not their thing.'

Megan smiled indulgently. 'We usually let them stay in and babysit.'

Janine looked down at her coffee. She stopped herself saying it. *It's not babysitting if it's their own kids.*

'When the dads have a night out, they prefer to go to the pub.' Megan rolled her eyes.

Janine looked up slowly. 'But when you get to have a night out, it's the school quiz.'

Megan smiled. 'The men wouldn't want to be doing school stuff in the evenings, would they?'

Janine had a flashback to the racoon play. The way Katie's teacher expected the girls to hand out crisps while the boys were allowed to play on the crashmats. The way the girls had to collect the donations at the end.

Janine stirred her coffee jaggedly.

She thought of Phil. A man who had unquestioningly agreed to come to the school play of a child who wasn't even biologically his. Admittedly, that was because he was laidback and agreed to most stuff for an easy life, but it still counted.

She stirred more gently now.

Maybe Janine should go easier on Phil.

Maybe she'd start making him a lunchbox again.

The mum with the cheek filler and eyelashes, the one whose name Janine still didn't know, leaned forwards. 'Janine, I've been meaning to ask. How's Katie feeling now, after the pirate/princess mix-up?'

The movement was minute, but Janine noticed. The way the cheek filler mum glanced at Cass as she said it. Something blink-and-you-miss-it.

But Janine hadn't blinked. She definitely hadn't missed it. 'Katie's fine. She rallies.' Janine gripped the chair arm. 'You know.'

'And how's your father-in-law?' Cheek Filler Mum glanced at Cass again. 'Is it all back to normal? Because you live with him . . . right?'

Janine dug her fingers into the chair arm further. She wasn't imagining it – there was something in the woman's gaze. Too much interest in Janine's situation. Too much *knowledge*.

'He's fine.' They knew about the forum. They all knew. And they were laughing at her. 'You know what?' Janine stood up quickly. She bumped her thighs into the table painfully, making teaspoons rattle on saucers. 'I've got to go.'

Back at Roy's, Janine put the key in the lock. She pushed the door open and listened.

There was a whooshing sound.

A newspaper closing? A footrest being pushed under a chair?

Janine unlaced her trainer and tapped it against the wall, releasing a tiny stone that had been there the whole morning. She tied her shoe back up.

She pushed the door open and went inside.

Her delaying tactic worked. She just saw the back of Roy's shirt as he turned at the top of the landing. There was a rushing sound of wood against carpet, and the click of a door.

Behind Janine, there was a knock at the front door.

She opened it. 'Hi!'

The postie handed a parcel over.

'Thanks, Jim.' She'd asked his name already. 'You must think we get a lot of parcels! Thing is, I keep noticing things we need now we've moved house. Not *moved* house, not permanently. As I explained last time. Humans just need so much more stuff to function than you think, don't they, Jim? Don't you find that, Jim?'

Jim held out his electronic machine with the little wired pen.

Janine took it. 'Do you find—'

'Just sign here.'

Janine signed. She took the parcel inside and pulled the door shut with her foot.

Jim wasn't as friendly as their old postie – but then, Janine needed to put the hours in. You couldn't just strike up a friendship with a postie overnight. She'd just keep chatting, and it would come. Maybe tell him she knew Esther who did the Appleton Road area, so he'd know Janine came with another postie's approval.

She unpacked the box and pulled out her heated gilet. A label fluttered out of the packet – *battery not included*.

Janine put the gilet on and zipped it up.

She sank onto the sofa and leaned down to pick up the *battery not included* label.

What now?

Janine tried not to let the feeling of pointlessness permeate her. This feeling was normal, of course. It wasn't a problem, it was just her mind, and Janine controlled her mind. It was essential to keep the feeling on the surface, not to let it soak through. STOP SOAKING, STOP—

Janine got out her phone, flicked onto the forum and started to read.

Two hours later, Janine looked up from her phone. Her neck felt tender where she'd been scratching it.

Of course, this post was definitely still a good idea. Just because there was the odd critic, that didn't mean it wasn't a good idea.

@savethepandanow: shame on you, denouncing an elderly man with dementia

Janine replied to each one calmly, and with reason.

He hasn't got dementia – he's perfectly lucid. He wins at Scrabble every time.

Janine also found herself having to disagree with people who thought she wasn't angry *enough*. She kept adding replies to her original post, feeling her jaw stiffen.

She stretched, looking up into the gilt-framed mirror over Roy's fireplace. Red friction marks tracked the skin above her collarbone.

For a second, Janine held her own eye contact.

Her phone rang in her hand. Marky.

'J!' She could hear the battering of wind in the background. Was that *a seagull?* 'You good?'

'Fine.' Janine deliberately didn't ask where he was. 'I've been meaning to tell you there's a fundraiser quiz at the school on Friday night. But it'll be shit and you'll be busy, so—'

'I'm not busy.'

Janine set her jaw. 'It's an evening thing and Katie won't be there, so there's really no need.'

'We'll be there to support the school. We were gutted to be in Lanzarote for the racoon play.'

Janine tried to remind herself Marky being interested was a great thing. That was what good parents thought – that the other twat being interested was a good thing. 'Great.'

'I'm phoning because Katie told me about the princess party and I'm worried. You really want Katie living *there?*'

Janine said nothing.

'I would have let you keep the house longer if I'd known you didn't have any other good options.'

Janine set her jaw. 'You never said that.'

'I would have let you if you'd asked.'

'Convenient you say that now.'

'You didn't tell me! Why are you always so stubborn?'

'I'm not stubborn,' Janine said. Stubbornly.

'Why won't you let anyone help you?'

'Marky.' Janine stared into her own reflection. 'You understand I've moved into my father-in-law's house. You know I let him arrange a party for my daughter because you're berating me about it. And you still say I don't let anyone help?'

'I was worried already, but now I'm really worried. The man's clearly a chauvinist.'

Janine stared at herself.

'That stuff really matters to me, as the father of a daughter.'

'Oh good.' She stood up. 'Does that mean you've finally learned how to clean the toilet? And use the washing machine?'

Over the wind in the background, Marky said, 'I don't want her living there.'

Janine grabbed her coat and handbag. 'It's a storm in a teacup.'

'It's all fine between you? No bad feelings in the house?'

She left the house and turned towards town. 'It's fine.'

'I've heard you've put a post on *Am I the Villain Here?*'

Janine gave a deep intake of breath. '*How?*' What was it about this public internet forum that meant everyone knew about it?

'Molly was telling someone about the car crash of a party, and they put two and two together. Pirates and princesses, pretty racoons.'

Janine never should have mentioned the pretty racoons.

'I don't want her growing up there, Janine.'

'She's not growing up there.' Janine crossed the road. 'It's just for a matter of weeks while we get sorted, so I don't know why you're making such a massive deal out of it.'

'You have my full support in being angry with Phil's dad.' Janine moved her jaw to the side.

'And I want Katie out of that house.'

'She will be. Very soon.'

Janine switched off the phone and stared at it. She scratched her neck in an extended flurry, Labrador-style.

She put her phone in her pocket and kept walking.

Somewhere.

Anywhere.

Anywhere that wasn't 'home'.

25

Roy sat on his bed, listening to Janine, talking on the phone to someone she clearly found irritating.

With Janine, that could be anyone.

Roy heard the front door bang. He watched her walk towards town, still talking on the phone, trying to put her coat on with one arm, her movements sharp and angular.

With the house to himself again, he padded downstairs. He saw a parcel on the side, addressed to Janine. Some item of padded clothing.

He took the parcel upstairs and placed it on Janine's and Phil's bed. The room smelled different now – sweeter and faintly of cucumber.

Roy was out of sorts.

He set up the shredder on the kitchen table – a good bout of shredding always helped him think. He opened a letter from his local MP about proposed new cycle lanes. He placed it in the shredder and watched it turn to satisfying ribbons.

Despite the comforting whirr, his thoughts came back to the anonymous note.

The note had said there was a poll.

Now, Roy had a deep respect for a poll. He'd read Surowiecki's *The Wisdom of Crowds*. He answered anything

Ipsos Mori wanted to know, however long they kept him on the telephone, however cold his tea was getting. Replying to a poll was an important social duty.

Roy picked up a letter from the bank that started *Dear Friend*. The letter went on to offer him an overdraft, suggesting this *friend* didn't know him very well.

Into the shredder it went.

Roy watched ribbons of paper snake into the plastic tub, piling like cooked fettuccini.

By early afternoon Janine still hadn't returned, so Roy risked making parsnip soup. He put some in the fridge, and one portion into a thermos flask. He made himself a sandwich which he put into some Tupperware, and took it and the flask up to his bedroom.

He wasn't preparing to hide in his own home – nothing of the sort. He just had a sense he might like some quiet time that evening.

At 5 p.m., just before Katie and Janine were due to arrive back from Katie's Street Dance, Roy set his ironing board up in the front-room window and got started on his ironing pile.

He glanced up, checked the road in both directions, and sprayed a cloud of steam at his shirt sleeve. He looked up again. And again.

At the sight of Janine walking down the road, Katie lolloping next to her, Roy took a deep breath.

At the click of a key in the front door, Roy tensed.

'. . . and Max has got eighteen gold stickers!' Katie said breathlessly, walking into the front room. 'Hi, Roy!'

'Good for Max!' Janine nodded at Roy. 'Katie, let's do your

reading homework in the kitchen.' She ushered Katie away and closed the door.

Roy kept ironing. He looked up every few moments, continuing his street surveillance.

A white delivery van pulled up, obscuring Roy's view. A man jumped out of the driver's seat and hurried up their path.

Roy stood the iron on its heel.

He opened the front door before the knock and took the flat cardboard parcel from the delivery man. 'Thank you.' He looked at the label. *Janine Pierce.*

Roy took it to the kitchen table. 'For you.'

'Thank you.'

Janine ripped the parcel open. She removed a potato peeler.

Roy frowned. 'I've got a potato peeler.'

'I wanted a better one.'

'Mine is perfectly adequate.'

'Not for me.' Janine looked back down at the book. 'Shall we keep going, Katie?'

Roy tidied the packaging and cellophane away.

'I can do that, Roy.'

'I'm here now.' He put the peeler in the cutlery drawer, next to his own absolutely functional peeler, and returned to his ironing board.

Roy glanced out of the window for the thousandth time. It was after six. He had finished all his shirts, his duvet cover and sheets, and moved onto his pyjamas.

Janine walked out of the kitchen holding a half-empty bin bag.

'Surely you're not emptying that?' Roy couldn't stop himself. 'It's not full.'

'I know, but it smells.'

'A bit of a smell is fine. It's wasteful.'

'I'll buy more bin bags, if that's what you're worried about.'

'That's not the point.'

Janine turned to face him. 'What is the point, Roy?'

Roy said nothing. She walked out of the house. Roy heard the metallic clang of Janine dumping the rubbish outside. It sounded like someone had put some cans in with general waste.

She walked back through to the kitchen. 'We'll get a take-away tonight, Katie. Pizza. We can eat it upstairs, like we're camping.'

Roy heard Katie whoop before Janine slammed the door.

At the ironing board, Roy shook his head. Parcels of clothes arriving. Duplicate potato peelers. Excessive use of bin bags. Over-large glasses of orange juice. *Takeaways.* It was eye opening, how extravagant Janine's habits were, for a woman who was short of money.

Roy saw a figure round the corner with a lopsided gait.

He stood the iron on its heel and hurried out of his house. 'Darsh! Could you wait, please!'

Darsh stopped and turned.

Roy scooted up to him. 'If I could presume upon one more moment of your time.'

Slowly, Darsh took out his earpieces.

'Don't invite me in, I'm not stopping.' Roy was alarmed to realise he was still wearing his house slippers. 'I'd just like your advice about this delicate situation.'

Darsh glanced towards his front door.

'And I'm all at sea, whereas you grasped the situation im-mediately. And you're young—'

'I'm thirty-four.'

'Exactly. Did you look?' Roy gave a stiff smile. 'At what Janine put on this forum?'

Darsh took a moment. He shook his head hard.

'It's fine if you did look, of course,' Roy said. 'It would be human nature.'

'I had a glimpse.' Darsh blinked at Roy. 'The briefest of glimpses.'

'Good.' Roy smiled at Darsh.

Darsh returned the smile weakly.

Roy watched Phil's van pull up outside the house. Roy waved.

'Have you got a plumber round?' Darsh's voice was eager. 'Do you need to—'

'My son is staying with me.' Roy watched Phil head inside and turned back to Darsh. 'So Janine *has* written something?'

Darsh pressed his lips together. 'The high road, Roy. You were gonna take the high road.'

'Oh, I've no intention of looking. It's just a question of establishing the note's accuracy.' Roy looked down at his house slippers. Seeing them outside their natural habitat was disconcerting. 'But, from your response, we've established it was true.'

Darsh looked down.

Roy nodded. 'I'd like to know how this forum works, please. This is not my comfort zone.'

Darsh took a second. 'Of course.' He put his rucksack down against the wall. 'You're good to us, always putting our bins out when we're away.'

Roy gave a small smile. 'What else would you expect from Bin Captain?'

'Roy!' Darsh's eyes flared. 'We don't mean anything—'

Roy gave a faint smile. 'It's in jest. I know.'

'It's a compliment! You should have seen us that time you were away.' Darsh pointed at the pavement. 'The streets around here were a free-for-all. Pure carnage.' He looked up. 'So what do you want to know?'

'I'm to understand Janine put together a poll? For people to vote in?'

Darsh nodded.

Roy clasped his hands together. 'But to vote on *what*?'

'Whether it is fair that she's raging about a princess party.'

Roy took this in. 'But why would anyone choose to put their dirty laundry online?'

Darsh shrugged.

Roy had so many questions. 'How does this forum work?'

'It's a minor, anonymous thing. *Anonymous*,' Darsh repeated with emphasis. 'These forums move at a pace. Loads of posts every day, and they're on to the next one before you know it. Gone and forgotten in minutes. Digital fish-and-chip paper.'

Roy thought about this. 'Thrown away and never to be found again?'

Darsh took a second. 'Kind of.'

Roy gave a firm nod. 'I'm thinking about the word itself – *forum*.' He found himself addressing Darsh's hedge. 'It was first used to describe a public square in the Roman municipium, primarily for the exchange of goods.'

He glanced at Darsh. Darsh nodded.

'The forum was a medium of civilisation.' Roy turned to address the hedge again. 'An asset to society. A good thing.'

Darsh gave another nod.

'And is this online forum the same?'

Darsh shoved his hands in the pockets. 'The same?'

'Conducted in the same vein.' Why did Darsh insist on repeating everything Roy said? 'An exchange of ideas, shared with optimism and best-practice principles, in the spirit of John Stuart Mill?' Roy glanced at Darsh and back at the hedge. 'What Janine and I are experiencing is a transactional tussle within the marketplace of ideas – and a healthy competition of ideas is good for society. I assume this forum is conducted in that same manner?'

Darsh took a breath. 'Yes. kind of.'

'Yes?' Relief made Roy close his eyes briefly. 'It's a place people go to exchange their ideas?'

Darsh nodded more firmly now. 'Oh, it's definitely that.'

'An extension of civilisation, where they respect the voices of their fellow man? To test their hypotheses and learn from others?'

Darsh paused before nodding again.

'I suppose I am asking you, Darsh, as a friend . . .'

Darsh licked his lips.

' . . . is this forum a good thing?'

Darsh looked at his phone. 'That's definitely the plan.' He jiggled the phone. 'There are even moderators. People who filter out any comments that aren't respectful.' He took a second. 'Not that anyone would do that, though, so I don't know why they have them.'

'Moderators.' Roy tapped his chin. 'I'm trying to think if they had an equivalent in the Roman marketplace. The town elders perhaps?'

'The forum doesn't mention you by name.' Darsh sounded strained. 'And people are able to give feedback anonymously.'

'Perfect for removing the bias of social expectation from the decision-making process.' Roy gave a series of nods. 'So this forum is . . . a decision-making utopia. Almost.'

'Yes. Almost.' Darsh's eyes widened. 'I'VE GOT A WORK CALL!'

Roy looked at the phone buzzing softly in Darsh's hand.

'How wonderful you're still so keen to answer after a long day! What is it you do?'

Darsh stopped smiling. 'I'm a surveyor.'

'Excellent. And thank you, Darsh.' Roy touched Darsh's arm. 'This has been an extremely helpful conversation.'

'No problem.' Darsh put the phone to his ear. 'Hi, Greg. Yes, let's talk water boundaries. It's the perfect time.'

Roy watched Darsh let himself into the house, feeling slightly envious. How much this man must enjoy his job, to be so enthusiastic about taking a work call in the evening!

Roy headed back towards his house, his step newly light in his slippers.

He had been needlessly worried all day, but now he understood.

He didn't need to avoid Janine anymore. He would just be polite, and smile, and let the situation play out.

After all, the wisdom of crowds was a wonderful thing.

And now Roy knew – with certainty – that everything was going to be fine.

Wednesday

Am I the Villain Here? Post 35915

CantBeArsed8: Am I the villain here for being furious my partner's father changed my daughter's pirate party into a princess party?

4,937 votes, 4 days left

You're the villain here: 14%
Not the villain here: 86%

Latest reply:

@unionjack1: You do not deserve this man! Have some respect. You are erasing his values – and the values of a whole generation!

26

Roy was in such a good mood, so forgiving of Janine for understanding her own limitations, that by seven thirty the next morning, when Janine walked blinking into the kitchen in her long T-shirt, Roy was waiting in his apron at the hob.

'Good morning.' Roy made a dramatic flourish with his spatula. 'I've made kedgeree.'

Roy sat with Katie, Janine and Phil at the table, eating. Even Phil ate some kedgeree, after Roy had pointed out he had weighed out the ingredients for four.

Roy watched Janine pour out orange juice. Again, she didn't use the small orange juice glass provided, but filled a water glass with a quantity that was alarmingly excessive. She didn't appear worried about either economy or her blood sugar.

Still, he was feeling generous today. 'Got a busy day planned?'

She looked down at her plate. 'Yep.' She chased a piece of rice round with her fork. 'Loads of things planned.'

'Do you want a lift to the library, Dad?' Phil jerked his head towards the window. 'It's pissing down.'

'I've got my golf umbrella.' Roy raised his voice over the sound of rain battering the window pane. 'I'll be fine.'

*

When Roy reached the library, Tessa and Yvonne were both standing at the counter.

He lifted his dripping umbrella. 'I'll put this up in the kitchen. Shall I do the coffees while I'm in there?'

Yvonne beamed at him, and Tessa said, 'That would be great, thanks, Roy,' because even Tessa couldn't get annoyed about someone offering her a coffee.

On his way to the kitchen, Roy passed the *New in Stock!* stand. *How to Think* and *The Little Book of Thinking* were both still there, which was surprising.

Roy set up his umbrella to dry in the corner of the back room and made the coffees. He placed the three mugs on the counter, and headed for the Technology section, surveying the stacks.

He pulled out *The Internet for Dummies* and flicked to the index page.

It was first published in 1995, with this version from 2004. Not ideal.

Roy put the book down on a side table. He flicked other past titles – *The Joy of Code, Data and Me, Java for Beginners.* He reached *The New Age of Enlightenment: The internet as the future of sharing and collaboration.*

Roy turned to the back copy.

Tim Berners-Lee was a man with a utopian vision. He wanted to give a gift to the world, a tool to benefit mankind, so all the people had access to all the information, all the time. He—

'Roy!'
At Yvonne's hush-shout, Roy looked up.
'Your coffee's going cold.'

Roy took *The Internet for Dummies* and *The New Age of Enlightenment* over to the counter. 'Thanks.'

Yvonne watched him beep the books out. Her jumper today was a pleasing shade of mauve. 'I reckon you borrow more books than the rest of our customers put together.'

'These books are exactly what I'm looking for. That's a very pretty' – Roy panicked at his choice of word – 'jumper.'

'Thank you! It's my favourite.' Yvonne picked up his coffee and offered the handle to him. 'You have a spring in your step.'

'I was worrying about something. And now I feel much better.' Roy looked at the *New in Stock!* stand. 'Has anyone borrowed any of my other books yet?'

'It's early days, Roy.'

'It's because people can't see them.' Roy moved two romance books from the top to the lower shelves of the stand. He moved *How to Think* and *The Little Book of Thinking* into their place. 'Don't tell Tessa.'

Yvonne put a forefinger to her lips. 'Your secret's safe with me.'

After finishing his shift, Roy called in at the bookshop.

'Back for more?' The manager smiled at him. 'You've read all those philosophy books *already*?'

'Have you got anything about trains?' Roy asked. 'Nothing too wordy. I'm looking for a picture book.'

'I'm sure we'll have something.'

The manager walked under a painted ladybird's open wings to a section of the shop with a lower ceiling. It had a tiny chair and table, and a miniature pink tea set, arranged with stuffed bears in some kind of Teddy Bears' Picnic.

With unease, Roy followed the manager.

'Something at the more adult end of the spectrum,' Roy said carefully. 'For a teenager, perhaps.' It still felt like betrayal.

The manager plucked a book from a shelf. 'How about this?'

Roy flicked through the book. It was mainly pictures of steam trains, with captions beneath. He looked up, smiling. 'Perfect.'

On the sofa at the nursing home, Roy leaned towards Joseph. 'The other book is called *The New Age of Enlightenment: The internet as the future of sharing and collaboration.*' Roy turned the page of the picture book in Joseph's lap. 'There are advantages to this technology we never dreamt of, Joseph. Look!' He tapped the page. 'The Flying Scotsman!' When Joseph didn't respond, Roy tapped again. 'You forget they made all this steam, don't you?'

Joseph ran his fingers faintly across the page.

Roy nodded. 'The internet is *fascinating*, Joseph. We should have embraced the possibilities earlier, but it was the newspapers' fault. They focused too much on the pornography, and the risk of societal breakdown in year-two-K. They hardly said anything about the emancipation of the people.'

Joseph turned a page in the picture book. 'It's all about the right stimuli with you, isn't it?' Roy patted his back approvingly. 'I'll get you something on architecture next. They must have lots of picture books about Brutalism.'

A shadow fell in front of Roy. A pair of red brogues shuffled into his eyeline.

Roy looked up. It was, of course, the lady with the baby.

Roy recognised this old dear from previous visits and here she was – again – carrying a man's shoe in the crook of her arm like a newborn.

The lady leaned forwards, holding out the shoe for Roy to admire.

Hurriedly, Roy petted it. 'Lovely.'

The woman gazed at Roy from under a thick white fringe.

Roy patted the shoe again. 'What a handsome chappie.'

He shifted position, hoping the woman would get the message.

The woman shuffled away to show her baby to someone else.

Roy lowered his voice. 'They should have a different wing for people like that. You must find it very distracting.' He turned back to see Joseph hunched over in concentration. 'Ah, so you like the book? I knew that you—'

Roy saw what he was doing. 'No, Joseph. Not like that.'

Joseph was captivated by a promotional leaflet tucked into a cardboard pocket on the flyleaf, inching the paper out of the pocket and pushing it back.

'No.' Roy reached over and took the book from Joseph. 'That's a leaflet.' He tucked the leaflet back in its pocket and closed the flyleaf. 'The book's the thing.'

Roy turned to another page. 'Ah, now we're talking!' He placed the book open in Joseph's lap. 'Stephenson's Rocket. A wonderful feat of engineering.'

Joseph stared at the picture.

'As I was saying ...' Roy straightened his shirt sleeves. '... the internet is a cyber utopia, enabling an emancipation of the people that has never been possible. It's so wonderfully anti-Hobbesian!'

Roy watched Joseph looking at the picture.

'And the reason I'm doing research is because it turns out Janine has put a poll on an online advice forum. She knows she can be hot-headed, so she's asking for help in forming a judgement.' Roy turned another page in Joseph's book. 'She's recognised her own weaknesses and is curious to learn. So in that spirit, I'm going to do the same.'

Joseph looked up slowly into Roy's eyes.

'No, Joseph, I must. Janine has shown humility – and I must show humility too. I will let this matter be decided by a technological *twelve good men and true*.' Roy beamed at his old friend. 'I'll sit back and receive my judgement in good faith. Because it turns out we live in a cyber utopia, Joseph.' Roy felt a warmth fill his chest – the warmth of social pride. 'And I'm going to let the people decide.'

27

Janine was feeling pointless. Again.

She checked for jobs first thing, but her job alerts didn't seem to be working. The only email she'd got was a reminder – *Networking Event – today!* – and Janine *still* wasn't that desperate.

By 11 a.m. she'd clingfilmed that night's traybake meal and placed it in the fridge. She'd even made tomorrow's lunchbox for Phil.

She sat on the sofa, looked around and saw – nothing.

Roy was out – but he only did half days at the library, didn't he? Which meant he'd be back soon. Where the hell was she going to go?

She looked at the email.

Wearily, Janine stood up.

She dressed in anti-superhero grey for maximum bland, and got the bus to the city centre. She drifted around the stalls, ignoring the free branded pens, lingering only to pick up a pack of chocolate buttons provided by a company who were clearly more in sync with the needs of the people.

Janine pushed three chocolate buttons into her mouth and ambled up to a busy area, where a woman in a paisley scarf in front of a cool tech logo talked to a crowd.

'And we don't see our colleagues as employees.' Paisley Scarf Woman smiled. 'We see them as friends and family.'

Janine touched her bare neck. Perhaps she should get a scarf to add to her interview costume? After all, a scarf screamed dull competence.

'*Joy* is one of our values, and it's baked into our company DNA. We're currently trialling sleep pods for our staff rooms.' Paisley Scarf Woman smiled. 'We even let staff bring dogs into the office.'

The woman caught Janine's eye. Janine nodded and smiled. Obviously, these ideas were nuts – but if anyone was going to be napping or stroking dogs on work time, it was Janine.

'We encourage our people not to look at their emails outside office hours. We know our colleagues are more than employees. They are people's partners. Parents. Friends.'

Janine threw another few chocolate buttons into her mouth. She inched her phone out of her pocket.

'Current vacancies in the North-West,' the woman on stage said, 'include contact centre workers, telesales executives, an area sales manager—'

Slowly, Janine slid her phone back away.

At the end of the talk, Janine went up to the woman in the scarf.

'Hi! You said you've got an area sales manager role? I've recently been made redundant.' Janine paused. 'A proper redundancy. I wasn't rubbish.'

The woman nodded. 'Would you be able to start straight away?'

'Immediately.'

The woman raised her eyebrows. 'Interviews are this week,

but we might be able to slot you in.' The woman picked up her phone. 'I'll look now.'

Janine kept her gaze on the woman's phone, willing it to give good news. 'I can be flexible with timing. Early starts. Late nights. I can be—'

The woman looked up. 'Let me go and check with my colleague. One sec.'

Janine watched the woman walk away. It was all Janine could do not to chase her. Janine could practically *feel* the office dogs' fur under her fingertips. She'd never seen a sleep pod, but she imagined snuggling into a womblike space. Maybe she could even take a dog inside the pod – they could nap together?

Paisley Scarf Woman came back. 'You're in luck! Interviews are on Thursday so it's tight, but because you're available now, Tracy says they'll squeeze you in if your skills fit.'

'Great!'

'If your skills fit,' the woman said again.

'They will,' Janine said.

They swapped email addresses and Janine forwarded her CV.

She leaned against the wall, taking it in. It was the first good thing that had happened to her in a long time.

She spotted her old company logo on a stall just in front of her. A woman stood beneath it, handing out leaflets, wearing wide-legged trousers with a sharp crease down the front. It was Nadia – the HR manager with the good eyebrows. A woman who had been conspicuously absent from the last few months of Janine's working life.

She considered the situation.

She still had nowhere else to be.

'Nadia! Hi! You won't remember me, I'm Janine Pierce. I

used to work at your place. I was Area Sales Manager.'

'I remember you.' Nadia made her face friendly but blank. 'Hi, Janine.'

Janine suspected they taught *friendly but blank* in HR school. 'Got any jobs?'

'Not sales managers, I'm afraid.'

'That's OK. I've got an interview this week anyway. I've been really busy.'

'That's good to hear. What have you been up to?'

'Loads.' Janine paused. 'Community stuff. Socialising. Also, I've been getting my head round death. Because you never have time for that stuff, do you?'

Nadia's good eyebrows moved up.

'You know, I never got contacted about an exit interview.'

'We don't do exit interviews.'

'But don't you want to hear what the leavers have to say?'

A beat. 'It's a resource thing.'

'Can I do one now, while I'm here?'

Nadia gave an apologetic smile. 'The thing is—'

'I want to tell someone about my experience. Do you want me to tell you here?' Janine indicated the people walking past. 'In front of all these potential candidates?'

Nadia indicated a meeting room behind her. 'In here.' She shut the door after them. 'To be clear, this isn't an exit interview.' She sat at the table. 'We don't do exit interviews.'

Janine sat opposite. 'That's fine.'

'And bear in mind before you tell me anything that I might have to do something about it – whether you want me to or not. Though I also might not.'

Janine considered this. 'Which?'

'I don't know what you're going to say yet. I'm just letting you know.'

'Oh, you HR people. It's like the police, isn't it? *Anything you say may be taken down and used in evidence!*'

'Just trying to be fair, Janine, that's all.' Nadia looked at her watch. 'I've got ten minutes.'

'Lee shouldn't have been in my pool. When I was made redundant.'

'Right.' Nadia maintained her *friendly but blank* expression. 'You have access to our formal processes as part of the redundancy portal which explain how you can raise—'

'No way. I won't get a good reference if I raise a grievance.'

Nadia stared at her. 'Of course you will.'

'People will say I'm difficult. You don't think sales directors talk?'

Nadia said nothing.

'Lee shouldn't have been in my pool. It only happened that way because Adrian hates me.' Janine paused. 'This isn't about Lee. He's great.'

'You know we have robust selection processes, Janine. Our managers apply strict, objective criteria.'

Janine waited.

'Why do you think Adrian hates you?'

Janine sighed. 'Because I wouldn't pour the coffee that time.'

Nadia's good eyebrows moved up a fraction more.

'There was a meeting about targets around a big table.' Janine leaned forwards. 'It was all the sales guys and me. His assistant wasn't there, so Adrian asked me to take the minutes – and why me? Because I was the only woman there. So I kept my mouth shut and did it, like a good little sap. But then Adrian asked me, specifically, to pour the coffee – but there were *four men* between me and the coffee trolley.' Janine shook her head. 'Four men, with three of them more junior than me. So why did he ask me, at the other end of the table? I said *no*. On principle.' Janine sat back in her chair. 'That was the start of it.' She took a beat. 'It wasn't the end.'

Nadia glanced at her watch.

'Work's not meant to be like that anymore! When I first started working, it was like *Don't get a taxi with* that *director'* – Janine made a double *handsy* gesture – 'and now it's like we've binned off the worst pervs, we've got a diversity policy, it's all good. But you know I never had any one-to-ones with Adrian, even *before* the coffee thing? He'd go out for one-to-one drinks with people to talk about their careers – but only the men. He'd promised his wife he wouldn't do anything outside work with any women.' She folded her arms. 'Like that was so respectful of him. Like we didn't all know it was because he'd had affairs with two admin assistants and an IT manager.' She took a breath. 'I know it's not the most important thing. I know there are worse things happening in the world every day. But it's still not fair I lost my job just because Adrian is a sexist. And this stuff is *insidious*. It all starts so young!' She leaned forwards. 'Nadia, what colour do you think a racoon is?'

Nadia stared at her.

'Nadia?'

'I'm struggling with the relevance.'

'The relevance is – my daughter's options are getting limited by the day, and people just want her to flounce about prettily and serve the crisps. And that's her *teachers*.' Janine stared at a crack in the coving above. She was losing her audience. 'I heard you got a new boss. So where did he spring from? There're no men in HR, then – *poof!*' She did an illusionist's hand gesture. 'And everyone acts like they're such a novelty, like they're a treat. *Ooh, man in HR, a nice change!*

Not at the top, it isn't. They bunch there.' Janine made an expressive dangling gesture. 'Like grapes.'

There was a long pause.

'This is why you don't do exit interviews, isn't it?' Janine nodded. 'I get it now.'

'Look, Janine.' Nadia leaned forwards. 'That all sounds . . . a lot. And no one wanted to lose you, you have a great track record. It's just—'

'Consolidation and streamlining, I know. I've written those comms.'

'But if you don't want to raise your complaint through the redundancy portal, then I'm not sure what you want.'

'I just want someone to give a shit. And make things better, for ever. And tell me it's going to be fine for my daughter.'

Nadia gave a faint smile. 'I think you overestimate the power of a part-time HR manager in retail.'

'Why did you meet with me, then?'

'In case you weren't aware of your rights.' Nadia looked up. 'And, also, Janine, because you were being quite loud.'

'I get it.'

Nadia stood up.

'Thanks anyway.' Janine stood up too. 'Say *hi* to your boss for me.'

'I'll tell him you wish him well. I won't mention the' – Nadia made Janine's illusionist's *poof!* gesture – 'and the grape thing.'

Janine gave a small smile.

'And I mean it when I say I wish you the best of luck with your interviews.' Slowly, Nadia tucked her chair under the table. 'But a word of advice. You know you said you don't want a reputation for being difficult?'

Janine felt herself redden. 'I know.'

'This.' Nadia spread her arms wide. 'Hugely inappropriate, Janine.'

'I know.' Janine nodded hard. 'I don't know why I do this stuff either. But trust me – I know.'

28

The wisdom of crowds. Twelve good men and true. It was perfect – just perfect.

Roy walked back home from the nursing home, picking up discarded cans and chocolate wrappers, full of goodwill towards his fellow man.

The only snag was that he wasn't sure when and how to find out the results of the poll.

Roy glanced at Darsh's house on the way past, but Darsh would be at work. Which was for the best, really.

Roy would take the journey from here alone.

Roy opened the front door and walked into the front room.

Janine jumped up from the sofa. 'I've just got in.'

Roy nodded. 'Me too.' He walked through to the kitchen, heated up his soup and poured it into a thermos. He made a tuna sandwich.

He took both upstairs to his bedroom and shut the door.

He put his food on the bedside table and moved piles of books from the desk onto the floor. He switched on the computer and Anglepoise lamp. He sat on the bed and swung his feet round, to get them under the desk. He had a good ergonomic desk chair, but that had had to go into the attic, for reasons of space.

His gaze fell on Lynn's urn on her dressing table, partly obscured by piles of books.

It was too late to phone Claudia, so he sent an email.

Dear Claudia,
I am looking at your mother.
Have you thought any more about dates so we can scatter her ashes? I'm sure you don't need me to tell you that your mother's birthday was the third of May. The soonest we can get in a date, the more notice we can give Phil and family.
Love, Dad

P.S. When I say, 'I'm looking at your mother', I mean I'm looking at her urn. I haven't gone senile.

Roy sent the email. He turned his desk pad to a fresh page, removed the lid from his biro, and placed it next to the pad.

He typed *Am I The Villain Here?* into the search engine.

Am I The Villain Here?
Welcome to a place of moral judgement. Ever wanted to know where you stand from a philosophical perspective?

At the word *philosophical*, Roy sat forward.

We're here to help adjudicate any conflict situation, as long as there's no violence or suggestion of abuse. Are you the hero or the villain? Let us be the judge!
    See our best (most controversial) posts here:

Roy started scrolling. He skimmed posts about weddings,

housemates, uncles. Neighbours, fridges, parking. Yoghurt. There were *thousands* of posts.

Roy clicked on the search box. He entered *Roy Frost*.

No results found.

Roy nodded. Darsh had said the forum was anonymous, but it was still a relief to have the hypothesis confirmed.

He thought for a moment, and typed *pirate*. Several posts appeared.

Post by OhNoItAint: Am I the villain for making pirate noises whenever my girlfriend wears her new hat?

Post by OnlyAHamster: Am I the villain for refusing to join in Talk Like a Pirate Day at work?

Post by CantBeArsed8: Am I the villain for being upset my partner's father changed my daughter's pirate party into a princess party?

Roy swallowed.

Yes, it was uncomfortable. But a well-operating marketplace of ideas was never meant to be comfortable.

Beneath the post, it said *4,937 votes, 4 days left*. That was what he came here for. Roy's reconnaissance mission was complete.

He would stop reading now.

Five minutes later, Roy hadn't moved. He glanced at Lynn's urn.

He looked back at the screen, trying to ignore the fluttering in his stomach. A thousand insects marched lightly around his stomach lining.

He glanced at Lynn's urn again.

He leaned towards the dressing table and pushed a pile of books completely in front of the urn, so he could no longer see it.

Roy sat back upright, staring at the screen. He clicked onto *CantBeArsed8*'s post.

My partner's father is always telling my daughter how pretty she looks, and buying her pink things, and expecting her to be passive. I have made several hints that I don't want her getting these influences and asked him clearly to stop calling her pretty after he said my daughter made a pretty raccoon. He hasn't stopped. And I don't think he forgets – he just chooses to ignore me.

I want us to have a good relationship. He's a widower, and I want to support a lonely man. He means well, and he's been really kind to us in lots of ways. We are currently living with him because of a brief blip in our housing situation. It's harder to pull someone up on their behaviour when they're doing you a favour.

Recently, he offered to arrange my daughter's birthday party. She'd asked for a pirate party, but when she got there, he'd changed the party theme from pirates to princesses because he thought it was 'more suitable'. My daughter was devastated.

Am I the villain here for pulling him up on his sexist outlook, when he's the one in the wrong? Is it fair to be furious, when he's doing me all these 'favours'?

EDIT – I am asked in the comments how my partner's father treats his grandsons. He does not have grandsons.

EDIT – People are asking his attitude to my daughter's weight. He has, on occasions, been known to say to her 'are you sure you need another slice?' but that is because he has a thing about processed food.

EDIT: For those who think he might have dementia, my partner's father plays the 'old' card, but he definitely has all his faculties. Recently, he told a waiter to add a 10% tip and they got the maths wrong, and he was on it like a hawk.

EDIT: there's some misunderstanding in the comments. It's never in a sexual way. Sex–ist, not sex–ual. Old school, fairly harmless sexist, you know?

EDIT: To people who say my 'story' is 'inconsistent' . . . I refer to this man as my partner's father because that's what he is. I refer to my girl as his granddaughter, but she is technically his step-granddaughter. I was trying to simplify, not 'changing my story'.

EDIT: OK, so a lot of you disagree with me saying 'old school fairly harmless sexist'. OF COURSE I think all gender stereo-types are harmful, why do you think I posted this? I am not an 'apologist for the patriarchy'. I'm going to stop doing edits now because this is getting ridiculous. No one is on trial here and frankly I'm starting to regret the whole thing.

Responses (3412)

Roy switched the monitor off. There was a roaring in his head.

He picked up his pen. He couldn't seem to break down the

detail of the post – it just entered his head as a single blur.

He watched himself write *lonely man*.

Roy put a heavy line through the words. He tried to think what to write.

But all he could think was: *Responses (3412)*.

He licked his lips.

This forum was a perfect cybermarket for the exchange of ideas. Collaboration, in the spirit of Tim Berners-Lee's utopia. The wisdom of crowds in action. Twelve good men and true. Yes, yes, yes – to all of the above.

Roy shook his head at his own ridiculousness. *Come on, man!*

Roy had been a shift leader in a factory, overseeing danger-ous machinery and chemicals for forty years. He'd once been trapped in a hairy situation while fixing an industrial paddle mixer. As a magistrate, he'd been targeted by hardened crim-inals, and even received a threatening letter at home. Three years ago he'd had his bicycle clipped by a careless driver and come away with only a broken arm. Roy was *practically bionic*, as they told him at the hospital. He'd even had a knife drawn on him in the street, by someone who was clearly under the influence and in need of pity as well as censure. Roy had lost his parents, his sister. He'd lost his *wife*.

Roy had survived life. He was logical, he was sensible. He had an Open University degree in philosophy – with distinc-tion. He'd been *a magistrate*.

He had no idea why he was being such a daft sod about this.

Roy stood up. He switched off the Anglepoise. His deci-sion was clear – and irreversible.

Roy would stop reading now.

29

Phil was sick of his family tiptoeing around each other. He was also sick of finding himself in the role of messenger. *Please ask Roy where he keeps his food waste bags. Please tell Roy the bathroom's free. Please remind Janine to switch the immersion off after showering.*

Phil just had to wait it out, so things would resolve themselves. Janine couldn't let this go on for ever – she had an inability to let things fester. It was a fundamental part of her make-up that she had to push things to a head – even if that head was an expanding mushroom cloud.

He got in from work to find Janine in the bedroom. 'All right.'

She looked up from her phone and gave him a smile. A proper smile. 'Are you still coming to the school quiz on Friday?'

Phil closed the door behind him. 'Why wouldn't I be?'

'You wouldn't prefer to stay in? Or go to the pub?'

Phil didn't answer straight away. 'Is this a trick question? Look, I'm coming to the quiz, unless you tell me not to.'

'I love you.' Janine got up. 'You're not too bad actually.' She put her arms round his neck. 'So I've made you a lunchbox for tomorrow.'

Phil raised his eyebrows slightly into Janine's hair.

'I'm still mad at you for not standing up for me enough.'

And yet – she had her face in his chest. 'OK?'

'But you're not absolutely awful. You have some redeeming qualities.'

'That's nice to know.' Phil pulled away from her. 'It's quiet downstairs. Where's Katie?'

Janine sat down and swung her legs onto the bed. 'Judo.'

'And Dad?'

Janine looked at her feet. She stretched her toes to a point. 'I don't know.'

'He's not downstairs.'

Janine kept looking at her feet. 'I might have seen him taking a thermos and a sandwich to his room earlier.'

Phil stopped smiling. 'Oh this is ridiculous! We can't just live in this room! We can't just keep eating pizza on the bed!'

Janine stretched her toes again. 'I like pizza in bed. Feels illicit and naughty. Comfortingly furtive, you know?'

'Dad is drinking thermoses of soup in his bedroom. In his own home. You can bet he doesn't feel *comfortingly furtive*. Do you think Dad has ever eaten in his bedroom in his life?' Phil shook his head in disbelief. 'Have you even seen it in there? He's got a computer desk wedged against the bed, books piled everywhere – he's doing us a favour and yet he's hiding in his room with preheated soup!'

'But we didn't want that favour! He tricked us into it – he doesn't feel vulnerable at all! And he's in the wrong, Phil. And he still hasn't apologised.'

'Can't you just be the bigger person?'

She was silent.

'I'll go and pick up Katie from judo. You talk to him. Make this right, Janine.'

She stared at her feet again. She wrinkled her nose. 'Don't

let the mums coo after you like they do after Danny Carswell.'

Phil gave a sniff of laughter. 'How can I stop them cooing if they want to coo?'

'Don't bask in it, then.' Janine folded her arms. 'Don't encourage them.'

Phil picked up his keys from the bed. He left the house.

He'd made a stand. Kind of.

And Janine had made him another unwanted lunchbox.

It was progress.

Phil sat outside the church hall in the van, waiting for judo to finish.

He heard a tap on the window.

Danny Carswell smiled and did two thumbs up at Phil. 'Coming in, pal?'

'Can't.' Phil made a sad face and held up his phone. 'I've got a call.'

He understood why Danny Carswell made Janine narrow her eyes. It was because of parents like him that Phil always waited for Katie in the van.

Maybe it was because Phil had got into parenthood late and via a right angle. Maybe he'd missed something fundamental. But there was something about these people in *parent* mode that repelled him. The too-loud, too-smiley, *Isn't parenthood a lovely hell* mode. It was something about the way they carried those sparkly rucksacks and tiny cardigans. Phil managed to think this, even if, at the same time, he was holding a sparkly rucksack and tiny cardigan.

So Phil stayed in the van. He could actively not engage with these people. Not engaging was his superpower and, when you had a superpower, it was disrespectful not to use it.

Katie headed towards him, trailing her coat, the same look

on her face as on the day of the party. Like she'd seen the future, and it was haunted.

Phil got out of the van to meet her. 'You OK?'

Katie shook her head. 'I lost all my best animal stickers.'

'Oh, mate.' Phil walked her towards the van. 'How?'

'I swapped them. I lost all my gold ones.'

They got in the van.

'I thought the gold ones were your favourite?' Phil said gently. 'I thought they were valuable?'

Katie stared at her lap.

'So why did you swap them?'

Kate kept staring.

'Is this like the mobile phone thing at Halloween?'

Katie started to sob. 'I don't know!'

Phil closed his eyes. At a Halloween party, Janine had only let Katie hold her phone for a few minutes, yet Katie had *still* managed to get digitally mugged. An older kid had got her to transfer over all her game's paid-upgrade pet outfits and Katie had cried for days. *All my waistcoats and bow ties! I thought I was just lending them. Now my animals are start-of-game naked!*

He was going to have to help her wise up these next few years, or she'd have an eventful time at high school. 'Which kid did you swap with?'

Katie pointed at a little boy standing with Danny Carswell.

Phil unbuckled his seat belt. 'One sec.'

'Danny!' Phil got out of the car and jogged over. 'Hi! Hi, hi. I think your lad has done some sticker swaps with our Katie.' He kept his voice light. 'And somehow, by accident, Katie lost all her best gold stickers. The valuable ones.'

Danny looked at his kid.

The kid was expressionless. 'She wanted to swap.'

Phil smiled, like this kid wasn't taking the piss. 'There must have been some confusion. They were Katie's favourites.'

The kid shrugged.

'She's sobbing her head off.'

Danny looked at his kid. 'Give him the stickers.'

The kid got a fat plastic pouch of stickers out of his trouser pocket. He rifled through it, and handed two stickers to Phil.

Phil looked up. 'Just two?'

'Just two,' the kid said, still expressionless.

Phil looked towards Katie in the van. 'I'll go and get your swaps from Katie.'

The kid shook his head. 'She can keep them.'

Danny smiled at the kid. 'That's nice.' He looked at Phil. 'So we're all done here?'

'Thank you.' Phil aimed the words at Danny. He was pretty sure this kid didn't deserve it.

Phil jogged back to his van.

Katie took one look. 'Those aren't mine. And he took about twenty. All gold. Those aren't gold.'

Phil looked down at the two stickers.

'They're still there, Phil, standing there – look!' Katie pointed through the window. 'You can go over now.'

Phil couldn't help noticing Katie was way more assertive on behalf of other people than herself. Phil watched Danny and the kid get into a car. Were you meant to tell a fellow parent their kid was a sticker rat? Or was that against the code?

Phil switched on the ignition. 'We'll buy you some more sticker packs on the way home. We'll go past the newsagent. You'll get some surprises!'

'Will they have gold ones?'

'I'm sure you can swap whole packs for more gold ones.'

Katie nodded. She looked a little less haunted.

Phil switched on the engine. 'Just . . . don't tell your mum.'

'Why not?'

Phil paused. 'I don't know.'

When Phil and Katie got back, Katie ran straight upstairs to sort her stickers.

Janine was in the kitchen, chopping vegetables for what smelt like a curry.

Phil took a piece of baby corn from the chopping board. 'And?'

'He hasn't come out of his room.'

Phil stopped crunching. 'But you've knocked for him?'

'I've been busy!' Janine indicated the vegetables with a sweep her knife. 'But you can tell him he's welcome to join if you like.'

Phil shook his head at her.

He walked upstairs and knocked on Dad's door. 'Dad?' He took a moment and pushed the door open.

Dad was sitting on the bed, his computer desk wedged against it, his screen lit up.

He jabbed the monitor off.

'Dad?' Phil said more softly. Dad looked even smaller than usual.

Dad cleared his throat. 'I'm just doing some paperwork.'

'Janine's making curry. Do you want to join us for tea in a bit?'

Dad stared straight ahead. 'I'm not hungry.'

'You've got to eat.'

'I've had soup.'

'But that's not a proper meal and Janine's making—'

'I'm busy, Philip!' Dad jerked his head up. 'I'm knee-deep

in important administration!' He banged the top of the desk with both hands. 'What about that is so hard to understand?'

'OK!' Phil put his palms up. 'Wow, Dad. I get the point.'

Phil reversed out of the room.

Well. He'd tried. And ended up pissing off both of them in the process – and all because he'd got involved. This would teach him not to go against his instincts.

Phil ate the curry with Katie and Janine, only occasionally looking at the ceiling, towards the silent upper floor. He forgot about Dad's outburst at the computer, and went to bed as normal.

But when Phil got called about an emergency leak, he got in the van at 3 a.m. – and couldn't help noticing there was a glow from behind one set of blinds.

Dad's bedroom light was still on.

30

At 2 a.m., Roy turned his head on the pillow. Slivers of moonlight peeped through the blind's slats in a faint, corrugated glow.

Roy turned his head back to look at the ceiling.

I want us to have a good relationship – he's a widower, and I want to support a lonely man.

Well, that was rubbish, for a start.

Yes, Roy had lost his wife, but he had a very full life. He had Phil. Claudia and her family were just a plane ride away. Roy had the library; he had tai chi; he had Joseph. He was an active member of the neighbourhood watch. She was talking nonsense.

He looked at the thin lines of moonlight and waited for sleep to come.

He said my daughter made a pretty raccoon.

Yes, he *had* said that – because Katie *did* make a pretty racoon. Roy said it as he saw it, and he hadn't wanted Katie to feel insecure in her orange Corn Flakes T-shirt. Only Janine could mind that. *Only Janine.*

Janine was showing her ignorance in public – and in so many ways. *Racoon* in British English only had one *C*.

I don't think he forgets, I think he's choosing to ignore me.

But what did she want from him? Roy sat up. How was he meant to behave when she was so *completely unhinged?*

Roy took a deep breath and switched on the bedside light. His heart couldn't have pumped harder if there'd been a burglar kicking down the front door.

Roy waited. No pain in his chest or arms. It probably wasn't a heart attack.

Roy stared at the framed wool picture on the wall ahead – the *Home Sweet Home* Lynn had crocheted decades ago.

It was ridiculous that Roy was torturing himself. Janine was wrong, and everyone reasonable would agree with him! Once you got to a statistically significant sample size, people had to disagree with Janine. They *had* to!

Roy threw back the duvet cover, pushed his feet into his slippers, and sat in front of his computer.

Since Roy had last looked three thousand, four hundred and twelve replies had blown up to 4,016.

@wendyshouse: He's a dinosaur.

@breathoffreshhair: My cousin's a clinical psychologist. So I know him using those words will have a lasting long-term impact on your daughter's subconscious.

@ellaishere: This is toxic masculinity at its worst, and it's <u>not</u> harmless. The man is clearly a danger to your child.

Then, there were people who stuck up for Roy.

@nineteensixtysix: This man is clearly a kind grandparent with good intentions. Your undermining of him is unnecessary and cruel. Shame on you.

Reading that comment should have made him feel better, obviously. And it might have done – if it hadn't felt like someone was peering through a gap in Roy's living-room curtains. Saying *I like Roy's coffee table. Do you like his coffee table?* And someone else replying, *I preferred it when it was over there by the hearth, next to the coal scuttle. Do you think he has enough coasters?*

Then there were the other types of supportive comments. The ones that were *so* supportive, they didn't feel like they were really about Roy at all.

@paulclover51: These women have gone too far. They can't just accept being equals. They won't be happy until we're all in gulags.

@yourticketinspector: The man is a hero, flying the flag for trad-itional values and refusing to be cowed. Look what this country has become. We are British! We will not surrender!

Roy slammed his fist onto the desk, catching a box of paperclips with the heel of his hand. The box skittered into his keyboard.

@revolution76: You are doing the right thing pulling him up on this – it is your obligation to speak out. If you don't say any-thing, you are remaining silent. Silence is complicity. Tell him

to read some Simone Weil and Foucault. Tell him to educate himself.

Roy threw the box of paperclips across the room. It hit the wall, broke open, and showered its multicoloured contents over the carpet.

All Roy had ever wanted was for people to talk about French philosophers. He'd kept trying to introduce them into conversation – on buses, in pubs, at weddings. All he ever got was a polite, *'That's interesting, now have you tried the canapés?'*

Roy got up. With shaking hands, he gathered the paperclips together. He tried to put the lid back on the box. After several tries, he threw the box and clips into the bin.

There was the sound of a door opening across the landing. Roy froze.

He heard footsteps padding around. The flush of the toilet. Steps on the stairs; the pulling back of the front door chain. Someone leaving the house.

Roy stood up, putting one hand on the bed to support himself. He leaned round the desk and tweaked the blind to the side.

On the driveway, Phil was getting in his van in his overalls.

Roy let the blind fall back with a clatter. He sat back down.

@checkmybio: Textbook toxic masculinity in action

Fingers of cold snuck round the bottom of Roy's back. He pulled the hem of his pyjama top down, tucking it into the elastic waistband of his bottoms.

He typed *toxic masculinity* into the search engine.

About 12,900,000 results.

Toxic masculinity *refers to a group of behaviours that are used to categorise manliness, perpetuating domination, homophobia, aggression and physical . . . '*

Fingers of cold tickled his lower back again. Roy went to tuck in his pyjama top, but it was already tucked. He closed the search engine and clicked back to the forum.

@janey44: The results of the poll say it all.

Roy stared at this comment for a long time.
He clicked *Frequently Asked Questions* and scanned the list.

How do I see the results of a poll?
The results of a poll appear when you have voted.

Roy stared, wearily. It hadn't even occurred to him to vote – it felt like interfering with due process. He considered it poor form MPs voted for themselves at general elections, slotting their self-ticked slips into the box on camera with no shame.
Roy scrolled back to the post. He looked at the two buttons at the side of the screen.

You're the villain here
Not the villain here

Roy placed his cursor over **You're the villain here.**
He took a second, letting the cursor hover. This was it:

Roy was entering enemy land. He was Caesar, crossing the Rubicon.

Roy clicked the mouse. He stayed smugly powerful for the whole second it took to read the percentages that appeared on the screen.

Thursday

Am I the Villain Here? Post 35915

CantBeArsed8: Am I the villain here for being furious my partner's father changed my daughter's pirate party into a princess party?

7,782 votes, 3 days left

You're the villain here: 19%
Not the villain here: 81%

Latest Edit:

EDIT: 10% is actually quite a standard tip in the UK. I know it's different in the US, but I think we pay a higher basic wage to waiting staff, or something – either way, I'm not saying he's tight. Can we please stick to the topic in hand?

31

'I know I said I'd let the people decide, Joseph, but the people are *wrong*!'

Other visitors glanced over.

On the sofa, Roy shifted position. 'You've got the right idea, Joseph, staying in here with all the puddings. You don't have to go *out there* – where no one cares about innocent till proven guilty. Where the deranged and the barmy and the cuckoo interact at will!' Roy banged his palms against his thighs. 'They put all of you in this nursing prison, but it's the people walking around out there, the public, who are *actually* demented!'

It was only 11 a.m., but Roy had had a long day.

He wiped his forehead with his handkerchief. They kept this room as hot as a sauna.

'Eighty-one per cent to Janine!' Roy reached for Joseph's hands. 'Eighty-one per cent! That's over *six thousand, three hundred people* who say I'm wrong. The wisdom of crowds can't possibly apply! Surowiecki clearly stated the quality of the crowd mattered in achieving the right conclusion, and *this* crowd' – Roy shook his head in despair – '*this* crowd—'

'Hello again!'

Roy whipped his head up.

The nurse, Elena, stood over him, smiling, like the world

hadn't turned on its axis overnight. 'You're here a lot this week!'

Roy tried to smile back. Or he bared his teeth – he wasn't sure. He really didn't know how to function in public anymore. Not now he knew how *the public* behaved.

'You're here more than me this week!' Elena kept smiling. 'Roy, is it?'

Roy gave a stiff nod.

'Joseph's very lucky to have such a good friend. Would you like me to get the two of you a book?'

Roy looked at the selection on the table. 'No. I left a special book in his room, on engines. Joseph likes engines.'

Elena kept smiling. 'Joseph really likes the Touch and Feel books.'

Roy spoke immediately. 'No, he doesn't.'

'He likes to feel the textures.'

'No. No, he definitely doesn't.' Roy tried to stare some sense into this ridiculous woman. 'I'll go and get his proper book.'

Roy headed towards the bright magenta door of Joseph's room. What these prison nurses didn't understand, with their crispy, jangling children's books, was who Joseph *was*. Joseph would never be able to fight this if he didn't remember himself, would he? Joseph was a man of substance and dignity. He was not a man of *felt*.

In Joseph's bedroom, the wardrobe door was slightly ajar. Roy pushed it shut. He adjusted the photo of Joseph and Audrey, so it was directly facing the bed. He pulled his handkerchief out of his sleeve and wiped his fingerprint from the glass.

He picked up the steam trains book and re-entered the lounge.

Joseph was standing up, holding hands with the shoe-baby lady.

Elena touched Roy's sleeve. 'That's his girlfriend, you know!'

'That's *not* his girlfriend.' Roy had had enough of this. 'His wife of forty-five years was a respected GP, and Audrey *wouldn't have countenanced* treating a shoe as a baby.'

Finally, Elena was silent.

His face reddening, Roy walked over to the lady and petted her shoe briefly. He steered Joseph over to the sofa and placed the steam trains book open in his lap.

'I don't know what to do, Joseph.' A wall of exhaustion hit Roy. 'What would you do if you were me?'

Joseph didn't answer.

Roy turned the page. India's *Fairy Queen* shone out in its glorious reds and greens.

'I know what you'd do. You'd rise above it.' Roy clapped Joseph softly on the back. 'You can stand all this indignity in here because you know you're better than them.'

Around them, nurses gathered inmates into eating positions, wheeling out the food tables, herding the mobile people into a central area.

'I'll leave you to your pudding and come back tomorrow.' Roy stood up. 'But I'm going to take a leaf out of your book and exercise self-discipline. I can take the moral high ground. Until Janine comes to her senses, I'll just wait it out.' He patted Joseph's shoulder. 'Wait it out, like a sniper.'

32

After yesterday morning's unexpected kedgeree-making, Roy had reverted to not coming down at breakfast time, which made the whole situation easier. It was a lot nicer for Janine to drink coffee and scroll through the news without the sound of an electric screwdriver in the background. She could even pour herself a cup of orange juice in a normal glass without being frowned at, not one of the thimble-sized ones Roy kept especially for the purpose and pushed towards her, muttering about economy and the importance of controlling blood sugar levels.

Even Katie looked happier than usual, sorting her animal stickers with one hand while eating toast with the other.

Katie's toast hand wavered. 'Rosa said her mum's said I can come for tea tonight.'

Janine looked up hopefully. Did this mean Janine had been making progress with the mums after all? 'What's Rosa's mum called?'

Katie shrugged. She moved a sticker from one pile to another.

'What does Rosa's mum look like?'

Katie shrugged again.

Janine took a bite of her toast.

'Rosa said her mum has got lots of questions. She really wants to know if we live with Roy.'

Janine stopped chewing.

'And whether he's ever called me a pretty racoon.' Katie shrugged – *people* – and focused on moving stickers between piles.

Janine put her toast down. 'Under no circumstances are you to go to Rosa's for tea, Katie.'

Katie looked up. She had antennae for trouble.

'We've got plans.'

Katie narrowed her eyes. 'What plans?'

'Good plans. Fun plans.'

Katie took a slow, suspicious bite of toast.

Janine looked at the wall calendar, where Roy marked all his activities – even the ones that could be done at any time. *Change Bedding. Check Oil and Tyres.*

Today, Roy's calendar said:

10 a.m. Visiting time, Joseph
1 p.m. Library

Janine nodded. She had time to think of fun plans. And she just had to kill time until after the school run, and then she'd be able to dodge Roy and his electric screwdriver until at least tea time.

Janine stopped at the end of the road. 'You can make it from here, surely?'

Katie looked at her school, still a hundred metres away. 'We're not even close!'

'You're a big girl. I'm watching!'

Janine watched until Katie had stepped through the gates, and hurried off before she could make eye contact with anyone.

She decided to kill an hour on the bench in the park, watching a particularly fat pigeon groom its feathers. Sal had asked Janine not to call round in the workday, so Janine tried phoning instead.

The voicemail message kicked in. *Hi, it's Sal. Please don't leave a message. If you're still thinking of it, just stop. Just don't.*

Janine considered leaving a message since she was here, but – no. She had to do things on Sal's terms now. Janine was not busy, and therefore the lesser party when it came to friendship arrangements.

Janine scrolled through other names on her phone, trying to find someone who would want to hear from her at this time of day, and someone she wanted to speak to. There was surprisingly little crossover in that Venn diagram.

Janine watched the pigeon lift its wing and burrow its head in its own armpit.

She flicked onto *Am I The Villain Here?* for some validation.

There were over *seven thousand* votes now – and nearly as many replies. At the bottom of the screen, a new section had appeared – *Latest Twitter Comments.*

Janine looked up at the burrowing pigeon.

Of course, she knew some of these posts moved onto Twitter. It was fine.

But when she followed the link there were over a thousand replies.

@pennythefoxterrier: This is exactly what's wrong with our country

Janine nodded. The comments on the forum had changed focus lately, and it made sense now. The move to Twitter meant the batshit cavalry had got involved, and they were charging over the digital mountain, flying the flag for bendy bananas or for policemen wearing helmets, or whatever the fuck these people cared about.

Janine scrolled through the replies. *Nutter. Nutter. Nutter, nutter, nutter. Nut—*

@intotheforest: The man's called Roy and he used to be a magistrate.

Janine stared. Cold flooded her body.

But who even knew?

Rosa's mum. Asking Katie for tea, for the first time ever.

That woman at the pedestrian crossing, looking up from checking her bag. *'A pirate party? Instead of a princess party?'*

Then there was that look. That look that had crackled between some of the mums in the café yesterday.

Janine had to face it. There was no anonymity anymore.

Her phone buzzed in her hand. An email notification slid across the screen.

Urgent – interview tomorrow

Janine was so distracted, and so unused to getting good news, it took a surprisingly long time to process the message.

Janine hurried back home and tried on her skirt suit in front of the mirror on Roy's landing. She frowned at the bland woman reflected back. The kind of woman you would call *harmless*. The kind of woman you would call *a safe pair of hands*.

She heard the front door go. 'Phil!' She ran downstairs. 'I've got an interview tomorrow! For a job I actually want!'

The *v* between Phil's eyebrows shrank. 'Brilliant!'

'They have sleep pods and dogs in the office!'

He looked at her. 'And you're planning to sleep in that?'

'I'm trying on disguises.'

'You mean outfits.'

'I suppose. How come you're back?'

'Forgot my lunchbox. Thought I should eat my sandwiches, seeing as you've gone to the trouble of making them.' Phil kept studying her. 'You look nice.'

'I don't. But thanks. What do you think?' She stood in his eyeline. 'Skirt suit, like a lady.'

Phil looked at her for a moment. 'Perfect.'

'Tights or no tights?' She did a sweeping gesture with the backs of her hands. 'This is *tights*.'

Phil nodded.

'And this is *no tights*.' Janine removed them and put her hands on her hips in a Wonder Woman stance. 'Which is more me, I think. If you ignore the skirt suit bit.'

'I think you look great. Both ways.'

'No, you don't. You think I look like *a safe pair of hands*.'

'No one wants to employ a maverick.'

'I just think the whole outfit reeks of desperation. Especially with the tights.'

'I think you read way too much into tights.'

'I could just get a badge saying *desperate*.' Janine took her suit jacket off. 'I could print out all my rejection emails and sew them into a nice coat to wear for interviews. What do you think?'

'I think I should get back to work.'

Phil got his lunchbox from the kitchen. He kissed Janine

on the cheek, and Janine forgot she was angry with him, so let him.

After he left, Janine ran upstairs. She stared at herself in the mirror again.

Tomorrow was *everything*. If she got this job, it would all be different. She wouldn't worry so much about money. She wouldn't have time to overthink. She would be able to call Sal from a position of equal busyness and friendship equality. She'd legitimately be able to leave Sal the voicemails Sal didn't want to hear.

And Janine would be happier after tomorrow too, which meant she'd be calmer. And because she'd be calmer, she'd be better able to make Roy understand what he'd done wrong. And then Roy would apologise and see the error of his ways. And then they'd move out. And then everything would go back to normal.

The post outing Roy on Twitter wasn't ideal. But then, it just said his first name, it wasn't a full belts-and-braces outing. Besides, neither Roy nor Phil went anywhere near Twitter.

Janine took a breath. She stared at herself in the mirror.

She'd get this job. And then it was all going to be OK.

33

Roy stood with Tessa and Yvonne at the counter. 'Quiet, isn't it?' He watched a lady with too many shopping bags browse the audiobook selection. The library was silent, but for the tapping of keyboards.

Roy glanced at the library computers.

Lately, computers had taken a new, sinister shape in his life. Anything could happen on there. Anything *was* happening.

Roy shifted his weight from one foot to the other.

Three of the four computers were busy, but the last one was free. Free – and convenient. And not more than five metres away.

Roy shifted his weight again. Of course, he'd told Joseph he'd wait it out, like a sniper.

But the thing about snipers was they had to stay alert. Or how would they know when it was time to fire?

Roy cleared his throat. 'Quiet in here.'

Yvonne smiled at him.

Roy shuffled his feet. 'Not much to do.'

Tessa glanced up. 'You're welcome to go home, Roy.'

'A Frost always meets his commitments. Though, as it's *so* quiet . . . is there any harm in me using that free computer to look something up?'

He was about to formulate a convoluted story about

a chiropractor appointment and a forgotten address, but Tessa said, 'Roy, you're a volunteer. You can do what you want.'

Roy headed to the free computer in the corner, next to where a man in his sixties with a distinctive smell was completing a job application. Smelling of marijuana certainly wouldn't help his prospects, but Roy didn't say anything. It was none of his business.

That was how the world was meant to work. People minding their own business – without the need for any commentary from others. The world had worked perfectly adequately like that for millennia.

Roy's hands briefly curled into fists.

He stretched his fingers out, glanced at the marijuana-smelling man, and typed the forum address.

Over a hundred more comments had appeared since he'd last looked.

'The textbooks are over there, treasure. By the classical music.' Yvonne walked past Roy's computer, smiling at a customer, a stack of books in her arms.

Roy waited until Yvonne was safely behind the stacks. He looked at the screen.

@alltheowls: *The man's an anachronism. He doesn't know it's the twenty-first century.*

Roy narrowed his eyes. He certainly *did* know it was the twenty-first century, or how would he be using the internet?

@iansmith12: *Traditional British values are dying out. Honour and Empire. Our values MUST. BE. SAVED.*

Roy coughed with frustration. It was worse, somehow, when the unhinged ones were on his side.

At the bottom of the screen, there was a new section – *Latest Twitter Comments*.

Roy had heard of Twitter. They were always talking about it in the newspapers.

He clicked on the button.

The screen changed to a different format, and Roy started reading the comments. They were still, apparently, talking about him, but more angrily now. These people seemed even more sure of themselves.

@intotheforest: The man's called Roy and he used to be a magistrate.

Invisible needles prickled up Roy's back.

'Roy!' Yvonne smiled over the top of his screen. 'Can you help this gentleman with Shakespeare? Unless they made it into a film with Leonardo DiCaprio, I'm useless!'

Roy took a second. He clicked the *X* at the corner of the screen. 'No problem.'

He got up slowly, his fingers tingling with adrenaline. He let Yvonne walk him to the Education section.

'My daughter's been told to read Shakespeare comedies,' a scruffy man said to Roy. 'But which are the comedies?'

'*Measure for Measure*,' Roy said automatically. Usually, he lived for this kind of question. '*As You Like It. The Merry Wives of Windsor. Love's Labours Lost.*'

Yvonne nudged Roy. 'Isn't he brilliant? We don't even *need* a computer!'

'*The Comedy of Errors. Much Ado about Nothing.*' An overweight man with a too-short jumper walked towards Roy's computer. Roy widened his gaze. '*All's Well that Ends Well.*'

Don't sit down, don't sit down, don't sit . . .

He sat down.

Roy felt his shoulders slump. '*Twelfth Night.*'

'Thank you.'

'I haven't finished.'

'I'll start with those. Thank you.'

Roy watched the man turn to look at the books in the stack. He looked so normal – if scruffy. But then, most people *did* look normal.

How could you tell if he was one of *them*? Did *this man* call people dinosaurs and anachronisms? Did this man use the term *toxic masculinity*? Was he secretly *@intotheforest* – the person that had just given Roy's name to the world?

And if he was *@intotheforest,* how would Roy know?

Roy made a noise of frustration in the back of his throat. He glanced back at the computers.

The man in the short jumper had logged into a site called *Wicked Bingo.*

The marijuana man was getting notes out of his bag.

Roy pushed up his sleeves impatiently. He looked up – to see Tessa watching him.

His face burned. 'Coffee, I think.' He strode to the staff room. He made three coffees and carried them to Yvonne at the counter.

She beamed at him. 'Wonderful! I'll take this one to Tessa. Don't go anywhere!' She came back and sipped her coffee. 'Lovely. It must have been nice to have that man to ask you about Shakespeare. I know you like book questions.'

'Plays. Shakespeare wrote plays.'

Yvonne laughed. Roy was vaguely conscious of her saying something else, but he couldn't concentrate. Not with everything going on.

@intotheforest had inside information.

Could *@intotheforest* be the same person who put the note through Roy's door?

If not, could this mean Roy had *another* nemesis – on top of Janine, the windscreen man and the anonymous note writer? Could it be that *everyone* was out to get him?

Yvonne nudged him. 'You're miles away!'

Her face swam into focus. 'Sorry.'

'I said, are you going to the school quiz? Right up your street!'

'Sorry. Yes, I am going to the quiz.'

'I was thinking, maybe we could be on the same team? Wouldn't that be fun? You being able to reel off all those Shakespeare plays just like that. Me being good for morale.'

Roy nodded absentmindedly.

He had a new enemy. But who?

'We don't have to be on the same team, if you've already got one.' Yvonne cupped her mug between her hands. 'I was just thinking it would be nice to spend time together outside work. Maybe we could do something fun together some time.' She looked up from her mug. 'Companiable, like.'

Roy stared at the computers, willing one to become free.

'Roy?'

Roy wound back what she'd said in his head. 'Companiable?'

Yvonne gave a tiny smile. She sipped the coffee.

Did she mean *a date*?

'NO! No, no!' He shook his head in embarrassment. 'That wouldn't work at all!' He tried not to look too horrified at the suggestion – from this woman, with her fluffy pastel cardigans, her too-strong scent and her *sweethearts* and *treasures* and *poppets*. 'Lynn's hardly been gone any time!' Yvonne was *a smoker*. She only ever borrowed books with covers of women in Regency dress with heaving bosoms. 'I've still got her ashes!' Roy added desperately, because surely Yvonne would understand *now*?

There was a silence.

Yvonne took a long sip of her coffee. 'No bother.'

Roy shuffled his feet. 'I didn't mean to—'

'Least said, soonest mended.' She placed her mug down. 'That gentleman needs some help at the printer.'

Roy wrung his hands. He turned towards the printers. 'Yvonne!'

But Yvonne was at the other side of the library, pushing open the door to the Ladies.

Roy wrung his hands again.

He leaned to pick up the contents of the returns bucket. He tried to place the first book back on the shelf without making eye contact with Tessa – which was hard, when she was only standing a metre away, in *General Fiction A to C*, glaring at Roy, gripping the long window pole like there was nothing she wanted more than to skewer him with it.

34

Phil took his lunchbox and thermos and headed back to his job on the new estate.

Janine had an interview now and *thank Christ*.

He parked. Michael, the project manager, stood in the front drive, chatting to the lads.

Michael saw Phil and glanced instantly away.

He looked back. He gave Phil a slow, strange nod.

Phil nodded back. Michael hurried into the house.

Phil got out of the van and locked up. He walked past the two young roofers in the driveway. 'Lads.'

They both nodded – too casually. One roofer put his phone slowly in his pocket.

Phil put his headphones on and went into the house. He switched on his music and headed into the kitchen.

He sensed someone behind him. He turned.

Michael faced him, holding a newspaper. Silent.

Phil took his headphones out. 'If this was prison, I'd be about to get shivved.'

Michael still said nothing.

Phil frowned. '*Am* I about to get shivved?'

'Do you know?' Michael held out the paper. 'Page eight.'

Phil took it. 'Everyone's behaving very oddly today, you know that?'

'My wife said I had to tell you.' Michael hurried up the stairs. 'Keep it!'

Phil watched Michael disappear out of sight. He turned the pages of the *Mail* to page eight.

He stared at the headline.

Princesses And Pirates – A Family At War!

Phil couldn't get his key into the front door fast enough. 'JANINE!'

He shoved the door open. It banged into the wall, rattling the photo frames on the hallway table. 'JANINE!'

He rushed through to the front room, into the empty kitchen, back into the hallway.

She had better be in. She needed to hear how *fucking furious* he was. 'JANINE!'

Janine appeared at the top of the stairs, back in jeans and a hoodie. 'You've heard.'

'Of course I've heard!' Phil threw his hands in the air. 'Everyone's heard! And by everyone, I mean – actually everyone. Buddhists on mountaintops. Engineers on space stations. They've all heard about Janine Pierce and her hot take on princesses and pirates and PRETTY FUCKING RACOONS!' Phil took a breath. 'You coming down?'

Janine took a moment. She shook her head.

'How could you do this to us?'

'*He* did it! *He* did this to us. And if you'd been there for me, I wouldn't have had to go elsewhere for support, would I?'

Phil gestured between them. 'Are you coming down or am I coming up?'

Janine took a moment. She walked down the stairs and past him, into the kitchen.

Phil followed her in. 'How could you do this?'

She pushed the door closed. 'I thought it would stay on the forum. I didn't think you'd see.' Janine leaned against the kitchen unit. 'I never thought it would go onto Twitter.'

'Twitter? And the rest.' Phil threw the newspaper down. 'You've seen the *Mail*?'

Janine blanched.

Phil waved his hand over the paper. 'Fill your boots.'

Janine glanced at him. She picked up the paper.

'Page eight.'

Janine turned to the page. She put the paper down. 'I can't.'

'Christ, Janine.'

'It shouldn't have made the *Mail*. You know I don't believe in the *Mail*.'

'It's a newspaper, not the Easter Bunny.'

'I'm sorry. But you can't control how these things blow up.'

'You *can* control it, though. It's easy. You just don't put personal shit out there. Why would you do this to us?'

Janine pushed her fringe out of her eyes. 'I never expected this.'

Phil shook his head. 'This explains some of those weird conversations I've been having lately. And for what? So a few people on the internet can tell you you're right.'

'Eighty per cent.'

'What?'

'Eighty per cent think I'm in the right.'

'A *hundred per cent* of me thinks you've lost your fucking mind.'

'This is serious.'

'It's really serious. For us.'

'What does that mean?'

Phil didn't answer. He didn't know.

'It's no longer acceptable to both sides this, Phil!'

'It's *no longer acceptable*? I'm not your fucking employee, *Janine*.'

They stared at each other.

'I'm right, though.' Janine's voice was soft. 'The internet people agree with me.'

'But they aren't here!' Phil tried to lower his voice again – it was a struggle. 'They aren't the ones expected to make their dads change their whole personalities, like you can make a man who's nearly eighty think like he's twenty! You expect the whole world to change to suit you – it just doesn't work like that! Do you think it works like that?'

There was the sound of a key in the front door.

Phil and Janine froze.

Light, quick footsteps hurried up the stairs. Roy's bedroom door banged shut.

Janine rubbed the arms of her hoodie with both hands. 'He hasn't even apologised.'

Phil shook his head. 'He took us into his home.'

'You need to support me.' Janine's voice was barely audible. 'Or what's the point? What do you think, Phil? What do you think?'

'I don't know what I think!'

'Then work it out.'

Phil took a breath. 'You need to fix this, Janine.'

'No, *you* need to fix this.'

'We can't stay here. Not in his house. Not like this.'

Janine rubbed her arms again. 'Me and Katie definitely can't.'

There was a pause. This was where Phil was expected to argue, of course.

Instead, he folded his arms.

A silence stretched between them.

Janine looked up. 'I'll find somewhere else to go, then.'

'Fine.'

'Just me and Katie.'

'Fine.' Phil tensed his folded arms. 'In fact – good.'

'I'll take Mum up on her offer of the caravan.'

Phil stared at her. If this was a game of chicken, he was too angry to lose. 'If that's what you want.'

'It's exactly what I want. There!' Janine shouted. 'We've made progress, haven't we?'

She threw the kitchen door open and stormed out of the house.

35

Janine marched down the road in the direction of Marky's house. She mustn't cry. She mustn't cry.

And she mustn't think either. She'd focus on the practical side, and just take this one step at a time.

She tried Marky first. *Pick up, pick up, pick up . . .*

He did.

'Marky, have you sold that car yet?'

He didn't answer straight away. 'This is a turn up for the books.'

'Can I borrow it? Just for a few days? I've got third party insurance. I need to . . . move some things.'

'Sure, Janine.' His voice was neutral. He didn't crow. He didn't even ask.

That was when Janine realised just how much she'd fucked up her life.

No thinking. 'OK if I pick it up right now?'

'Sure.'

'See you in twenty.'

She took a deep breath. She'd leave a few minutes to regroup before making the next call.

*

Mum's voice was clipped. 'So my caravan's good enough for you now?'

'It's just for a few days. While I sort something long term out. Is that still OK?'

'I just wish you'd said.'

'I am saying. Now.'

'If you'd said, I would have cleaned it for you.'

'Now I *have* said, and I can clean it myself.'

'It's going to be tight, with all three of you.'

'It's just me and Katie.'

There was a long pause.

'It's not a thing, Mum. Don't make this a thing.'

Mum said nothing.

'It's just for a few days.'

For a while, Mum was quiet. 'I'll be back from the garden centre by four, so you can pick up the keys.'

'Thanks, Mum.' Janine paused. 'I mean, properly. Thank you.'

Katie looked excited at first, when Janine turned up at school in Marky's car. 'Daddy's given it to us?'

'He's not given it.' Janine helped Katie into her booster seat. 'He's just lent it to us for our holiday.'

Katie squealed. 'Holiday!'

Janine got into the driver's seat. 'We're going to Grandma's!' She turned to look at Katie. 'To live in Grandma's caravan! I mean – *holiday* in her caravan!'

Katie's smile switched off. Janine kept her smile firmly on.

'*That's* the holiday?'

Janine nodded.

'Where are we going in the caravan?'

'We could go anywhere! The whole world's our oyster!'

She switched on the ignition. 'But somewhere within a good distance of school and your father, obviously. Isn't it freeing?'

She made eye contact with Katie in the rear-view mirror.

Katie's blank silence gave Janine chills.

'But we'll just stay on the drive for now,' Janine pulled away from the kerb, 'while we decide.'

Half an hour later, after the quietest car journey Janine could remember, they pulled up on the road Janine had grown up on.

Janine gazed at the sixties semi. Her dad had left this house when Janine was younger than Katie, and her mum had done everything. Had Janine ever appreciated enough what her mum had done for her, bringing her up alone?

Katie stared at the caravan.

'It's bigger on the inside. Like a Tardis.' Janine wondered if she'd ever stop gaslighting her daughter.

Her mum opened the door, wearing exercise leggings and a TV presenter's full face of make-up.

'Grandma!' Katie ran up and hugged her legs. 'Don't make me live in there.'

Janine made eye contact with her mum. 'It's just a holiday.'

Her mum smiled at Katie. 'It's just a few days, love!' She ruffled Katie's hair. 'Can't wait to have you living next door to me. We can make biscuits. You can help me water my hanging baskets!'

'But *why*?'

Janine made her voice singsong. 'Because it's fun!'

Her mum looked up at Janine. 'Hi, love.' She held out the caravan keys.

Janine took the keys, her throat thick with emotion. She touched the sleeve of Mum's sweat-wicking gym top.

'Thanks, Mum.' It still wasn't enough, so she said it again. 'Thanks, Mum.'

Half an hour later, Janine had scrubbed the surfaces. She was mopping the floor with the energy of a dancer. 'It's an adventure!'

Katie had been stationary on that caravan seat for a long time, like a Victorian ghost kid in a horror film. It was getting sinister.

'A lot of people would love to live on holiday!' You can even eat at the table in bed – what about that?' She slapped her mop from side to side, splashing grey water onto her trainers. 'Do any of your friends have a bed where they can eat at the table?'

'No,' Katie said quietly.

Janine continued brightly. 'I bet they don't!'

'Do I get to sleep under a duvet?'

'Of course!' Janine looked around. 'I'll just go and ask your Grandma. She'll have some bedding.'

'Mum—'

'This is fine, Katie.' Janine opened the door. 'It's exciting.' She avoided her daughter's gaze. 'We're going to have so much fun!'

Janine rushed out of the caravan, still beaming.

She shut the door and leaned back on it. She closed her eyes, just for a second.

Her mum would have spare bedding, wouldn't she?

Of course she would. If the worst came to the worst, Janine could go back to their storage unit.

This was fine.

It was all absolutely fine.

36

At the end of his shift Roy marched home, pacing the streets like a soldier.

He'd been rude to Yvonne, but it wasn't his fault. It was essential he conveyed the message clearly.

Lynn had teased him once about it. *'If I go before you, then be on your guard. You'll have women flocking!'*

Roy had just frowned. *'Surely not.'*

'A man at your age is a catch!' Lynn had leaned back on her armchair, so the mechanism lifted the footrest, raising her socked feet. *'Remember when Cousin Andrew went into sheltered accommodation? He had a different lady trying to make him dinner every night!'*

The memory of this conversation now, the callousness of Lynn joking about her own death, stopped Roy's breath.

How could she have joked about it?

He knew how, though. Because they never thought death could happen to them. Even in his third age, having lost parents, friends, siblings, Roy had never believed it. Not in his core.

Not until the night of the rushing water. Perhaps not even then. Roy wasn't even sure it had sunk in now.

Of course, Roy *acted* the part of a widower. But the idea of Lynn – Lynn the party organiser, the calendar-filler, the life-force – gone? *For ever?*

Roy swallowed. He reached the main traffic lights, crossed the road and—

'Hey! Judge!'

The windscreen man in the bobble hat leaned over a black car, sponge dripping suds onto the tarmac.

Roy stared.

He had *forgotten*. He'd been so wrapped up in his thoughts, he'd *forgotten*.

The windscreen man straightened up. 'You here to apologise?'

Roy turned and walked in the opposite direction.

'You think you can run away from me?'

Roy turned his walk into a half-jog.

'Hey! I will find you!'

Roy hurried down the main road and through the park. He circled back by the busy bowling green. He dodged a lady with a tray of cakes and took deep breaths, trying to blend in with the crowd of bowling seniors.

He waited in the small alley between the bowling hut and the park toilet, trying not to inhale the acrid drain smell, waiting for his chest to stop heaving.

He peered out at the park. No sign.

A woman in an apron came round the corner, carrying empty boxes.

Roy nodded *hello*.

The woman put her boxes down. She went away again.

Roy concentrated on his breathing. He listened to the murmurs of pleasant conversation and the calming click of bowling balls.

He envied these old people their conversation. About grandchildren. Haircuts. Cricket scores. These people were full of the small pleasures of the day, not a care in the world. Surrounded by friends.

Not like Roy. Who was only surrounded by enemies.

When Roy got back to the house, Phil's van was in the drive.

He opened the front door to the sound of Phil's raised voice. 'You need to stop this. Right now!'

There was no response. Just silence from the kitchen.

Roy shut the door quietly behind him. He hurried upstairs and shut the bedroom door.

He sat at the computer and found the message on Twitter.

@intotheforest: He's called Roy and he used to be a magistrate.

@grahamthekidd: A magistrate? Like a judge? That says it all. Rape apologists, the lot of them. They think anyone in a short skirt is asking for it.

Roy slammed both hands on his desk. His biro rolled onto the floor.

Of course, Roy agreed that some of his fellow lawmakers weren't the most *with it*. There had been some regrettable judgments over the years from people who'd spent too long on the bench – people deeming it reasonable for a man to have sex with his wife while she was asleep, that kind of thing. But Roy had always been a modern magistrate. He'd always been clear in his mind that no one – no one of any gender, of any marital status – should be having sex while they were asleep.

Roy heard the front door bang. He got up.

Janine was rushing down the street, head down. She stumbled and righted herself. She disappeared round the corner.

Roy sat back down. He kept scrolling through Twitter messages.

There was a knock at the door. Roy jabbed the monitor off.

Phil pushed the door open and frowned. 'Are you still doing that paperwork?'

Roy nodded.

Phil sat on the bed. 'I need to head back to a job.'

'You look exhausted. Are you sure you shouldn't finish for the day?'

'We're on a deadline. The plasterers are in tomorrow.'

'You can't work at this time.' Roy looked at his watch. 'The light will be going soon.'

'I'll be fine.'

Roy glanced at the black monitor screen. He wondered how long Phil was planning to sit here.

'So Janine and Katie are going away this afternoon for a few days.' Phil didn't meet Roy's eye. 'To Janine's mum's caravan.'

'On holiday?' Roy stopped himself saying *I thought she had no money*. Here was Phil, working so hard, late into the night. Supporting Janine, who was flitting off without a care in the world.

'See you later.' Phil stood up. 'Don't wait up.'

'I'll leave some food in the top oven for when you get back!'

He switched the monitor back on and felt his smile fade. It was still there. *Of course* it was still there.

@intotheforest: He's called Roy and he used to be a magistrate.

Roy felt his heartrate thunder back up. He clicked on *@intotheforest's* bio.

Einstein
@intotheforeʒt

Joined February 2022
3 Following   **0** *Followers*

Roy tried to scroll down *@intotheforeʒt's* posts. There was nothing else to see.

Roy took a breath. He clicked back to the original post.

And he started reading again, from the top, everything the world thought about him.

A while later, Roy was staring at *@intotheforeʒt's* message again. *Show yourself, you scoundrel!*

At the sound of a car on the drive, he pulled the blind to one side.

Janine got out of a fancy-looking silver saloon car. She opened the back door.

Katie slid off a booster seat and followed Janine towards the house.

Roy glanced at the bedroom door. He got up and pushed it shut.

There was the sound of footsteps on the stairs. 'Be quick, please.' Janine's voice.

Roy turned the key in the lock. He leaned against the door, breathing heavily.

*

Half an hour later there was a knock on the door.

'He's not in,' Janine said. 'Don't go in his room!'

Roy watched the handle turn. It turned back.

'Why does he lock the door when he goes out?' Katie asked.

'Who knows why Roy does what he does? Hurry, love!'

There were rushed footsteps. Bottles being thrown into a bag. The opening and closing of drawers. Pacing across the landing and down the stairs. 'Have you got your gym kit? Have you packed a spare school skirt?'

Eventually, the front door slammed.

Roy walked to the window. He watched Janine throw two holdalls into the boot of the silver saloon. Katie handed her a set of school clothes on hangers, which Janine laid carefully on top.

Roy stood at the window. He watched them drive away.

He was about to go back to the computer, to read the comment again and try to fathom *@intotheforest*'s motives when, across the street, he saw a familiar loping figure.

Darsh.

Roy stared.

Darsh knew the post was about Roy. But surely Darsh wouldn't . . . ?

Roy sat at the screen, scrolling. He left an agonising few minutes.

He threw his pen down and hurried down the stairs.

Darsh answered the door wearing a T-shirt and shorts.

'It's gone onto Twitter.' Roy could hear the desperation in his own voice.

'Ah.'

'But I have concerns about anonymity. You said it was anonymous.'

Darsh squinted at Roy. 'Still taking the high road?'

'Someone's given out my personal details in response to Janine's post.'

'I'm so sorry.' Darsh took a moment. 'Hang on, are you asking if it was *me*?' His voice went up at the end.

'Of course not.'

Darsh shoved his hands in the pockets of his shorts.

Roy's face flamed. 'That's not what I came over about.'

Darsh stared at him.

Roy coughed. 'I came to ask, did I lend you my hedge trimmer? I gave it to a neighbour, and I can't remember who.'

Darsh shook his head. 'Our hedges are wild.'

Roy nodded. 'Then I must be having a senior moment.' He'd never used that phrase in his life; something within him withered. 'I'll let you get on with your day.'

Darsh gave a slow nod. 'Bin day tomorrow.' He smiled at Roy. 'Black and green!'

Roy made himself smile back. 'You're learning! Anyway, can't stand here all day.' He patted Darsh's arm and turned. 'Busy, busy.'

'I'll let you know if I hear about your hedge trimmer!'

Roy lifted his hand in acknowledgement. Back in the house, he slammed the front door hard. So hard that a picture frame on the hallway table fell flat on its face.

Roy righted it.

Everything about that conversation was excruciating. And unnecessary.

Darsh wasn't the note writer. He was just a person who'd been in the street at a coincidental time.

It's just Darsh had been his only lead. But he wasn't even a lead. He'd never been a lead.

Roy had an enemy.

And he didn't have a clue who it was.

Friday

Am I the Villain Here? Post 35915

CantBeArsed8: Am I the villain here for being furious my part-ner's father changed my daughter's pirate party into a princess party?

12.4K votes, 2 days left

You're the villain here: 28%
Not the villain here: 72%

Latest reply:

@proudtobelibra: When all's said and done, you've got to ask — where is the partner in all this?

37

Roy lay in bed, listening to the grandmother clock strike two.

No chance of sleep again.

He needed to *do something*.

But he couldn't keep looking at the forum – not at night. There was something about reading the forum at night that made him wonder . . . did these people have a point?

He felt powerless. He couldn't work out who *@intotheforest* was. He couldn't work out who put the note through his door.

He pushed his duvet back.

Because there was one thing he could do.

Roy had once had the notion of using his retirement to write up his time at the bench. For a jolly newspaper column, perhaps – maybe even a book. He even had a working title: *The Wheels of Justice*. He'd kept diaries of his cases, redacting as he went, rendering the individuals unidentifiable for ethical reasons.

Roy spent most of the night with papers spread all over the front-room floor, trying to unredact the information.

What did that windscreen man think Roy had done to him?

And whatever it was . . . had Roy actually done it?

His Third Age had taken an unexpected turn.

By four a.m., Roy had been going through his old *Wheels of Justice* diaries for hours. He was reading through notes from August 2013 about a D. N. who'd been charged with handling stolen goods – A David? A Derek? – when he heard the sound of footsteps.

Phil scanned the room. 'Wow.'

Roy looked at the room through Phil's eyes – at the papers strewn on the rug, on the coffee table, on sofa cushions. 'I'm looking for something important.'

Phil walked into the kitchen. 'I couldn't sleep either.'

Roy watched Phil take a glass to the sink. A coldness gripped his stomach. 'Phil?'

Phil looked at Roy quizzically.

Roy wanted to say *be careful*. 'Your mother used to get water in the night.' Why did Roy's mind insist on going to sinister places in the early hours?

Phil filled the glass. 'I can't do conversation at this time, Dad.'

Roy held up a hand. 'Understood.'

Phil took one last long look at Roy, then headed back upstairs.

Two hours later, Roy's back was aching, his thighs stiff. He boxed up his *Wheels of Justice* diaries and locked himself in his bedroom.

He scrolled through the forum comments, listening to the dawn chorus.

He still hadn't worked out who the windscreen man was, but it didn't matter – not anymore. In the night, he had been worried that he – he, *Roy Frost* – was in the wrong.

But it wasn't dark anymore. The dawn light was creeping through the blinds, and Roy knew. He was not the one in the wrong. Because *look at these people.*

Dinosaur.

Roy clucked his tongue at the lack of originality.

Ignorant.

Roy gave that comment the sniff it deserved.

Misogynist.

Roy shook his head, sad for this poor, misguided individual, apparently roaming the earth with no semblance of understanding.

As he read, Roy started humming *The House of the Rising Sun.* He reached a particularly rousing section and found himself thumping his slippered foot on the carpet, keeping time.

There were so many comments, Roy was inured to them now. Hero or villain – it was all the same. As Kipling once said:

> *If neither foes nor loving friends can hurt you,*
> *If all men count with you, but none too much . . .*
> *you'll be a man, my son!*

Old-fashioned and unhelpful – WRONG! *Perniciously ig-norant* – farcical!

Roy wasn't ignorant – perniciously or otherwise. He was

wise; he was curious. This person calling him *ignorant* would be eating their words if they knew Roy was *mentally quoting Kipling* right now.

It looked like Janine had added another edit, two days previously – one he'd missed at the time.

EDIT: 10% is actually quite a standard tip in the UK. I know it's different in the US, but I think we pay a higher basic wage to waiting staff, or something – either way, I'm not saying he's tight. Can we please stick to the topic in hand?

This edit had received a direct reply.

@themightypen76: He's tight.

Roy stopped humming.

Roy Frost was not *tight*.

He always tipped exactly 10 per cent. Even the time that waiter spilt a bowl of soup down his back – when Roy had smiled supportively at the teenager while his spine was on fire and had to eat the rest of his meal in a T-shirt the restaurant had provided, with the slogan *We Love Carbs!* – even *that* time, Roy had still tipped exactly 10 per cent.

At a pub, Roy *rushed* to be the first to get a round in. He sponsored everyone for their charity runs, and had even set up complicated internet accounts to do so.

Roy was not tight.

But he mustn't respond – not now. It was a mantra he took from the bench: *one mustn't pass sentence when one's emotions are high.*

Still, Roy found his mouse had moved over the *comment* button.

New Commenter? **Log in** *or* **Create an Account**

Roy clicked on *Create an Account*. He created the name *Justice0305* and clicked *New Comment*.

The wisdom of crowds can be a useful tool to overcome ill-education, but Surowiecki was clear the method has limitations if the make-up of the collective brain is flawed. In this case, we have the obvious problem of self-selection bias. Plus, there are educational flaws evident, at both the collective and individual levels. How do we spell racoon *in the UK, Janine?*

Roy clicked *Post* – and there it was. His comment, subtly nesting among the others. The cuckoo in the nest.

He kept scrolling.

At a soft knock at the door, Roy jerked his head up.

He listened to the bongs from the grandmother clock downstairs.

Nine a.m. How could it be . . . ?

'Dad?'

'Dad? Are you in?'

Roy watched the doorhandle turn. The locked door didn't move. The handle turned back.

'Dad?'

The handle turned again.

On Roy's desk, the phone rang.

Roy stared at the phone. The ringing stopped.

Eventually, there was the sound of Phil going back to his room. Sounds of him getting ready. Leaving the house.

Roy looked at the comments. He started scrolling again.

*

What must have been only a few minutes later – surely? – the phone trilled.

Roy started. He leaned over a pile of books and picked up the receiver. 'Four nine five three oh two.'

'Is it too early, Roy? It's Sue.'

'It's fine. I've been up for hours.' Roy switched off the monitor and shuffled out from behind the desk. 'How are you, Sue?'

'I'm fine, I just haven't heard from you. Have you been to see my dad this week? I know it's a lot to ask to keep me updated, and you've been so good, going so often. I'd understand if—'

'It's not that. I've been going to see Joseph. Sorry, Sue. I've got a lot on, and I've forgotten to email you. I've been several times this week, in fact.'

'Several times?' Sue paused. 'Is he all right?'

'Oh, yes!' Roy stepped towards the window. 'Fit as a fiddle. Enjoying his puddings. He's keeping busy.'

The line was silent.

'And I took him a picture book about trains. He loved it.'

'Did he?' Sue's voice caught. 'That's nice. I've taken in old photo albums, but he seems more interested in the plastic bags I carry them in.'

'It's all about catching him on a good day. This new train book went down a storm.'

'Right.' Sue sounded brighter. 'And thank you. I didn't mean to sound like I'm checking up on you. I just appreciate your updates so very much.'

Roy stared out of the window. He wondered whether Claudia would be so diligent.

Claudia hadn't even replied to his email about her mother's ashes.

Roy coughed his emotion away. 'I'm going to take Joseph a book about Brutalist architecture next.'

Sue laughed. 'He did love that big hilltop estate in Sheffield. Before they renovated it.'

'It got renovated?'

'Ages ago, Roy! Don't tell Dad though. He doesn't need to know Mum died, and he doesn't need to know they've done up the Park Hill flats.'

Something outside the window registered in Roy's eyeline. A large moving vehicle.

Roy stared. For the first time he could remember, he had forgotten to put out the bins.

'Roy?'

Roy gripped the waistband of his pyjama bottoms, about to make a dash for it.

He stopped.

Darsh was running across the street. He held up a hand to the bin lorry and opened Roy's back gate. He wheeled Roy's green and black bins out to the street.

'Roy?'

'Sorry.' Roy kept hold of his pyjama waistband and watched Darsh jog back across the street. 'I'm still here.'

'Anyway, thanks Roy.' Sue's voice was warm. 'It's so good to know he has you there. It means the world.'

'Well. It means the world to me too.'

They ended the call, and Roy sat down and switched on the monitor.

He'd got a reply.

@bullsbullsbulls: Raccoon is spelt with two Cs, you fool

Roy sat up straighter.

Not in British English it isn't. The United States of America isn't the whole world, and it would serve you well to remember that. Good day.

Roy posted the comment with a frisson of righteousness. He scanned more comments.

@intotheforest: The bigot Roy works at Brook Street Library. You'd think a man who works at the library would educate himself.

Roy's chest flamed.

YOU IMPUDENT ROGUE! HOW DARE YOU? UNMASK YOURSELF, VILLAIN!

Roy posted the comment. Instantly, his body temperature dropped. In seconds, he was shivering.

He reached forwards and jabbed the computer monitor off.

The screen turned black. A static buzz lingered, and the air around Roy popped.

There was silence. Just a shaking Roy sitting there, unbreakfasted and in his pyjamas, at nearly ten in the morning.

Terrified.

38

Phil usually slept well. *Like someone with a clean conscience,* Janine would say. *Like someone who has a proper job,* Phil would say in reply – but only back when she had one too.

And now Janine didn't have a job, and she wasn't here. And Phil's family row was in the *Mail*.

After staring at the ceiling for hours, Phil got up for a glass of water. He found Dad in the front room, papers spread everywhere, like in the scene in a TV show before the patient gets sectioned.

At six-thirty, with his alarm due to go off in half an hour, Phil gave in to the inevitable.

He shuffled up in bed, opened the *Am I the Villain Here?* forum, and started to read what people thought about his family.

It turned out a lot of people thought a lot of different things. The one thing they had in common was their certainty.

@deeperthought: If you don't say anything, you are remaining silent in the face of misogyny. Silence is complicity.

Phil didn't *think* silence was complicity. But was that what a complicit person would (silently) think?

266

He wondered why he had never felt as strongly about anything as these people felt about this thing that wasn't even their fucking problem.

He had one thought about this – one consistent thought – which was *I want this to go away.*

Did Phil even have opinions? Was he a whole functioning person?

Or was he ... he picked up his phone and googled *creatures with no spines* ... Phil the invertebrate? Phil the flatfish? Phil the coral?

Phil kept scrolling.

All these comments, from all types of people. But where were all *Phil's* people? The ones who sat somewhere in the middle and said *but – context*. Phil's people were all being (complicitly?) silent. The opinions shared here were from people at either ends of the curve. The bell curve.

No – the bell*end* curve. Because it was at the ends of this curve that you found the bellends.

He gave a sour sniff of appreciation at his own joke.

He closed the forum and googled, *How do I know what I think?*

He clicked on an article headed *Psychological indeterminacy.*

In Metaphysics, *Aristotle says that if you don't think something determinate, you think nothing at all. But beliefs and ideas are individuated by their content. A lot of what we believe can be incomplete, partial, confused, or even contradictory. In Wittgenstein's view, the single-proposition-plus-individual-belief-state ...*

Yeah, he wasn't reading that. Phil didn't know who Wittgenstein was, and he didn't care what he thought – not unless he was telling Phil *exactly* what to think, in simple terms, and

Phil suspected Wittgenstein wasn't that kind of guy.

Phil sighed. Couldn't someone just tell him what to think? Of course, lots of people had done exactly that on the forum – but he meant someone *normal*. Couldn't someone normal tell him what to think *properly*?

@revolution76: This man's words are epistemic violence. He is acting from a position of pernicious ignorance.

Phil didn't need to understand everything to draw the conclusion that the more strongly people felt, and the longer the words they used to explain it, the less he'd want to go for a drink with them.

@justice0305: The wisdom of crowds can be a useful tool to overcome ill-education, but Surowiecki was clear the method has limitations if the make-up of the collective brain is flawed. In this case, we have the obvious problem of self-selection bias. Plus, there are educational flaws evident, at both the collective and individual levels. How do we spell racoon *in the UK, Janine?*

Phil felt like he was being lowered into icy water.

He threw back the duvet, got up, and knocked at the bedroom door. 'Dad?'

The grandmother clock chimed nine times downstairs.

Phil tried again. 'Dad? Are you in?' He'd never still be asleep at this time, and that comment was fresh, typed just minutes before. Had he left when Phil had been in the bathroom?

Phil tried the handle. The door didn't move.

Phil frowned. 'Dad?'

He tried the handle again. He called Dad's landline. He

listened to it ring out in stereo, from his phone and in the house.

There was no answer.

Dad couldn't have *died*, could he?

But then – a dying man didn't lock his door. A man who'd had a fall didn't either.

There was no way Phil could break into Dad's room – he'd be so affronted if he knew Phil thought he might have had a fall. Dad had a special form of disdain for anyone who acknowledged his age. The icy tone of his reply that time a young woman had offered Dad her seat on a train – *'I'm afraid you've made a clear error of judgement'*. He couldn't have been any more hostile if that poor woman had offered to take him to Dignitas.

Dad couldn't have died. After all, hadn't he just posted a passive aggressive message? He was clearly fine. Sort of.

Phil took one last look at Dad's door and, thoughtfully, got ready for work.

Ten minutes later, Phil got in his van.

Dad's bedroom blinds were still drawn. As were the front-room curtains. After nine in the morning.

Unprecedented.

Phil got his phone out of his pocket, still staring at the house. He texted the project manager of today's job – *Something came up, will be there in a bit* – and started the engine.

Five minutes later, Phil pulled up at the library and looked at his phone.

The good news was Dad was definitely not dead. There had been two more comments from *@justice0305* on the forum.

@justice0305: Not in British English it isn't. The United States of America isn't the whole world, and it would serve you well to remember that. Good day.

@justice0305: YOU IMPUDENT ROGUE! HOW DARE YOU? UNMASK YOURSELF, VILLAIN!

Phil just stared at the screen. He had to pick a side, and pick it now. Phil was a *man* – a human man. He wasn't shrimp, flatfish, *or* coral.

He strode up to the older lady in a fluffy pink jumper at the counter.

'Morning, poppet!' The woman radiated goodwill, and a cloud of floral perfume. 'How can I help?'

'Is my dad in today? Roy Frost?'

The woman's smile faltered. 'You're Phil.'

'I am.'

She took a beat and refreshed her smile. 'I'm Yvonne and I know everything about you. Your father's not rostered on today. You'll see him at the quiz later though?'

Phil jiggled his van keys in his hand. 'I'd forgotten the quiz. Do you know where he is?'

'Not a clue. I love quizzes! Do you?'

'Kind of.' There was something about this woman's friendliness that made him want to answer honestly. 'The problem is, Yvonne, I never really know what I think. Sometimes I just stay silent.'

Yvonne smiled again. 'Open-mindedness is an admirable trait. It means you're curious. And willing to learn.'

'I like that way of looking at it.' He looked at the *New in Stock!* stand. His gaze fell on the two books on the top shelf:

How to Think. The Little Book of Thinking.

'You know what?' Phil picked the books off the stand. 'I'll borrow these while I'm here.'

'How wonderful. Can I have your library card?'

With some surprise, Yvonne helped Phil register to be a library member, perhaps reviewing her assessment of *curious and willing to learn.*

Phil waved goodbye.

Maybe, if he read *How to Think* quickly, the learning might kick in right away. Time was tight, of course. But if Phil could read the book at lunchtime, process everything he knew, and decide what to do – and ideally all before the quiz tonight – that would be ideal.

But, first, he'd try Dad one more time. And keep trying him on the hour until he answered.

39

Roy stared at the blank monitor screen.

He had forgotten who the windscreen man was. He had forgotten to put the bins out. And he was still in his pyjamas at two in the afternoon.

Was this a breakdown?

The electronic chirrup of the telephone registered vaguely again. Someone *really* wanted to speak to him.

Shaking, Roy lifted his head from his hands and picked it up. 'Four nine five three oh two.'

'Dad!' There was something like relief in Phil's voice. 'Is this a good time?'

'I'm afraid not. I'm quite busy.' Roy looked down at his pyjama bottoms. 'Doing the garden. The hedges, specifically. Down the bottom end.'

'We need to talk.'

'I'm busy, Phil. I told you.'

'I'll come back home to see you.'

'NO! I'm due at . . . the dentist. Then I'm going straight from there to the quiz.' He paused. 'It's a long appointment. Will Janine be at the quiz?'

Phil didn't answer.

'If you don't want me to come to the quiz, I won't come.'

'Dad. If you want to come, come. It might help if you see each other.'

Roy felt his eyebrows inch up. 'I very much doubt that.'

'I'll see you there.'

'Phil, before you go.' Roy stood up and got out from behind the desk. 'Will you call your sister?' He pulled the urn out from behind the pile of books. 'And get a date out of her. She needs to come back to scatter your mother's ashes.'

Phil didn't reply.

'Or she needs to know we'll do it without her.' Roy took a tissue from the bedside table and wiped dust from the urn. 'Which would be very upsetting for Claudia, and would be extremely upsetting for her mother if she knew.' Roy stared at the urn. 'Which, in one way, she will.'

Roy wondered what he meant. His words were a logical fallacy, of course.

But Phil didn't pull him up on that. 'It's a long way for Claudia to come, Dad.'

'I'm aware of that, Philip.'

'See you at the quiz.'

Roy clicked the phone off. He switched on the monitor.

@intotheforest: The bigot Roy works at Brook Street Library. You'd think a man who works at the library would educate himself.

@justice0305: YOU IMPUDENT ROGUE! HOW DARE YOU? UNMASK YOURSELF, VILLAIN!

@intotheforest: Me, the villain? That's a case of projection, my friend. What do you think, fellow 'rogues'? 'Dare' we march through Brook Street library in protest?

Roy put his shaking hands on top of the urn. Surely they weren't allowed to do that? *Surely?*

There was another chirrup from the phone.

Still staring at the urn, Roy picked up the receiver.

'Dad, I said I'd let you know about a date – you didn't need to set Phil on me.' Claudia's voice was clipped. 'And he never thinks to check what the time is here – we're in bed!'

'Did he phone? I'm sorry.' Roy wasn't sorry. 'So let's get that date in.'

'I said I'd let you know.'

'You *did* say that, but you haven't.' Roy covered any emotion with brusqueness. 'Did Phil say anything about Janine?'

Claudia paused. 'What about Janine?'

Roy said nothing.

'Is something wrong with her?'

Roy wanted to say *very much so*.

'Is it cancer?'

'Nothing like that, Claud. No, Janine's being completely ridiculous about a tiny thing, and I need you to talk some sense into her when you come over.' He took a breath. 'Which will be when, please?'

There was a silence.

'Mum's gone.'

'I know she's gone, which is why I want you to help me scatter her ashes.' Had his children always treated him like an imbecile, or was this a recent development?

'I know it's important to you, Dad, but she won't know whether I'm there or not.'

Roy stared at the urn. 'You're not coming home?'

'We've just been back for the funeral.'

'*Just?* I'm sorry to burst your bubble, Claudia, but that was six months ago.'

'It's just hard to get the—'

'You both work in private equity, I gather, and have the money for a double-storey over-garage extension. I've looked at the proposed plans online. But I'm sure I can help financially, if necessary.'

'It's hard to get holiday that fits in with both schools.'

There was a long silence.

'Right.' Roy kept staring at the urn. 'Then that appears to be that.'

Claudia said nothing.

'You know, when you were little and got an earache on holiday in Menorca, your mother took you halfway across the island for those injections every day. No lazy days relaxing in the sun for your mother that year.'

The other end of the phone was silent.

'All those times she waited for you, shivering outside your netball practice.' Roy felt his hands bunch into fists. 'All those trips to A and E after you inserted marbles and pen lids into unsuitable orifices.'

'Dad.'

'We get the message. You just mustn't mind that Phil and I will do it without you.'

'Don't be like that.'

'Don't do it without you, you mean?'

'No. I mean'—Claudia's voice was quiet—'please understand.'

'I need to go. This is inconvenient timing. I'm in the middle of trimming the hedges.'

Roy hung up.

He stared at the screen.

*

@intothefore5t: Me, the villain? That's a case of projection, my friend. What do you think, fellow 'rogues'? 'Dare' we march through Brook Street library in protest?

@fisforflorence: Direct action – great idea

@chchchchanges: I'll bring my DSLR camera, they might even put a picture in the paper

@themainjohn: I'm in!

Roy sat there for the rest of the afternoon, no longer reading the comments. Just staring straight ahead, aware only of his thoughts and the ticking clock.

The clock that was ticking just for him.

Because Roy knew it now – and knew with certainty.

His time of judgement had come.

40

Janine smiled at the three interviewers. 'If I have any faults' – she shifted position to avoid the glare of sunlight from the window – 'which, of course, we all do' – she gave what she hoped was a self-effacing laugh – 'I might care a bit *too* much about my job. You know?'

Janine wondered whether she should tone it down. Whether she was saying *the only problem might be that I'm a little too excellent.*

Still, the interviewers were writing down what she said, doing that half smiling thing that told her she wasn't doing too badly. It was their fault, really, that Janine was laying it on so thick. If you set up a puppet show, you couldn't be surprised if the puppets started to dance.

Janine answered all the interviewers' questions, trying to sound perky, but not so perky she'd be a nightmare to work with.

She felt anything but perky. She had hardly slept on the slim caravan sofa bed with thin foam cushions. With every car passing or rattling bin, Katie woke up. Again and again, Janine saw her daughter's silhouette jerk up in the moonlight.

'What's that noise outside?'

'It's probably just a fox.'

The orbs of Katie's eyes glinted.

'A *harmless* fox. A friendly one.'

'It's a witch.'

'It's not a witch.'

'Why are we even here?'

'It's not for long.' Janine reached up and stroked Katie's hair. 'Go to sleep, angel. I'll protect you from witches.'

Janine watched the interviewer finish writing. The female interviewer was the only one doing any writing, but Janine tried not to notice that. Today was a day for her brain to stand down. If Janine could just *think* less, this interview would go so much better.

The interviewer with the neat beard looked up. 'And what would your last employer say about you?'

'That I had a strong sales record. And that I was passionate and ethical.' She thought of Nadia's face at the networking event. 'That I stand up for what I believe in.'

The female interviewer scribbled some more. 'Any questions for us?'

'Can you tell me a bit about the structure of the department, please?'

Janine pretended to listen. She waited for the woman to finish.

'Thanks!' Janine made her voice bright. 'That's it!'

The woman looked at the other interviewers and back. 'We're hoping to wrap this up very quickly.'

'Great!' Janine's tone contained too many exclamation marks.

The three interviewers had a conversation with their eyes.

'We want to do a final video interview tomorrow afternoon.' The interviewer with the neat beard leaned forwards. 'And we'd like to see you again.'

Janine sat up straighter. 'Amazing!'

'We can't get any time in the board members' diaries other-wise, and we don't want to hold this up. Would tomorrow be possible? Would you be available on a Saturday?'

'Absolutely.'

'Do you want to check your diary or—'

'No need.'

Back in the caravan, Janine sat at the foldaway table with her phone.

Phil hadn't called.

Janine sighed and looked out of the plastic-lined window.

The forum edits didn't seem to be working. Janine kept being accused of *changing her story*, as though she was the defendant. And she wasn't the defendant. She wasn't the prosecution either. She was – just Janine!

Janine came off the forum. She felt lighter immediately.

She took a breath and rang Phil.

He took a long time to pick up.

'Hi.' Janine made her voice soft. Grown-up soft. 'How are you?'

Phil said nothing.

'So I had my interview.'

He didn't ask.

'You don't have to go to the quiz later. But can we talk?'

'I told Dad I'd be there.'

'He's still coming?'

'*Of course* he's coming. He's never cancelled a plan in his life.'

'Right. We can talk there.'

The long tone told her Phil had hung up.

Janine sat there for a moment.

This was the calm before the storm or something. No – the other way round. The darkest hour, just before the dawn.

Because it was going to be fine. She'd get this job, and it was all going to be fine.

41

Phil pulled his wet hood down and blinked the rain away. He'd deliberately arrived at the school hall twenty minutes later than advertised, and the room was already full.

Small chairs and tables had been set up in front of the stage, arranged in groups of four. Phil walked past people standing in small clusters, holding plastic cups of what had better be alcohol.

He'd pick up the van in the morning. There was no way he'd get through tonight without booze.

He spotted Janine at the drinks table in a belted dress with a V-neck that she wore for weddings. He wondered if she'd put it on to send subliminal messages. *We used to go to fun places, Phil. We used to be happy.*

Danny Carswell fell into step beside him. 'Evening, Phil.'

Phil shoved his hands into his pockets. 'All right, Danny.' He glanced up. This was when he should bring up the stickers.

'Your girl happy to get her stickers back?' Danny asked.

Phil paused. 'Yes.'

Danny patted his back. 'I just need to catch Mrs Vaughan.'

Phil watched Danny greet the teacher. *Phil the invertebrate,* his brain whispered. *Phil the coral.*

He strode up to where Janine was pouring red wine at the drinks table.

She put down the bottle. 'Hi.'

'Hi.'

'It's good to see you.'

Phil looked at the display wall, covered with sugar-paper pictures of the planet in distress. Hand-painted earths cried rivers of tears, their continents covered with bandages and red first aid crosses. Phil studied those pictures with the quiet focus of an art critic.

'Phil. I know you're angry – so am I! And we need to talk. But can we play nice for tonight?'

Phil stared at the crying earths. 'Are you going to be nice to Dad?'

Janine took a sidestep so other parents could reach the bar table. 'Of course. But it's you I want to talk to.'

Dad entered the hall, shaking out his golf umbrella. His face was redder than usual, his hair more buoyant. He looked around uncertainly.

Phil waved. 'Dad!'

Dad took a beat. He strode up to Phil and Janine.

Janine picked up a plastic cup of red wine and one of orange juice. 'Hi, Roy.'

Dad picked up a cup of tea. 'Janine.'

Phil licked his lips and looked from one to the other. The silence extended, filling the air.

Should he say something?

Yes. Yes, he should say something.

Or maybe he shouldn't say something. Maybe this tension would just all go away on its own. Sometimes problems did go away on their own, didn't they? Or maybe Phil should call it out, right now. Maybe—

Janine gave a sniff. 'Here comes Marky.'

Marky and Molly walked up, Molly's hair swishing,

looking, as she always did, Instagram perfect. Janine had once said to Phil, 'I know I tell Katie there's no such thing as *perfect* but there definitely is if you've got Molly's genes, hours to waste in salons, and a fuckload of cash from your parents' import/export business.'

'Evening.' Marky wore baggy jeans of a deliberately odd shape that were too young for him.

'How are you doing, Mark?' Dad asked. 'How's the musical career?'

Phil felt himself frown.

Molly gave Marky an admiring look. 'He's going to be in the studio again soon!'

Dad smiled. 'How wonderful.' It didn't even sound sarcastic.

Janine made a funny twist of her mouth.

'How's the car?' Marky asked.

'It's great.' Janine gave a tight smile. 'Thank you so much again.'

'Oh, it's your car, is it, Mark?' Dad sniffed into his beaker of tea. 'That makes sense.'

'You can return it whenever, J,' Marky said. 'We've got two others.'

Janine stared at her cup of orange juice. 'I know.'

'It's very generous of you, Mark.' Dad turned to Marky. 'You're clearly a responsible man, who is always only trying to do his best for his extended family.'

Phil stared at Dad.

Marky raised his eyebrows a millimetre. 'Anyway. Are our brains fired up?'

'Dad's will be.' Phil nodded at him. 'Kings and Queens, Suez Canal – Dad knows absolutely everything.'

Dad smiled. 'Not *absolutely* everything.'

'And Latin. Anything about Latin.'

Dad tipped his head. '*Gratias tibi ago.*'

Phil turned to Janine. 'And, of course, Janine is good at music and TV. And celebrities.'

'Not just those,' Janine said quickly. 'I know the brown questions too. And green – Science and Nature. I don't always pick the pink questions.'

'You always picked the pink questions when we were together.'

'I didn't, Marky, you're remembering wrong.'

'Team quizzes are wonderful. The wisdom of crowds in action.' Dad glanced up. 'That's how it works, isn't it, Janine?'

Phil felt a prickle up the back of his neck.

Dad turned to Marky and Molly. 'The wisdom of crowds is a wonderful concept. Though Surowiecki expressly said it has limitations if the collective brain is flawed. And some individuals have blind spots when it comes to their own education.' Dad paused. 'Like spelling.'

Janine moved her lower jaw a millimetre to the side, then back.

Marky looked from Janine to Dad.

Janine glanced at Phil.

'Dad . . .' Phil gave a minute shake of the head. He stared deliberately at the pictures on the wall.

Finally, Janine held Dad's gaze. 'Spelling?'

'I'm useless at spelling,' Phil said quickly. 'Give me plastering or a broken socket any day.'

Janine crinkled her forehead. She looked like she was still trying to process what Dad meant. But . . . did that mean she *hadn't even read* the latest comments on the forum? She'd laid a bomb – yet hadn't bothered to watch it go off?

Janine indicated the beaker of wine in her hand. 'I said I'd take this over to Sal.'

Phil waited till she was out of earshot. 'Dad? Are you OK?'

'I'm quite well, thank you.'

Phil studied Dad. He looked the same, with his shirt carefully ironed, his chin recently shaved. He was sipping his tea in his usual careful way, the *V* of his top lip jutting out to check the temperature before fully committing.

But appearances lied.

Because there was something very wrong with Dad.

And Phil knew, for certain now, that Swiss neutrality was a failed strategy. Dad was not himself. Not *anything like* himself.

Phil should have intervened sooner. He *definitely* should have intervened sooner.

And he had a really bad feeling about this quiz tonight.

42

Roy sipped his tea as he watched Janine walk towards Sal. He felt a small rush of victory.

'Dad, are you OK?'

'I'm quite well, thank you.'

Roy wondered if it had been worth it. He wasn't sure. Congratulating Mark on his musical career had felt unclean.

Phil nodded over Roy's shoulder. 'Dad, there's your friend. From the library.'

Roy turned. Yvonne wore a fancy black jacket with a silver sheen, which suited her better than the usual pastel jumpers. She was in conversation with someone he didn't know. With her head thrown back in laughter, Roy could see her fillings.

'What a great lady she is,' Phil said.

'Yes,' Roy said thickly. 'She is.'

Roy waved to get her attention. Yvonne smiled faintly. She turned back to her conversation, like he was an occasional postman she vaguely knew.

No. That was how *Roy* would smile at an occasional postman he vaguely knew. Yvonne would smile brightly, coo over what the postman was wearing – *a very sharp shirt, very snazzy* – and give him a cutting from the paper that had made her think of him, and ask how his son Finn was getting on with his grade five piano.

'She works at the library.' Phil turned to Mark and Molly. 'Dad volunteers at the library. Doing his bit because he's a decent guy.'

Molly smiled.

Mark said, 'Volunteering, as a concept, is interesting.'

Roy looked at him. There was something about Mark's tone. 'Is it?'

'Ignore me,' Mark said.

'Ignore you what?' Roy said.

'I'm sure you mean well. I don't want to ruin it.'

'Ruin what?' Roy couldn't quash the sharp edge to his voice.

Mark glanced at Phil. 'It's about jobs, isn't it?' He looked back at Roy. 'If you didn't volunteer, for free, the library would have to pay someone. And there would be meaningful work for an unemployed person.'

Roy stared at him.

Mark took a sip of his drink. 'Work is freedom. And dignity.'

Phil licked his lips. 'And yet you choose not to—'

Roy cut across him. 'Are you saying I'm wrong to volunteer at the library?'

'I'm not saying anything.' Mark gave a reassuring smile. 'It's just something to think about.'

Roy felt his chest tighten. 'I think Yvonne's trying to get my attention. Excuse me.'

He walked over to where Yvonne was not trying to get his attention. 'Yvonne! That's a lovely jacket.'

She took a moment. 'Thank you.' She turned back to her friend.

Roy stared at the floor. He raised his toes, straining them upwards, forming two pressure mounds on the leather of his wet brogues.

Yvonne touched her friend on the shoulder. 'One moment.' She turned to face Roy. 'Your Phil was in the library earlier.'

Roy frowned. 'Really?'

'He borrowed two of your books from the *New in Stock!* stand.'

'My books? My *philosophy* books?'

'Did he find you?' Yvonne said pointedly.

'No, but' – Roy couldn't get a handle on any of this conversation – 'I've just seen him now.'

'Then I've passed the message on.' Yvonne turned back to her friend.

Roy stared at the back of her shiny jacket.

'And I don't know what you're talking about, pet.' Yvonne's voice was back to its usual level of warmth. 'You never need Slimming World! You're built like a racing snake!'

Roy hovered behind Yvonne while she and her friend chatted about yoghurt.

Usually, Roy had a lot to say about yoghurt.

Today, everything he knew had deserted him.

'The quiz will start in fifteen minutes.' A lady on the school stage spoke into a microphone. 'Get in your teams of four and get your pens and paper from the stage.'

Roy stepped forwards. 'Do you ladies have room for one more in your team?'

Yvonne didn't even look up. 'We've got a four already.'

Roy swallowed. 'Maybe we can have teams of five?'

Tessa appeared next to her mum. 'Teams of four. They were very clear.' She took a long drink. Her straw made an empty gurgling noise. 'No waifs and strays.'

Roy kept smiling through *waifs* and *strays*. He took a step away. 'Good luck, then.'

He looked at Phil, standing with Janine and Sal.

He tapped the tip of his golfing umbrella on the parquet floor. *Tap, tap, tap.*

He was hit by a sudden force in his chest. *Lynn.*

Lynn would have sorted things out with Janine ages ago. Lynn would have explained that Roy didn't mean any harm. She wouldn't have made any digs about spelling, or told that wastrel Mark that he was a responsible man with his family's best interests at heart. She would have dealt with all this *well.*

Roy felt his lungs shudder.

And Lynn would have known how to go up to strangers and say, *Excuse me, sir, madam, I know we've never met, but do you have room for a little one? I don't know a lot, but I can do Henry the Eighth's wives in order, and garden birds.*

Roy just stood there, lightly tapping his umbrella.

Being the last one to be picked in this school hall wasn't a new experience. And Roy didn't care about being popular – he was *seventy-eight.*

But as he stood there, tapping his umbrella tip, he felt more alone than he ever had. The sensation of not getting picked felt more powerful now than it ever had when Roy's classmates had looked past him, seventy years before.

43

Janine watched Beth's mum team talking animatedly on the other side of the school hall. She tried to catch their attention with a wave, to show she was with them in spirit, but it was hard to wave with a cup in each hand.

Maybe that was why none of them acknowledged her. She hoped so.

She walked up to Sal. 'Why don't you answer my calls?'

Sal indicated the cup of wine Janine was holding. 'Is that for me?' She tried to take the cup.

Janine kept hold of it. 'I'm having a really shit time.'

'I've been up since five thirty.' Sal's voice was firm. 'Hand me that wine.'

Janine pursed her lips. She handed the cup over.

Sal took it. 'Don't use those looks you use on Katie, I *invented* those looks. I've been busy! But I know you're under stress, so I forgive you for leaving a voicemail. This once.' Sal swigged from her plastic cup. 'Work's a binfire. The board are hinting at more redundancies, so your Scott's trying to butter me up, talking about *cross-departmental collaboration*.'

Janine sniffed. 'Looking for a new Bad News Bear.'

'He thinks I was born yesterday. Still can't believe you did all his people stuff for him.'

'I didn't do it for *him*. I did it for the people getting the bad news, because he was so bad at it. I was being altruistic. I used to be someone who did stuff for other people, Sal. And I used to be good at my job. I used to *be* someone.'

There was a pause. Sal made a pained face.

'What's that face?'

'You're being weird.'

'It's a weird time!'

'It really is.' Sal indicated across the room. 'And Roy knows about your forum post.'

'What?' Janine stared at Sal. 'Did he say something?'

'Darsh over the road says Roy got an anonymous note through the door.'

'WHAT?'

Sal shrugged.

Janine stared at her. 'But who would even do that?'

Sal sipped her wine. 'I don't even pretend to understand people.'

'Shit,' Janine said. 'So Phil knows. Roy knows. The mums at school know.' Janine caught the eye of a woman in a yellow T-shirt, who had looked at Janine for a moment too long. '*She* knows.'

'Just get more drinks down you, then you won't care.' Sal looked at the orange juice in Janine's hand. 'You're driving? The whole four hundred metres?'

'I've got to drive. Me and Katie live in Mum's caravan now.'

Sal stared at her.

Janine blew her fringe out of her eyes. 'Yeah.'

Sal glanced at Phil and back. 'For how long?'

'I can't talk now or I'll cry.' Janine gave Sal a bright smile. 'And let's not do eye contact either, hey?'

Sal nodded. She looked deliberately over Janine's shoulder. 'Can I say anything sympathetic?'

'No. Let's change the subject. I've got a second interview tomorrow.' Janine brightened her smile further for a teacher walking past. 'For a job I actually want. Apart from the fact they do interviews on a Saturday. Can I ask a favour?' Janine took a step out of the way of someone moving a table. 'Can I do the video interview from your house? I won't have time to get back to the caravan after dropping Katie off at a party.'

'Of course.'

Janine made eye contact with a thin woman. 'People are definitely looking at me, Sal.'

'I said *don't be weird*.' Sal indicated Marky and Molly with her cup. 'I take it that's Molly?'

'Yep. I hugged her earlier and Sal, *the smell*! Her *hair*. Her *skin*. She smells like when I accidentally go into a shop that's too expensive.'

'Money does smell good,' Sal said.

'I think I'd prefer it if Marky hadn't fallen on his feet. Which means I'm a crap mother.' Janine turned back to Sal. 'Which was fine before, but I've got no excuse anymore.'

'Says who?'

'Now I don't work, I'm meant to be a better mum.'

Sal frowned. 'You can't be thinking you've got to be a great mother, all of a sudden. You've got to sort your head out, Janine.'

Janine nodded. 'I know.' She tried to drink, but her cup was empty.

Phil headed in their direction.

'Phil.' Sal took a sip of her wine. 'How is Marky. Still a tool?'

'He's just made my dad feel bad about volunteering in the library.'

Sal shook her head. 'Still a tool.'

'What are you doing here anyway?' Phil asked. 'Alfie goes to high school.'

Sal shrugged. 'Janine's here. Night out, isn't it?'

A woman standing on the stage tapped a microphone. 'The quiz will start in ten minutes. Get in your teams of four and get your pens and paper from the stage.'

Sal looked from Janine to Phil. 'I reckon we could take it as a three.'

Phil stared across the room, and Janine followed his gaze.

Roy was alone, tapping the tip of his umbrella on the floor, head down.

Phil turned to look at Janine.

Janine sipped at her non-existent orange juice.

'Dad's on his own,' Phil said finally. 'I can't just leave him on his own.'

Janine pretended to drink again.

Phil made a noise of frustration. 'You're not even *trying*, are you?'

He walked away.

Janine pressed her lips together. She caught Marky's gaze. He made a V with his fingers, pointing at himself and Molly, then pointed the V at Janine and Sal. He raised his eyebrows in a question.

Janine nodded.

'*What the hell?*' Sal glared at Janine. 'Oh, for fuck's sake, they're only coming over!'

'I panicked.' Janine kept smiling in Marky's direction. 'He's done me a favour, lending me his car, so I panicked.'

Sal took a large swig of wine and shook her head. '*Christ*, Janine.'

Marky and Molly stopped in front of them.

'Hi! I never see you anymore, do I, Sal?' Marky said.

Sal raised her glass an inch in acknowledgement. 'Weird, that.'

Molly smiled at Sal. 'I'm Molly.'

Sal looked at the leather bracelets on Marky's wrist. She gave Molly a shoulder pat of sympathy. 'Sal.'

Molly turned to Marky. 'Let's get the pens.'

Sal watched them walk away. 'Marky's gonna be on my team for the next two hours?'

'I'm making bad decisions. Sorry. Everything's really getting to me.'

'I know you don't want to talk about things tonight but, whatever's going on, you've got to sort it out, mate. For me.'

'I know. I know.'

44

'Come and pick up your pens and worksheets from the stage.'

Phil was in No Man's Land.

Across the room, Dad stared at his umbrella, tapping it on the floor like he was about to launch into a minor key version of 'Singin' in The Rain'.

And Janine still wouldn't even try to fix this. She'd messed up everything – and wouldn't even *try*.

So, finally, Phil made a decision. He walked away.

He approached Dad. 'Dad. Shall we be a team?'

Dad looked up from his umbrella tapping. 'I thought you were—'

'We just need to find two more people.'

'Right, then.' Dad gave a faint smile and looked around. 'Your mother used to be good at things like this. Approaching strangers.'

Around them, people were sitting at tables in groups of four. Marky and Molly were – inexplicably – standing with Janine and Sal. Danny Carswell was walking out of the gents, adjusting his belt, looking around.

Phil turned away from Danny quickly. 'I'm sure we can enter as a two.'

They found a spare table and Dad lowered himself gently into a chair. He'd been moving more tentatively these last few days, and watching it hurt. This was the man who had taught Phil how to sprint. How to get out the last of the bath sealant. How to catch a ball, and use a tape measure.

'Phil?'

Phil closed his eyes. He took a second before opening them.

Danny Carswell stood with his hand on the back of one of Phil's chairs. 'Shall I join your team?'

'Questions twenty-eight to thirty-two. In the traditional Linnaean system of classification' – the woman on stage spoke into her microphone – 'what are the five kingdoms of living things?'

'Monera, Protista, Fungi, Plantae and Animalia.' Dad stood up. 'I need the gents.'

Danny stared after him.

Phil wrote down his best guess at the five words, hoping his spelling wasn't too bad. Being in a school hall and having Dad express disappointment in Phil's spelling was not a new experience for Phil, but not one he wanted to revisit in his forties.

Danny watched Dad leave the hall. 'Your dad's a quiz machine!'

The teams around them were still discussing the five kingdoms. At Janine's table, she was trying to grab the pen from Marky, with Marky not releasing it. Sal had got up for more wine.

'Question thirty-three.' The lady with the microphone looked down at her piece of paper. 'Under which of the five categories does coral fall?'

'Fungi.' Danny made a shape with interlinking hands. 'It's definitely fungi.'

'It's the animal one,' Phil said. 'Animalia. I read about coral just today.'

'No, fungi. It's obvious.' Danny made that shape with his hands again. 'Mushroomy.'

Phil wrote *fungi* on the answer sheet and downed his wine.

It was only a quiz. As the library book explained, there was such a thing as the marketplace of ideas and today Danny had a bigger stall, or a better goat, or something.

But how had Danny even got hold of that better goat? How did Danny get to be so confident, even when he was wrong? And how did Phil get to be more like this smug bastard?

But – no. Phil could take a position, he'd proved it. Phil had finally picked a side.

His dad's side.

The woman on the stage spoke again. 'Which author's classic book featured Jim Hawkins?'

Phil leaned forwards, but Danny was quicker.

'*Treasure Island*!'

'Big fan of the muppets, are you?' Phil asked.

'I knew it before.'

'Who wrote it, then?' Phil asked.

'That guy.' Danny waved a hand. 'You know the one.'

Dad hurried back to the table. 'Robert Louis Stevenson's *Treasure Island*, obviously.' He slid into his chair. 'But I assume we got that.'

'We'd got it,' Danny said, as Phil wrote *Robert Louis Stevenson*.

Eventually, the questions finished. Phil didn't bother to stay for the answers, he just went straight to the bar table and poured himself more wine.

'Well, that was a fun evening.' Sal appeared at his side, her voice deadpan. 'Watching Marky and Janine arguing over music, it was like their wedding day, all over again.' She held her plastic glass out for Phil to top up. He refilled it, and put the bottle down.

The woman on stage was reading out answers. 'The five kingdoms of living things are Monera, Protista, Fungi, Plantae and Animalia.'

Sal sniffed. 'Marky said it was animal, vegetable, mineral. And herbs and spices.'

'Coral is a member of the animalia kingdom.'

Dad shot up in his chair.

Phil took a big swig of wine.

Dad appeared at his side. 'Coral is *fungi*, Philip?'

'I know it's an animal, but Danny wanted to write *fungi* so I let him. It's the marketplace of ideas and Danny had a better goat.'

Sal took her cup away from her mouth. She stared at Phil.

Dad stared too. 'The marketplace of ideas?'

'Coral's an invertebrate,' Phil said.

'Yes, colonies of polyps.' Dad looked at Phil carefully. 'Phil, you know what Mark said before. About the library.'

'Whatever Marky, said, don't listen, Roy. It'll be bollocks.' Sal took a tactful step away, pretending to study crying earth pictures while she drank.

'Sal's right,' Phil said. 'Don't listen to Marky.'

'It can't be wrong to volunteer, can it?'

'No.' Phil could put this in language Dad would understand. 'Marky's idea does not deserve to sell big in the market of ideas.'

Dad frowned. 'Why do you keep talking about the marketplace of ideas?'

'I got a book out of the library.'

Dad buttoned his coat. 'But . . . why?'

'I was trying to figure something out.'

Dad finished buttoning. 'I'll see you at home.'

Phil watched Dad walk away. 'Sal, can I ask you something?'

Sal turned back from pretending to look at the wall. 'If you must.'

'I knew that one about coral.'

'That's not a question, but nice one.'

'I let Danny overrule me even though I knew he was wrong. Is that me all over, Sal?'

Sal turned away, studying the wall pictures again. 'Phil. Mate.'

Phil looked up.

'I don't know what's going on, and I don't care what anyone in your family thinks about anything.' She kept looking at the pictures. 'But if it means you're going to ask me these questions when I'm trying to have a nice drink, and I'm going to have to spend two hours listening to Marky bicker with Janine and talking about how his new car's electric, then understand your family need to sort your shit out. For me. Right now.'

Sal patted him on the shoulder and walked away.

'Hey.'

Phil turned to see Janine holding his coat. She pushed her fringe out of her eyes. 'Can I give you a lift home in Marky's fancy car?'

Phil took his coat. 'I want to walk.'

'Please.'

Phil shook his head. He strode towards the exit.

'I'll walk with you, then.' Janine hurried to keep up. 'I'll come back for the car.'

Phil said nothing.

Outside, the darkness was thick with damp. Phil flipped his hood over his head.

Janine did the same.

They walked in silence. Phil tucked his chin in further to keep the rain from his face.

'Why are you being like this?' Janine's voice was small.

'You left me no choice.' Phil struggled to keep his voice low as they walked past another set of parents. 'The way you've treated him.'

'So you've finally chosen a side.'

'You were the one who *made it* about sides. Dad isn't the one who put this online. And now he's having to read what people are saying about him. Have you read what people are saying about him?'

Janine scratched her neck hard. 'He wasn't meant to read it. You weren't meant to either. That was meant to be just for me. It was private!'

Phil shook his head in disbelief.

'It was *for me*,' she repeated.

'You haven't even been reading it!'

She reached for his arm, but he shook her off. The bottom of Janine's dress was soaking, the bare skin on her legs speckled with mud.

'Roy shouldn't have known. He *wouldn't* have known except—'

Phil stopped walking. 'Except?'

He turned to look at her.

Despite her hood, the rain had plastered her fringe to her

forehead. 'Sal said someone put an anonymous note through his door.'

Phil just stared at her. 'You see what you started?'

'*He* started it, Phil!'

Phil looked into her eyes. Her black make-up had smudged around her lower eyelid. He used to look at that wonky-lovely face and feel warm. Right now, he felt – disgust.

'I don't want this. Leave me alone.'

Phil started walking again, past the chip van at the park. He felt Janine hurrying next to him. They didn't speak for a long time.

They turned into Dad's road. Janine looked up. 'Phil—'

'I'm too tired for this. All of this.'

'I get it. It's raw.' There was a waver in Janine's voice. 'Let's talk tomorrow.'

'No.'

They reached Dad's house. Phil pulled his keys out of his pocket.

Janine tugged on his sleeve.

He stopped. He turned to face her.

Raindrops ran down Janine's face and dripped from her chin. 'Please don't be like this.'

Phil stared at the faint glow from the blinds of Dad's bedroom window. 'I'm so tired, Janine. It's enough.'

Janine wiped the rain from her chin. 'What does that mean?'

'It's not right anymore. *We're* not right. This doesn't work any more.'

Her black-smudged eyes were wide with sadness. 'No. Please.'

'We'll sort details out later.' Phil stared at the ground. 'Don't follow me in. I'm putting the chain on.'

'Phil!'

Phil let himself into the house and slammed the door, deliberately not turning back to see the figure standing motionless in the pouring rain.

Saturday

Am I the Villain Here? Post 35915

CantBeArsed8: Am I the villain here for being furious my partner's father changed my daughter's pirate party into a princess party?

24.6K votes, 1 day left

You're the villain here: 37%
Not the villain here: 63%

Latest reply:

@playnice: This is the grooming behaviour of a paedophile. Keep your kid safe. Cut this dangerous man out of your life and report him to the police. Safe not sorry.

45

For seventy-eight years, Roy had thought volunteering was a good thing. Right up to switching off his bedside light the night before, Roy still thought volunteering was a good thing.

Mark was an idling ne'er-do-well. He might have added an extra *y* to his name, but he didn't know the first thing about right and wrong. Because how could volunteering not be a good thing?

But by 4 a.m. the darkness had done its nighttime shape-shifting, and Roy's thoughts had started to mist and swoop. So Roy switched on the monitor and the Anglepoise and put *volunteering* into the search engine.

Instantly, he was confronted with crowds of smiling faces: people digging gardens and painting refuges, and running. Lots of running.

Roy read comments of gratitude – *Thanks for generously giving up your time!* – and started to feel a bit better. So much better, that he kept reading – partly for reassurance, and partly for good sample sizing. He wanted to have read a statistically significant portion of the internet before he could tell Marky to take a running jump.

Roy put *volunteering good or bad?* into the search engine.

The ethics of job substitution.

Roy clicked on the first article. Instantly, the tone was different. There were no more bright colours or smiling faces and *thanks for your time!*s anymore.

Volunteering decreases the number of roles available – roles unemployed people would value. To compound the problem, well-meaning volunteers doing unpaid work affects free market forces, devaluing the work by performing it for nil reward. Any staff the volunteers work alongside, the skilled, salaried workers, get paid less as a result.

Taking meaningful jobs, putting some people out of work, while ensuring others get paid as little as possible – volunteers may feel altruistic, but they are the unwitting agents of capitalism at its most brutal.

Roy put his head in his hands. It stayed there for a long time.

Eventually, he reached for the mouse. He scrolled through comment after comment on the forum, barely taking them in. Until one word registered.

Paedophile.

@playnice: This is the grooming behaviour of a paedophile. Keep your kid safe. Cut this dangerous man out of your life and report him to the police. Safe not sorry.

Roy stared. And stared.

A PAEDOPHILE? He, Roy – ex-judge, first aider, life-time friend of the National Trust – a PAEDOPHILE?

He pushed himself to his feet.

There was a gentle knock on the door. 'Bye, Dad!' Phil didn't try to come in. 'I'm off to work.'

Roy stared at the screen. The comment was still there.

'Dad?'

He made himself shout, 'Bye!'

Roy sat down. He was late for the library. But he couldn't not answer *this*, could he?

He typed his reply stiffly, his pecking fingers bone-straight with injustice.

I am Roy, the subject of this post, and I can assure you I am absolutely NOT a paedophile!

He picked up the phone. He punched in the number for the library and waited.

When there was no answer, Roy replaced the receiver. He blinked at the screen.

@playnice: You are not him. And you are not called Roy.

Roy roared.

He glanced at the clock – still late – and typed:

I have no need to argue with you. As Kipling wrote:
If neither foes nor loving friends can hurt you,
If all men count with you, but none too much...
you'll be a man, my son!

The reply came instantly.

@playnice: Kipling was a colonialist and an anti–Semite.

Roy was so very, very late.

Janine's lost her mind. Never mind the racoon play – she's not been right in the head since the redundancy. I am NOT a paedophile! What is wrong with you people on the internet? What is wrong with you all?

He shook his head. How could he make these people understand?

He created a new post.

Am I the villain here to mind that my daughter-in-law, Janine Pierce, has taken private family interactions and posted them on the Am I the Villain Here? *website? Meaning that I, Roy Frost, ex-magistrate and an upstanding member of the local community, am now accused of being a paedophile in the internet kangaroo court of public opinion? WHO IS THE REAL VIL-LAIN HERE, JANINE?*

Breathing heavily, Roy clicked *Post*.

Forty-five minutes later, Roy rushed up to Tessa and Yvonne at the library counter.

Yvonne smiled at a lady walking past. 'Yes, treasure, can I help?'

Roy put his coat on the rack. 'I'm sorry I'm late.' He paused. 'There's something very wrong with the people on the internet.'

Tessa licked her lips. 'And that's the best you can do.'

Roy shook his head. 'It's complicated.'

'You'll be pleased to know we've coped without you. We always cope without you.'

'That's as it is.' Roy took a deep breath. 'Tessa, have you heard of the term job substitution?'

'I've heard of the word *late*.'

'Because it means—'

'My patience with your monologues wears thin at the best of times, Roy. I have no interest in learning whatever you want to teach me today.'

'No, I . . .' Roy held up his hand and collected his thoughts. 'I'm handing in my letter of resignation. I'm afraid I won't be working here anymore.' He paused. 'I haven't actually written the letter. I got distracted.'

Tessa's face was expressionless.

'Also, you need to pay someone to do my job.'

Tessa raised her eyebrows a fraction.

'And pay them a decent wage,' Roy said. 'A *living* wage.'

'I will certainly not pay someone to do your job, and do you know why?' Tessa held his gaze. 'Because you are very, very slow. It is only because Mum follows you around that you get anything done at all. Six months you've been here, and you can't even work the printers!'

Roy turned to Yvonne, who was standing by the shelf of reservations. 'Yvonne, I need to explain. If you just . . .'

Yvonne picked up some books from the returns trolley and carried them into Personal Development.

'We've managed without you this morning.' The disdain in Tessa's gaze made Roy crunch his toes in his shoes. 'I'm sure we can cope without you for the rest of today.'

Roy vaguely registered noises outside the library entrance.

Wood clacking against wood, like someone was gathering a collection of skittles.

'I'll work whatever notice you want. I'll put it in writing.'

'There's really no need.'

A voice travelled through the front doors. 'Everyone got their sea legs?'

'Then I shall take my leave.' Roy clicked his heels together like Dorothy's red slippers. 'But I will work my remaining shifts. A Frost meets his commitments.'

'Isn't that *Game of Thrones*?' Tessa stared at Roy. 'You know that family were the baddies?'

'When I come in on Friday, I'll do admin. I can stay in the back office all day. In the dark.'

He looked from Tessa to Yvonne, waiting for one of them to say something.

'Goodbye, Tessa.' He gave a small nod. 'Goodbye, Yvonne.'

When neither answered, he turned to leave.

'Batten down the hatches!' The voice outside the library was a rallying cry. 'Buccaneers – assemble!'

Roy looked towards the double doors.

With yells and hoots, people rushed in.

The library burst into life.

There were placards and banners. Eyepatches, bandanas and tricorn hats. Skull-and-crossbones painted on every placard and T-shirt. Cutlasses made from cardboard and tinfoil, held aloft in triumph.

Yvonne's voice was soft with wonder. 'The library's being taken by *pirates*?'

There must have been twelve pirates, with more coming through the doors. Two of the pirates strode back and forth, arm in arm, chanting the words on their placards.

'Why can't girls get to be pirates too?
Why can't girls get to be pirates too?'

One pirate with a camera and a painted-on wooden leg crouched down, clicking at the scene through his telephoto lens.

One pirate was less active than the others, skulking at the back, wearing a plastic mask made up of a tricorn hat and eyepatch.

Someone with a cutlass ran in Roy's direction. Roy stumbled back.

'Hoist the Jolly Roger, me hearties!' The man jumped onto the wheeled library step, springing from it onto Tessa's counter. He appeared to be wearing a chef's white jacket and checked trousers under the skull and crossbones accessories. 'Pull up the rigging!'

'What on earth are you doing?' Tessa strode towards him. 'GET OFF MY COUNTER!'

'There's a lily-livered scurvy dog here' – the pirate jumped down as Tessa approached – 'who needs a-keelhauling.'

'I don't know what that means!' Tessa roared.

The chef-pirate let his cutlass droop. 'Don't you believe in equality for girls?'

'What a ridiculous thing to – GET AWAY FROM MY AUDIOBOOKS! Why on God's earth are you protesting *here?*'

Roy swallowed. He took a step backwards, towards the door.

'We had to protest' – the chef-pirate gave a wave of his cutlass – 'in this very library.'

'But WHY?' Tessa roared.

Roy took another step back.

'Because there's an old chauvinist who works here. One who's caused a stir online.'

Tessa blinked at the chef-pirate.

Slowly, she turned to look at Roy.

Yvonne turned to look at Roy.

'Someone called Roy.' The chef-pirate put one hand to his forehead, as though checking the horizon. 'Is he here?'

There was a hush. The scene finally fell library-quiet.

The chef-pirate followed Tessa and Yvonne's gazes. 'Is this the landlubber?'

A camera flashed in Roy's face.

'Pirates not princesses!' A red-faced woman waved a placard at him. 'Pirates not princesses!'

Roy rubbed his eyes. 'To summarise,' he turned to Tessa, 'I will get my resignation letter to you promptly.'

Roy grabbed his coat and walked home, as fast as he could.

He crossed the high street, his despair turning to outrage. He circled the roundabout, his outrage turning to fury. As he walked home, his thoughts shrank to a single, burning pinprick.

This was one person's fault.

One person. One person, who had destroyed his family, his job, his relationships, his sleep. His sanity. His life. Janine.

46

That morning, Janine drove Katie to a classmate's ceramics party. 'You know, if you don't feel like telling your dad you're staying in a caravan, that's fine.'

She risked a glance in the rear-view mirror. She looked quickly away. Katie's eye contact had a laser effect, penetrating Janine's very soul.

Damn it. 'No.' Janine looked back at the road. 'Ignore me.'

They drove a bit further.

When finally she spoke, Katie's voice was quiet. 'You said there was nothing wrong with the caravan.'

'I know I did, and there isn't. Which is why I'm telling your father today.'

After dropping Katie off at the ceramics shop, Janine pulled up at a traffic light. She pushed the buttons on the car's system to call Marky.

He sounded like he was walking. 'Hi.'

'So, I've just dropped Katie off at the ceramics party.'

'Ceramics is a good choice. We should do that for Katie next year.'

Janine tapped her hand against the steering wheel. 'It's a little out of budget.'

'Obviously I'll pay, Janine. I'm going to do her parties from now on.' Marky sighed. 'I'm going to start making a stand.'

'No stands needed. None at all.' Janine gave the left indicator a hard flick. 'I've got a final interview this morning and I'm the only candidate they've put forward. Everything will change soon.' She pulled up over Sal's drive. 'I'll come in when I drop Katie off later. I have some stuff I have to discuss.'

'Please God tell me you're moving out of that awful man's house.'

'I can't talk now.' Janine tried to pull a handbrake that didn't exist. She looked down and pressed the button. 'I've got that interview.'

Sal had cleared her hallway desk of junk, so all that was left was her computer and a lamp.

Janine put her handbag on the desk. 'Thanks so much for this.'

Sal nodded. 'No problem.' Her voice sounded clipped.

Janine glanced at her. 'Something up?'

Sal paused. 'We can talk after.'

'Is that a yes?'

'After. Good luck.'

Sal took her laptop upstairs, and Janine set up her meeting. She adjusted the monitor, and used her phone's camera as a mirror. She had nothing in her teeth.

Janine put her phone down and her hands neatly in her lap. She stared at the screen.

Please wait for your host to start the meeting.

It was *essential* Janine didn't panic. Or remember she hadn't slept. Or remember that Phil was leaving her, or that she was living in a caravan on her mum's drive.

The message on the screen changed.

Just a moment.

Three men in individual boxes appeared on the screen. Janine sat up straighter, and summoned her most trustworthy smile.

Forty-five minutes in, the interview was going surprisingly well. Even when Sal started doing a slow commando crawl under the desk to unplug a phone charger, it hadn't thrown Janine off her game.

'...which means I'm available immediately.' Janine leaned forwards. 'Not that I've been out of work for long. The redundancy was very recent.'

The doorbell rang. Janine kept smiling.

The procurement director looked up. 'Do you need to—'

'No.'

'And for salary expectations' – the procurement director pushed up his Penfold glasses – 'can you give us an indication of what you're looking for?'

The doorbell rang again.

The procurement director looked up.

'Please ignore it,' Janine said.

The bell rang again.

'Honestly, it'll just be Jim – the postman. He can deliver tomorrow. It's fine.'

The bell rang again. And stayed ringing continuously.

Janine glanced at the door. 'He isn't usually this persistent.'

The procurement director coughed. 'Do you want to answer quickly so we can carry on?'

'Of course.'

Janine stood up. She looked at the shape outlined through the textured glass pane. It was the top of someone's head, someone shorter than the postman, with white hair, not brown. The man's head was moving in what looked like agitation, a piece of hair floating above his crown.

Janine paused.

She glanced behind. The interviewers were watching. Waiting.

She opened the door.

'JANINE!' A speck of Roy's spittle hit her cheek. 'I saw your borrowed car outside the house, you bullying shrew! You've destroyed my life!'

'No, Roy – *please*! Not now.' She screwed up her eyes. 'Please not—'

'Not now? NOT NOW?' He took a step forwards in his anorak, his unironed shirt visible through the zip. 'Pray tell, my busy *busy* Janine, when would be the most convenient time?' Another fleck of spittle hit Janine's cheek. 'You put our family's dirty washing all over the internet and now you're saying *I need to make an appointment*?'

In tiny movements, Janine inched the door backwards towards the frame.

He jammed a brogue in the doorway. 'Oh no you don't.'

He banged the door wide open.

'I'm in an interview, Roy.' Janine's voice was a whisper.

'And I'm on the moon, eating pieces of cheese.'

Something caught Janine's attention at the top of the stairs – Sal, taking her headphones off, frozen. It took a lot to make Sal look horrified. But this had done it.

'It's onscreen, Roy. The people are—'

'Yum, yum.' Roy put one hand to his mouth. 'Yummy, yum, yum.' He pretend-gnawed at the invisible cheese and dropped his hand. 'If you're going to ruin someone's life, you can at least learn to spell. *Racoon* has one *c* in British English, Janine. *One c.*'

'Roy, please. *Please.*' Janine's whisper was barely audible. 'The interviewers are on the screen.'

'What screen?'

Janine made a tiny arm movement.

Roy looked. Slowly, his mouth closed. The wisp of hair floated back into position.

Behind Janine, the screen was silent.

Roy looked at Janine. He looked back to the interviewers.

He gave a curt nod. 'Gentlemen.' He gave a dramatic turn, and strode down the path.

Janine shut the door with a soft click. She pressed her face up to the glass pane, feeling the cold against her cheek. She closed her eyes.

The room was silent.

She turned and walked back slowly to the desk. She sat down, and carefully adjusted her position.

She pushed her fringe out of her eyes. 'I'm sorry about that.' She smiled directly into the lens. 'My father-in-law isn't well.'

She kept her gaze firmly on the computer's camera, trying not to see the faces of the people in the boxes beneath.

She waited. She kept smiling. And smiling. And smiling.

Finally, the procurement director looked up. 'I think we've got everything we need here.'

'Yes.' Janine nodded. 'Yes, I expect you probably have.'

47

It took Roy three tries to get his keys into the front door.

Phil would never forgive him for this. How could he?

Roy needed a distraction. Anything.

A shepherd's pie.

He closed the door with shaking hands. He'd make a shepherd's pie.

Twenty minutes later he was peeling carrots, still trying to control his breathing.

There was a knock at the door.

He stopped peeling.

There was another knock at the door.

The squeak of the letterbox opening. 'Roy?'

Roy froze.

'Roy?' Janine said again.

Roy didn't move.

The letterbox closed with a snap.

With trembling hands, Roy jaggedly peeled another strip from the carrot.

When he'd finished the pie, Roy sat in his armchair and picked up the nearest book: *Thought Experiments: Philosophical Puzzles for Young and Old.*

He'd borrowed the book to read with Katie, of course.

In his mind's eye, Roy saw the flash of a plastic cutlass.

He made himself look at the book. He flicked past The Trolley Problem and The Big Man on the Bridge. He reached The Fish That Asks You to Eat It.

Roy stared at the illustration of a cartoon fish handing a knife and fork to a confused man. The fish stood like a human, walking on its tail. A fishtail transformed into feet, like in *The Little Mermaid*. The film that Janine said contained *dangerous messages*.

Roy slammed the book shut. Wasn't there anything he could do that wouldn't remind him of the disaster he'd made of his life?

He thought.

The kitchen roll dispenser was squeaking. He'd noticed that this morning.

Roy jumped up and grabbed his Phillips screwdriver from the window ledge. He went to work, unscrewing the bolts.

At the sound of the key in the lock, Roy stopped.

Phil walked into the room. 'Afternoon.' He placed his keys by the toaster. 'Can't believe we didn't win the quiz.'

Roy coughed. 'It was the questions about modern music. And coral.' He stayed bent over the dispenser and tried to sound casual. 'Have you spoken to Janine today?'

There was a long silence. Roy stared at the dispenser.

'I might as well tell you. Janine isn't coming back. Me and her isn't working.'

Roy straightened up. 'What?'

Phil said nothing.

Roy put the screwdriver down. 'For good?'

Phil didn't answer immediately. 'It's for the best. And I'm going to move out of here for a while. Clear my head.'

Roy stared at the kitchen roll dispenser. 'Where will you go?'

'The pub's got availability. I'll pack up my stuff now.'

Roy stared at him. 'I'll give you a hand.'

'Thanks, Dad.' Phil patted his arm. 'But there's no need.'

Roy paced the front room as Phil packed his things upstairs.

Eventually, he came into the front room. 'I'm off, then.'

Roy couldn't bring himself to make eye contact. 'Take care.'

The door slammed. Roy looked around, desperate for anything to take his mind off the mess he'd made of everything.

A pile under the side table caught his eye.

Roy pulled out one of his *Wheels of Justice* diaries.

After an hour of reading, Roy sat back on his heels, conscious of the intense stretch in his thighs, notes and exercise books spread all over the front-room carpet.

He didn't remember.

Whoever the windscreen man was, he was right: Roy was fallible. The evidence had been piling up for a while, piece by piece. Today, that pile had toppled.

Roy was now a liability. A man who got things wrong. He'd been falsely confident of his own ability to navigate the world – it had only been Lynn keeping him safe this whole time.

'What Roy meant was that he thinks you look very smart.'

'What Roy meant was thank you for such a lovely gift.'

'What Roy meant was that he doesn't agree with your logic, but he respects your decision and he's sure the new business will work out brilliantly.'

It had only taken six months of Lynn's absence for Roy

to ruin his family – and to destroy the only real long-term relationship his son had ever had.

Roy pictured Katie in her racoon outfit, dancing sideways across the stage, her tail trailing after her. He saw her eyes wide with excitement, squealing at Roy's Captain Hook *arr*-voice when he read her *Peter Pan*.

To become a grandfather-by-proxy, after all this time, had been a gift. He barely knew his Singapore grandchildren.

Roy made a gruff noise in the back of his throat. He collected his notes and reboxed them. He started ironing as his next distraction.

But he was only two minutes in when pain flared in his hand. He'd caught it with steam from the iron's starboard bow.

Roy placed the iron down on its heel. 'Damnation!'

He put the fat of his hand in his mouth and sucked it.

He headed to the bathroom and opened the first aid cupboard, pushing past bandages and boxes of plasters and paracetamol.

Roy took the tube of antiseptic cream and sat on the side of the bath. He unscrewed the cap and took in the sweet, familiar smell. A smell that, until now, Roy didn't even know he knew. One that smelled so completely of Lynn.

Roy found his mouth opening in pain.

He pushed himself forwards from the side of the bath. He dropped onto his knees on the hard vinyl floor and sobbed, wedging his mouth into his shirt sleeve, his chest shuddering as he finally let himself understand the scale of everything he'd lost.

48

Janine stared at the screen.

Meeting ended.

'Fuck!' She pushed her fringe out of her eyes, leaving her hand pushing hard against her forehead. 'Fuck. Fuck, fuck, fuck!'

Sal hurried down the stairs.

Janine looked up. 'Is there any way this could possibly be OK?'

Sal pressed her lips together. She patted Janine's shoulder.

Janine's forehead was clammy against her palm. 'Another Classic Janine anecdote. One for the grandkids. How long before I'm telling this one in the pub, do you think? How long till it'll be funny?'

Sal just stared at her.

'Roy's proper lost it, hasn't he?' Janine said.

Sal nodded.

'Can I stay here and hide?'

'As long as you like,' Sal said.

'One second.' Janine picked up her phone and opened her forum thread. 'This ends now.' She didn't look at the sea of messages, just clicked *reply*.

Pirates – sheath your cutlasses. It's a storm in a teacup. My father-in-law is a good man and there is no need for this circus. He made one mistake and does not deserve to be dragged. I made a mistake too, by posting about this online. I don't know what I was thinking. If you're reading this, Roy, this is my formal, sincere, public apology.

Janine looked up at Sal. 'You wanted to talk about something.'

Sal shook her head. 'Not now.'

'Really?'

Sal shook her head.

'So. A cup of tea, I reckon.' Janine stood up. 'Then I probably need to go next door.'

Janine knocked on Roy's front door.

The door's shiny black paintwork was almost perfectly clean, with just a trace of Blu-tack left over from the party decorations.

There was no answer. She knocked again.

The Blu-tack looked so wrong on Roy's pristine door. With a fingernail, Janine scratched it away, and flicked the scraping into the hedge.

She crouched down and pushed the letterbox open. The hard brushes of the letterbox spiked her fingers.

She could see the hallway table, covered in photographs, but no movement. 'Roy?'

Janine waited.

'Roy?'

She let the letterbox door flap shut.

*

Janine gave up. She drove to the ceramics shop to pick up Katie.

Janine walked up to the group of mums, too tired to care whether she was ostracised.

She looked from Beth to Cass. To Megan. To the woman with the cheek filler. 'OK, let's get it all out there while I'm having the worst week in the world. I know you all know about the forum. And Twitter. And the *Mail*.' Janine wrapped her arms round herself in a hug. 'It's fine that everyone knows.' She paused. 'You do *know*, right?'

Beth looked at Cass. Cass looked at Megan. Megan rocked her shih tzu pram, and looked at the woman with the eyelashes.

As one, they nodded.

'And you've been talking about it?'

They all nodded again.

'Appreciate it. It's a relief to know I'm not paranoid.' Janine tapped the side of her head. 'You start to doubt yourself, you know?' She gave a tight laugh. 'So anything you want to know, just ask me. I don't care anymore. You can have all the gossip, direct from the horse's mouth. Just please let Katie keep going to parties, OK? It's not her fault I'm her mum. I mean, she's suffering enough – surely?'

There was a tinkle of a bell. Janine turned and hurried back to the car.

Kids poured out of the ceramics shop, pulling on coats, smiling at parents. All cradled hand-painted mugs sellotaped in bubblewrap, holding their prizes like the most precious antiques.

Katie saw Janine and scooted up. They got in the car.

'Did you have fun?' Janine asked.

'We painted our grown-ups on mugs.' Katie patted her

bubble-wrapped parcel. 'Then a lady put our mugs in the oven, and then it was just like a normal party.'

Janine smiled. 'Can I see?'

Katie picked carefully at the Sellotaped bubble wrap. She held up a black mug, her cheeks flushed with pride.

Janine took it. She took in two hand-painted figures with sinister Jokers' smiles.

The first figure held a guitar, his eyes blacked out with sunglasses. Beneath, an adult had written *Marky is a musician*.

'Nice.' Janine gave an admiring nod. 'Good work with the fretboard. Good tuning pegs.' She mimed twisting a peg. 'And your father does wear sunglasses in the dark, so that's a nice detail, Katie.'

Janine turned the mug to look at the figure on the other side. This figure wore a triangular red dress, an apron and high heels. She held something that looked like a big grey hairdryer. *Janine is a housewife.*

Katie tapped it. 'The lady in the shop helped me with the word.'

Janine glanced at the shop. 'And what is it I'm holding?'

Katie's face hardened in outrage. 'A *hoover*!'

Janine stared at the picture. 'It's obvious now you say it.'

She glanced up at the shop again. She flicked her seatbelt off – and stopped.

She clipped her seatbelt back in. 'Come on.' She handed the mug back. 'Wrap it back up, and you can give it to your dad as a present. He'll love it.' She smiled at Katie. 'Especially the guitar.'

Janine sat in Marky's landscaped garden, listening to the trickling of the water feature. At the other end of the garden, Molly was pushing Katie on the swing.

Marky looked up from Katie's musician/housewife mug. He'd liked it just as much as Janine knew he would. 'You can't be living in your mum's caravan.'

'We're not living there. It's just for a holiday.'

'A holiday on your mum's drive?'

'You wanted me to move out of Roy's, didn't you? I listened.'

'How long for?'

Janine brushed dandelion pollen from her jeans.

'If you get that job from this morning, then . . .'

Janine took a second. She nodded hard. 'Exactly.'

'It still isn't OK. You must see it isn't OK.' Marky glanced up, checking Katie still couldn't hear. 'I can't have Katie living in a caravan when I've got all this space.'

'It's a holiday. Just a stopgap. Katie loves it. Turning the furniture into beds every night. It's an adventure.'

'Would Katie say it was an adventure if I asked her?'

Janine glanced at the herb garden. Marky had a *herb garden*. 'You can never predict what any kid will say on a particular day, so—'

'No, Janine.' Marky thumped the mug down on the latticed iron table. 'I know when we first split up, I didn't think I could manage to do much—'

'You said you couldn't commit to overnights, because what if you skipped a gig and missed the A and R guy who was going to make your career?'

Marky stared across the garden, at Katie on the swing. 'I just needed to get sorted. And I did.'

'I needed to get sorted too. But Katie wasn't an optional extra for getting sorted. Not to me. She was the core I built my life around.'

'You know it's different now.' Marky indicated around him

with his arm. 'Look what we can offer her. We've got fields at the back. We've got swings, Janine.'

Janine shook her head.

'We need to change the arrangements,' Marky said.

'No, we don't.' She got up. 'And we've got somewhere to be.'

49

Roy stopped sobbing. He got up from the bathroom floor and washed his face.

Half an hour later he walked into town, cradling the urn in a boxy cardboard bag. Under his smart coat of charcoal wool, he wore his best suit and his crispest white shirt. Gently, he massaged the burn on his hand.

If Claudia wasn't going to come back, and Phil wasn't going to speak to him again, there was no reason to delay any longer.

Roy might have alienated his whole family. He might have alienated Yvonne. But he still had one friend he could rely on.

Roy made his voice authoritative. 'Where's his coat?' This was how you dealt with obstructive forces – by giving clear, unequivocal direction.

'I don't think it's wise,' the security guard said. Who was actually the nurse Elena.

Roy placed his feet wider apart. 'I'm breaking him out for the day. Fresh sea air will do him the world of good.'

Joseph shuffled on the spot, looking at the floor.

Elena stared at Roy. 'He doesn't understand.'

'Does he even *have* a coat?' Roy asked. 'Or have you taken that, as well as his liberty?'

Silently, the nurse Angelo moved to stand next to Elena.

Roy put the bag down. 'Joseph can have my coat.' He slipped his arms out of his sleeves. 'He'll like it when he gets there.' Roy rested the coat onto Joseph's shoulders. 'Give me a hand here, old man.' He lifted one of Joseph's arms and tried to twist it into the sleeve. 'Make yourself a bit floppier.'

Joseph gave a quiet moo.

Roy wrestled with the arm and the sleeve. 'Think blancmange. Think those inflatable men at car dealerships.'

'You're upsetting him,' Elena said.

'How can I possibly be upsetting him?' Roy tried to wedge the arm into the sleeve. 'We're going to St Anne's! He loves the beach.'

Did Joseph like the beach? Roy couldn't remember. He managed to get one arm into a sleeve and lifted the other. 'One to go.'

He glanced up.

Joseph's eyes were watery. His mouth moved in slow agitation.

Roy let his grip slacken.

'You're upsetting him,' Elena said slowly. 'Please.'

Roy took a step closer to Joseph. He whispered. 'Come on, man!'

Joseph looked past Roy. With one coat sleeve on and one sleeve off, he shuffled towards his usual sofa.

Elena put her arm around Joseph. Roy watched, helpless, as she eased Joseph out of the coat.

'That's better, isn't it?' Elena's voice was calm.

She turned to Roy. 'I will have to phone his daughter, I'm afraid.' She folded the coat and put it over a chair arm. 'We'll have to discuss this visit.'

Elena took Joseph's hand and helped him sit down. She pulled a Touch and Feel book from the table.

Elena opened the book. 'See this bee?' She tugged a pop-out wing. 'Is this a nice bee?'

Joseph gripped the wing, crinkling it slowly between his fingers. He hunched further over the book. Softly, he crinkled the wing again.

Roy looked at the scuffed lino floor. At his waterproof hiking shoes, that he'd cleaned especially.

Elena turned a page. 'Here's a centipede! Look at all these feet!' She jiggled the book; a plastic foot on a rope jiggled too. 'Gosh!'

Joseph leaned forwards. He reached for the roped foot.

Angelo was also watching. 'He's calmer now.'

Roy pulled his own coat on, still not taking his gaze from Joseph.

Joseph held the roped foot, his hand unmoving.

'Goodbye, Angelo.' Roy picked up his bag of ashes. He signed himself out of the visitor's book and strode into the warm lunchtime air.

And he set off for the coach station, alone.

Roy sat on the coach, the urn in its cardboard bag on the seat next to him, watching the cars speed by on the motorway below.

A young woman holding a bag of sweets indicated the urn's seat. 'Excuse me! Can I sit there?'

Roy lifted the bag. 'Of course.' He put the ashes on the floor.

'My nephew has spilt a can of Fanta over our seats.' The woman sat down. 'I warned Jinny he was too excited, but she never listens.'

'That's probably why they have these.' Roy indicated the sign on the seat back. *No eating or drinking.*

The woman laughed. 'He can barely sit still – he's buzzing. Kids love the beach, don't they? Even in this weather. But we can't wait for sunshine in this country, can we?' The woman held out her bag of sweets. 'Skittle?'

The aroma of manufactured fruit filled the air.

Roy wrinkled his nose. 'Thanks, but I don't.'

'Don't . . . what?'

'Don't . . . skittle. I only eat real food.'

The woman raised her eyebrows in amusement. 'Are Skittles not real food?'

'They are certainly not.'

'How about M and Ms?'

Roy shook his head. He stared straight ahead.

'What about the ones with the peanut in?'

Roy shook his head again.

'More for me, then.' She threw some skittles into her mouth. 'I'm addicted.'

Roy glanced at the bag, which was too big for one person.

'I'm worst at about nine o'clock. In front of the telly.' She munched audibly, the shells cracking between her teeth. 'Sometimes it's Skittles, sometimes it's other things.' The woman wiggled back into her seat. 'Skittles are my favourite *sweet* sweets, I think. Are they?' She put her head to one side. 'Yes, they are. Now with chocolate sweets, it's harder to pick a favourite. It depends how many you're planning to eat. Some can be delicious at first, but get claggy if you have too many. And some . . .'

Roy tuned out. He should have waited until he had his car again, so he could give this occasion the dignity it deserved. Sitting here now, Lynn's urn on the floor, with this woman crunching sweets and talking nonsense, felt wrong.

Roy glanced down at the urn.

Except . . . maybe that wasn't true.

Because Lynn probably wouldn't have minded this conversation. She definitely would have shared some of the sweets. Lynn had always liked coach journeys. *'It feels like a lovely adventure. And you never know who you might meet!'*

'If you don't eat sweets, what do you snack on?' The woman kept munching. 'Don't tell me you're one of those people who eats *fruit*?'

Roy couldn't let that go. 'I do eat fruit. But only as a dessert.' He turned to look at her. 'I don't eat between meals.'

The woman widened her eyes. 'Never?'

'Never.'

The woman stared at him. 'You're superhuman!'

'There's no super about it. It's about discipline.'

'But what do you eat?'

'Well. I usually start the day with fish. Or eggs. You need a protein base. Then, of course, you have to make sure you get your roughage and your greens.'

To his surprise, Roy found himself talking to this woman for the rest of the journey.

The coach pulled up in St Anne's. The door opened with a pressurised *shush*.

Roy got off the coach and raised the collar of his coat against the wind. He waited for all the other passengers to disperse and headed towards the beach.

He took a long, deliberate breath, taking in the unmistakeable smell of seaweed and wet sand.

Lynn had loved it here.

In his mind's eye, Roy pictured toddler-sized Phil and

Claudia on this sand, holding spades and smiling up at him, while Roy hammered in the windbreak.

Overhead, seagulls cawed. The sandy breeze stung his cheeks as he watched the birds dip and soar.

Lynn had always fed seagulls, though Roy told her they were vermin. On one holiday in Aberdyfi, Lynn had fed a seagull pieces of sandwich from their hotel window. It kept returning, tapping its beak on the window to demand more food. Roy had told Lynn that this was clearly an established menaces racket, and that the seagull shouldn't be encouraged.

Lynn fed it anyway.

Roy stepped onto the sand. On this bleak, damp day, this stretch of beach was emptier than usual, mainly dogwalkers and joggers, no windbreaks and picnickers. The tide was out, the water a distance away.

Lynn would have laughed to know Roy had cleaned his walking boots just to step onto wet sand. But Lynn had always teased him about his standards. His ironing, his shoe cleaning, his sock darning – she'd teased him about it all. Lynn had—

Lynn had—

Roy stopped.

He looked down at his empty hands.

He turned back towards the road and started to run.

Sunday

Am I the Villain Here? Post 35915

CantBeArsed8: Am I the villain here for being furious my part-ner's father changed my daughter's pirate party into a princess party?

60.5K votes, 16 hours left

You're the villain here: 46%
Not the villain here: 54%

Latest reply:

@respectisearned: Everyone seems to be wilfully ignoring the real issue, which is that we DON'T NEED a British spelling of racoon. Racoons are native to North America and it's essential they're never introduced into the UK, or it'll be grey squirrels, all over again. It's an environmental genocide, waiting to happen.

50

Roy waited for the beep. 'Hello, it's Roy Frost again. I know you don't open until nine, but just to remind you, I'm looking for an urn of ashes in a silver cube-shaped carboard bag with ribbon handles. Dawn has my details and she'll remember me. My number is four nine five three oh two. Thank you.'

Roy sat back in his armchair. Dawn would definitely remember him.

'Sir,' she'd said on his third call the day before, 'I can understand you're distressed. But I've told you several times now we've got your details, and we only have skeleton staff at the weekend. Trust me, it is in my interest to get the urn back to you as soon as I can. I will be dreaming about that urn tonight.'

Roy stood up.

He'd get to the lost property office half an hour early, to be on the safe side.

An in-person visit would help them appreciate the severity of the situation.

'You can't!' Dawn threw up her arms in frustration. 'You can't stand here all day!'

'I can.' Roy hoped it was true.

'But what are you going to do all day?'

Roy looked at the corkboard next to him. *Travel in style and comfort. Let us take the wheel!* There wasn't much space on the customer side of this desk but, still, needs must. He shifted his weight from one foot to the other. To maintain stamina standing all day he'd keep moving, like a shark. 'I'm going to wait.'

Dawn sighed. 'I'll give you a chair from the back, but please try not to block the door when the drivers come in.'

Roy sat in the chair provided by Dawn. He waved his news-paper at the driver. 'Thanks again for the paper. It's very thoughtful.'

'No problem.' The driver left.

It was a tabloid, and Roy turned to the crossword. He pondered the first clue, *Loved man about the house (7)*, for longer than necessary, assuming it must be an anagram. But it wasn't a cryptic puzzle and the answer was, disappointingly, just *Husband*.

Ten minutes later, Roy pushed the finished crossword aside, feeling sorry for the setter, whose job must be very unrewarding.

He wondered if he should write a letter to the newspaper. 'Dawn, do you have writing paper? And a pen?'

'I'm working, Roy.'

Roy thought. A minute later, he stood up.

'I'm sorry to impose on you one more time, Dawn. I don't suppose you know where I could access a gents?'

On his return, Dawn glanced up.

'Someone's left the *Mail* from yesterday so I put it on your chair.' She paused. 'Not *your* chair. Just your chair for today.'

'Of course,' Roy held her gaze meaningfully. 'We both hope I won't have to come back tomorrow.'

Dawn flicked on the kettle. 'I'm not making you any tea. I don't want you getting too comfortable.'

Roy unfolded the local newspaper and sat down.

'Though I can probably find a spare mug.'

Roy smiled. 'That would be lovely, Dawn.' Roy had been terrified of the public earlier this week, but his terror was lessening. Dawn had been kind. The woman on the coach yesterday might have had an unfortunate sugar addiction, but she'd been pleasant. The public were infinitely nicer in human form than online.

He shook the paper out. He glanced at the paper's headline. *Mutiny on the Brontë!*

He felt Dawn's gaze on him. He looked up.

'I've got everyone on it, Roy.'

She held up the bag of sugar in a question.

'Just milk. Thank you.'

'No one would take an urn. *No one*. It's just a case of tracking it down.'

Roy looked at his feet, trying to stem the wave of emotion threatening to overtake him.

'I'd have been gutted if I'd lost my dad's ashes.' Dawn raised her voice over the boiling of the kettle. 'Though not much chance of that – he'd have haunted me. That man could hold a grudge. Didn't speak to his brother for half his life, and all over a retractable awning.'

Roy smiled. 'It sounds like your father was a man of principle.' He looked down at the paper.

Mutiny on the Brontë!
Pirate Activists Storm Local Library

Roy pushed the newspaper's pages together in fright.

Dawn looked over. 'Roy?'

Roy didn't move.

Dawn looked at the newspaper in interest. 'What's in there?'

'Nothing.' He crunched the pages more tightly. 'Nothing.'

Dawn gave a slow nod. She put Roy's mug of tea on the counter.

'Thank you.'

He waited until Dawn was on the phone and safely distracted. He began to read.

Mutiny on the Brontë!
Pirate Activists Storm Local Library

There was no quiet section in Brook Street library this morning when a group of women's rights activists infiltrated the building in pirate costumes.

'It's about the imbalanced societal expectations we place on children,' said one of the protestors, identifying only as Toothless Jack. 'Who says girls can't have pirate parties? Why do our girls always have to be princesses? Why is it we tell our girls they must only aspire to pretty domesticity?'

Library manager Tessa said, 'People have a right to protest, but this is nothing to do with us. Libraries are quiet, calm spaces. Woe betide any pirate who tries to cross the threshold of my establishment again.'

Roy looked at the accompanying photograph – of himself, balking at the end of a chef-pirate's cutlass. Behind Roy stood the pirate with the mask. Something about his jawline looked familiar.

'Roy!' Dawn slammed the phone down. 'We've found Lynn!'

Roy let the paper fall to the floor.

'She's on the way from Colchester! The driver, Steve, says he's got the ashes right next to him. He's not going to let them out of his sight.'

'Oh, Dawn.' Roy's chest shuddered with emotion. 'Thank you.'

She smiled. 'We couldn't have you cluttering up the office again tomorrow, could we? I'm busy here! I've got a job to do!'

'You're wonderful, Dawn! I can't thank you enough.' Roy picked up the newspaper. 'You know, Lynn might have liked that, sitting at the front of the coach.' He shook the pages of the paper back into place. 'We always thought she'd be good at driving an HGV. She had excellent spatial awareness. She could park in the tiniest of spaces.' He folded the paper. 'Shall I wait for the driver here?'

'Colchester, Roy,' Dawn said meaningfully.

'Still—'

'But I can give them to you first thing tomorrow.'

'Thank you, Dawn.' He took a final glance at the newspaper and, light with relief, shoved it decisively into the recycling bin.

51

On Sunday morning Janine pulled back the caravan's tiny, crinkled curtains. She lit the hob with a match and put the kettle on.

With Katie at Marky's, the caravan felt emptier than should be possible for somewhere with barely more square footage than a toilet cubicle.

But Janine needed to get used to being alone. She knew what Marky was hinting at. He wanted primary custody.

Her stomach rolled.

And if he did want primary custody, was it even fair of Janine to fight? She couldn't offer Katie what Marky could. That much was clear.

And she couldn't do anything about it.

But there was one thing she could do.

She tried Roy's landline. There was no answer.

She messaged Phil.

I'm leaving you alone, but I want to go and apologise to your dad while Katie's at Marky's. A proper apology. Is there any time today that you're out? x

The reply came more quickly than she expected.

Do what you need to do. I've moved out of Dad's.

Janine frowned. There was so much she wanted to ask. *Where have you gone? How long for? How are you feeling? Do you forgive me? Are we OK, Phil? Are we going to be OK?*

She typed and deleted and typed and deleted. Eventually she stood up, turned the hob off, and grabbed the car keys, her message unsent.

Half an hour later, Janine knocked at Roy's front door.

She was just crouching down to look through the letterbox when there was a voice from next door.

'I saw him go out first thing.' Sal stood in her doorway with her arms folded.

Janine let the letterbox flap shut.

Sal gestured with a jerk of her head. 'You coming in?'

Janine nodded and got up.

'How's Phil?'

Janine shrugged. 'Still not talking to me.' She sank on the corduroy sofa in the lounge. 'And Marky wants to go for primary custody.'

Sal sank down on the sofa opposite. 'He wouldn't.'

'He's in a stable relationship now, with time and money, living in a massive house with a woman who loves Katie.' Janine stared at the fireplace. 'Whereas I'm single, jobless, with no savings, and living in a caravan on my mum's drive.'

Sal didn't say anything immediately. 'That's a particularly bad spin.'

'You think there's a better spin?'

'It's just not the full picture.'

Janine looked at the floor. 'I feel like I've failed this life thing so badly, Sal. I just want to curl up into the smallest of balls. For ever.' She paused. 'Go the full foetal, you know?'

Sal moved to sit next to her. 'Phil will come round.'

They sat in silence.

'It's weirder when you're being nice. Freaks me out. Let's me know things are really bad.' Janine looked up. 'What did you want to talk to me about yesterday?'

Sal wrinkled her nose. 'Still not the right time.'

Janine glanced at a newspaper on the side table.

Sal reached for the paper and turned it face down.

'Is it the *Mail*? I've seen the *Mail*.'

Sal said nothing.

Janine frowned. 'Hand it over, Sal.'

Sal picked the paper up. 'I suppose you'll see it eventually.' She gave the paper to Janine.

Mutiny on the Brontë!
Pirate Activists Storm Local Library

Janine looked up. 'Oh, God.'

There was no quiet section in Brook Street library this morning when a group of women's rights activists infiltrated the building in pirate costumes.

'It's about the imbalanced societal expectations we place on children,' said one of the protestors, identifying only as Toothless Jack. 'Who says girls can't have pirate parties? Why is it we tell our girls they must only aspire to pretty domesticity?'

Library manager Tessa said, 'People have a right to protest, but this is nothing to do with us. Libraries are quiet, calm spaces. Woe betide any pirate who tries to cross the threshold of my establishment again.'

The spark for the protest was a poll posted on the Am I the

Villain Here? *forum by local housewife Janine Pierce, forty-two,* *who was furious her father-in-law had arranged a princess party* *for her six-year-old daughter, rather than the pirate party Janine* *had asked for.*

Party organiser Vince Kemper commented: 'What a shame it *was. The kids usually love my princess party! The little one was* *just confused on the day, after her mother told her she wanted a* *pirate party. If only the family had said! At Party Vince's we're* *delighted to arrange bespoke parties for anyone – whether that's* *boys in the enchanted castle, or girls in eyepatches. We cater to all* *your individual needs, and that's why we have a five-star rating* *on* Trust My Clown.

'*Party Vince!*' Janine shook her head. 'If I ever see that snake again' – she flapped an invisible hand-puppet – 'him and his fucking squirrel are gonna get it.' She pushed the paper away. 'Oh, God, Sal, what have I done? No wonder you wanted to talk to me.'

There was a pause.

Janine looked up.

'That was it, wasn't it?'

Sal shook her head.

Janine took this in. 'There's another bad thing?'

Sal didn't reply.

'If it's bad, let's just get it all out of the way today. On the worst weekend of my life.' Janine put her hands either side of her on the sofa, bracing. 'Hit me.'

'OK. I'm cross with you.'

Janine nodded. 'Everyone is.'

'Alfie didn't want to see you yesterday. He wouldn't come down when you were here. I could tell something was wrong.'

Janine looked up.

'I worked at him, and eventually he told me.' Sal didn't break eye contact. 'He said you want to watch porn with him, Janine. He thinks you're going to make him sit beside you and look at *vulvas*. He's fucking *petrified*.'

'Shit. Really?'

'He says he's scarred for ever. That he can't even look at a girl on Instagram without your face looming into view.'

Janine took that in.

'And that's not all.'

Janine gripped the sofa cushions beside her. Why had she made Sal tell her? Why couldn't she, for once, let something go? Why couldn't she change her whole personality, just this one time?

'I had a bad feeling, that there was something else Alfie wasn't telling me. So I went to see Roy last night and asked if I could see this anonymous note Darsh mentioned.'

'No!'

'It was Alfie's handwriting.'

Across the room, the clock ticked.

'He was so scared of you,' Sal said, 'that he sent an anonymous note to create conflict so you'd have to move out from next door! A note! On paper! Can you imagine what it takes to get a teenage kid in this day to write a note *on paper*?'

'Oh, God. Alfie!'

'He's absolutely terrified of you.'

'Is he upstairs?'

'He's out.'

'How can I apologise?'

Sal took a moment. 'Maybe through me for now. I think it needs a third party. He might not be able to be in a room with you for quite some time.'

Janine gave a long sigh.

'Sighing. Again.'

'I know, it's just ... I don't think I could take it if we weren't friends, on top of everything.' Janine looked up. 'Are we still friends?'

Sal nodded.

'Thank God.' Janine put her face in her hands. 'I've fucked everything else up, Sal.'

'I know, mate.' Sal pulled Janine towards her. 'I know.'

Monday

Am I the Villain Here? Post 35915

CantBeArsed8: Am I the villain here for being furious my partner's father changed my daughter's pirate party into a princess party?

104.1K votes, Final Results

You're the villain here: 49%
Not the villain here: 51%

Latest reply:

@imlindabates: 'Sheath your cutlasses?' 'It's a storm in a teacup?' You're a coward and a traitor @CantBeArsed8. You're an apologist for the patriarchy, and even worse than him. What a terrible excuse for a mother you are. How do you sleep at night?

52

Roy desperately wanted to pick up the ashes first thing, but he couldn't. He trusted Dawn, and a Frost always met his commitments.

He looked at his reflection in the mirror. He fastened his tie carefully. He got ready for his first post-pirate-march shift at the library with the solemnity of a man going to war.

He adjusted his tie. He adjusted it again.

He took one last look in the mirror and left the house.

Yvonne was standing at the front desk when he arrived. 'Roy.' Her voice was cool.

'Good morning, Yvonne.'

Tessa appeared at Yvonne's side.

Roy rubbed his hands together. 'Shall I get the kettle on?'

'No need.' Tessa picked up her mug. 'If you remember, you said you were going to work your notice in the stockroom.'

He tried to smile. 'So I did.'

'You said you were going to sit there all day. In the dark.'

Roy looked from Tessa to Yvonne. He coughed. 'I should explain—'

Tessa's voice was harsh. 'There's no need.'

Roy shuffled his feet.

'Those bloody pirates broke my ergonomic keyboard.' Tessa glared at him. 'Which I brought in *from home*.'

'So maybe there *is* a need to explain?'

'There's nothing you can say.'

'But I want to apologise. I'm truly very sorry for bringing all that nonsense to this wonderful place.'

Yvonne lifted her mug to her mouth. She looked over Roy's shoulder at the stacks behind.

Roy shuffled on the spot. Of course she would want nothing to do with him now – not now he was famous. No, not *famous* – not like Paul McCartney. *Infamous*, like Pol Pot.

'I apologise for any toxic masculinity I may have inadvertently displayed. And for rousing the wrath of the pirates. And about your special keyboard, Tessa – good ergonomics are extremely important.' He swallowed. 'I'm just going to the stockroom and I may be some time.'

Roy headed into the stockroom and closed the door. He switched on the overhead light. Sitting in the dark wasn't necessary, and neither was the Captain Oates line. They were both a bit of melodrama on Roy's part, and surely Tessa wouldn't really expect him to work with no light?

Roy looked at the stack of books on the desk, waiting to be sent on to other libraries. He started labelling the books, determined not to think about how he'd ruined his life.

Because how was this even fair? He was seventy-eight! You weren't meant to be able to ruin your life at seventy-eight! Bets were meant to be off by then, the value of a life weighed and counted, good deeds long banked. Hadn't F. Scott Fitzgerald said *There are no second acts in American lives* – and wasn't that surely even more applicable for unshowy British lives?

Roy's last few days had been anything but uneventful.

Here he was, sliding down snake after snake. Seventy-seven years of good behaviour counting for nothing.

This was not the life-enhancing Third Age the educational materials talked about.

He realised he wasn't parcelling up the books, but he couldn't focus – not until he'd got Lynn's ashes back to the house. Straight after this, he'd go to the coach office. Then she'd be safe, at least. Safe from Roy, who could no longer be trusted.

Roy headed for the staff room.

'Ah, Roy.' Tessa's voice was deceptively pleasant. 'It's you.' She switched the kettle on with a hard flick. 'Out here, in the light. How many of those packages have you put in the post?'

'I haven't.'

'You – haven't.'

Roy licked his lips. 'I don't pack the books up one at a time, you see, I have instituted a better system for sending stock. I—'

'I told Mum you wouldn't be able to just sit quietly out of the way.' Tessa turned back to the kettle. 'If you want a drink, you'll have to wash a mug.'

Tessa stood there, waiting for the kettle, her back to him.

Roy coughed. 'You're cross with me.'

Tessa spooned out coffee grounds into two cups. 'Whatever gives you that impression?'

'You're on the pirates' side, and that's why you're being frosty.'

Tessa reached for the sugar bowl. 'The pirates, Roy, were a bunch of self-righteous clowns. They broke my keyboard and, if I ever see them again, I'll have their library cards.' Tessa spooned sugar into the mugs. 'I'm being *frosty* because you were rude to my mum.' She looked up. 'See, I can put up with all sorts from you, Roy – and I did. From you not being able to work the printer after months, to turning up hours late for work, to flooding the library with unwanted books' – Tessa seemed to be gaining alarming momentum – 'to long-winded monologues on topics I haven't asked about' – Tessa held his gaze – 'to spending hours in the stockroom without packaging up a single parcel to, and let's not forget this one, bringing a horde of angry pirates to my door. But being rude to my mum?' Tessa sliced the air with her hand. 'That's my line.'

Roy closed his eyes. 'I handled that badly. I was very distressed that day, for pirate-related reasons. Your mother is quite wonderful.' He shook his hands in frustration. 'What can I do to make it better? Right now?'

Tessa studied him for a moment. 'Mum's gone to meet a friend for lunch. She's got the afternoon off.'

Roy swallowed again. She hadn't even said goodbye. 'How can I make it up to her?'

'Roy.' Tessa leaned against the sink. 'Do you remember promising that when you came in today, you'd be in the stockroom—'

'In the dark.' Roy doffed an imaginary cap. 'Got it.'

Roy remained in the stockroom for the next hour. At the sound of the door opening, he looked up.

Tessa jerked her head towards the counter. 'Someone to see you.'

'Right.' Roy dusted off his hands and followed her.

He barely dared look up. Could it be Phil or Yvonne? Or even Janine, here to make up?

He reached the counter, still with his head down. He took in two work boots. Two legs clad in dirty denim.

Roy looked up with a smile. 'Phil!'

'Hello, *Judge.*' The windscreen man's cheeks flushed with satisfaction. 'I saw the photo in the paper.'

He pulled back his fist.

A bright shock of pain flooded Roy's eyes.

He staggered backwards, collapsing against the *New in Stock!* display. He brought the stand and all the new books tumbling down around him.

Roy managed to generate two thoughts before the blackness took over.

That, after so much mental agony, the white heat of pure physical pain was something of a relief.

And that *thank God* Lynn had been spared the horror of having to live through Roy's Third Age.

53

Janine dropped Katie off at school on Monday morning and drove to the supermarket. She was just reaching for a basket when she got the email notification.

Your application

Janine sniffed. It was considerate of the company not to drag it out. Like those gentlemen executioners in Tudor times – the ones who promised to make the beheading swift and accurate.

Dear Janine,
Thank you very much for attending the interview on Saturday. Unfortunately, we will not be taking your application further at this time. If you would like to receive feedback, please contact . . .

Janine closed the email. No, she would not be taking up the offer of feedback on this occasion. But, all round, it was a good execution. Now, at least, she could get on with her life.

Janine wondered what form *getting on with her life* would take.

She ambled up the vegetable aisle, the chilled air making

the skin on her arms goosebump. She leaned against a wall and flicked onto the forum.

She had thousands of notifications – mainly angry ones. The *storm in a teacup* comment hadn't gone down well with her fans.

Janine deleted the thread.

She deleted her account.

And deleted her Twitter account.

"Scuse me.' A woman leaned past to get some raspberries.

Janine stepped out of the way. 'Sorry.' She slid her phone back into her pocket and, at the leisurely pace of someone with all the time in the world, started perusing the broccoli.

Janine was back at the caravan unpacking her shopping, when her mobile rang with an unknown number.

'Hello?'

'I'm calling from Manchester Royal Infirmary.' The woman's voice was gentle. 'Can I speak to Phil Frost, Roy Frost's next of kin?'

Cold fear gripped Janine's stomach. 'I'm Phil. Kind of.'

The other end of the phone was silent.

'Is Roy OK?' Janine leaned against the counter. 'What's happened?'

'Mr Frost has received a head injury after a suspected assault. He's conscious and breathing, but we're keeping him here for observation.'

'Assault? Is he OK?'

'He's alert. And able to form reasonable responses.' There was a pause. 'In general.'

Janine leaned back against the counter. 'In general? What aren't you telling me?'

A pause. 'He does seem to have a circular obsession with a window cleaner.'

Janine took this in.

'He keeps saying it was just what he needed, to be punched by a window cleaner. There's an element of confusion in his responses. And euphoria.'

'Right.' Janine stood up and stared out of the window. 'But you think he's all right?'

'He's in very good spirits. He's sitting up in bed now, watching a film. He's concentrating on it intently.' There was uncertainty in the woman's tone. 'He keeps shushing people if they try to talk to him.'

'What's the film?'

A pause. '*The Little Mermaid.*'

Janine swiped her car keys from the counter. 'I'm coming right now.'

Janine left a message for Phil and drove to the hospital. She hurried into the ward.

Roy was sitting up in his white hospital gown, talking to a nurse. 'It's worth checking the ingredients carefully, because not all kitchen sprays are equal. Bleach isn't always—'

At the sight of Janine, he stopped.

The nurse moved away from the bed. 'I'll leave you to it.'

'Roy, I came as soon as I heard.' Janine took a step closer. 'Are you all right?'

Roy cleared his throat. 'They said Phil was coming.'

'They had my number as an alternative. You know he never answers his phone. I've left him messages.'

Roy stared at the front of his gown.

'I'm so sorry.' Janine stopped at the end of his bed. 'For everything. I mean it.'

'Yes. Well.' Roy kept staring at his gown. 'This has not been my finest hour either.'

'But—'

'Least said, soonest mended.' Pointedly, Roy moved a newspaper off his visitor's chair.

Janine sat down. 'Are you OK?'

'Better than OK.' There was a light in Roy's eyes. 'I've been punched in the face by a windscreen cleaner!'

'Right.' Janine spoke carefully. 'It doesn't sound *that* great.'

He sat up straighter. 'It's absolutely marvellous.'

'A window cleaner?'

'A wind*screen* cleaner. And *I know him*! I remembered! I didn't deserve it, Janine!' Roy leaned forwards and grasped her hands. 'It's simply the best thing that could have happened! And the doctors think I'll be heading home today. They don't think I've got a head injury.'

'Right.' Janine gave a weak smile. 'Have they done any ... actual tests?'

'My mind's as sharp as a saw! Because I now know that man was an absolute scoundrel. Alistair Edwards. He lived at 240 Acton Court.' Roy shook his head; a section of hair floated up. 'Aggravated bodily harm and spousal battery. A rock solid case. No miscarriage of justice there! I threw the book at him and I'd do it again – delightedly!'

Roy's chest was puffed up with passion, his cheeks flushed with pride. He was breathing heavily.

He didn't *look* confused.

Janine looked at the broadsheet on the side table, folded to reveal a crossword, completed in Roy's neat block capitals. *Rudimentary. Phalanx. Turpitude.*

'Janine, now, I need you to phone a woman called Dawn. I know the number by heart.'

'Of course.'

Roy glanced up. 'I wonder if Phil will come.'

'*Of course* he'll come. He's just not answering his phone.' Janine looked down at her hands. 'And definitely not to me.' Janine felt her cheeks redden. 'Roy, it goes without saying that I'm so, so sorry.'

'I played my part.' Roy brushed something invisible from his gown. 'And I am very sad this ridiculousness has come between you and Phil. Very sad indeed. This is not an outcome I anticipated. Or wanted.'

'I've apologised to you online. A public apology. And I deleted the post.'

'Thank you.' Roy dusted something invisible from his gown. 'And I am also very sorry about your interview.' He raised his head briefly. 'Did you . . . get the job?'

'I didn't.' Janine patted his leg. 'But I *did* learn how to spell racoon. So, every cloud.'

'Don't joke.' Roy shook his head. 'This is unforgivable. This has been an awakening for me. I dismissed your concerns out of hand. Arrogantly – and erroneously, it seems.'

Janine raised an eyebrow.

'You were correct about *The Little Mermaid*, Janine.' Roy's eyes widened. 'I've just watched it, and it was shocking. A completely irresponsible production. As you warned me – dangerous messages. *Extremely* dangerous messages.'

'Thanks for getting it.'

'It would be impossible *not* to get it. Your point jumped right out of the screen.'

'And while we're doing apologies, I need to say I'm sorry about the library,' Janine said softly. 'I know how much you loved it there.'

'It's not your – I'd handed in my notice anyway. Even before The Mutiny on the Brontë.'

Janine wrinkled her nose. 'You saw the paper?'

He nodded.

'And the *Mail*?'

'What male?'

'So you've resigned?' Janine asked quickly. 'Why? You seemed so happy at the library?'

'It's for the best. A library's meant to be a calm place of learning. Not a place of rampaging buccaneers or irate windscreen cleaners.' Roy looked up. 'But I'm going to keep busy in other ways. If you'll allow me, I'm going to throw Katie a pirate party. Much better than Party Vince's. Look.'

Roy turned the newspaper over. On a blank section, he'd written a list.

Katie's Pirate Party Ingredients
Cutlasses – silver foil and cardboard
Hooks for hand – coat hangers, bubble wrap and silver foil
Eye-patches – black elastic and felt
Skull and Crossbones flags – bamboo poles, pillowcases and black paint
Sea – blue bed sheets on top of pillows and sofa cushions on top of groundsheets
Crocodile – Phil and Claudia's holiday lilo from Majorca '89
Cat o' nine tails –

Janine looked up. 'Cat o' nine tails?'

'I'm struggling with the safety angle,' Roy said. 'I'm thinking bungee cords, with sponges to slow the trajectory.'

Janine patted his shoulder. 'Maybe we don't need a live whip for a six-year-old.'

'We can't have a pirate party without a cat o' nine tails. I told Party Vince that.'

'That man!' Janine sat up straighter. 'Was it him who talked you out of the pirate party?'

Roy shook his head. 'I'd already decided to overrule your request, Janine. It was all my fault. Completely and unequivocally.'

Janine blinked. 'I've never heard you say that before.'

'Surely . . .' Roy frowned. 'Surely I apologise regularly?'

'Maybe I've just not been there at the exact time.'

Roy appeared to be taking this in. 'Because I know I am not perfect, Janine.'

Janine gave a small raise of her eyebrows.

Next to them, a nurse drew a curtain across the next bed. There was a murmur of chatter.

'So you deleted your post,' Roy said thoughtfully.

Janine nodded.

'Out of interest,' Roy's voice was over casual. 'Was that before or after the poll had closed?'

Janine gave a small smile. 'After.'

Roy lifted his chin in acknowledgement.

A nurse pushed a woman in a wheelchair past.

Roy coughed into his chest. 'And the final—'

'Fifty-one, forty-nine.'

Roy jerked his head up.

Janine just smiled.

'Oh, come on, girl!' Roy sat forwards. 'To whom?'

'It doesn't matter, does it? It's fifty-fifty.'

'It's not fifty-fifty. It's fifty-one, forty-nine. Though, depending on the number of votes, that may not be a statistically significant difference. We'd need to determine the p-value.'

'It was fifty-fifty, Roy.' Janine leaned forwards. 'Now did

Sal tell you Alfie was the one who put the note through your door?'

'She came to see me yesterday. I couldn't believe it.'

'Did she say why?'

Roy nodded. 'She was critical of you, which I didn't think was completely fair. Alfie shouldn't be watching *any* porn.'

'It wasn't that . . . he's a fifteen-year-old boy, Roy.'

'Exactly!'

Janine pushed her fringe out of her eyes. 'I just don't understand who was giving your details out on the forum. Surely that wasn't Alfie too?'

'Oh yes!' Roy sat up straighter. 'Mr Into the Forest! I'd forgotten, with everything else, but there was something about one of the library pirates. He had a mask over the top of his face, but there was something familiar about his jaw. And then I saw the photo of him again in the paper and I got it, Janine!' Roy beamed. 'I got it!'

54

Phil stood in the supermarket after work, checking out the sandwiches. He picked up a chicken salad, clearly made for the long-gone lunch crowd. He studied the thin wet bread and limp lettuce and put the sandwich back.

He picked up a bacon roll and was about to assess its condition when he saw Danny Carswell by the bakery counter. Phil watched him choose a loaf and place it in his basket. He headed round the corner and into Tinned Goods.

Phil put the bacon roll down. He followed Danny through Tinned Goods, through Household Supplies. Danny was in Frozen Food, opening a high freezer door, by the time Phil made a decision.

He stepped into Danny's eyeline. 'All right.'

'All right.'

'Danny. I'm sorry to grass, but your son's a sticker rat.'

Danny hunched his eyebrows.

'A sticker rat. He lies about stickers. He took so many more from Katie than he said he had, and he owes her gold ones. See you soon.'

Phil walked out of the supermarket, past the sandwich section and, suddenly, knew exactly what he had to do.

*

He was just parking down the road from Janine's mum's house when a low, sleek car pulled up over the drive.

Phil watched Marky shut the driver's door and help Katie out of the back.

Phil switched off the ignition. He got out of the van, but hung back. He didn't feel like seeing Marky today.

Janine opened the caravan door. Phil took in her faded sweatshirt and her soft house jeans, tucked into her fake-fur-lined checked slippers.

'All right, J.' Marky opened the boot and handed Katie her travel bag. 'Had a good weekend?'

'I hope you had a good time at Daddy's.' Janine gave Katie a tight smile. 'Go inside the house and see Grandma, please. I need a word with your father.'

Katie looked from one parent to the other.

Janine stared at her. 'Grandma's got you a chocolate eclair.'

Katie handed Janine her bag and hurried inside.

'YOUFUCKINGBASTARDCLOWNMARKY!' Janine strode down the driveway towards him. 'You think it's funny to put Roy's details on the internet and arrange a pirate march through the library? What is wrong with you?' She threw her hands up. '*Everything's* wrong with you. Are you actually broken?'

'Whoa.' Marky held his hands up. 'It's an important matter, Janine. I was making a stand! And I can't believe you've backed down.'

'You're not even denying it?' Janine shouted. 'You're proud of it?'

'I'm a feminist, Janine! I take sexism very seriously, as the father of a daughter.'

Slowly, Phil got out of the van. He shut the door.

'Where was your fucking feminism when you never cleaned

the toilet for three years? Where was it when you never did a wash or changed the bedding? I paid for everything, all that time, and you *still* did fuck all around the house. Roy's a better man than you'll ever be. As if I'd let you have primary custody of Katie! What was I thinking? You're pathetic! And you're FLAKY AS FUCK!'

Marky pushed his lips together. 'Katie told me you've split up with Phil, and I'm sorry, but that means you haven't even got Phil's income to fall back on now! You live in a caravan!'

Phil gave a small cough.

Marky and Janine looked up. Janine went completely still.

Phil stepped forwards and stood next to Janine at the caravan. 'Honey, I'm home!'

Marky blinked at Phil. 'You live here too?'

Phil nodded. 'We're caravan people now.'

'No, we're not caravan people,' Janine said. 'It's just a blip.'

'But while we're having that blip . . .' Phil reached for her hand – 'we're here together.'

There was silence.

Phil gave Janine's hand a small squeeze. She squeezed back so hard.

Marky looked from one to the other. 'But Katie said—'

'So you can take your car home, Marky.' Janine waved at the car dismissively. 'Right now, please. And thank you for the loan.'

She stomped into the caravan. A set of keys flew out of the caravan door and landed on the drive.

'I can't drive two cars home at once!' Marky shouted after her. 'How do you think I'm meant to drive two cars?'

There was no reply.

Phil turned to Marky. 'You were the one who outed my dad online? And what's this about a march?'

Marky's jaw slackened. 'I thought I was doing the right thing.'

Phil made his voice polite. 'Did you? Really?'

A redness crept up Marky's neck. 'A man's got to do what he believes. He's got to do what's morally right.'

'What's morally right,' Phil repeated.

Marky held his hands up.

'Thanks for the loan of the car.' Phil picked the keys off the drive. 'We'll drop it back round tomorrow.'

Phil turned, walked into the caravan, and shut the door.

Inside, Janine was waiting, perched against a wood-effect central table. She flicked her forefingers and thumbs against each other in a nervous twitch.

Phil took in the elastic-bound jazz-floral curtains. He looked at the tiny hob. 'It's cosy.'

Janine kept flicking her fingers and thumbs.

He put the keys on the counter. 'Hi.' He put both arms around Janine.

'I can't believe you're here.'

He felt the tension leave her body as she rested her head against his shoulder.

She gripped him tightly and nuzzled in. 'You're back?'

He kissed the top of her hair. 'I'm back.'

'This means the world. *You* mean the world.' Janine lifted her head from his shoulder. 'Are we really going to be caravan people together?'

Phil nodded.

'Because there're only two beds. And no floor space.'

'We'll sort something.'

Janine snuggled back into him. They stayed in a silent hug for some time.

Janine made a noise in her throat. It sounded like frustration.

Phil didn't move. 'What?'

'I don't want to ruin this moment.'

'Then don't.'

Janine lifted her head. 'You haven't listened to your messages? I've left loads.'

Phil stared at her. He shrugged.

'You're as bad as Sal.' Janine snuggled further into him. 'But let's just stay like this for a moment longer before I have to tell you about the window cleaner.'

Tuesday

Error

Something went wrong. We can't find the post you're looking for.

Please try again later.

OK

55

At 8 a.m., Roy was locking the door behind him when he saw Darsh leaving for work.

'Darsh!' Roy hurried across the street. 'What felicitous timing!'

'Roy.' Darsh adjusted the position of his rucksack. 'Have you seen the film *Groundhog Day*?'

Roy indicated he would walk with Darsh. 'I wanted to say thanks for putting my bin out last week.'

'No problem.'

'I've never missed bin day before.'

'I was surprised.'

'I wasn't myself. I even started replying to people online. Did you see?'

Darsh took a second. 'Well. It's surely important everyone knows how to spell *racoon*.'

'Very droll.' Roy clapped Darsh on the back. 'I owe you an apology, Darsh. I know you're not the person who put the note through my door.'

Darsh frowned. 'I told you that.'

'Yes, but that's what the culprit would say, wouldn't they?'

'Roy, I'm ... why would I ever put a note through your door?'

'In the absence of any other suspect, I couldn't rule you out.' Roy gave a small bow. 'I have now.'

'Am I meant to say *thank you*?'

'In an unrelated note, Alfie next door has offered to deep clean all the street's bins.'

Darsh lifted his chin. 'So the note was from—'

'Someone who made a mistake under pressure. Someone who should be allowed to learn from his mistakes in anonymity, as we all should, in a just world.'

'If you say so, chief.' Darsh nodded. 'If you say so.'

In the coach company's office, Dawn lifted the silky handles of the cardboard bag and handed it over the counter.

Roy bowed his head. He took the bag. 'Thank you.'

'I took very good care of her.'

'I know you did. I appreciate it very much.' Roy looked down at Lynn's urn. 'I'm going to scatter these at the beach next weekend with my son and his family. Then we're going to go for a meal and talk about Lynn. Janine thinks we should do karaoke. Lynn liked karaoke. But I think a meal is better. We're going to have Molotov cocktails.'

Dawn stared at him.

'That's not actually what they're called. That's just what Lynn thought they were called.'

A man came out of the back office. His necktie was carelessly tied and too short, only hanging down to his navel. 'Is this the gent who left the ashes?'

Roy nodded. 'I am.'

The boss, Dawn mouthed.

Roy looked back at the man. 'Your employee Dawn has provided me with impeccable customer service.'

The man leaned his elbows on the counter, giving the effect

of peering down. 'Now you take good care of those ashes, sir.' He spoke as though he was addressing a toddler. 'We don't want another incident like this one, do we?'

Roy clenched his jaw.

'You have to check around you for personal items before leaving the coach.' The man continued in the same tone. 'That's why we do the announcements, you know.'

Roy stood there and let the man patronise him for a bit longer because – well, Roy *had* left Lynn's ashes on a bus. And this man could patronise Roy all he liked, but it didn't change anything. Roy was still a respected ex-magistrate. This man's tie was still too short.

And Roy had his ashes back. And his family back together. This man could patronise him as much as he liked.

'So it ended up being quite the day, Joseph!' Roy leaned into Joseph's lap and tapped the book. 'And the best thing was, he deserved it!' Roy crinkled the felt bee's pop-out wing. 'An absolute scoundrel. Alistair Edwards. He lived at Acton Court. Guilty of actual bodily harm and domestic battery. Open and shut case, he was bang to rights!'

Joseph looked down at the book in his lap. His hands were still.

'Not in the mood for the bee today? Your call.' Roy flicked through the pages. 'Oh, now. This ladybird. What a handsome fellow!'

Roy watched his friend stroke the ladybird. He turned the page; a frog the colour of absinthe stretched concertinaed legs out of the book. 'What flappy legs! Wouldn't get much meat off those.' Roy pulled a paper leg. 'Do you remember when the four of us ate frogs' legs on that trip to Lyon? Absolutely revolting things.'

'Everyone OK over here?'

Roy looked up. Elena stood over them, holding a tray of plastic cups.

'We are absolutely fine. Thank you. Elena.'

'Planning to stay here today?' Elena's gaze was kind. 'No excursions planned?'

Roy shook his head. 'We like it best inside.'

She smiled. 'Then you're welcome here any time.'

She walked away, and Roy watched Joseph pull the frog's legs. 'Good man.' Joseph let the legs spring back. 'That's the spirit.'

When Roy felt Joseph was ready, he turned the page and the frog disappeared. A pop-up silver fish gaped out of the book's spine. Roy pulled the book flatter, making the fish's mouth gape further. The tail's sequined scales stirred his consciousness.

'Oh, now, listen to this!' Roy sat forwards. 'Janine had warned me about *The Little Mermaid*, Joseph. She said it had dangerous messaging. And I didn't believe her because I was being pig-headed, but I watched the film yesterday and she was spot on!' Roy stroked the fish's scales. 'It was horrifying. A minor exchanges a body part in an unconscionable contract with unbreakable terms? An unelected prince dispenses vigilante justice? The rule of law is officiated by a vengeful sea witch?' Roy shook his head. '*Thank Christ* I never showed that film to Katie.'

He smiled at Joseph. Joseph smiled back.

There was the sound of shuffling, as the lady with the shoe-baby headed over. She offered her baby to Roy for inspection.

Roy patted the shoe. 'Very handsome. What's his name?'

'Neil.'

At the unexpected deep voice, Roy looked up.

'At least, I'm pretty sure it's called Neil.' A middle-aged man with a greying beard leaned against the wall, holding a mug of tea. 'That baby's me.'

'Well, Neil.' Roy stood up. 'It must be a comfort to know you were so well looked after.' Roy held out his hand. 'Roy Frost.'

'Neil Ferguson.'

Roy shook Neil's hand. 'And your mother's name?'

'Diana Ferguson. *Dame* Diana, actually – she has an OBE.' Neil watched her hold the baby out to Joseph. 'If she could see herself now.'

Roy spoke softly. 'Don't.'

Neil stared at his mother.

'They're content. And we've still got them.' Roy kept his voice low. 'Which is such a privilege.'

Neil took a moment. He gave a small nod.

Roy made his voice hearty again. 'A Dame, hey?' He jerked his head at Joseph. 'Joseph was an award-winning structural engineer. Brain like a scythe. He designed that bridge over the M60 near the old viaduct.'

'My mum was an architect.'

'*Really?*' Roy turned to stare at Diana. 'Joseph was a *huge* fan of architecture. I don't suppose she did Brutalist?'

'Before her time.' Neil scratched his face. 'She's only sixty-two.'

Roy tried not to blanch. 'Well, she looks content right now,' he said quickly. 'Very happy caring for baby Neil. Very diligent.'

Neil smiled. He steered his mother to a sofa, leaving Roy with Joseph.

Roy watched Diana stroke her shoe-baby. *Sixty-two!*

He had assumed this woman was from the generation above him. Not the generation below.

It was disquieting.

Roy watched Diana hold out her shoe. Neil patted 'himself' good-naturedly. Roy stared at them for a moment longer.

'Well, that's a turn up.' Roy turned back to Joseph. 'A celebrated architect, *and* a knight of the realm. A younger woman, to boot.' He turned the page in Joseph's book, revealing a grasshopper. 'Which shows, again, that I really should have learned my lesson by now.' Roy shook his head fondly, as he watched Joseph reach for the grasshopper. 'I don't know why I ever question you.'

56

It was an odd arrangement, Janine and Katie staying in the caravan and Phil staying at Roy's. But it was also fine.

Phil came to the caravan in the evenings. They played Chase the Ace with Katie and shared fish and chips, supermarket sandwiches, or, occasionally, the hot pies Roy sent round in an insulated bag.

After Katie went to bed, Phil and Janine sat on Janine's mum's front wall and drank wine like teenagers.

It was strangely – strangely – fine.

Incredibly, it was all OK at the school gates too.

The other mums had taken Janine up on her *you can ask me anything* gambit.

'And you're still living with your father-in-law?' Megan asked Janine, rocking her shih tzu pram.

'Phil is for now. But Katie and I are living in a caravan.' Janine enjoyed the reactions of shock. 'A stationary one. It's tiny. Two berth. From 1998.' She smiled at the horrified faces. 'The best bit – it's on my mum's drive.' She could get *loads* of anecdotes out of this. 'Now, did I tell you what happened at my job interview?'

The interview story was a good one, and Janine was able to tell it with lightness, and almost find it funny. It was something about having Phil back. And Marky no longer making noises about custody of Katie.

Everything was still shit. But it was a better kind of shit.

'We'll have sorted something else out before the weather turns, I'm sure.' Janine looked from one face to another. 'Anyway, loads of people live in caravans. Look at the travelling community – there's a dignity to it, when you think about it. It's fine. We're doing fine.'

'What about Katie's dad?' Megan asked.

Beth rolled her eyes. 'The guy with the car?'

Janine stared at her. 'What was that?'

'Nothing.'

'Did you just roll your eyes?'

'I'm sorry.'

'No, you misunderstand me. No apology necessary.' Janine patted Beth's arm. 'Absolutely no apology necessary.'

'If he's got all that money, can't he help more?' Cass asked.

'I don't want any more help from him. The man's a tool.'

'You can tell.' Beth turned to the others. 'He wears sunglasses when it's dark.'

Janine widened her eyes. 'YES, HE DOES!' She took a deep breath. 'He wants to see Katie loads now. Now he's got a rich girlfriend. When we first split up, he wouldn't even take Katie overnight, but lately he's been hinting about primary custody.'

'Ri-ight.' Cass made the word long with sarcasm. 'Now he's got a woman to help, you're meant to think he was reliable all along.'

'Oh, my God.' Janine's eyes widened further. 'You get it!'

'And you have to let him, for Katie's sake.' The woman with the cheek filler stepped forwards. 'And be grown up about it.'

'YES!' Janine practically shouted. 'I'm sorry, I don't know your name?'

The woman put out her hand. 'Ronnie.'

Janine smiled and took it. 'Janine.' She paused. 'I didn't think any of you would understand.'

'Why not?' Megan asked.

Janine paused. 'I don't know.'

'Come on.' Beth jerked her head. 'Let's go to the café.'

An hour later, Janine was leaving the café and saw a red van driving past. 'OY!'

She hurtled down the pavement, rushing past buggies and pedestrians. Past a charity stand, and a teenager on a scooter. 'Hey!' She ran, keeping pace with the slow-moving traffic. 'I want to talk to you!'

She shouted at an alarmed-looking woman at the roadside, next to a pedestrian crossing. 'Press that please!'

Obediently, the woman pressed the button.

'Thanks so much!'

In front of the van, the traffic light turned amber.

'Party Vince!' Janine ran up to the passenger window and banged on it. 'I want to talk to you!'

Vince stared straight ahead. His Adam's apple bobbed.

'Vince!' She banged again. 'You know I'm here!'

Janine glanced ahead to see the light changing.

Vince, still staring ahead, shifted the gearstick jerkily. There was the sound of the accelerator.

'You won't even speak to me? Fine.' Janine banged the side of the van. 'But I'm going to put a review on your website!'

She watched the van speed away. 'It's not just going to say *sexist*. It's also going to say *spineless*!'

She turned. She took in the crowd of shoppers.

'Never arrange an event with Party Vince.' Janine shook her head. 'Trust me. Whatever rating he gets on *Trust My Clown.*'

Janine smiled at the crowd. She walked towards the bus stop and pulled out her phone.

She had a new email. From Nadia at her old work.

Vacancy – Area Sales Manager, North-West

Janine lowered herself slowly onto the bus shelter seat.

Hi Janine,
Due to an internal reorganisation, we are looking for someone with experience of managing people and an exemplary record in retail sales . . .

Janine opened the attachment. It was a job description Janine had written for her own job, two years previously.

She rang the number on the email.

'Nadia speaking.'

'Nadia, It's Janine Pierce.' Janine jumped off the seat. 'You've just sent me a message?'

'Janine. How did your interview go?'

'Nadia, are you shitting me?'

There was a pause.

'You'd have me back after that exit interview?'

'That wasn't an exit interview. We don't do exit interviews. Lee wanted you to know about the job opportunity. He's been promoted to head of sales. If you were to get the job, he'd be your boss.'

Janine took this in. Her ex-trainee Lee had had quite the year. 'But where's Scott gone?'

'He's been promoted too. He's now vice-president.'

'But he can't even give anyone bad ne ...' Janine shook her head. *Not now.* 'And Adrian? Adrian who thinks women should take the minutes and pour the coffee? Don't tell me he's CEO!'

Nadia paused. 'No. He's not CEO.'

Janine waited.

'After years of loyal and valued service, Adrian has left the business.' Nadia's voice was even, like she was reading the news. 'He will be taking the opportunity to spend more time with his family. We are grateful for everything he has done for the company, and we wish him all the best for the future.'

For a moment, Janine couldn't speak.

'Janine?'

'Adrian's been *sacked*?'

'Janine, I said *so he can take the opportunity to spend more time with his family.* Don't you listen?'

'Is this because of what I said to you at the exit interview?'

'It wasn't an exit interview, and *of course* it wasn't.'

'Wow.' Janine shook her head. 'This is incredible. I'm actually speechless. I'm super speechless.'

'Not *super* super speechless, it seems.'

Janine watched a woman walk past with a buggy. 'Left with a nice tidy settlement agreement, did he?'

The woman with the buggy gave Janine an odd look.

'He's gone, Janine. I thought you'd be pleased. Especially because of the domino effect of the vacancies. Scott and Lee have been promoted in backfill, so we now need an experienced Area Sales Manager.'

Janine looked into the middle distance. 'I can't believe this.'

'It's not all good news. You'd have the same sales targets, but the team working for you would be half the size.'

'But you're saying the job's mine if I want it?'

'Janine, I'd never say that. I work in HR.'

'Scott would have me back?'

'He was the one who suggested contacting you. Though it's worth noting he didn't want to make the initial contact with you himself.' Nadia's voice was deadpan. 'Just in case you were still angry.'

'*Vice president!*' Janine sniffed. 'You need to get that man on an assertiveness course, Nadia.'

'While I've got you, though, I'm fascinated to know. Did you ever manage to get your head round death in the end?'

'I didn't, and it sounds like I might not have time now. Nadia, I can't thank you enough.'

'I've done nothing.'

'You've done loads.'

'Nope.'

There was the sound of a dial tone.

Janine just stood at the bus stop for a moment, taking it in, and lifted her phone to dial Phil.

Epilogue

Tessa was at the desk, making notes in a pad, as Roy pushed through the library doors.

'Tessa.'

Tessa looked up. She took in the bouquet of flowers in one hand, the carrier bag in the other. She looked back at her pad. 'Roy.'

'May I have a moment of your time?'

Tessa scribbled hard, a muscle working in her jaw. She put her pad down and leaned both palms on the counter. 'Yes?'

Roy rested the flowers on top of the returned books trolley. 'This is for you.' He reached into his carrier bag, and handed Tessa the box. 'It's top of the range, the gentleman in store said. Brand new.' He watched Tessa turn the box over. 'I know it will take time to get used to a new one, but I couldn't leave you without an ergonomic keyboard.'

Tessa studied the box. 'Thank you.' She looked up. 'That's actually very kind.'

'It's the least I could do.' Roy paused. 'Have ... they been back?'

Tessa pulled off the cellophane. 'It's all quiet on the pirate front.' She lifted the lid. 'This looks perfect.'

Roy watched Tessa run her fingers over the keyboard's

hump. 'Today is a day for making amends.' He picked up the bouquet of flowers. 'I'm going to make things up to your mother.'

When Tessa didn't acknowledge the flowers, Roy moved the bouquet further into her eyeline.

Tessa sighed. 'Mum's next door, in the supermarket.' She sounded strained. 'I'll message her to pop by.'

'That would be extremely helpful.'

A man came up to the desk. 'The printer's stuck.'

Roy laid the bouquet back on the returns trolley. 'Allow me.'

Tessa called after him. 'You don't work here anymore, Roy!'

Roy helped the man with the printer, opening all the doors. He removed the crunched-up piece of paper and pushed the door closed.

Roy headed back to the desk and waited.

Tessa looked up from her pad. 'Well, I'm sure you have a busy day planned, so I can give her the flowers.'

'It's fine.' Roy waved at the trolley of returned books. 'I can put these back while I wait.'

Something in Tessa's cheek twitched. 'Why are you still helping?' She threw her pad down. 'Haven't you got a new volunteering job somewhere better?'

Roy gave a sad smile. 'There's nowhere better than a library.'

'But if you like being here so much' – Tessa's voice was tight with strain – 'why did you resign?'

Roy arranged the books in the trolley in alphabetical order, moving a Bryson in front of a Cookson. 'Because I'd always thought volunteering was a good thing. But then I learned that it wasn't. That I was taking away someone's paying job. And ensuring other workers got paid less as a result.' Roy kept sorting the books. 'As Dante wrote in *The Divine*

Comedy, Amor sementa in voi d'ogne virtute, e d'ogni operazion che merta pene.' He looked up. 'Which translates as *No good deed goes unpunished.'*

Tessa waved her hand, swatting away the Italian. 'Taking away someone's paying job?' She stared at him. 'Where on earth did you get that?'

'From the internet. It's a concept called *job substitution.'* Roy felt his voice getting quiet. 'You don't think it's true?'

'Roy,' Tessa's voice was firm, 'I don't know what you read on the internet. But I can tell you – for sure – that if no one volunteered here, the council wouldn't start paying people. I promise you, one hundred per cent, that if no one volunteered here, the council would close this library.'

Roy stared at her. 'Surely not.'

'We're not an essential service.'

Roy's voice climbed high with disbelief. 'Not *an essential service?'*

'Then *I* wouldn't have a job then either, and nor would the other salaried staff. We'd be at the job centre, taking jobs other unemployed people could do. There's your job substitution – right there.'

Roy let the books in his arms droop. It was positively dystopian.

'Of course' – Tessa scratched her chin – 'the more people read books digitally, the less need there is for physical libraries. In fact, I expect soon—'

'Tessa.' Roy stood taller. 'I'd like to formally retract my resignation.'

Tessa sighed. 'Right.'

'I'll put it in writing this very afternoon. For your records.'

'No need.'

'And I'll see you bright and early tomorrow.'

Tessa shook her head. 'We've got a full rota.'

'Next week, then.'

Tessa closed her eyes – a long, meditative blink. 'Next week, then. And you're right.' She turned and pulled her chair closer to the computer. 'No good deed goes unpunished.'

Roy was about to explain how Tessa had misunderstood that reference when Yvonne strode through the double doors, a carrier bag of groceries in each hand.

She saw Roy and stopped.

Roy put his armful of books back down on the trolley, having returned none to the stacks. 'Good afternoon, Yvonne.' He picked up the bouquet. 'This is for you.'

Yvonne bent her knees, lowering her shopping bags to the floor.

'An apology. For being so unforgivably rude.'

Yvonne said nothing.

'I had a lot on my mind. I'm not excusing myself, because it was unacceptable. But I was entirely in the wrong.'

Slowly, Yvonne took the bouquet. She didn't look at him.

'It was a shock – it felt so soon. But I just needed to re-flect. Lynn would have wanted me to *carpe diem*.' Roy looked down. 'Though I can understand if you're horrified by the idea now. After making such a fool of myself with the' – he looked down – 'pirates.'

He stared at the carpet. He waited.

He risked a glance up.

Yvonne was sniffing the flowers.

Roy coughed. 'It's nearly six decades since I've asked anyone on a date, so please bear with me.' He felt his cheeks warm. 'Yvonne, would you do me the honour of coming to the cinema with me some time?'

Yvonne studied him.

Roy looked at the floor again. Warmth crept towards his neck and his ears.

Eventually, she spoke. 'Can we watch a romantic comedy?'

Roy felt his shoulders relax. 'Why not?'

'Well, then. I'd love to accept.' Yvonne beamed at him. 'Gosh. This is a turn-up!'

Roy beamed back. 'Tessa made me realise what an idiot I'd been.'

They both looked over at Tessa, who was typing furiously at the computer. 'No good deeds,' she muttered.

'She's probably on the phone.' Yvonne made a gesture next to her ear. 'On her little earpiece.' She looked at her shopping bags at her feet. 'Would you like to walk me home?'

'I'd be delighted.' Roy bent his knees and picked up the shopping bags with a weightlifter's jerk. 'Also, Yvonne, I'm coming back to work at the library. I've retracted my resignation. It was another thing Tessa put me straight on.'

'Hurrah for Tessa! What a hero.' Yvonne smiled at her daughter. 'Bye, love!'

Tessa raised her hand without looking up. Her face was clouded as she muttered something, presumably at something unsatisfactory on her screen.

Roy waved her a cheery goodbye, turned sharply on his heel and, carrying Yvonne's shopping bags, followed her happily out of the library.

Credits

Caroline Hulse and Orion Fiction would like to thank everyone at Orion who worked on the publication of *Reasonable People* in the UK.

Editorial
Sam Eades
Emad Akhtar
Celia Killen
Sahil Javed

Copy editor
Sophie Buchan

Proof reader
Marian Reid

Contracts
Dan Herron
Ellie Bowker

Design
Charlotte Abrams-Simpson
Joanna Ridley

Nick May

Editorial Management
Charlie Panayiotou
Jane Hughes
Bartley Shaw
Tamara Morriss

Finance
Jasdip Nandra
Nick Gibson
Sue Baker

Audio
Paul Stark
Jake Alderson

Production
Ameenah Khan

Marketing
Helena Fouracre

Publicity
Alex Layt

Rights
Rebecca Folland
Flora McMichael
Alice Cottrell
Marie Henckel

Sales
Jen Wilson
Esther Waters
Victoria Laws
Toluwalope Ayo-Ajala
Rachael Hum
Anna Egelstaff
Sinead White
Georgina Cutler

Operations
Jo Jacobs
Sharon Willis

If you loved *Reasonable People*, don't miss Caroline Hulse's brilliantly original previous novel . . .

The Fair is the only good thing that happens every year. And Fiona Larson is the only person in town who's never been.

This year, everything will be different.

Fresh and hilarious, *All the Fun of the Fair* is a deeply poignant coming-of-age novel from sensational talent Caroline Hulse.

If you loved *Reasonable People*, don't miss Caroline Hulse's hilarious and heartwarming debut novel . . .

Two exes. Their daughter.

And their new partners.

What could possibly go wrong ...?

'Funny, dry and beautifully observed. Highly recommended for anyone whose perfect Christmases never quite go according to plan!'

Gill Sims, author of *Why Mummy Drinks*

Another achingly funny, uncomfortably relatable novel from Caroline Hulse . . .

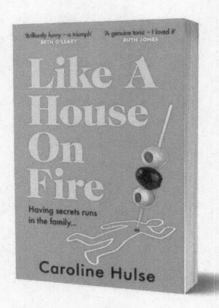

Stella and George are getting divorced.

But first, Stella's mum is throwing a murder mystery party.

All Stella and George have to do is make it through the day without their break-up being discovered – though it will soon turn out that having secrets runs in the family . . .

'Part Fleabag, part Agatha Christie, Like A House On Fire *is everything I love in a book . . . I was hooked from page one.'*

Josie Silver, bestselling author of
One Day in December